Chrysabelle was already walking to meet Creek. "What's going on?"

Bad news. There have been two humans murdered, both by vampires and the KM think Mal's to blame."

Her spine went cold. "Why would they think that?"

"Because they know something's changed between you two. You didn't give me the full story the other day, did you?"

"No." She sighed. "It's not something I want to get into, especially if I can make it go away."

"That's not all." He shot a look at her car. "Are you going somewhere?"

"I have some out-of-town business to take care of." Out-of-town business that would hopefully bring Mal back to her.

"Good, that's good."

"Why?"

He glanced at the gate behind him before answering her. "Because as of last night, Tatiana is back in Paradise City."

PRAISE FOR
HOUSE OF COMARRÉ

"Prophecy, curses, and devilish machination combine for a spellbinding debut of dark romance and pulse-pounding adventure."
—*LIBRARY JOURNAL* (Starred Review)

"Gripping, gritty, and imaginative. If you love dangerous males, kick-ass females, and unexpected twists, this is the series for you! Kristen Painter's engaging voice, smart writing, and bold, explosive plot blew me away. Prepare to lose some sleep!"
—LARISSA IONE,
New York Times bestselling author

"Kristen Painter brings a sultry new voice to the vampire genre, one that beckons with quiet passion and intrigue."
—L.A. BANKS,
New York Times bestselling author

BY KRISTEN PAINTER

House of Comarré

Blood Rights
Flesh and Blood
Bad Blood
Out for Blood
Last Blood

Forbidden Blood (e-only novella)

LAST BLOOD

House of Comarré: Book 5

KRISTEN PAINTER

orbit

www.orbitbooks.net

This book is a work of fiction. Names, characters, places, and incidents are the product of the author's imagination or are used fictitiously. Any resemblance to actual events, locales, or persons, living or dead, is coincidental.

Orbit
Hachette Book Group
237 Park Avenue
New York, NY 10017
Visit our Web site at www.orbitbooks.net

Orbit is an imprint of Hachette Book Group. The Orbit name and logo are trademarks of Little, Brown Book Group Limited.

Printed in the United States of America
First edition: July 2013

10 9 8 7 6 5 4 3 2 1

ATTENTION CORPORATIONS AND ORGANIZATIONS:
Most HACHETTE BOOK GROUP books are available at quantity discounts with bulk purchase for educational, business, or sales promotional use. For information, please call or write:

Special Markets Department, Hachette Book Group
237 Park Avenue, New York, NY 10017
Telephone: 1-800-222-6747 Fax: 1-800-477-5925

For Rocki and Louisa,
my sisters from other misters.
I love you guys!

LAST
BLOOD

Heaven has no rage like love to hatred turned—nor hell a fury like a woman scorned.

—WILLIAM CONGREVE

Chapter One

Paradise City, New Florida 2067

Twenty-four hours. That's how long it had taken Chrysabelle to get herself together after finding out that the raptor fae had devoured Mal's love for her, leaving him cold and uncaring, only to then discover she was also pregnant with Mal's child. Twenty-four hours as a sobbing wreck curled in her bed. Then she'd run out of tears and passed another twenty-four hours there, staring blindly at the ceiling, thinking about nothing and everything, rationalizing her choices, and trying to make sense of her future. On the third day, she'd gotten out of bed with the resolute knowledge that whatever she had to do to protect that future wasn't going to get done in bed.

If there was anything she'd learned from her mother, it was that strong women pushed forward, no matter what the circumstances, and strong women protected their children. Even at the cost of their own lives.

Being able to protect herself and her child meant being ready for anything, and that meant training. Lots of it.

Beating the daylights out of an opponent had always given Chrysabelle a sense of peace. Even now, when the opponent was her brother, it still worked. The focus of landing each hit and avoiding his incoming blows almost made her forget about the life-changing secret growing in her belly.

Almost.

It was still better than moping in bed, staring into space and trying to figure out how to make sense of a life without Mal when the child she carried was a constant reminder of everything she'd lost.

She ducked too late to avoid Damian's bokken. The wooden practice sword caught the side of her headgear, spun her off balance, and knocked her to her hands and knees.

"Hey." He straightened, bokken falling to his side. "Pay attention, will you? The last thing I want to do is concuss the sister I just found." Under his own headgear, he smiled as he offered his hand. "More accurately, who just found me."

She took the help and he pulled her to her feet. "Thanks."

"You want to stop? You seem a little distracted." Concern sparked in his blue eyes. "I realize we're just getting to know each other, but I *am* your brother. If there's anything you want to talk about . . ."

"Thank you." His offer meant a lot, but this wasn't something she was ready to share. "I'm fine." Other than the gaping hole in her heart. She lifted her bokken. "Let's keep going. I like having a partner again." And she liked maintaining her edge.

He tipped his head to one side. "You're sure? We've

sparred more in the last day than I used to in a week at the Domus."

She allowed a tiny bit of what she was feeling into her face. "I need this." Because stopping meant dealing with her reality.

"Cool with me." He went back to first stance.

"Cool? I think a little Fi rubbed off on you." She matched him, shifting most of her weight onto her back foot and bending her knees slightly. She pointed the tip of her bokken at his eyes and forced herself to concentrate on the present.

"There are worse people to hang out with." He nodded at her and took the same stance.

What did he mean by that? Mal? Before she could unravel that thread any further, knocking interrupted them. They both turned toward the door.

"Speak of the devil." Damian came out of fighting stance. "Not that you're the devil, Fi." He laughed. "Nice to see you."

Fi smiled and gave a little finger wave. "You too, Damian. You seem like you're settling in okay."

"You too from what I hear." He planted the tip of his sword against the gym mats and pulled off his face mask, tucking it beneath his arm. "I guess you're here to see Chrys?"

Fi's brows rose a tiny bit, maybe at his shortening of Chrysabelle's name. She nodded. "Yep. You cool if she and I chat for a bit?"

Chrysabelle glanced at Damian. He took her bokken. "Sure. It's almost lunch anyway. I'm going to get a shower, and then I'll come back over and eat." He winked at Fi. "If you two aren't still having your super-secret girl talk."

"Guys never change no matter how old they get." Fi rolled her eyes. "I'm sure we'll be done by then."

Damian nodded, but the humor faded from his face and he glanced at Chrysabelle. "It's okay if I come back for lunch, isn't it?"

She tugged off her headgear. "Of course it's okay. You know half of all of this is yours. House included. You don't have to ask for permission to come over here and you certainly don't have to stay in the guesthouse." Again, she wondered if his reluctance had something to do with Mal. Or her relationship with Mal. Not that there was any current relationship to speak of.

"I know, but I'm comfortable there. And I feel a little responsible for Amylia."

"She the comarré you brought back from Čachtice?" Fi asked.

"Yes," Chrysabelle answered, but she kept her eyes on Damian. "And you shouldn't feel responsible. I would have brought her back anyway."

He shrugged, walked to the weapons rack, and notched the first bokken into place. "Then you're a better person than I am." He dropped the second one into its slot, hung up his face mask, then headed for the door. "I would have left her. After Saraphina...you just never know. See you at lunch."

"Okay." She watched her brother leave, sighing with frustration.

Fi spoke after the door closed behind him. "Things not going as planned?"

"Does anything?" Chrysabelle prayed Fi didn't see that as an opening to ask about Mal. She pushed some stray hair behind one ear and quickly moved on. "How are you? How's Doc? I'm sorry I missed the wedding."

Fi shrugged. "So did everyone else. It was just me, Doc, his council members as witnesses, and Isaiah, Doc's— I mean, our butler, who happens to be a minister of the Church of Bast, so he married us. Really, we just wanted to make it official and get on with our life."

"I understand that. And I have to say, marriage suits you. You look... different. But in a good way." Fi's formerly long wavy hair was pin-straight and cut in a precise chin-length bob, her makeup impeccable, her clothes—which had always been good—seemed even better. "How's Doc doing with his new position as pride leader?"

"He's good. Busy. Running a pride is a twenty-four-seven job." Fi looked down at her sleek little navy dress. "As for the rest of me, being the pride leader's wife comes with access to all the best stuff, including a personal beauty team." She laughed nervously. "Who knew?" Her smile washed out. "There's so much stuff to go to. Meetings. Appearances. Dinners. It's a *lot* of work."

Which would explain the dark smudges under her eyes. Chrysabelle tipped her head to one side. "Sounds like it. Is there anything I can do to help?"

"Actually, yes." Fi took a deep breath. "I want to learn to fight. More than that. I want to learn to *win* a fight."

A slight alarm sounded in Chrysabelle's head. "Why? Who's threatening you?"

"No one. Yet. But that's the point." She hugged her arms around her body. "Barasa—he's one of Doc's council members and the pride's main physician—he says a pride leader's wife needs to know how to fight. And that opposition 'rears its head' at least once a year. More when the wife is new."

"But I thought the only challenge that counts is one issued by the pride leader or his wife, right?"

"Yes, but..." Fi stared at the ceiling. "I'm not known for my even temper." She shook her head and twisted the toe of one coral stiletto into the gym mat. "And it's occurred to me that I might be a target. Doc isn't always with me. I have a bodyguard almost all the time now when I go out."

Chrysabelle looked over Fi's shoulder. "Where is he now?"

"I made him stay with the car. I know how Velimai feels about strangers in her house. Sorry, your house. Yours and Damian's. *Whoever* it belongs to now. You know what I mean."

Chrysabelle rested her hand on top of Fi's arm, hoping to ease some of her anxiety. "I'd be happy to help you."

"You will? Awesome! Doc's had his council members trying to teach me, but they're varcolai. I don't have that same strength or speed. Plus they're guys. Who knows better how to fight like a girl than another girl?" Fi grinned. "I've seen you fight. You go hardcore. I wanna do that too."

Dropping her hand, Chrysabelle laughed. "Hardcore it is then." She raised her brows. "There's a catch."

"Does this have to do with—"

Before Fi could say "Mal" Chrysabelle spoke. "Remember how you offered to help me with changing my look? I'm ready."

Fi's eyes widened. "You are? Sweet! This is going to be so much fun." She reached into the expensive-looking handbag hanging off her shoulder and pulled out a small bejeweled rectangle. She tapped the face, causing it to light up, then tapped another button and held it up to her mouth. "Pull samples for Chrysabelle." Then she dropped the device back into her purse. "I love that phone. So much better than the comcell I used to have. I'll be over in the morning and we'll get started."

"I'm looking forward to it. Bring a change of clothes and we can have your first lesson afterward."

"I will." Fi started toward the door, then stopped and twisted back. "It's probably none of my business, but have you talked to Mal? I've been by the freighter but either he hasn't been home or he's avoiding me. I know things went south for you guys. I'm sorry about that. I really am."

South? If hell was in that direction, then yes, things had gone south. Chrysabelle took a deep breath, willing it to calm her. "Thank you. No, I haven't talked to him." She turned a little, hiding her face. "He doesn't love me anymore, Fi. I don't have the slightest idea what to do about that. He was pretty adamant when he left here that I stay out of his life."

Fi walked back. "I know Mal and if he loved you once, he'll love you again. You still love him, right?"

There was no holding back the hitch in her breath that time. A shuddered exhale and when she found her voice, it wavered with the emotions she was trying to put behind her. "Of course, I love him. That's why this hurts so much." She closed her eyes, partially to hold back tears and partially to shut out the pain, but the ever-present ache she'd felt since losing Mal only blossomed in the dark.

"Then we'll find a way to remind him of that."

Opening her eyes, Chrysabelle shook her head. "I don't think—"

"He feels things more deeply than you can imagine. Trust me. I used to live in that tortured head of his, remember? His curse would have never worked if he'd been completely without remorse. Somewhere deep inside, his love for you still exists just like yours does. Love doesn't just go away."

She stared at Fi. "Yes, it does. That's exactly what happened."

The ghost girl shook her head. "I don't believe that."

"Fi, you didn't see the way he looked at me." She swallowed, the memories she'd been working so hard to shut out now engulfing her. "He called me...*food*."

With a soft whimper, Fi put her arms around Chrysabelle and hugged her. "That's awful. Awful. But it sounds like the voices talking, not Mal. Don't write him off completely, okay?"

Chrysabelle nodded, but it wasn't a promise of anything. If Mal had truly reverted to the monster he'd once been, then he really was lost to her. There was no way she was letting that version of him near her. Or their child.

She'd kill him first.

Corvinestri, Romania

Tatiana clutched the pillows to her face. Octavian's side of the bed still held his dark, sweet scent. An exhausted sob shuddered through her as she inhaled what was left of him, punishing herself for falling in love with yet another man who'd betrayed her.

"My lady?"

Tatiana ignored Kosmina and stayed face down in the pillows, grief pressing her into the bed, betrayal raking down her spine.

"My lady, Daciana is outside with Jonah."

The mention of Daci's young, *willing* comar led to thoughts of Tatiana's own missing comar. Another male added to the list of her betrayers. An angry growl built in her throat. Somehow, he'd escaped her again. If she ever captured him, she would kill him the instant she could. She forced the growl down to speak, her words muffled by the bedding. "Leave me."

"It's been three days, my lady." And over the course of those three days, Kosmina's voice had gone from soothing to frustrated. "You must feed."

"I will feed when I'm ready. Leave. Me." Another word and she'd snap. Already she teetered on the knife edge of insanity. Blood would spill if she was pushed further.

"Yes, my lady." Kosmina's pulse faded as she walked away. The doors to Tatiana's quarters opened softly, then began to swing shut. A second later they burst open and a new presence flew through them.

"Tati, please get up." Daciana. The only companion Tatiana had left. The only one she could still trust. "I know you're grieving, and my heart aches for you, but you can't give up. There has to be something we can do to get Lilith back." She sat on the side of the bed and took Tatiana's hand. "And you need to feed. You're as cold as marble. You're only weakening yourself further."

Tatiana pulled her hand away. "He *betrayed* me."

"Octavian loved you." Daciana sighed. "Whatever he did, I can't help but believe he was forced to do it."

Tatiana swallowed the anguish creeping up her throat. "No one forced him to kill himself." The bitterness of those words almost undid her. "I made him my consort, Daci.

I would have *married* him." She twisted herself upright, pulling her knees to her chest and leaning back against the padded leather headboard. She rocked back, her eyes filling with cold tears. "I'm such a fool. I believed every word he fed me. And the whole time, he was just stringing me along, using me for Hades knows what."

Daciana's shoulders slumped. "Tati, you don't know—"

She stopped rocking. "Like hell I don't. Why do you think he killed himself? Because he knew I'd do it for him when I found out what a traitor he was." She tore the bed linens off and jumped out of bed. "He cost me my daughter." She was shaking now, her body trembling with grief that had no outlet.

Silver glinted in Daciana's eyes, turning her soft expression hard. "Then consider his suicide a gift."

The words bit into Tatiana's soul, freshening her pain. "How can you say—"

"Enough." Daciana stood and planted her hands on her hips. "This isn't the Tatiana I know. The strong, determined woman who fought her way to the top. You're the Dominus of the House of Tepes."

"I know who I am."

Daciana narrowed her gaze. "Then act like it."

Tatiana froze in shock. Few spoke to her that way, but Daciana wasn't just anyone. She was the only family Tatiana had left.

"You know I'm right," Daciana said. "You need to do something, not lie around in bed moping."

Tatiana wrapped her arms around her body. Daciana spoke the truth, but Tatiana wasn't ready to put the pain behind her. It had bitten too deep. Taken too much.

Daciana's harsh expression softened. "I know you're

hurting, but you're not alone in this. Whatever you want to do to get her back, I'm with you."

Tatiana swallowed, letting Daci's offer wash through her. She nodded and the darkness shrouding her soul lifted enough to let the light of possibility shine through. "I know what needs to be done, but getting there, finding a way out of this..." The image of Lilith in Samael's arms, followed by Octavian's ashes strewn across the floor, flashed in her head. She turned away. "You don't understand."

"I do understand." Daciana strode forward and grasped Tatiana's shoulders, forcing her to meet Daciana's gaze. "What has happened to you is more horrible than words can describe, but you're a fighter. You've always been a fighter."

"And I will be again." Tatiana shook her head. "Just not now. I need more time."

Daciana's lip curled. She drew back and slapped Tatiana across the face. "You've had enough time. The nobility is beginning to talk."

Stunned from Daciana's attack, Tatiana reeled back, the first frissons of anger breaking through the pain. "Why did you—"

Daciana followed and struck her again.

Before Tatiana could react, Daciana lifted her hand a third time. Rage moved Tatiana forward. She grabbed Daciana's arm, bent it behind her, and took her to the ground. She crouched overtop Daciana, fangs bared. "Hit me again and I'll—"

"Finally." Daciana smiled up at her. "There's the Tatiana I know. Channel that anger. Let it motivate you." She lifted her free hand and flattened it over Tatiana's heart. "Who caused you all this pain?"

"Malkolm," Tatiana hissed. "And his comarré whore."

"Yes." Daciana nodded.

Tatiana freed Daciana and sat back. "I have let this grief make me soft. No more."

"That's it," Daciana encouraged.

Tatiana stood and lifted her head. "I am *so* sick of them interfering with my life. My plans." She growled softly, weaving her grief into a suit of armor to protect her for the fight to come. Because fight she would. "If it means sacrificing everything I have left, I'll get Lilith back and put an end to Malkolm and Chrysabelle once and for all."

Daciana grabbed Tatiana's hand and squeezed. "That's the Tatiana I know and love. Come, feed from Jonah and renew your strength. Then, together, we will find a way to make all of this happen." Her eyes went bright with promise. "I will never leave your side. You have my word."

The pledge broke the last of Tatiana's doubts, opening the way for her anger to take full rein. "If only everyone in my life were as faithful as you." The wicked smile bent her mouth. "We have work to do."

Chapter Two

Mal followed the human woman, keeping enough distance so she couldn't see him, but close enough that the dying roses scent of her blood still teased his senses. Human blood. It had been too long. *Too long,* the voices agreed.

Catch her. Drain her. He didn't need the urging. The fae who'd taken his love for Chrysabelle had done him a favor, leaving a hole inside him that the beast had slipped into as easily as a knife through flesh. The voices no longer mocked him as they had in the past, perhaps content that he was theirs to control once again.

Ahead of him, the human continued without a clue that she was about to become his dinner. Mesh shopping bags swung from her hands. Food that would never be eaten. Milk that would spoil.

The remaining shreds of control on his humanity had disappeared with the day's setting sun and the increase in his hunger. He was lost to the bloodlust, severed from the threads of mortality that Chrysabelle had begun to weave into something whole again.

Whore. Mal didn't argue. She was a comarré and

comarrés gave their blood to anyone with enough funds. That left him out. Anger gnawed at his bones. She'd never been anything but an anchor tethering him to his humanity, keeping him from fulfilling his immortal destiny. He was a vampire, not a pet to be chained and fed when she deemed it so.

The beast hovered just below the surface of his black-inked skin, crouched and ready. Feral need flexed his muscles and he inhaled again, the perfume of his quarry stirring the chaotic pleasure in his head to new heights. He anticipated the succulent pressure of the human's flesh beneath his fangs. The way she'd struggle and mewl, her feeble attempts to escape only fueling his predatory intentions.

The joy of the impending kill ran hot and electric down his spine, winding him like a spring.

She entered her apartment building without a glance back. Stupid humans. So unsuspecting. Then another dark figure followed after her. This one smart enough to look around before going in.

Fringe vampire. Mal snorted. No fringe was going to thieve his kill. He shot forward and latched onto the fringe faster than the lesser vampire could react. He snapped the fringe's neck, then vanished into an alley as the ash settled to the sidewalk. He waited a few beats, but the act hadn't caused the slightest ripple in the evening.

Satisfied he remained undetected, he went to smoke, slipped under the closed door, and hugged the ceiling. He found his target as she made her way up four flights of stairs. Garbage littered the landings and graffiti covered the dirty walls. Greasy food smells wafted from other apartments along with shouted arguments and blasting holovisions.

She should be happy he was about to take her away from all this.

One after the other, she pressed her thumb into the locks buttoning up her apartment, then opened the door. He stayed in the hall to give her a few minutes to relock her door and settle in. Experience had taught him a mark who felt safe was an easy mark to take. His smoke form blended with the lingering remnants of someone's burned dinner and her junkie neighbor's hash addiction. How perfect. In a building like this, in a neighborhood like this, it might take a week before anyone discovered her body.

He was smarter now than all those years before when he'd killed without thought. Now he knew how to leave no trace. To make it look like a suicide. He'd give them no reason to wonder about the locked door or the lack of forced entry.

The voices clawed at him, eager for their take. He filtered through the gap under the door but kept his smoke form once he got in, unsure of where she might be. The cacophony of heartbeats in the building made it impossible to pick out her pulse.

The kitchen was lit only by the dim bulb burning over the range. Her shopping bags sat on the counter. He returned to his physical body and went to find her. It was a small apartment; she couldn't be too far away. The kick of the hunt shot through him like the spike of good whiskey.

He was moments from devouring her, moments from tasting the hot spill of blood he craved like nothing else. *Yes yes yes…*

A smiled creased his mouth and he was unable to stop it. Too long, he'd been shackled by the curse. *By the comarré*. Yes, she'd kept him from this as well. But those cares were gone. Nothing mattered but the blood and the righteous satisfaction of a kill.

Somewhere in the depths of his mind, the word *ghost* surfaced. He shrugged it off and pushed forward. Soft singing met his ears. He went after the sound, using it like a beacon to locate her.

A door at the end of a narrow hall stood ajar. He walked toward it, pushed it open silently, and stopped cold.

No. Take her. Now. Anger reverberated through the voices, but his feet were planted.

She sat on the edge of a twin bed, singing quietly and petting the hair of a sleeping child. A boy. No more than four or five.

Mal backed up a step.

Kill her. Drain her. Drink!

He stared at the two of them while the voices spun into a frenzy. So innocent and unaware. Images flitted through his brain. An angelic face surrounded by brunette curls. Big brown eyes that stared up at him like he ruled the world. Pale skin torn and bloodied. Her body lifeless as a rag doll.

He went to smoke and left.

Creek paced expectantly. Every night since he'd told Annika about the mayor making him Paradise City's enemy number one, the two of them had gone on patrol and made sure that the city's othernatural residents remained as law-abiding and behaved as possible.

Tonight, she was late.

He pulled out his phone and checked it for the second

time, but there was still no message from her. She was a basilisk and could definitely take care of herself, but that didn't stop him from being concerned about his sector chief.

Not that he'd ever worried about Argent, except what the old dragon shifter might have thought about a few of Creek's screwups.

Annika was different. He stopped pacing to sit on the steps that led down from his sleeping loft. Thanks to his grandmother, he and Annika had developed a much better relationship than he'd ever had with Argent.

He laughed softly. If Mawmaw had her way, she'd probably get them married off. Not that he felt like that about Annika. He preferred his women...human. Or comarré, but that door wasn't just closed; it was nailed shut. And he knew Mawmaw well enough to know that inviting them both over for dinner wasn't just her friendly way of saying thank you for saving her from Yahla, the soulless woman. He shook his head. Oh no. She made plans, that one. Plans she liked to see realized.

He'd pulled out his phone again and started a text to Annika when three short knocks sounded on the door of the repurposed machine shop he called home. He jumped up and went to slide the door back.

Annika stood on the other side, draped in shadows. She nodded and her ever-present black shades reflected the two solar lamps lighting his home. "Creek."

Relief erased the tension in his shoulders. "I was starting to think something had happened."

"No, I..." She looked down the street. "I just had some things to take care of." Then she checked the other side. "I'm not alone."

His brow furrowed. "Who's with you?"

"Another operative. Everything clear?"

"Yes." Another operative? Was he being moved? Given help? He pushed the door open a little wider. "Come in." And explain.

She looked to her side again and motioned to someone, then stepped through the door. "This is the highest level of security, you understand?"

"Absolutely." What wasn't with the KM?

A shadow filled the doorway behind her. Taller, darker, and reeking of the dirty, spicy scent only one creature carried.

"Vampire," he muttered.

She nodded and turned toward her guest. "It's clear."

The operative stepped into the light and Creek's gut twisted hard. He swore softly under his breath. "Octavian."

Chapter Three

Doc signed the last of the papers in front of him and set them aside. "All right. Bring him in."

Barasa nodded and opened the office door.

A few moments later, Remo Silva strolled in.

With the same apprehension he'd feel toward any newcomer to his pride, Doc eyed the man entering his office. Even Omur and Barasa, Doc's existing council members, seemed on edge. Despite being the son of the leader of São Paulo's largest pride, Remo would still have to prove himself as a member of this one. His guaranteed position on Doc's council didn't come with built-in trust.

But Doc had agreed to Remo joining his pride and he would not go back on his word. He stayed seated, the proper position for any pride leader, and extended his hand. "Maddoc Mays. Good to meet you, Remo. Your father spoke highly of you."

Remo shook Doc's hand with unnecessary vigor. "I doubt that." He laughed and a shiver of unease rippled down Doc's back. "The old man was just happy to pawn me off." He shook Barasa's and Omur's hands as well, then turned back to Doc. "Good to be here, though. I like new places. New people. New experiences."

"Please, sit." A flash of yellow flickered through Remo's eyes so quickly Doc was barely sure he'd seen it. "Just so long as those new experiences don't include sleeping your way through the female membership of this pride."

Remo took the chair on the end, beside Omur, who looked like he'd rather not be so close to the Brazilian varco-lai. "I see my father has shared more than he should have."

"It's his job to inform me about the newest member of my pride."

"It's also his job to protect his son. To make it possible for me to have a fresh start. So much for that." Remo sat back, threw his ankle over his knee, and peered at Doc in a way that sent red flags up. "So..." He drew the word out. "Where is this wife of yours? The one who murdered my sister?"

Doc clenched his teeth to keep from snarling. Heat snapped along his veins, a reminder of the witch fire that still lingered in his system, although he'd been learning to control it with help from Barasa. With a deep breath, he leaned back and answered. "Is that the São Paolo pride's official stance? Because if your father has changed his mind—"

"No." The smugness on Remo's face was gone, momentarily replaced by panic. A second later, he flipped his hand through the air like he was flicking a bug away and smiled. "I am just playing with you."

Doc didn't return Remo's good humor. "I don't play. Ever." He stood, pulling up to his full height before coming around to lean on the other side of the desk. Crossing

his arms, he stared down at Remo with as much intensity as he could without causing fire to leap off his skin.
"You've been here three minutes. So far you've called me
a liar and my wife a murderer." He let his eyes go gold
with anger. "Have you ever played baseball, Remo?"

The man looked genuinely confused. "Yes."

"Good." Doc smiled. "Then you understand the three-
strike rule." Remo shifted in his seat. "You have one left.
Do you get where I'm coming from?"

Remo nodded. "Y-yes." His voice cracked. He cleared
his throat. "I understand. I am just tired from my trip."

Doc got up and went back behind his desk. "Barasa and
Omur will give you a tour of the building and show you
to your apartment. I suggest you rest before dinner." He
looked up and made eye contact with Remo one last time.
"I wouldn't want you to be so *tired* you end up with that last
strike." He glanced at Barasa. "A word before you leave."

Remo nodded and followed Omur out. Doc waited
until the door was shut before speaking to Barasa. "I
want eyes on him and a full report of your conversations
with him."

"Absolutely." Barasa glanced toward the door. "How
much of a problem do you think he's going to be?"

Doc thought of Fi and all she'd been through. "No
more than we let him."

Lola Diaz-White waited while John Havoc, her personal
bodyguard, knocked on the heavy church doors. Even here
in the car, the place's proximity made her skin tingle. She'd
fed from Hector, her comar, before they'd left. How much
worse would the effects of the place be if she didn't have

his sweet, rich blood fresh in her system? Until now, she'd never understood how incredible it was that the vampire, Preacher, could live on such hallowed ground until now. He was indeed one of the most unique of their species.

John started back to the car. "He must be out. We'll have to come back."

"Wait." She scooted toward the window. One of the doors had opened a few inches. "Preacher," she called out. "Are you there?" She motioned to John. "Talk to him."

With a nod, John returned and had a few words. Quiet words, because she couldn't make them out over the hum of the car's air conditioner. Assuming it was Preacher on the other side of those doors, he wasn't being very friendly. The doors still hadn't moved more than a few inches.

Finally, John came back and leaned his head down to speak through the window. "He says he'll meet you soon, but not now."

She frowned. She was the *mayor* and he was going to tell her when they'd meet? "I don't like that. I need to know when and where. Tell him I'm busy, that I'm—"

"I told him that." John shrugged. "He's not exactly biddable."

Lola leaned closer to the window. "Tell him if he wants to know what's going on with his daughter, he'll be at my house in an hour. After that, I'll refuse to see him."

"Be right back."

While John relayed the message, she sat back, crossed her arms, and stared at the ceiling. The letter she'd received from Dominic had said only that the mission had failed and that her grandchild was now in the untouchable hands of the ancients. In other words, he'd told her to forget getting the baby back. Like hell she would. She'd hoped to enlist Preacher's help before going to see Dominic, but that didn't look like it was going to happen. Once again, she had only herself to rely on.

John got back in the car. "He says he'll be there."

She hit the button and closed the window, staring at the abandoned church that housed the father of her grandchild. The little hairs on the back of her neck had been on alert since they'd parked in front of it. She shook her head. "Get us out of here."

This was Preacher's loss. She'd given him a chance and he'd squandered it. When—if he showed up, she'd cut him out of this equation once and for all. Better now than when she finally had Mariela back.

What if she'd come here because Mariela needed him? What if there'd been a real emergency? She took her gaze off the building as the car pulled away. There was no place for him in Mariela's life. Fortunately, she knew just how to get rid of him.

As Jonah left the office, Tatiana reclined on the chaise where she took most of her feedings. The power of his blood ignited within her, making her heart beat and lungs fill with air. She exhaled and nodded at Daciana, seated across from her. "You were right. This is exactly what I needed. I feel whole again. There really is no substitute for comarré blood."

"None better," Daci said. She watched the door shut behind Jonah. "He is especially good. Young and compliant and happy to serve."

Tatiana tipped her head back to stare at the coffered

ceiling. "They're all like that in the beginning. So full of purpose and pride of place. Gah! Then they get full of themselves, think they're worth so much more. That's when the trouble starts."

She smiled gently at Daci, who'd only meant to help, and softened her tone as she straightened. "I really must get another comar, as much as I am loath to." She ran her fingers over the silk upholstery. "You did such a wonderful job picking out Jonah. Would you be willing to act as my emissary and go to Madame Rennata on my behalf? I have no desire to face that old witch. I know she blames me for *her* comar's desertion. And I trust your judgment. I'm sure you'll bring back the very best comar she has to offer."

Daci's eyes brightened. "I would be honored to! After all, you taught me everything I know about choosing one." Her chest puffed up a bit. "And I am your Elder. That certainly seems like a job I should handle. Has Rennata replied to you on the issue of Damian?"

Tatiana nodded toward her desk. "Her letter is on my desk. Somewhere among the flowers and apologies there is her word that I am to be given full credit for his blood rights." She shook her head. "I'm sure that will still leave money owed as I doubt she'll let me have another for the same price, but I don't care. Whatever it costs, I want the best." She tipped her chin toward Daci. "The one you deem best."

"I'll take care of it immediately. Right now if you wish me to."

Tatiana nodded reluctantly. "I do. I want to feed again soon. Build my strength a little more until I'm fully confident in my ability to face the ancient ones." Thoughts of her dear, sweet missing Lilith dampened her mood.

Daci came to sit beside her. She laid her hand on Tatiana's leg. "I know you're thinking of Lilith. We *will* get her back. I promise you. Whatever you need me to do, I will do it."

Tatiana slid her hand over the top of Daci's. "I know you will. And I appreciate your loyalty." She gave Daci's hand a squeeze, then looked deeply into her eyes. "My dealings with the ancient ones have never been easy. If I don't... survive their demands, I want you to know that I would be happy to see you as Dominus of the House of Tepes."

Horror marred Daci's pretty face. She yanked her hand out from under Tatiana's. "Don't say such things!" She stood and shook her head. "You need more blood. It's clear you're still not yourself. Where is that letter? I'm going to the Primoris Domus immediately."

Tatiana pointed to her desk. "Right on top."

Daci grabbed the letter and waved it like a flag. "I'll be back as soon as I can. Then we'll get you up to full power and make our next move."

"Thank you. You're too good to me."

Daci smiled and gave a little nod as she left. Tatiana reclined on the chaise again, listening as Daci's footsteps faded. As much as Tatiana agreed that she needed a new comar, she'd wanted Daci out of the house more.

Daci was too dear a friend to put in harm's way. With a sigh, Tatiana resigned herself to what needed to be done. She pushed to her feet and went to the office door, opened it, and stuck her head into the anteroom, where one of the house servants awaited her needs. "I'm not to be disturbed until I come out again, understood?"

The servant nodded without making eye contact. "Yes, my lady."

Tatiana went back in, locked the door, and walked to the front of her desk. With a few deep breaths, she forced away her residual anger toward the ancients. She needed to be calm. Confident. Respectful, despite the fact that they had stolen her child from her arms. But more than just respectful, she must appear worthy of the power and position that had been bestowed upon her. The ancients were fickle, as they'd proved. She must not give them reason to strip anything else from her.

She pulled the chairs aside and stood in the small clearing, girding herself for what was about to happen. Then she tipped her head back and spoke to the one she'd worked so hard to please, the one who owed her so much for her undying loyalty, the one who'd betrayed her just as Octavian had.

"Samael, my liege. I respectfully request your company."

Chapter Four

The weather had cooled enough that Chrysabelle tugged one of Maris's long white cardigans over her tunic and pants before heading out to sit by the pool, but the change in temperature wouldn't keep her from taking in the evening's quiet. If anything, the calm only seemed to reinforce her determination to move confidently forward with her life while the soft lap of the bay against the new dock and the occasional grunt of a cormorant helped soothe the pressure of everything she might not be able to resolve.

Like Mal. She loved him, more than was wise, but the hard truth was the Mal she loved was gone, replaced by a creature more monster than man. Her heart ached for herself and the child in her belly who would never know a father. Just as she had never known a father.

Sad how the circumstances of her life seemed inescapable, even for her unborn child. She pulled her sweater a little closer. Losing Mal like this was worse than when she'd thought he'd died in the city square. It would have been better if that had been his end than knowing he might now actually be her enemy. She shook her head, her vision blurring slightly. How would she fight him if it came to that?

Her hand slid to her stomach. She knew how. With strength and resolution, because protecting this child meant more than anything. She understood now why her mother had sacrificed so much and been willing to fight so hard. She also understood a part of her would die with him. There was no other way to survive something that horrific.

"Chrysabelle?"

The voice yanked her from her thoughts. She turned. "Mortalis. I didn't know you were coming by."

The shadeux fae blinked, his expression unchanged. "Sorry. Is it a bad time?"

"No, it's fine." She pointed to the chaise next to her. "Join me."

He sat, perching on the edge like he might have to leap into action at any moment. He scanned the perimeter beyond where the security lights around the property faded into blackness. "I came to see how you're doing. Nyssa's been asking about you."

"You told her about..." She didn't mind Nyssa knowing about the pregnancy, but the more people who knew, the harder the secret would be to keep.

His gaze stayed fixed to one distant spot for a few counts. "No, she just wanted to know how you're adjusting to life with Damian. That's all she knows."

Chrysabelle exhaled. It didn't surprise her that Mortalis had kept the secret of her pregnancy from his partner. The fae was stalwart in his loyalty to those he considered friends. "You can tell her. I trust her like I trust you."

A slight upturning of his mouth and Mortalis finally

made eye contact. "Thank you." He moved back on the chaise a little. "You're well then?"

"Well enough. Thanks again for helping me buy that plane and find that pilot. Not that I plan to travel any time soon, but Damian might." She shrugged. "It's nice to know it's there if we need it."

"You're welcome. Although I think Amery wishes he could have taken the pilot's job."

She smiled. "He's a good kid. I like him. Tell him I said hi next time you see him."

Mortalis's gaze dropped to her stomach before shifting away suddenly like he'd heard something. He slanted his eyes toward her, looking past the horns that curled from the top of his head to his jaw line. "Without any alarm, stand up and walk back to the house."

She sat up, her body tensing. She took a breath and relaxed as he'd asked, then stood. "Velimai made a gorgeous chocolate cake for dessert. Why don't you come inside and I'll pack up a few slices for you to take home to Nyssa."

He nodded, still surreptitiously watching the horizon. "Sounds good." He gave her elbow a nudge, pushing her forward.

She tried to keep a casual pace, but the tickle of fear at the base of her spine made casual difficult. Once they were inside, Mortalis punched the panel beside the sliders to close the curtains and give them privacy.

Her breath stuck in her throat. "What's going on?"

Nothing about his expression said his answer would be good news. "Has Mal tried to contact you?"

"No. Do you expect him to?"

After a long breath, he nodded. "I think he's outside right now. Watching you."

She reached for the curtains, but he caught her arm. "Don't. It's better if he doesn't know you know."

"Why is that better? What does he want with me?" She put her hand over her heart to feel it race beneath her skin. "Do you think he knows about the baby? Velimai, bring me my sacre."

Mortalis grabbed her arms and held her still. "Listen to me. There's no way he could know about the baby. You're not in any danger right now."

She stared at him. "Really? Because you know I've invited him in. There's nothing to keep him from entering the house." Panic clawed at her throat, making it hard for her to breathe.

Velimai ran in with Chrysabelle's sacre, her eyes rounded with concern. *What's happening*, she signed.

"Mal's outside," Chrysabelle shot back.

Mortalis held up one six-fingered hand. "Nothing's happening. I *think* Mal's outside. Could be another vampire."

"Like that's better." Chrysabelle shuddered. Something was wrong with her to react like this. She pulled out of Mortalis's grasp and sat on the couch. "What is my problem? I don't normally freak out like this."

Hormones, Velimai signed after setting the sword on the sofa table before her. *How about a glass of warm milk?*

Chrysabelle nodded, not really wanting the milk but knowing Vel would feel better with something to do.

Mortalis sat on the ottoman across from her. "You going to be okay?"

"I'm fine." She pressed her palm to her forehead. "Or as fine as I can be considering I'm going to be high-strung for the next few months. Holy mother, help us all. I don't like this one bit." She closed her eyes for a moment. "What am I going to do about Mal? I can't live with him stalking me. Or whatever else he might be up to."

"Whenever you leave the house, I want you to wear your body armor."

"Mortalis, I have the gold from the ring of sorrows sewn into my back. Death isn't a permanent thing for me anymore, remember?" She picked up her sacre, comforted by the sword's height in her hand.

He raised his brows. "You carry another life inside you now. Do you trust that gold to protect your unborn child's life as well?"

She closed her eyes for a moment, knowing he was right. "No. And this child is everything to me." Including her only connection to the Mal she loved. She looked toward the sliders. "Wearing that armor isn't going to keep Mal from coming back, though."

Mortalis followed her gaze. "He's drawn by the memory of your blood, I'm sure." He sighed. "We need to take the threat level down."

Her hand tightened around the hilt of her sacre. "I'll do it." She'd known this moment might come, just hadn't expected it so soon.

Mortalis frowned. "Do what?"

She tipped the blade toward the sliders. "Reduce the threat level."

"I didn't mean kill him." Mortalis looked a little shocked, which for him meant slightly elevated brows. "I meant find a way to reduce his cravings for your blood."

She grimaced, but let the weapon drop to her side. "You want me to leave a glass of blood on the porch for him? Because I don't feel like that's a step in the right direction." Although, if it meant helping Mal, she was all in.

A light turned on in his eyes. "In a way, that's exactly what you need to do." He nodded, clearly thinking through what he was about to tell her. "Let me explain…"

As soon as Chrysabelle went inside, Mal dropped over the security wall and onto the unoccupied neighboring property. No matter how much he wanted to sink his teeth into the comarré he owned, he wasn't about to take on a wysper or shadeux fae to do it. The voices chimed in agreement.

For all the grief Chrysabelle had put him through, for the hell she'd made his life, she *would* give him blood. She owed him that much. *Yesss…*

He pushed through the overgrowth that had once been manicured landscaping. Whoever owned the property had let it fall into disrepair. He glanced toward the house. No lights, no sense of life inside. Was it completely abandoned? If they were winter people, they'd be here now. He peered through the branches of a bottle brush tree. Certainly more comfortable than the rusted freighter he called home. And so conveniently located. Chrysabelle had asked him to move into the new yacht she intended to buy. How would she feel about him living next door? Like he cared. With a twisted smile, he started forward to investigate, but an odd rustling caught his attention. He looked up. A flicker of white glimmered in the sprawl of palmettos a few yards ahead. He inhaled.

Warm fresh blood. Just under that, the tang of wet animal.

Launching toward the source, he caught the buck around the throat. It was wet and slippery from its swim to the island. He squeezed harder. It thrashed in his grip, punching the tip of one slender antler through his shoulder. He flipped the deer over and threw his weight onto it to hold it down. Its dark eyes went wide and it let out a loud, whistling snort.

Mal's fangs punched through his gums and he struck, biting into the animal's neck with one swift contraction. The struggling beneath him weakened as he drank, the taste of blood and salt water mixing. Finally the creature went limp. Mal sat back, fed if not satisfied.

He pulled his jacket away from his shoulder. The wound had begun to knit closed, but he recognized the signs of weakness. Animal blood was a poor substitute for human.

He twisted to look toward Chrysabelle's house as he pushed to his feet. And human blood was a poor substitute for comarré. The taste in his mouth wasn't even close to the taste he craved. He scrubbed his hand across his face, wiping away the last drops of blood.

He would get what he wanted. Even if he had to wait.

Chapter Five

Creek whipped out his halm, snapping his wrist to open the titanium weapon to its full length. "What the hell are you doing here?"

Annika stepped in front of Octavian. "He's one of us. He's the operative."

"A vampire." Creek knew the mistrust in his voice bordered on disrespect, but he didn't care.

"Yes," she answered. "You know we employ them." She glanced back at her guest. "Octavian has given much to the cause. He was human when we first recruited him."

Weapon still raised, Creek studied the vampire's face, memories coming with Annika's words. "I know who he is. I've seen him with Tatiana. How can you be sure he's not working for her?"

Annika pushed the halm down. "He's loyal to us. You have my word and that's all you need. Put your weapon away. Now."

Inhaling, Creek twisted the center of the halm and retracted it. Annika's word would have to stand. And as much as he trusted her, he couldn't shake the feeling that there was more to Octavian than she thought. The Florida State Prison had honed his ability to assess people. Getting released hadn't changed that.

Octavian held his hands up. "I've been through enough to get here. I don't need to have my loyalty questioned."

Annika shot him a look. "No one's questioning your loyalty anymore. Now enough of this. You two have to work together. I suggest you get past your doubts. Both of you."

Creek tucked the halm back into his belt. He nodded for Annika's sake. "If Annika vouches for you, that's all I need."

"Is it?" Octavian lifted a brow. "I wouldn't want to find myself unexpectedly staked."

"Not going to happen," Creek reassured him. Not as long as Octavian kept his fangs to himself. Creek nodded to the pair of secondhand chairs he'd added since Mawmaw had taken to visiting. Duct tape patched the tears in the fabric, but they suited him just fine. "Make yourself comfortable. Anyone want a beer?"

"No." Octavian snorted.

"Yeah," Creek said. "I guess you wouldn't. Don't have any blood to offer you either." He looked at Annika as he opened the fridge door. "Beer?"

She shrugged. "Why not."

He grabbed two long necks and twisted the top off hers before handing it over. She took it and joined Octavian in the chairs, so Creek moved around to the steps and crouched there. He took a long pull from his bottle, wiped his mouth with the heel of his hand, then leaned his elbows on the step behind him. "What was it like working for Tatiana?"

Octavian took a moment before answering. Like he was choosing his words. "Hard. She's demanding. And crueler than you can imagine."

"I doubt it." Creek took another sip. "I can imagine some pretty cruel things." Another thing his time in prison had helped with. He turned his attention to Annika. "What's our mission?"

Annika set her beer on the empty cable spool currently serving as his coffee table. "Octavian is going to become invaluable to the mayor. We know what she needs and he's about to provide it. Once that happens, we'll be able to use him to find out who turned her. As soon as we have that information, we'll know whom to exterminate. A vampire that's siring humans cannot be allowed to live. That way lays the makings of an army, and armies are needed for only one thing. War."

Creek raised a brow. "What's my part in that plan?"

"Very little, since we know she's gunning for you. I need you to find Preacher, the father of the vampire baby, and make sure he's not planning a rescue mission of his own. Tell him whatever he needs to hear, but keep him under control. We know the ancient ones have the baby and the grand masters are working on a way of luring them out. Until that happens, your task is business as usual. Protect the citizens of Paradise City."

Octavian raised his brows. "Hasn't it been pretty quiet since the mayor lifted the curfew?"

So he'd been filled in on what had been happening. Annika was good about keeping her people in the loop. She tilted her head toward the double agent. "We don't anticipate that quiet lasting much longer." Then she looked at Creek again. "It never does in this town."

* * *

Fi shifted from one foot to the other, her new heels too high to be comfortable. Not that she cared. Shoes this pretty didn't need to be comfortable. Besides, most of the evening would be spent sitting down after the cocktail hour was over.

"Nervous?" Doc asked, glancing down at her with a smile.

"Does it show?" He looked amazing in his tux. She could think of a lot of other ways to spend the evening with a man that fine. None of them included making party talk with the brother of a woman whose death she'd played a part in.

"A little." He squeezed her hand. "Is it because of Remo?"

She nodded.

Doc's face went serious. "Don't let him intimidate you. You rank higher than he does."

She looked away. "Too bad that rank doesn't come with fangs and claws."

He yanked her hand to bring her attention back to him. "Hey. If anything happens—anything—you go ghost, you understand?"

"I know." Once Chrysabelle taught her to fight, she'd feel better.

Isaiah, their butler, approached. "Omur just called up. Everyone's arrived, Maddoc. They're ready for you and Mrs. Mays downstairs."

Doc tipped his head. "Thanks. Go 'head and call the elevator. We'll be right there." He turned back to Fi, the devilish charm she loved so much glinting in his eyes again. "Have I mentioned you look like a million bucks, Mrs. Mays?"

She glanced at her strapless black gown. "You're just saying that to distract me."

"I'm saying it because it's true." He winked. "Did it work?"

"I'll be fine. Stop worrying about me." The elevator chimed and she gave him a playful shove toward it, following after him.

When they stepped off the elevator, cocktail hour was in full swing. Barasa and Omur each had small groups of upper-crusty varcolai and social types gathered around them. Fi scanned the crowd for familiar faces besides theirs, but found none.

Doc leaned in to whisper. "That blond woman in the red suit? That's the state senator's wife. She's from a long line of puma shifters. Old, old family. I definitely want you to meet her. And the man next to her with the buzz cut is a former JAG we're considering hiring as the pride's attorney."

Fi nodded. "What kind of shifter is he?"

"Lynx." He tipped his head toward a man standing beside Barasa.

"That's the police chief over there with Barasa."

"Why was he invited after what happened with you getting arrested for violating curfew?"

"The curfew was the mayor's idea, not his. And he's been fairly sympathetic to varcolai causes. It's a relationship we want to maintain."

"The mayor's not here, is she?"

He sighed. "No, but the council thinks it would be a good idea to talk with her at some point."

"Screw that."

"Fi." He looked at her, his expression half shock, half amusement. "It's in the pride's best interest."

A stranger walked up to them. "What's in the pride's best interest?"

Doc straightened. "Hello, Remo. Our relationship with the mayor, but that's a conversation for another time."

Fi tensed. So this was Remo. She didn't like him just from looking at him.

"Indeed." Remo smiled at Fi. "You must be Fiona. If I can call you that?" He stuck his hand out. "Call me Remo, please."

She didn't want to shake his hand any more than she wanted him to call her Fiona, but what choice did she have? "Nice to meet you," she lied. *Sorry your sister's heart gave out.* "How do you like New Florida so far?"

He leaned in, still holding her hand. "I like it very well." His eyes gleamed. "Very well."

He was too close, too strange, too...everything. She backed up, pulling her hand out of his. "Glad to hear it. I'm sure you and Doc have a lot to talk about. Council stuff and...okay, I have to go say hi to someone." She broke away and headed for Barasa.

"Hi," she breathed, aware she was interrupting, but not caring.

"Hello, Fiona." Barasa bent his head. "Have you met Chief Vernadetto?"

"No." She smiled, this time genuinely. Anyone was better than Remo. "Nice to meet you, Chief. Can I call you chief? Is that allowed?"

The stocky man laughed. "Peter is my first name, but you can call me Pete if you like, ma'am. That's what my friends call me."

"Whoa. No 'ma'am' here. Fiona is just fine, Pete." Calling the police chief by his first name was kind of strange, but she liked him a little more for it. He seemed like a genuinely nice man.

He nodded. "Fiona it is. Truth is, you remind me of my niece so calling you 'ma'am' does feel a little odd." His smile disappeared and a sudden seriousness took over his face. "Thank you for not holding what happened with your husband or the vampire against me. I was opposed to the curfew and was only following orders."

She reached out and rested her hand on Pete's arm. His suit wasn't expensive, but it fit him well enough. Something about that made her want to be kind to him. "I know that. But I appreciate you saying it all the same."

Barasa clapped the chief on the back. "Can I leave Fiona in your capable hands? I see someone I need to speak with."

"Absolutely." Vernadetto beamed like he'd just been given a prize. He leaned in. "They usually make me watch the dangerous ugly ones. Not often I get the young and pretty."

Fi's insides stopped churning and Remo was completely forgotten. "I like you."

Pete laughed. "I like you too. I hate coming to these things because I always feel so out of place. You don't make me feel that way, though." He dug a card out of his jacket and handed it to her. His big fingers swamped the small rectangle. "You ever need anything, you call me, okay?"

She studied the Paradise City seal embossed on the crisp white stock. "Thanks. I will. Having the chief of police on speed dial isn't such a bad thing." She tucked it into her evening bag. "So what kind of varcolai are you?"

The color drained from his face. "W-why would you ask that?"

She shrugged. "Most of the people here are, but you, I

can't tell." She'd made him uncomfortable for some reason and that made her feel bad. "I'm a ghost, you know."

"I've heard." He swallowed and cleared his throat. "I'm not a, well, that is, I'm…" He sighed. "To be honest, I don't know what I am. Probably just a few stray bloodlines that got mixed in generations back. Nothing to even talk about." He smiled, but it was weak and forced. "I'd actually prefer it if that didn't get around. Being police chief is tough enough without people questioning where my loyalties lie, you know."

She nodded. "I won't say anything to anybody. I'm really good at keeping secrets." Poor guy. It was clear he was either afraid of what he was or ashamed of it. She wanted to do something to put him at ease. "Look, if you ever want to talk, just call me up. I'm a great listener."

"Yes, you are." He nodded hard, like he was thrilled to change the subject. "And you know, if there's anything I can do for you, just name it."

She smiled and patted his arm. "Thanks, Pete. I'll remember that." And she would, because with Remo around, having the police chief on her side might come in handy.

Chapter Six

Nothing. Not a hint of brimstone, not a wisp of shadow or smoke. Samael had ignored Tatiana's repeated requests for his presence. Requests that had quickly turned into pleas, and after the second hour, had eroded almost to the point of begging.

Tatiana didn't beg. But for the sake of Lilith...she might. Hands clenched at her sides so tightly that her metal one creaked, she called out to the father of her kind once again. "Samael, liege of darkness, lord of all vampires, I beseech you come to me."

The only reason for his absence that made sense was that she was still too weak from grief to call him properly. She clung to that, because the thought that her liege, her source of power, had abandoned her was...unacceptable.

"Please, Samael. I-I...beg you." The word soured in her mouth, a bitter reminder of how far she'd fallen. Because of Malkolm and his comarré pet.

The air stayed still while she vibrated with anger. She picked up a vase and hurled it across the room with a snarl. "Damn you, Malkolm. Damn you and your meddling whore."

Kosmina came running in. "Is all well, my lady?"

"No, all is not well." Tatiana tucked the rest of her emotions away as best she could, but Kosmina knew what these last days had brought to the House of Tepes. She would certainly understand Tatiana's frustrations. "I asked not to be disturbed."

"My apologies, my lady." Kosmina's gaze skipped to the shards of Chinese porcelain decorating the carpet. "Shall I have that cleaned up or leave it for later?"

"Clean it." Tatiana stalked out of the room, the overwhelming need to hold her child burning through her body like sunlight. She wrapped her arms around herself as she headed down the hall and into the empty nursery.

The faintest tang of Svetla's ashes still lingered, but not enough to drown out Lilith's sweet scent.

Tatiana sank into the rocker where she'd often sat with Lilith, closed her eyes, and inhaled. She could sense Lilith's weight in her arms, hear her soft coos and demanding cries, feel the delicate silk of her skin. Heat stung Tatiana's eyes. She opened them and stared skyward. Not tears, she told herself. Anger. Righteous, indignant anger at what had been done to her and her child.

One of the rocker's wooden arms groaned under her grip. She released it and stood. It was time to make something happen. There had to be a way to summon Samael, but just in thinking that, she knew there wasn't. Even the council had been unable to call him when they'd wished his decision on whether or not to name her Dominus.

The father of all noble vampires only came when he wanted. That was the trouble with the ancients. They only did what they wanted, not what benefited their children. As parents went, they were wretched examples. How would they know how desperately she wanted, no, needed Lilith back? How could they begin to understand?

A knock on the nursery door dispersed her thoughts. "Yes?"

Kosmina stuck her head in. "My lady, Daciana has returned with your new comar."

"That didn't take long. I guess Rennata didn't want to deal with my emissary any more than she wanted to deal with me." The tickle of anticipation trilled down Tatiana's spine. Her sorrows temporarily pushed aside, she nodded and pointed out the door. "Send them to my office. I'll be there shortly."

"Yes, my lady." With a short bow, Kosmina left.

Tatiana took a long look in the nursery mirror and arranged her expression into one of calmness and serenity. She would drink from this new, unspoiled comar until her strength was completely returned to her, until power rippled over her skin. Then she would call Samael again, and this time, he would come to her. She hoped.

"Faith," she whispered, nodding solemnly at her reflection, seeing the woman who had defied her human life to rise through the ranks of her vampire brethren until she'd been named head of her House. There was no one above her. No one who had the power she did, power that had been given to her by the very creature who now refused her beckoning.

She smiled, showing her fangs. "This time, my liege, you will not deny me."

Creek approached the old Catholic church with caution. He knew Preacher wasn't a big fan of company. The front doors didn't look well used, so he went around to the side. He knocked twice. No point in overloading the man's vampire senses.

"Who's there?" The door stayed closed.

"Name's Thomas Creek. I have information about your daughter."

The door moved, but only an inch, the light from inside casting Preacher in shadows. "What kind of information?"

"Where she is and what's being done to get her back."

"You work for the mayor?"

Creek made a face. "Hell no."

The door opened all the way. "Come in." Preacher stood back, watching him. His nostrils flared. "Your blood smells strange."

Creek came in but not too far. "Most vampires think it smells sour."

"No," Preacher said. "Smells sweet to me."

Creek laughed once. "Figures you'd think that considering where you live. I'm Kubai Mata. You know what that is?"

"Nope. Should I?"

Creek shook his head. "Most vampires don't and those that do don't believe in the KM. I guess you could say I'm part of a secret society organized to protect humans against othernaturals."

Preacher's stony expression cracked into a grin a few seconds later. "You mean you're a vampire slayer?"

Not the reaction he'd expected, but then nothing was expected when it came to a vampire like Preacher. "You could say that."

Preacher crossed his arms. "Prove it."

"You mean you want me to try to kill you?"

He laughed. "I think we both know that's not going to happen, so I'd find a different way if I were you."

Creek thought for a moment, then shucked his jacket and his weapons holster. As much as that went against his self-preservation instincts, he had a feeling showing Preacher the brands on his back would do the trick. He turned and yanked his shirt up.

"Latin."

"You read that, don't you? You were a priest, right?"

"A chaplain. I read a little."

More than most. Creek helped him out anyway. "*Omnes honorate. Fraternitatem diligite. Deum timete. Regem honorificate.* Translated that says, 'Honor all men. Love the brotherhood. Fear God. Honor the king.' It's the code of the Kubai Mata and it comes from—"

"The New Testament," Preacher finished. "1 Peter 2:17."

Creek pulled his shirt and gathered up his holster as he turned around. He nodded. "Proof enough for you?"

Preacher stuck his hand out. "Good to meet you, son." Creek shook his hand, and then Preacher turned on a dime and headed into the church's interior. "We can chat in here." He took a spot on one of the front pews.

Creek sat a few places down from him. "The KM would like you to know that we have some intel on your daughter's location and we're working on getting her back but that it would be in everyone's best interests if you let us handle it. The ancient ones that have her are more powerful than you can imagine. Chances are if you went after her, you'd end up dead before you got close."

"You want me to agree to this, you'd better keep me

informed." Preacher stared at him. "I'm not without skills. You keep me out of the loop or lie to me, and I will do whatever I feel necessary."

"Understood." Creek decided to test the waters a little further. "You asked if I worked for the mayor. I take it you don't get along with her?"

"She may be the mother of my late wife, but she's got bad ambitions. That ignorant woman tried to get me to turn her into a vampire."

"Interesting. I can tell you she found someone else to do it."

A muscle in his jaw jumped and his eyes lit with anger. "She is *not* getting her hands on my child."

Creek nodded. "The KM shares your sentiment on that."

Preacher twisted to stare at the altar. "The mayor was just here not long ago. She wants me to come see her at her office. Says she has information on Mariela."

"That's your daughter's name?" Creek asked. "I didn't know." He leaned forward. "Go meet with her. See what she has to say, but don't let her know that you and I talked. She's not a big fan of me anyway. We know she wants Mariela for herself, but let's see what else we can find out."

Preacher nodded without looking at him. "Will do."

Creek stood. "I'll be back when I have information to share. Until then, keep a low profile." The guy seemed all right. Not entirely normal, but not bad for a vampire. "If you need me, I live in that old machine shop."

"I know the place." Preacher rose. "And don't worry. I won't do anything stupid. I have a daughter to live for."

* * *

"I didn't think you'd show." Lola didn't get up as the housekeeper brought Preacher into her office. She glanced at her watch. "You're almost four hours late."

"I said I'd come. I didn't say when." The dog tags around his neck gleamed against his dull green T-shirt and camouflage jacket.

"But you were too busy earlier? When I came to you?"

He sat, his expression neither pleased nor displeased. A hard man to read. "Yes. Too busy."

"Doing what?" Because honestly, she couldn't imagine what filled his schedule.

"I see you got what you wanted. Found someone to sire you." He snorted. "Can't sense you, though, so I'm guessing you must be some kind of vampire I don't know about."

Fine. Play it that way, don't answer. Once again, his loss. "House of Paole," she told him. "It's the inherited power all nobles of that house receive. We are undetectable to others."

"Can you daywalk?"

"You know very well that is a gift you and you alone possess."

He stared at her, a hint of impudence in his eyes. "What did you want to speak to me about?"

"I thought you might want to know. I had a team go after Mariela."

He sat forward. "Why wasn't I brought in? I'm trained for that kind of thing. I could have been an asset."

She held her hand up. "This was more of a diplomatic exercise than a military one." She lifted the prepared letter. "Unfortunately, it wasn't successful."

"They didn't bring Mariela home?"

Lola pushed her tongue against the tip of one fang until the pain made her eyes water. "I am very sorry to inform you that Mariela perished during the mission."

The muscles in his neck tensed and his eyes seemed to grow slightly brighter, more liquid. "What do you... mean... perished?" His voice was throaty and rough.

"You know what I mean." Even as she imagined Mariela really being gone, she bit down, tasting blood. The combination was enough to cause her eyes to well. She let the emotions fill her voice. "She was killed in the escape." She held the letter out to him. "It's all right here. You can keep this copy, if you like."

He took the letter, folded it up without looking at it, and tucked it into his jacket. Then he stood, his body rigid with military stiffness. One nod to her and he turned sharply and walked out.

She waited until she heard the front door open and shut, and then she leaned back in her chair and nodded with satisfaction. That had gone so much easier than she'd anticipated. Now Mariela would be truly hers.

If she could just find out how to get ahold of the ancients Dominic claimed had taken Mariela. They would be harder to deal with than a crazy daywalker who lived in a church, but how much harder?

She flexed her hands into claws, wishing she had something to grab hold of. She had worked around Preacher; she would find a way to work around the ancients. Mariela would be hers soon. She could feel it in her bones.

Chrysabelle stood her ground as Fi came at her again. For the second time, Fi failed to flip her over. "Come on, Fi.

You've got to bend your knees and use the power of your legs."

Fi snorted out a breath. "I can't do it! You're way taller than me. You can't expect me to hoist you over like that."

"It doesn't have anything to do with height. It's all about leverage, which is really important when you're fighting an opponent who's bigger than you." Chrysabelle pursed her mouth, trying to think of how better to explain it. "Do you want to wait until Damian's back? He and Amylia should be home soon, and then he and I can demonstrate. Or maybe Amylia could help. She's closer to your size." Damian and the new comarré had left with Velimai to get groceries just as Fi had arrived that morning. The excursion was Damian's idea, part of his effort to learn to live on his own and help Amylia come to terms with the new life that had been thrust on her. Chrysabelle understood all that, but the idea that Damian might move away from her after she'd just found him only added to her stress.

Fi sighed and fussed with the belt of her gi. "Maybe I should just get a gun."

"Unless the bullets are silver, it's not going to do much good against a vampire or a varcolai."

Fi frowned. "But at least I'll have the satisfaction of tearing holes in something."

Chrysabelle lifted a brow. "You're in a fun mood today. How about we reschedule?"

"No, sorry." Fi sat cross-legged on the floor, then lounged back on her hands. "We had one of those super-boring formal dinners last night to introduce Heaven's brother Remo to everyone as the new council member."

Chrysabelle sat beside her. "I take it you didn't have a good time."

She made an impolite noise. "Other than getting to know the police chief, it wasn't exactly a laugh-fest. Having Remo there just made it worse." She shuddered. "I do not like that guy. He gives me the creeps." She came off her hands to lean forward. "He looks at me like he wants to skin me. Or eat me. Or both." She grimaced. "I know he blames me for his sister's death, but what can I do?"

Chrysabelle sat back. "If he bothers you that much, say something to Doc."

Fi shook her head. "I don't want to add to his stress."

"Do you think Remo would actually hurt you? Does he have a history of violence?"

"No clue."

Chrysabelle dipped her head to stare directly at Fi. "You're the wife of the pride leader. You said you got to know the police chief. Do you think he could help you out? Get a little background on this guy?"

Fi's jaw popped to one side and her eyes took on the distance of thought. "He did give me his card."

Chrysabelle straightened the hem of her tunic. "Is Remo why you want to learn to fight? Because you think he's going to try to get revenge for his sister's death?"

"No. Maybe a little." She sighed. "At first, I felt awful about what happened. That fight wasn't supposed to end in anyone's death. But Doc and his council guys kept telling me not to feel guilty, that challenges and fights are part of life in a pride, and as I healed up, I realized that what happened *was* perfectly within pride laws—which I didn't break—and by winning that challenge, I showed everyone what I was capable of. I was kind of proud of myself." Her fingers went to her neck and a slim leather cord that disappeared beneath her gi.

Chrysabelle nodded. "I get that. And you should be proud. In your human form, you went up against a varcolai. A creature stronger and faster than any human could ever be, and you came out the winner." She reached over and squeezed Fi's leg. "Even I would have been scared in that situation."

Fi perked up a little. "You would have?"

"Absolutely."

Fi smiled and dug under her gi to pull out something dangling off the long, black cord. "I made this to remind myself of what I'd accomplished." She held a little glass vial in her hand. Something shimmered inside it.

"What is it?"

"It's sand from the arena. It was in my boots. Every time I get intimidated by my position as the pride leader's wife, this reminds me that I've already proved myself worthy."

Chrysabelle held the vial, turning it under the light. "It's actually really pretty. I've never seen sand that looked so sparkly." She let go of it. "I think it's a great idea. It's like your talisman."

"Thanks." Fi tucked it back into her training uniform. "I haven't shown it to Doc. I'm afraid he'll think it's silly, that I should just automatically have confidence like he does." She propped her elbows on her knees. "I think he forgets that I was just a regular old human college student when I was killed. I didn't grow up on the streets like he did. I don't know how to handle myself in a lot of these situations that seem to come so naturally to him. He was raised in the pride. It's been his life except for the years

Sinjin threw him out." She leaned her head into her hand. "I'm rambling. I'm sorry. You have enough problems without me adding mine."

Chrysabelle smiled, but the smile wasn't whole-hearted. "We all have problems."

"What are you going to do about Mal?"

"Nothing. I have to move forward." While she waited and watched and prayed she didn't have to kill him.

"There's always something you can do. Don't you love him? He needs you."

"I told you I did, but Fi, I don't think you understand what happened."

"I do. The fae sucked out all his love for you. I promise, I get it. Now answer the question. Do you love him? Not did you, *do* you."

Chrysabelle struggled to keep her mind off the child she carried. "Yes. That's the hardest part of moving forward."

Fi's eyes narrowed. "You don't just stop being in love with someone."

"I don't see what choice I have." Chrysabelle stood, ready to get back to work. As she came to her feet, the floor twisted beneath her. The world had suddenly gone off balance. She put her hand out, but found nothing to grab onto. She stumbled, going down on one knee. Her stomach revolted and her mouth watered. She doubled over and pointed to the corner of the room. "Trash can."

"What?"

"Trash. Can." She swallowed, trying to hold herself together. "Now."

Fi scurried to get it, sliding back to Chrysabelle's side

just as her control left. She vomited into the metal bin. Relief settled in immediately. Fi stuck her hand on Chrysabelle's forehead. "Are you sick? You don't feel warm."

"No, I'm fine, just something I ate, I'm sure."

Fi's brows arched in disbelief. "Really? Because when I got here, Damian told me there were plenty of leftovers since you'd skipped breakfast." Suddenly, her eyes widened. "Holy crap. You're pregnant. Are you pregnant? You're pregnant!"

Chrysabelle was about to deny it when her stomach heaved again. She sighed and wiped her mouth on her sleeve as she lay down on the gym mats. She crooked her elbow over her eyes, wishing she could block out the reality of what was happening just as easily as that.

Fi didn't get the hint and kept talking. "Whom did you sleep with? Not that it's any of my business, but that's never stopped me before."

Chrysabelle lifted her arm long enough to shoot Fi a look. "Mal. Who else would I sleep with?"

Fi's jaw dropped open and for a few brief but glorious moments, she was speechless. Anticipating the questions, Chrysabelle dropped her head back down and explained. "He drank my blood during...our time together, which brought his body to life. That's how."

"Does Damian know? Holy crap, is he going to go all big brother and go after Mal? Defend your honor and all that?"

Chrysabelle kept her head down. The cool mat felt good against her neck. "No, he doesn't know and my honor doesn't need defending. The only people who know are Vel, Mortalis, maybe Nyssa, and now you. And I'd like to keep it that way."

"Mum's the word. Or not, seeing as how mum means—"

"I get it." Chrysabelle felt Fi lay down beside her.

"You should at least tell Damian. He's family. And he's about to be an uncle to a half-vampire kid. You should give him a little time to prepare for that."

Chrysabelle sighed into the air. "I know. I'm just worried about how he'll react."

Fi was quiet for a long second. "You know this means you *have* to find a way to fix things between you and Mal."

Chrysabelle turned her head enough to see Fi. "It doesn't mean that at all. My being pregnant doesn't make the impossible any more possible."

"Really? Because your getting knocked up by a vampire seems like the definition of that." Fi frowned. "Look. Mal's daughter was killed by a vampire. You can't take this child away from him too."

"He's not the Mal he was a few weeks ago, Fi. He's the Mal who killed you. The Mal the nobility wanted to erase. He's become a monster again. He was here last night, watching me. If Mortalis hadn't intervened..." She sat up a little, causing her insides to slosh unpleasantly. "The house next door was broken into and the alarm was set off. When the police came, they found one of those white-tailed deer dead on the property. Its neck was slashed open and it had been drained of blood. Do you understand what I'm saying? That would have been me." She lay back down. "The best I can do right now is pacify him, something I'm going to see Dominic about this evening."

Fi grunted. "I've never known you to be a quitter."

"I'm not quitting. I'm—"

"You want to be safe? You want this child to be safe?"

"Of course I do." Anger skipped along Chrysabelle's nerves. She blew out a breath and forced herself to remember Fi was only trying to help. She pushed to her elbows and met Fi's gaze. "Look, if there was a way to fix Mal, I would do it. Whatever it was, short of sacrificing the life of this child, I would make it happen."

Fi's eyes glittered with determination. "Then we have to figure out what that is."

Chapter Seven

Things were oddly quiet in Paradise City. Lola tapped her fingers on her desk, knowing it wouldn't last. In fact, it would probably end the moment she announced she'd been turned into a vampire at this evening's press conference, but the citizens needed to know how far she'd gone to bridge the gap between the othernaturals and the humans. Word was starting to spread. Better they heard it from her own lips.

They would see how much she was willing to sacrifice for them. And how things were going to change for the better because of it.

For one, she couldn't keep traditional office hours and it was becoming more obvious that the city needed to be open twenty-four hours to service the needs of all its citizens. And some of those citizens of the othernatural variety were perfectly suited to nocturnal time schedules. Not only would employing a second shift of othernatural workers for city hall fulfill their needs, but it would bring more jobs to the city and show how hard they were all working to create a place where everyone could live in harmony.

Paradise City would set an example for the rest of the country. She leaned back in her chair and put her feet up on the desk. The big networks would want to interview her. Maybe she'd even write a book.

"Mayor?" Valerie, her administrative assistant, pushed the office door open.

She dropped her feet back to the floor. "Yes?"

"There's *someone* here to see you."

The way Valerie stressed the "someone," Lola knew that person wasn't human. She inhaled and immediately scented another vampire. Preacher? Hopefully not. After giving him that letter, she'd assumed that situation was resolved. "Give me two minutes."

Valerie nodded and pulled the door shut.

Lola closed her eyes and focused on what she was feeling. Immediately, she realized she could detect the new presence. Luciano had told her she'd be able to but that it would take time to develop her senses. She really needed to visit with him again. He'd been so helpful. Odd that he hadn't contacted her in the last few days.

Valerie knocked again.

"Come in."

She entered with a handsome, well-dressed vampire behind her. Definitely not Preacher. Valerie looked a little uneasy. She had no issue with varcolai so maybe it was just that he was a vampire? She'd have to get used to the othernaturals eventually, just as the othernaturals would come to accept their human counterparts. That balance was necessary for peace to continue.

Lola stayed seated as Valerie introduced him. "This is Octavian Petrescu."

"Mr. Petrescu, how can I help you?"

"Call me Octavian, please." He smiled and glanced at Valerie. "May we speak privately?"

Lola nodded to her assistant. "Thank you, Valerie. That will be all."

She seemed relieved to be dismissed.

Once the door closed, he gestured toward the chairs in front of her desk. "May I sit?"

"Of course. Now, what brings you to my office?"

He eased into the seat, small lines of tension bracketing his mouth. "I am new to your city. As you have no doubt noticed, I am also a vampire, but my understanding is that this city is not exactly . . . friendly to my kind."

She nodded. "You're referring to the curfew incident. I assure you that is well behind us and not to be repeated. I was under the influence of a very dangerous man." She smiled, hoping to reassure him. "Perhaps you didn't realize, but I am vampire also, having recently been sired." She let her eyes silver. It was a skill she'd mastered almost instantly, although keeping her human face in place without a regular feeding schedule remained difficult. Fortunately, Hector, her comar, was always willing and on hand when she needed him.

"I had heard a rumor, but there is nothing about you that indicates such." His body language relaxed and he leaned forward. "You are House of Paole, then?"

"Yes. I guess it takes another noble to understand something like that."

"Indeed." He splayed his fingers against his chest. "I am House of Tepes, not so long ago sired either, but I have been in the company of nobles all my life." He dropped his hand to rest on the chair's arm. "Perhaps this is a bold statement, but I have come here to make a new life for myself and I feel like fate has brought us together. I believe you and I could help each other."

"Mr. Petrescu—"

"Octavian, please."

She nodded. "Octavian. I am extraordinarily busy. I have a city to run." And a granddaughter to find. "A city that is tenuously holding on to a modicum of peace between its othernatural and human citizens." Some of his enthusiasm left his face. "However, what you're suggesting appeals to me. I have no other real vampire acquaintances and as I am young, I know you could be valuable to me." She sighed. This was an opportunity she did not want to pass up, but she could not ignore the needs of her city. "I have several pressing matters to address before I can allow myself any personal time. Until then..."

"May I ask what kinds of pressing matters?"

How much should she reveal? He was one of her own, after all, and her plans would soon be obvious. "I am trying to turn Paradise City into an example of how humans and othernaturals can live in harmony. A big part of that plan is making sure the city is open and operating around the clock so that the needs of all its citizens can be met. That means hiring a second shift of workers to keep city hall running. My administrative assistant, Valerie, is going to be difficult to duplicate. I need an othernatural who is organized, knowledgeable of both sides, and capable of getting things done. Plus, they must be compatible with me as we'll be working very closely together since I'll be taking that second shift and letting the city council handle matters during daylight hours." She studied him, wondering what he thought of such ambition. "As you can see, my plate is full."

"This is fate indeed." He smiled broadly. "I was the assistant to a very powerful, very old vampire in my city. For years before I was sired, I ran her vast estate, managed the extensive staff and her schedule. I know how to work with mortals and othernaturals alike." His face went very serious. "I can do this job. It may very well be the reason I felt compelled to come here. Please, give me a chance."

She sat back, taking in everything he'd said and mulling it over. The wheels in her head began to spin. "How old and how powerful?"

"She was in direct connection with the most ancient of our kind."

She tried not to react to his statement, but it was as if he'd known what she wanted to hear. She played it off, fussing with some papers on her desk as if his words meant nothing to her. "If you were so good at what you did, why aren't you still working for this vampire anymore?"

Sorrow tarnished his eyes. "The burden of eternity became too much for her to bear. She lost someone dear to her and, in her grief, walked into the dawn." He swallowed and looked away for a moment. "Forgive me. I still miss her."

Lola understood what it meant to lose someone so close to you. She nodded in sympathy. "I'm sorry for your loss. I would be happy to offer you the job. Maybe the work will be good for you. Give you something else to focus on."

He smiled gently, his eyes still liquid and yet happy. "Thank you. I will not let you down."

Exactly how powerful and connected was the vampire

across from her? She needed to know what he was capable of, because what she really wanted from him wasn't for him to become her nighttime assistant.

What she wanted from him was the knowledge of how to access those ancients he spoke of. The ancients she knew were holding her grandchild.

"Mariela," Preacher whispered, letting the breeze take her name like a prayer. His military and religious training had taught him enough about lies and confession to know that Creek was telling the truth and the mayor was not, but even without that, he knew in his heart that his daughter was alive. He could feel that the bond between them remained unbroken.

The wind whistled past, barely registering. He stood high in the church's belfry, the bells long ago stolen by hoods looking for a few quick bucks off the scrap metal. The view from here made the church impossible to sneak up on. When Mariela was first born, he'd spent every night up here, coming down only to eliminate the bands of fringe who came nosing around, sniffing after the scent of newborn.

Damn vampires.

He'd killed as many as he could. Each one an example of what he'd do to anyone who tried to harm his child.

He laughed softly, bitter and disgusted at himself. He still hadn't been able to save her. And now, he was forced to sit on his hands or sacrifice his life. Patience was a difficult thing, especially when it came to Mariela's life.

But he would wait. At least a little while longer.

* * *

Creek leaned against the kitchen counter while Annika and Octavian stood across from him. He wasn't crazy about his place being the new meeting spot for KM business. All the coming and going attracted too much attention. He also didn't like Octavian arriving before Annika. The vampire had been here half an hour before the sector chief, leaving Creek to play host. Not a job he excelled at.

Annika tipped her head toward him. "How did it go with Preacher?"

"He's not happy with the mayor being turned, but after I explained the KM to him and what we're planning, he agreed to sit tight. He wants to be included on whatever we do, though." Creek shrugged. "The kid *is* his. I can't say I blame him or disagree. Her name is Mariela, by the way."

"Whose name?" Annika asked.

"The child. Preacher called her Mariela. Also, he told me the mayor wanted him to meet with her at her office. I told him to go but keep our meeting a secret. Who knows, maybe we'll get some info off him the next time I visit."

She turned to Octavian. "Or you can find out what she wanted with him, assuming it went well with the mayor."

He almost laughed. "It did. Easier than anticipated, actually. The intel was dead on. She ate up the story about my past and hired me on the spot for the assistant job. As long as she perceives me to be loyal, I should be fine."

Annika nodded. "Good. Both situations are controlled, then. How much longer before you find out who sired her?"

"She needs companionship and seems very willing to confide in me. Twenty-four hours. Maybe less. I can confirm her sire was House of Paole."

"I knew it." Creek shifted to lean on his elbow. "When I saw her that first night, it was like she was a blank space. Couldn't sense a thing. Preacher told me she tried to get him to sire her, but he refused her. I believe him. He has no love for her."

Something buzzed. Twice. He realized it was his and Annika's phones. She reached into her jacket and pulled hers out as he did the same. She held the screen up so he could see the matching alert scrolling across the front. "New police scanner app. Part of the last KM upgrade to all communication systems."

She pressed her index finger to the screen, then scanned the message, shaking her head. "Not good. A body's just been found in an alley off of Biscayne Boulevard. Time of death is within the last two hours." Creek followed her words on his screen, surprised to be getting the same info she was at the same time.

He nodded. "Cause of death appears to be puncture wounds to the neck and exsanguination."

She made eye contact with him as he looked up. "There goes the quiet. We've got a rogue vampire."

Chapter Eight

Fi's driver brought the car to a stop in front of the pride headquarters private entrance. On the way, she'd made a call to Chief Vernadetto about getting more background on Remo. Pete had been happy to help, even offering to meet over lunch to discuss his findings. Such a nice guy. She felt fortunate to have met him. There had to be something she could do for him in return.

Her driver opened her door and she slipped out, leaving her bodyguard behind to discuss her schedule with the driver. She moved on autopilot, her thoughts turning to Chrysabelle's news. Fi's heart broke every time she thought about it. She couldn't imagine being pregnant *and* Doc not loving her, or worse, stalking her like she was a snack. Poor Chrysabelle. After everything she'd endured, now this? Fi resolved right then to stick with her and be there for whatever Chrysabelle might need. Besides, what good was being the pride leader's mate if she couldn't help a friend?

She sighed with the realization that Chrysabelle's secret was now her secret too. How was she going to keep it from Doc? That was going to be tough. She told Doc every—she smacked into a hard, warm body. A step back and she looked up into the eyes of...

Remo.

He grinned at her. "Hello, Fiona."

Barely controlling the urge to shiver, she looked behind her, but her driver had already disappeared and apparently her bodyguard had gone with him. She forced a smile to cover her nerves. "Sorry for running into you. I have a lot on my mind and I wasn't paying attention." She started to move around him. "Good night."

He stepped into her path. "What's got you so flustered?"

"Nothing. I'm fine." She made the smile bigger, causing her cheeks to ache. "If you'll excuse me."

He didn't move. "We should get to know each other better, you and I." He shifted slightly and somehow ended up blocking her path even more. "I had hoped to do that at the welcome dinner last night, but I barely saw you." A shimmer of gold slipped through his eyes. "Anyone else might think you were avoiding them, but I know you wouldn't do that."

"Of course not," she answered weakly. The fake smile was pointless now. "I was just so busy with the other guests." Where was Doc when she needed him? Her hand went to her necklace, hidden beneath the vintage rock band T-shirt she'd worn to Chrysabelle's. At least she didn't still have the gi on. Remo would know something was up then.

His gaze dropped to her shirt, scruffy jeans, and combat boots. "You looked so beautiful last night. I didn't expect to see you dressed like..."

"Like what?" His criticism irked her and she decided to let it show. She crossed her arms, waiting for his answer.

"Like a street urchin."

"Let me guess. Your sister would have never dressed like this and you don't think it's becoming for the wife of the pride leader to be seen—"

"Wait a minute. I never said any of that." His face colored. Almost like he was embarrassed.

"No, but you were thinking it."

His brow furrowed. "No, I wasn't. I was thinking how nice that you do not feel so confined by the role of pride leader's mate that you've lost yourself to it."

Her jaw went slack. "That's what you were thinking?"

"Is that so strange?" He threw his hands up and strode away. "Go about your business. I see what you think of me. What you all think of me."

Against her better judgment, she called after him. "Wait."

He stopped.

"I know it must be hard for you to be here, not knowing anyone, still mourning your sister, and I haven't been very friendly. I'm sorry."

He turned around.

"Maybe we could start over?"

"I would like that." He smiled and nodded, then sadness took his smile away. "Heaven would have never reacted that way. You are much better suited to this position than she. She was my sister, but even I admit she was too spoiled and self-centered to be the kind of partner a pride leader needs."

Amazed at his confession, Fi saw him with new eyes. He must feel like no one wanted him here. Like a complete outsider. Kind of the way she'd felt right after Doc had killed Sinjin and they'd found out that pride law stated Sinjin's wife was now Doc's. The spoils of war and all that. The general vibe from the rest of the pride hadn't exactly made her feel welcome. She still got a few stink eyes now and then. "Thank you for that."

He hesitated, then pointed toward the door. "I was headed out to get a drink. Bar Nine isn't really where I want to hang out at the moment. Do you want to come with me?"

"Where to?"

He laughed. "I actually don't know. I just thought I'd walk until I came to a place."

"How about the VIP section of Bar Nine? If the rest of the pride sees we can get along, maybe they'll get the idea that they should too."

"You'd do that for me?"

"Sure." Also, she had no intention of going anywhere outside headquarters with him alone. She might understand where he was coming from, but that didn't mean she'd lost her common sense. Doc could be very jealous when he chose to be and there was no point in starting unnecessary rumors. Or chancing it with Remo. This whole poor-me thing could be just an act. "Just give me a few minutes to run upstairs and change."

"Excellent. I'll meet you at the bar."

She nodded. "Back-corner booth. It's reserved for me. Tell them I said it was okay."

He stepped aside and as she started past, she caught an odd gleam in his eyes through her peripheral vision. She whipped her head around to look closer, but the expression was gone.

"Something else?" he asked.

"No." Nothing she could pinpoint. Other than the feeling she might be getting played.

* * *

Chrysabelle entered Dominic's office behind Mortalis, who'd set up the appointment for her. The anathema vampire sat behind his desk, but stood as she walked in. She nodded at him. "Thank you for seeing me on such short notice."

"*Cara mia, per favore*, you know you are like family to me." He came out from behind his desk and approached her with his arms out, but stopped a few feet away and wrinkled his nose. "You are wearing your body armor, are you not?"

"Yes, I am. Sorry, I know this much silver and holy magic so close to you must be very irritating."

Mortalis spoke up. "I told her to wear it whenever she leaves the house. We have good reason to think Mal is... after her."

Chrysabelle sighed. "He was watching me last night. The alarm in the house next door was tripped and when the police showed up, they found a dead deer on the property, throat torn out, blood drained." Just retelling it set her on edge.

Dominic's brows shot up and he mumbled something in Italian. He snapped his fingers and a lean, dark figure emerged from the sitting area at the far end of the room. "Luciano, you want to make things right with me? You will go to Chrysabelle's house and protect her. This is what you do, no? So do it."

Chrysabelle held her hand up. "No, please, I don't need that." She sat in the closest chair, her head swimming a little with the number of thoughts running through it. At least her morning sickness had really only hit her during the day. So far this evening, her body seemed fairly normal. She looked at the new vampire. "You're Dominic's nephew?" Then back at Dominic. "I have Velimai. I really don't need anyone else at my house protecting me."

"It's a good idea," Mortalis said. "Luciano is Paole. Mal wouldn't be able to detect him."

"He's also *caedo*," Dominic added with an edge of anger Chrysabelle didn't understand.

Luciano threw his hands up. "*Zio!*"

"Great," Chrysabelle muttered. "A vampire assassin. Just what I need." She rubbed her temples before speaking to Dominic again. "I'm still missing a piece of the puzzle, though, aren't I? You're angry at Luciano for something? What does he need to make right with you? If he's going to be at my home, on my property, I need to know the whole story."

Dominic went back behind his desk and sat. He crossed his legs and took a long, hard look at Luciano. "This one thought he was doing me a favor."

Luciano rolled his eyes skyward. "I meant no harm, *zio*. I swear it."

Dominic lifted a hand to silence him. "This one..." He shook his head as he turned his attention to Chrysabelle again. "Took it upon himself to help me. How? By giving the mayor what she wanted."

Luciano wrung his hands. "She dropped the curfew, didn't she?"

Chrysabelle's head spun a little harder. "What are you saying?"

Dominic sighed. "He *sired* the mayor."

"Holy mother." A nauseous chill sunk into Chrysabelle's belly. "Holy. Mother." Her mouth watered. She swallowed it down. "The mayor is a vampire?" She twisted to look at Mortalis. "How could you not tell me this?"

Mortalis cleared his throat. "I wasn't sure you could handle the news with everything else going on."

She stared at her lap, stunned and blinking as the weight of it settled over her. Abruptly, her head came up and she glared at Luciano. "And you're Paole. Which means the mayor is too. So the mayor is an *undetectable* vampire. That's bloody brilliant."

Luciano swallowed. "I am sure I could find a way to fix—"

"I think you've done enough," Chrysabelle snapped.

Silence filled the room like poison gas. It was clear that none of the men knew what to say to her. Finally, after a long exhale, she spoke a little more calmly. "I came here for a reason."

"*Si, si,*" Dominic said. He looked happy to have something new to talk about.

"I need a shipment of blood from your comarré sent to Mal's freighter every night. I want enough animal blood mixed in so that he won't be at full power. Do you understand?"

"*Si.*" Dominic nodded. "Consider it done."

"That's not all. Can you dope the blood with some kind of tracking system so that when he drinks it, I'll be able to know where he is? I don't need to know how you do it, just if you can."

"You grow more like your mother every day." He jotted something on a piece of paper. "Unfortunately, this is not something that can be done. However, if Mal has become this much of a threat to you, I can add something to the blood that will work just as well."

"Like what?"

Dominic lifted one shoulder. "A touch of this, a touch of that, a hint of laudanum. Enough to keep him so relaxed, he will not be a problem to anyone. And he will not even realize what's being done."

She hated the idea of drugging Mal, but... "Okay. I don't like it, but I like it better than him reverting to killing humans." If he hadn't already. *Please, holy mother, don't let him have come to that.* "Will you be able to get it to him in such a way that it keeps him from hunting?"

Dominic nodded. "I can enhance the aroma, make it irresistible, make it so that he is drawn to the blood and thinks of nothing else. And I'll be sure it's placed in his path. It will be done. You'll see."

"Good." She stood, ready to be home again. "One last thing. I don't care if Luciano guards my house, but I don't want to see him, I won't give him shelter from the day and under no circumstances is he to approach Mal if he shows up. Is that clear?" She knew she sounded harsh but didn't care. "I just... need my space right now."

"Absolutely. Perhaps I will find a better use for my errant nephew." The twinkle in Dominic's eyes said he found her commands either amusing or charming but she was in no mood to be either.

"Do you think this is funny? This is my life we're talking about. And the life of my—" She stopped cold, the word "child" dancing on her tongue. Her hand slipped to her stomach. "Brother," she covered.

The twinkle died, replaced by sudden curiosity. Dominic tipped his head. "How is your brother? And the other comarré? Amylia?"

Afraid she'd say something she'd truly regret, she

answered quickly. "They're both fine. If you'll excuse me, I really must go. I'm not feeling well." And with that, she hurried toward the door. Dominic could think what he liked as long as he sent Mal the blood as promised.

"Chrysabelle," he called after her.

She kept moving. It was that or vomit in his office.

Chapter Nine

The throb of bloodlust infiltrated Mal's daysleep with an undeniable force. The moment he moved, the voices started up. Their chant of *blood, blood, blood* multiplied his growing hunger until he could almost smell blood.

He sat up in bed. Actually, he *could* smell blood. Human blood. Still in the clothes he'd collapsed in when daysleep hit, he stumbled out of his room and down the freighter's long hall toward the scent. The solars had kicked on with the setting sun, but he could have found his way by the smell alone. It grew stronger as he approached the door to the main deck.

He swung the door open. A container sat a few feet away. Every sense alert, he checked the area but found nothing to indicate it was a trick. He inhaled. Beyond the thick perfume of blood, there was a faint trace of spice. The smell of vampire. Namely, Dominic.

A satisfied smile curled Mal's lips. About time Dominic started giving him what he was due.

He wrenched the top of the container off. Inside sat four bags of blood, still warm thanks to the container's insulation. He grabbed them and with one final look around, headed back inside. These would be just enough to fuel him for an evening of hunting. The deer he'd had at Chrysabelle's had barely scratched the surface of his need.

Squeezing one of the bags to tighten it up, he sank his fangs in and drank. The blood was definitely human, probably from Dominic's comarré, but a little flat tasting. Maybe because nothing compared to drinking straight from Chrysabelle's vein, something he'd do again, very soon. *Yes*, the voices urged. *Soon.*

Swallowing the last of the bag's contents, he tossed it away and started downing another. Halfway through it, his feet got harder to lift, his body less responsive. Still the voices urged him to drink more. *Blood, blood, blood.*

He struggled to keep his head up. The remaining two bags slipped out of his grasp. The one he'd just about emptied followed after, falling with a soft plop onto the metal flooring. Stooping to retrieve it made everything go sideways. He put his hands out to steady himself, but ran into the wall anyway. He dragged his feet over the threshold of his room. The light from the solars dimmed like they were running out of juice. Was dawn coming? He couldn't feel the sun approaching. No, definitely night. The sun had just set. The voices went quiet.

He lifted a hand to rub his eyes and missed. His lids drifted down, heavy as though he'd had no daysleep at all. Maybe he'd rest a little before he went hunting. Before he went back to Chrysabelle's and…

He stumbled onto his bed, closed his eyes, and passed out.

* * *

Luciano jumped down from the upper deck. All sounds of movement had ceased several minutes ago and judging by the way Malkolm had torn into the first bag of blood, he'd ingested enough of the drug for it to have taken effect. Luciano's lip curled at the rust and decay surrounding him. How could any noble vampire live this way?

He picked up the container's lid and tucked it into the empty vessel, then ducked inside to collect the blood bags. Considering that he'd gone from vampire assassin to vampire babysitter, perhaps he should be less critical, but this ship reeked of rats and rot.

One blood bag was empty, another still had a few ounces in it, and two were untouched. He picked them all up, then went a little farther down the hall to confirm Malkolm was safely out for the evening.

He was. Sprawled on his bed, arms akimbo, one foot still on the floor. Luciano smirked. When Dominic said he'd do something, he did it.

With a shake of his head, Luciano headed out. He stuffed the bags into the container, then tucked the whole lot under his arm and jogged back to where he'd hidden his car. Dominic's car, actually. Since he'd run from his noble life, he'd had little opportunity to take anything with him.

If not for Dominic, he would probably be in Malkolm's straits. For the hundredth time, he cursed himself for siring the mayor and angering his uncle and thought again about ways he could rectify the situation. He opened the trunk as a seabird flew overhead, shattering the quiet with its screech.

His skills lay in ending life, not creating it. He should have stuck to what he knew. After putting the container away, he closed the trunk and got in the car. Destroying the child he'd sired would be difficult, but nothing was as difficult as the reason he'd come to Paradise City in the first place.

He felt for the bottle of pills in his coat pocket before he started the car. He didn't have the alchemist skills of his uncle, but he'd learned enough over the years and Dominic's laboratory was a storehouse of supplies. What he'd put together should do the trick. All he had to do was convince Hector, which shouldn't take much. The comar would still be servicing fringe females at Seven if Luciano hadn't brought him in to supply the mayor with blood after her turning. He drove toward Lola's house. Starting tonight, he would begin to make things right, because there was no way he was going to ruin his chances of staying here.

Tatiana's new comar, Aaron, staggered from the room. She'd drunk from him until the ashen hint of death had tinged his blood, taking all he had to offer and then some. Daciana raised a concerned brow, but said nothing. Tatiana tipped her head against the back of her office chair and stared at the ceiling as her heart began to beat. "I know I took—" She gasped as the power of Aaron's blood gripped her. Icy hot pain coursed through her body. She tensed, bowing up off the chair with the sensation, teeth clenched, muscles contracted. Another gasp and it began to mellow into pleasure. A soft mew of contentment left her mouth. "Amazing. It's been a long time since I've felt this good."

She pulled herself upright, almost panting with the life inside her. "I started to say I know I took more than

I should have. I won't do it again. I just needed to renew myself." Heat suffused her being. "And judging by the power rushing through me, I have."

"You feel well, then? Enough to call the ancients?" Lines of apprehension snared Daciana's mouth.

"Yes, but you needn't be here. I know they are unsettling." Daci had done so much for her, there was no reason to put her in harm's way unnecessarily.

"No, I want to be here. I am your Elder." Daci stood a little straighter. "It's my duty to be at your side."

"Fair warning, then."

"I know what the ancients are like." Daci nodded. "Call him. I'm ready if you are."

Tatiana moved out from behind the desk to stand in the office's open space. Every fiber of her being thrummed with energy. If there was ever a time to call the ancients, this was it. She lifted her hands and called him by name. "Samael, my lord, my maker, please grant me your presence."

She teetered toward disappointment, expecting him to ignore her again.

Then shadows began to form, leaking out from the corners of her office. They coalesced into a dark, spiraling storm in the room's center. Lightning flashed over the whirling mass, shattering the blackness with bursts of heat and fire. The musty sourness of brimstone and unwashed flesh rose to an almost unbearable level. With a final crack of thunder, the storm split to reveal Samael in all his squalid resplendence. He wore his usual skirt of undulating shadows, the faces and hands of his victims visible as they failed to escape him over and over. From the waist up, his naked body was the burnished red of a flayed carcass left to dry in the sun.

But unlike the previous times he'd come to her, he was not alone. Another figure stood behind him, this one completely cloaked in shadows so that Tatiana was unable to determine anything except that the second being was closer to her size. A secondary Castus, perhaps? There were legions of them, but Samael was the only one she'd met face to face. The idea of what might lay in store for her with two of them made her stomach turn.

She immediately dropped her gaze and bowed, as overjoyed that he'd come to her as she was terrified. Time spent with him in the past had rarely been pain free. "My liege, thank you for coming to me."

"I know why you've called me," he growled.

To her side, Daciana was almost prone to the floor she was so low. Tatiana kept her head down but her gaze locked onto the razor-edged hooves visible beneath his shadowy covering. Respect was one thing; carelessness was another. She knew enough to stay quiet and let him speak, so she just nodded.

"You want to know about the child." A distant, eerie laugh followed his words. The second Castus?

"Yes, my lord." She lifted her chin a bit, her gaze still averted. As best she could tell, the figure behind him hadn't moved.

"Tell her," a high, feminine voice whispered. Definitely not Daci, as it carried traces of power unlike anything Tatiana had heard. Goose bumps rose on her arms.

Her gut reaction was to look up and see who'd spoken. When she did, she found herself staring at Samael. He'd gone oddly still and his eyes were slanted downward as if he was listening to the creature behind him.

Curiosity swept Tatiana like a wildfire. "Please, my

liege. I promise I am fit to raise her now. My enemies are behind me. No harm will come to her. I swear it. I need Lilith back. I need—"

More laughter.

Samael regained his stern countenance. "You don't know what you ask."

Tatiana stood her ground, making eye contact with a boldness that belied the nerves rocking her core. "Yes, I do. You gave her to me to raise and I let you down. I want to prove to you that I am not a failure. That I am worthy of the power you've bestowed upon me."

Samael was quiet a moment, his gleaming red eyes piercing her in a way that almost made her feel like he pitied her. "You take responsibility for her?"

"Of course." She straightened. "That is a mother's duty. That is the duty I accepted when you gave her to me."

Something like relief flickered over his face. He stepped aside and the being behind him moved forward.

The shadows surrounding the creature were actually a dark cloak. Slender hands reached up and pushed the hood back, revealing a young woman of such cruel beauty that Tatiana instantly felt lacking. Her eyes were the same blood red as Samael's, her skin so pale that blue veins etched the surface. She smiled at Tatiana, showing off a set of double fangs as wicked as the aura surrounding her. "Hello, Mother."

Chapter Ten

Creek hung back at the scene of the murder, hiding in the cover of the small crowd drawn by the flashing lights and yellow tape cordoning off the area. From his spot against the wall, he listened with one ear to the detectives, his KM-enhanced hearing making eavesdropping simple. In his other ear was a wireless bud with the running feed from the police scanner app on his phone. Both told him that, as suspected, the police were going on the assumption the killer was a vampire.

He couldn't imagine the mayor wouldn't respond to this in some way, but how would the population take it now that they were being led by a vampire? The careful peace that had followed the curfew was in danger of being disrupted.

One of the detectives scribbled something on an e-tablet, then tapped the stylus on the edge as he spoke to his partner. "Could be retaliation for the mayor killing that vampire."

His partner nodded. "Let's hope that's all it is, one and done. City'll get ugly if we have a killer vampire on the loose." He glanced at one of the uniformed officers working crowd control. "They're all over the place now. You know Janokoski in evidence is a vamp?" He shook his head. "Always thought that one was a little strange."

The other detective laughed. "Explains why he's so pale."

Creek had heard enough. He walked back to where he'd parked his motorcycle. He climbed on and fired it up. The mayor wouldn't welcome his visit, but it was his job as Paradise City's assigned Kubai Mata to question all known vampires. Might as well start with the newest one.

He hadn't expected to be let through the gates at her estate, but they opened for him after he showed his face to the security camera. He parked his bike outside the entrance of the house and walked up to the guard on duty. Fringe vampire, but not one Creek had met before.

The guard looked him up and down, probably assessing Creek's tattoos and Mohawk with the same impression most did. Trouble. Which wasn't far off if the guard didn't let him in. "The mayor wants to know if you've come to make amends."

"Sure, that's what I'm here for." If it got him in, who cared what she thought.

The guard went back to the intercom and relayed the message. There was no response, but a few minutes later, a maid opened the door. "Follow me."

He did and the woman led him to the mayor's office. Lola sat at her desk. Hector sat on the far couch, playing some kind of holographic handheld game. Creek nodded. "Mayor. This will be quick."

"Take all the time you like. I enjoy listening to apologies."

"I'm not here to apologize."

She frowned. "Then you'd better be here because you've finally brought me the information on Chief Vernadetto that I asked for." Nothing about her demeanor was friendly. She didn't even bother putting on her human face.

"No." He'd gotten a file from the KM, but he had no intention of handing anything over to Lola. He'd hoped she'd forgotten about it actually. The chief had never been a problem for him or the KM and the way Creek saw it, the man already had enough trouble with Lola as the mayor. "You may have already heard, but there was a murder this evening."

He watched her closely. If she had a pulse, it would have been much easier to use that as a gauge. "Victim was male, thirty-six years old. Died from puncture wounds on his neck and the lack of blood in his system."

No reaction out of her. Hector muttered something in Spanish, but Creek was pretty sure it was directed at his game since his eyes had never left the action. Finally, she pursed her mouth. "A vampire. I get it. What do you want from me? I'm sure the police are doing everything they can."

He leaned on her desk, closing the gap between them to a slim twelve inches. "Did you kill that man?"

"Now you have two things to apologize for." Her eyes went hard silver. "Get the hell out of my office."

He didn't move. "Is that a no on the murder then?"

"Yes, that's a no. Now get out." She got up and he backed away. "Tell your people I'm done dealing with the Kubai Mata, you understand? They've brought nothing good to this city. Nothing."

With a wave over his shoulder, he walked out. "You won't have to see me again." She wouldn't need to. Not with Octavian in place.

* * *

Fi slipped into nice jeans, a funky off-the-shoulder sweater, and heels. Casual, but not the grungy casual she preferred. She left a message with Isaiah to let Doc know where she was, then took the elevator to the VIP level of Bar Nine.

Remo stood on the landing, waiting.

"Did you change your mind?" Even if he had decided to go out after all, she wasn't going with him. She had boundaries, and that would be crossing a big one.

"No." A mix of anger and disgust crossed his face. "They won't let me into your booth. They don't believe me."

"Don't feel so bad. They wouldn't even let me in the building a few weeks ago." She jerked her head toward the lounge. "Come on."

The waitstaff stared openly as she walked in with Remo. She scowled at them. "I'm not sure why you denied entrance to one of your council members, but I'm going to assume it was an accident and won't be repeated again."

A round of nodding and mumbled agreements answered her. She walked past them to her reserved booth, sliding halfway around as Remo took the other side.

"Impressive," he said.

She shrugged. "I don't like that kind of nonsense." She gazed at the patrons in the VIP section, watching them slant their eyes and sneak peeks at her and Remo. She had the sinking feeling this was going to start rumors. Great. More to deal with.

A server came to take their order. She chose bottled water. Remo ordered coffee. Interesting. She'd expected him to drink. They sat in silence until the drinks came, which was so quick, Fi knew the staff was trying to get back on her good side. The server opened her water and poured it into a chilled glass for her. Oh yeah, definitely trying to make nice.

After adding an unnatural amount of sugar to his coffee, Remo stared out at the crowd, studying them just like she was. "What do you think they're thinking about us sitting here together?"

"Nothing good," Fi answered quickly. "Sorry. That came out too fast."

He laughed a little. "No, I'm sure you're right."

A woman in zebra-striped heels and a red dress openly flirted with Remo. Fi tipped her glass toward the woman. "That one especially."

"Do you know her?" He raised his coffee cup to the woman, who smiled brightly in response.

"Nope. I don't really know many of the pride members." Her hand strayed to the open neckline of her sweater. She hadn't exactly tried to make friends, but part of that was not knowing whom to trust.

"What's that?"

She peered into the crowd. "What?"

"No, that." He pointed at her. "Around your neck."

She looked at him and realized the cord holding the vial of sand was dangling from her hand. Without thinking about it, she'd wound the thin leather around her finger. She dropped it back beneath her sweater. "Nothing."

"It can't be nothing or you wouldn't wear it."

"It's just a memento."

"Of what?"

"Of nothing."

"You wouldn't need to be reminded of nothing."

The phrase *dog with a bone* entered her head. She got a little angry. "It's sand from the arena."

"Sand from the..." The slackening of his mouth told her the moment he understood. The twist of anger and sorrow in his eyes upset her, but it left his gaze as quickly as it had entered, replaced by something much darker. He held his hand out. "I'd like to have that."

"No." She sat back in her seat. "It means a lot to me."

"I bet it does." He pushed his cup away. "I should go."

"You asked," Fi said, but he was already walking away. She sighed and bounced her head against the padded booth. Exactly what she hadn't wanted to happen had just happened. She'd made a bad situation worse.

Chapter Eleven

Y ou sure about this?"

Chrysabelle met Jerem's eyes in the rearview mirror. "I'm wearing my body armor, you're coming with me, and I'm fully loaded." Besides her two sacres, she had a set of short blades. The daggers Mal had given her right before they'd gone into the Dominus ball. "I need to see him."

Jerem hadn't been her driver long, but it was clear the bear varcolai took his job seriously. "You know the risk."

"There shouldn't be any. Dominic told me Mal would be incapacitated."

He stared back at her. "And if he's not?"

If Mal was awake and attacked her, she'd kill him. If it came to that. "Like I said, body armor, you're coming with me, and I'm fully loaded." Jerem shot her a look that said he didn't believe she had it in her to take Mal down. Maybe she didn't, but she wouldn't know that until the situation arrived. Jerem also didn't know she had a child to protect.

He nodded. "We should go on foot from here then. Luciano didn't park any closer and he's undetectable."

They walked in silence the rest of the way to the freighter, communicating only with hand gestures and head nods. Chrysabelle's pulse kicked up as they climbed the gangway. This probably wasn't the smartest thing to do, but neither was falling in love with a vampire. Smart had long ago left the equation.

They stopped when they reached the main deck. Jerem put his hand up for her to wait, then tapped his ear to indicate he was listening for any sounds that might indicate Mal wasn't passed out cold. She waited, knowing his varcolai hearing was better than hers since she hadn't had the benefit of Mal's kiss or bite in a while. At last he nodded, then pointed toward the spot where he'd wait for her.

As planned, she'd be going in alone. She gave him the thumbs-up sign, hoping he understood she was good with all this. Even though he undoubtedly heard her pounding pulse. One last look, that's all she wanted.

One chance to say good-bye.

She twisted the latch, pushed the heavy metal door open, and stepped into the corridor. A faint coppery scent lingered. He'd definitely had blood recently. The solars gleamed, providing enough light to navigate the grungy passage. Now all she had to do was remember the direction Fi had taken her last time. Slowly, she picked her way through the labyrinth of the ship's interior. Mal's dark, spicy scent erased the blood smell the farther she went. She followed it until at last her surroundings looked familiar.

Mal's room was just ahead.

She went very still and tried to listen over the staccato rhythm of her pulse. All quiet as best she could hear. A few deep breaths and she found a measure of calm, enough to move forward.

The door was open. Mal lay on his bed like he'd fallen there and hadn't moved. Which was probably exactly what had happened. She stood at the threshold of his room, studying the figure of the man she'd once thought she'd have a future with. The solars penetrated the room's dark only so far, but what light there was outlined the hard angles of his body so that he seemed carved in stone. Or maybe "trapped" was a better word.

Her hands cradled her stomach as her heart clenched. This was a man she'd forever be linked to, no matter what he did or how he ended up.

She stepped into the room and held her breath. But of course, he didn't move. He was a light daysleeper, but this wasn't daysleep; this was drugged oblivion. She exhaled. In the soft wash of the solars, he seemed almost...peaceful in repose. Not at all like a man tortured by the voices of his victims. Although maybe it wasn't such torture now that he was giving into them. The thought made her heart ache anew. She bit the side of her cheek to quell her emotions. Had he given in? Or had Dominic sent the blood in time?

She prayed he hadn't killed again. If he had, there'd be a new ghost, wouldn't there? "Hello," she whispered as she checked the room for the sudden appearance of a spectral being.

But none came. And although the lack of response wasn't a promise of his innocence, she still took comfort in it. She moved closer, trailing her fingers over the bed. A bed he'd once tucked her into so she could recover from blood sickness and an injured ankle. She looked over her shoulder at the chair where he'd sat and watched her.

Amazing that those memories were now her happy ones. They raked through her, stirring up new pain.

She glanced back at him. He'd almost seem human if not for the unnatural stillness that held him. She sat gingerly on the edge of the bed, one hand firmly gripping the hilt of one of the daggers at her waist. Her heartbeat was almost back to normal now, the steady thump of it gone from her ears. She inched her free hand forward until her knuckles touched his. He was warm, further proof of the blood he'd ingested. Human blood purposefully diluted with animal blood to make him weaker. Purposefully doped to keep him subdued. She knew how necessary both measures were and yet she frowned at how much they bothered her.

Because it spoke to how much she loved him. To how much she knew he'd sacrificed for her. His voices were right about her. She'd caused him a lot of trouble that he didn't deserve. And now, because of that, he was going to miss out on his second chance at being a father.

She threaded her fingers through his and blamed her off-kilter emotions for the tears burning her eyes. Stupid pregnancy hormones. But those hormones didn't stop her from leaning down and pressing her lips to his. The lingering warmth almost undid her, crumbling the edges of her resolve.

"Oh Mal," she whispered. "Why did it have to come to this?"

She couldn't let him go this easily. Fi was right. She had to find a way to fix him and soon. Or the only thing left would be to kill him. And killing him just might kill her too.

"Why would you say that?" Tatiana stared at the powerful young vampiress before her. "Why would you call me mother?"

Daciana's mouth gaped open. She'd come to stand beside Tatiana, but was visibly trembling. Tatiana worried for her. Showing weakness was never a wise choice where the Castus was concerned.

The woman's smile widened into something grotesque. "Don't you recognize me? I'm your daughter. I'm Lilith."

Daci gasped.

"No, you're not." Tatiana shook her head. Fear gripped her core, wrenching down until tiny frissons of pain spiked through her bones. This thing before her was *not* Lilith. "My daughter is only a baby. You're an adult. Even at the rate she was growing, she wouldn't be your size." She stared at Samael. "What have you done with my child?" She pointed at the woman. "Who is this?"

"She is who she says she is." He stared at the new female vampire. "We fed her our blood. Turned her into the vampire you could not. Turned her into something... more than we expected." The tone of his voice didn't match his words. It was weak and shallow and full of... fear.

The Castus were afraid of this creature.

Tatiana's belly went cold. She looked at the woman, unable to find traces of the sweet baby she'd rocked in her arms. "You're Lilith? Prove it."

The woman's nostrils flared, perhaps at Tatiana's disbelief, but then she unbuttoned the top of her black leather pants and tugged them down to reveal one stark white hip. "Look. Here's your proof. Remember the birthmark?"

Tatiana stared at the crescent moon marking the woman's pale flesh. Her gaze slowly lifted back to the woman's face, her mind warping with the reality of who stood before her.

Daci's hand went to her mouth.

"Bloody hell," Tatiana whispered. "You *are* Lilith."

"Yes, and I'll be back to see you very soon, Mother." With a cackling laugh that cracked the marble hearth, Lilith spread her arms and disappeared in a burst of shadow and smoke, taking the Castus with her.

Daci turned to Tatiana, eyes round. "They're afraid of her, aren't they?"

Tatiana nodded slowly. "I think so."

"What does that mean for us?"

Tatiana shook her head, every plan she'd orchestrated these last few centuries unraveling before her like tumbling balls of yarn. "Nothing good."

Chapter Twelve

Mal woke up feeling like he'd slept under the freighter, not in it, and the fog thickening his skull showed no signs of dissipating. He blinked into the blackness, his sight adjusting instantly to the spare glow of the solars. They were almost completely tapped, but their weak light was more than enough for his eyes. In his bones, he could sense that beyond the painted and boarded-up porthole in his room, the sun still owned the sky for another hour. He shouldn't really be awake yet, but his need for daysleep had decreased since he'd been cursed and lessened even more once he'd started drinking comarré blood.

The voices snarled weakly at the white-and-gold image floating through his memories, too sated to make much of a fuss. He didn't remember a kill last night, but he wasn't hungry either. Maybe he'd mistakenly picked a human with alcohol or drugs in their system. That would explain why he felt slightly hungover. With a snort, he pushed up onto his elbows. The movement did nothing to dislodge the fog, but it did cause a familiar, honeyed perfume to waft up around him.

Chrysabelle.

He scrubbed a hand over his face. Her sweet scent intensified. He swung his legs over the side of the bed and grabbed a handful of the covers, lifting them to his nose. Her scent wasn't just on him; it was on his bed linens, too. Had she been his kill? He scanned the room, but there was no body. Closing his eyes, he tried to remember what had happened last night. Had he gone back to her estate? Tracked her somewhere? Nothing came to him. Except that Chrysabelle couldn't have been his dinner if he was feeling hungover. Comarré never touched alcohol, so drugs weren't even a remote possibility. He must have bagged a street person or a club-goer.

Which left only one explanation for why her smell was so present. She'd been here. On the freighter. In *his* space. Anger burrowed through his veins. What did she think, that she was going to make him fall in love with her again? That moment of weakness was not going to be repeated. He'd rather it disappear from his brain the same way his love for her had. What had he been thinking? What vampire fell in love with their meal? It disgusted him that he'd stooped so low. Made his gut ache with unpleasant feelings.

He stared down at the sheets crumpled in his fist. If she would just stay away from him, maybe he could forgive her for interfering in his life. *Weakling*. But no, visiting him was too much. Too bold for someone who was nothing more than a food source to him now. A small pain jolted through his chest. He rubbed at it, chalking it up to indigestion from last night's poor choice of blood supply.

Dropping the sheets, he got to his feet and smiled. Tonight would be different. Tonight he was going to dine on the finest blood he'd ever had and solve his biggest problem at the same time. The solar flickered and went dark. Twilight. Freedom.

He changed his clothes, then loped toward the exit, already anticipating the night that lay ahead of him. Throwing open the door, he stepped out onto the deck and stopped as the intoxicating aroma of human blood met him.

A shiny rectangular container sat a few feet beyond the door. The scent was so strong around the black box, it almost glowed red. He inhaled, scanning the area, but couldn't pick up anything that indicated another presence nearby.

Cautiously, he crouched and put his hands on the container. Warm. Almost hot. How long had it sat out here in the sun? There was no lock, so he flipped the latch and opened it.

The voices went crazy. Bags of blood filled it to the top. He grabbed one. It was warm enough to be body temperature. His fangs shot down and he grinned. This was just what he needed. Now he could feed before he went after Chrysabelle, which meant her blood wouldn't sway him and he'd be able to take his time with her.

He squeezed one of the bags to tighten it, then sank his fangs in. Definitely human. Not the best blood he'd ever had, but it was still rich and thick and perfectly heated. He drank deeply, emptying the first bag quickly. He tossed it and grabbed another. Near the end of that one, the ship seemed to lurch, throwing him off balance. He caught himself as he rocked to the side. What little light was left of dusk faded fast. So fast his eyes couldn't keep up. Unable to hold the bag to his mouth any longer, his arm went limp and the bag fell to the deck.

His eyes closed and a second later, he dropped to the deck beside it.

*　*　*

Fi pushed a piece of bacon around on her plate with her fork. She hadn't slept well since the incident with Remo, but she hadn't mentioned it to Doc either. She knew he wouldn't be happy that she'd spent time with Remo. Or would he? It *was* an effort on her part to get to know Remo better. She sighed and made a mound of her scrambled eggs.

Doc looked up from reading the morning news on his tablet. "You all right?" His gaze went to her plate. "Don't like Isaiah's cooking?"

She shoveled a forkful of eggs into her mouth, chewed, and swallowed. "No, it's great." She took a sip of coffee. "I think I'm going to go shopping today."

"You know you can have anything you want sent in."

She frowned at him. "How long have you known me? What's my favorite thing to do?"

He broke into a wicked smile. "Me?"

She laughed. "Besides you."

"Shop," he answered. "Probably not as much fun when someone does it for you."

"No fun at all. Plus, I told Chrysabelle I'd help her pick out some new stuff so she can start to ditch her all-white look."

"About time. How's she doing with … everything?"

"Okay." Fi bit her lip to keep from blurting out that Chrysabelle was pregnant. She tucked her napkin under the edge of her plate and stood. "I'm going to get ready. You busy all day?"

He nodded as she came around to his side. "All day every day, but dinner is just us."

She leaned down to kiss him. "Sounds good."

He grabbed her hand as she started away. "You know

if there's something bothering you—or some*one* bothering you—you can tell me."

She smiled, making light of his words. "Isaiah still hasn't baked that chocolate cake I asked for."

He laughed and pinched her side. "I'll speak to him about it."

Thirty minutes later, Doc was off to his office and she was in the elevator, headed down to see Remo. There was only one thing she could think of to make things right after last night. She would *not* be the cause of more tension in the pride, or worse, be responsible for creating some kind of rift between this pride and the Brazilian one.

The door opened and she stepped out onto his floor. Only two apartments here, both reserved for council members, just like the floor above it, except in this pride there hadn't been a fourth council member in years. Instead, the second apartment was kept for DVs. Distinguished visitors. Remo's father had stayed here when he'd come. Now his son was living in the apartment next door. She took a deep breath as she approached his door. Coming here was a risk, but not a big enough one to keep her away.

She knocked. After a long minute, the door opened a crack.

Remo peered at her, not far into his first cup of coffee, judging by his bed head and scruff. "What do you want?"

"To apologize."

His eyes and the door opened a little wider. He wore soccer shorts and a T-shirt emblazoned with a Brazilian team logo. "For?"

"Last night." She fished the vial of sand out of her

pocket and held it out. "You asked for this. You should have this."

He stared at it for a second before taking it from her.

She spoke before he could say anything. "I want you to know I wasn't wearing that as a symbol of your sister's death or some kind of trophy or anything like that. It was a symbol of strength to me. A reminder of everything I've been through and survived so that when things were tough or I doubted myself, I could remember what I've endured to be here. That I'd earned my place as the pride leader's wife no matter what some of the pride thinks of me. It was about my own journey, not your sister's end. I promise."

He opened his hand so the vial lay on his palm, gleaming under the morning light filtering in from behind him. "Thank you. That…means a lot."

"And I want us to be…maybe not friends yet, but at least not enemies."

He closed his fist around the vial and his expression softened. "We're not enemies. You're the only one who's shown me any genuine kindness." He glanced at his hand, the same odd gleam she thought she'd seen before dancing through his gaze. Just like the last time, it disappeared quickly. "This is the start of a new future for me. For us both."

"Fitting in takes time. I'm not entirely there yet myself."

Tucking the vial into the pocket of his shorts, he opened the door farther. "You want to come in for coffee? It's excellent. I brought it with me from São Paulo."

"Thanks, but I've got to be somewhere." Not entirely true, but she wasn't about to be alone with him in his apartment. "Maybe you could come to dinner at our place tomorrow night." Why had she said that? Doc was going to freak. Maybe.

Remo's face brightened at the invite. "That would be very good. Thank you."

"All right, seven o'clock then. The penthouse." Like he didn't know where they lived.

He nodded. "See you then."

She waved and headed back to the elevator as his door shut. She'd have to run back upstairs and tell Isaiah so he could plan the dinner. She should probably give Doc the heads-up too. The elevator chimed. She stepped in and leaned against the wall.

Shopping really didn't seem like it was going to be that much fun after all.

Chapter Thirteen

Chrysabelle was about to get in her car when Fi's vehicle approached the gates of the estate. The setting sun glinted off the windshield, causing her to squint, but she could just make out Fi's driver. "I must have a training session with Fi this evening. Give me a moment, Jerem."

He nodded. "Take all the time you need, boss."

The gates swung open and Chrysabelle approached the car.

Fi opened her door and hopped out before her driver reached it. "Hey, how are you? Are you going somewhere? I've got a bunch of clothes for you to try on. The trunk is full." She smiled. "I've been shopping all day."

Chrysabelle shook her head. "And yet you have all this energy left. How do you do that?"

Inside the car, Fi's bodyguard grunted like he agreed. Fi laughed. "Some people can hang, some can't." She jerked her chin at Chrysabelle's car. "You're leaving?"

"Yes. I'm headed out to an appointment with Dominic. I must have completely forgotten about our meeting."

"Oh." Fi shrugged. "We didn't have anything set up.

I just thought you'd be home." A new intensity filled her eyes. "What are you going to see Dominic about?"

Chrysabelle hesitated, but then Fi had been the one to push her in this direction in the first place. "I'm actually going to see Mortalis. To ask him if there's anything—"

"You can do about Mal?" Fi finished hopefully.

"Yes." She steeled her gaze as the emotions of the previous night threatened to overwhelm her. "I went to see him last night."

"Did you talk?"

"It wasn't that kind of visit." She blew out a breath. "I *have* to try to fix this."

Fi's smile was almost as blinding as the sun off the car. "Can I come with you to see Mortalis? Please? Mal's kind of my area, you know. I'm sort of an expert on him."

"True. No one knows him better than you." Chrysabelle was actually happy for the company. "But you're going to have to ditch your bodyguard. I don't want to make a big scene going into Seven. You won't need him anyway. I can protect you if something happens."

"Cool with me." She ducked her head into the car. "You're staying here." Without waiting for the bodyguard's answer, she motioned to her driver. "Pop the trunk? I want to get a few bags out." Fi rubbed her hands together. "I can show you a few of the things I think you'll really dig on the way over."

By the time they got to Seven, Chrysabelle wasn't sure Fi had left anything in the Paradise City boutiques. She liked most of it more than she thought she would, even sliding a soft beige duster on over her white top and pants.

"This too." Fi held out a simple gold link chain. "Trust me. It helps break up all that white."

Chrysabelle obliged, although she was starting to feel overdressed, considering she had her body armor on underneath everything else. Jerem parked the car at the employee entrance and came around to let them out. Chrysabelle glanced at Fi. "Stay close. You know how Seven can be."

Fi nodded and followed her to the door. This was the only entrance she used these days. Fighting the crowd up front just wasn't worth it. Chrysabelle punched in the code Dominic had given her, and then they went inside. A few corridors in and the club's music permeated the walls. When they reached the door into the club, Chrysabelle gave Fi another reminder. "Any trouble, go ghost."

Fi nodded. "I know, but I'm the pride leader's wife now. That alone should give me some protection."

"Or cause more trouble." Chrysabelle pushed through the door and the heavy beat washed through her, syncopating with her pulse. The place was packed with fringe and varcolai alike. Since Doc had lifted the restriction on pride members working at and patronizing Seven, Dominic's business had definitely benefited. A young female varcolai in half form, leopard by the spots decorating the expanses of skin visible beneath her tiny black top and boy shorts, danced on a platform nearby, her tail swishing as her hips gyrated.

Fi's brows shot up.

Chrysabelle shook her head. Now was not the time or place to comment. "Let's find Mortalis." She reached back, grabbed Fi's hand, and started pulling her through the press. Fringe turned as she went by, nostrils flaring as her blood scent announced what she was. Her free hand went to one of the daggers on her waist. If her sacres didn't draw so much attention, she would have worn them, but she also didn't want to cause Dominic any trouble. Besides that, if any of the fringe touched her, they'd get a shock once they came in contact with her body armor.

Fi squeezed Chrysabelle's hand and tugged, causing Chrysabelle to stop. "What is it?"

Fi's eyes were fixed on something farther into the crowd. Chrysabelle dodged a tall fae and found what Fi was staring at. Katsumi, coming toward them.

She released Fi's hand. "It's okay, nothing to worry about."

Katsumi glided to a stop before them and the crowd opened up a little. "Good evening, Chrysabelle. How is your brother?"

"He's fine, thank you." Chrysabelle couldn't help but wonder what new game Katsumi was playing at. She might have helped bring Damian home, but that was where their relationship ended.

"If he wants a job, we could certainly use a comar with his experience here."

So that was it. "I don't think he's looking for work." Especially since their mother had left them with a wealth of assets.

"Well, let him know I asked for him, will you?" Katsumi's smile never faltered as her gaze went to Fi. "I don't believe we've met."

Chrysabelle spoke up. "This is Fiona. She's Doc's wife."

Katsumi's head went back a little as she studied Fi. "Ah, yes, Maddoc. From outcast to pride leader." She arched a brow. "How interesting life is." She pointed a finger at Fi. "You are also Malkolm's ghost, yes?"

"Yes," Fi answered, her whole body rigid with either fear or anger. Chrysabelle couldn't tell.

Katsumi made a shallow bow. "Tell him we miss him next time you see him."

"I'll get right on that," Fi muttered.

Chrysabelle cleared her throat. "Is Mortalis on the floor or in his office? He's expecting me."

"I believe he's in Dominic's office." Katsumi waved a hand to attract a passing server. "Run to Dominic's office and let Mortalis know that Chrysabelle is here to see him."

"Yes, ma'am." The server took off.

"I know where his office is," Chrysabelle said. "Fiona and I will wait there."

"Very good." But Katsumi didn't move. Her eyes narrowed. "There's something…different about you. Your scent seems stronger."

"I'm wearing my body armor. I'm sure the silver is affecting my scent." And not the fact that she was pregnant.

"No." Katsumi shook her head. "I don't think that's it…"

"You're probably just used to smelling the fakes that work here." Fi grabbed Chrysabelle's hand and started moving. "Nice to meet you. Bye."

Katsumi might have growled, but Chrysabelle wasn't sure since Fi kept pulling her away. She redirected them toward Mortalis's office. "Thanks, but I'm pretty sure it's just the silver of my body armor, and wearing that in here isn't a big deal. Unless someone touches it."

"You really think that's what she was picking up on?" Fi glanced knowingly at Chrysabelle's stomach.

"Even if it was, she can't figure anything out by scent alone." She slowed Fi down. "Here. This is his office." She tried the handle but it was locked. "We'll have to wait." They stood with their backs to the door, watching the crowd. Mortalis appeared a few minutes later. At his approach, the few lingering fringe disappeared.

"Good evening." He nodded at Fi. "I didn't expect to see you, too. Nyssa's been asking about you."

Fi pushed part of her bob behind one ear. "I've been swamped and it sucks, but I promise to get in touch with her soon. Tell her I said hi and I'm sorry."

"Will do." He unlocked the office door, pushed it open, then waited for them to go in before entering and locking the door behind him. "Small quarters, but at least it's private." He went behind the narrow desk while they took the two chairs.

"Keep an eye on Katsumi," Fi said. "I think she picked up on Chrysabelle's condition."

Mortalis looked shocked for about a half second, and then his face went blank again. "What do you mean?"

"Fi knows," Chrysabelle told him. "She figured it out when I threw up in the middle of teaching her how to fight."

Fi laughed. "Yeah, that was kind of hard to ignore."

His expression softened as he spoke to Chrysabelle. "How are you doing? Are you . . . sick a lot?"

"It comes and goes. Right now I seem to be okay, but no telling how long that will last." She forced herself not to touch her stomach. "Do you think Katsumi would be able to tell?"

"By scent? No, but let me listen." He went quiet for a bit. "I can't hear a second heartbeat. I think the body

armor is blocking it. That may change as the baby grows."
He leaned back in his chair. "Don't worry about it. I'll
speak to her, see if she suspects anything." He tapped
his long fingers on the arm of the chair. "That's not why
you're here, though. What can I do for you?"

"Mal." Chrysabelle adjusted the chain around her
neck, trying not to feel like she was being strangled. "I
can't give up on him. Or us. There's too much at stake. I
need to know if there's anything I can do to get the raptor fae to release his emotions. Anything that will restore
Mal's feelings for me."

Mortalis stilled, but his eyes held great sadness.
"What's done is done. Undoing it is . . . there's no way—"

"There's always a way," Fi interjected. "What would
you do if the raptor had taken Nyssa's feelings for you?"

Mortalis swallowed. "What you're asking is beyond my
scope. It's so impossible there's no point in discussing it."

Chrysabelle's mood darkened. "Deep fae business,
then. How about you humor me and discuss it anyway?
Especially since you played a part in this."

His mouth thinned into a hard line. "It *is* deep fae business, so deep that telling you won't do anything but frustrate
you, because I can't give you anything you can use."

Fi slapped his desk. The noise was like a gunshot in
the small space. "Let her be the judge of that."

Mortalis propped his elbow on the desk and leaned
into his hand, his six fingers cradling his forehead. "Killing a raptor releases every emotion they've ever taken,
good and *bad*."

"How is that deep fae business?" Killing the raptor
seemed easy. Well, not easy, but she'd killed Nothos. How
different could it be?

With a sigh, Mortalis stared at her. "Because Amery and I brought him out of the Claustrum to meet with you. The Claustrum is on the fae plane, a place you can only access with the help of a fae."

"You or Amery can take me then."

"Absolutely not. Humans aren't allowed on the fae plane. Getting one into the Claustrum?" Mortalis snorted. "That's never happened and never will."

"I'm not asking you to get permission."

He leaned forward. "I don't think you understand. Doing something like that without permission would be to forfeit my life. Or Amery's."

"If you get found out. So we won't get found out."

He shook his head. "There's no way you won't get found out. You kill that raptor after the years he's been in the Claustrum feeding on all the hate and anger and rage in that place and those emotions will flood back to the rest of the inmates and turn that place into a maelstrom of destruction. It *won't* go unnoticed. " He stood and walked the few paces to the back wall. "Plus, you're talking about the fae plane. Humans don't do well there. You'd be lucky to get out alive."

"It's a chance I'm willing to take."

He turned. "You're risking two lives. Yours and your child's."

Chrysabelle's emotions betrayed her again. She blinked at the liquid welling up in her eyes. "What about Mal's life? If not for Dominic sending him drugged blood, he'd be trying to kill me. Or he'd be killing whatever humans were unlucky enough to cross his path. If that hasn't happened already." She wiped at her eyes. "If I can't save Mal, I'm going to have to…" Her throat closed. "Kill him," she whispered.

Mortalis didn't answer, telling her that was exactly what she'd have to do. Fi put her hand over Chrysabelle's, but she pulled away, unable to bear the contact. She couldn't even stand to look at Fi or Mortalis in that moment. The silence pressed so heavy she bent under it. "I need to go home."

"Chrysabelle." Mortalis's voice held a note of apology, but not acquiescence.

She held up her hand. "I understand your reasons for not helping. I do. Doesn't mean I agree with them." She stood. "You know I would do anything for you."

"Anything?" He raised one brow. "Then protect yourself and your child. Stay away from the raptor."

"Anything but that." She turned to leave, so disappointed in Mortalis that bitterness coated her tongue. "Let's go, Fi."

The ghost girl got up to join her, giving the fae an evil look.

"Listen..." He sighed. "Even if I could help, it puts too much at stake—"

"Message received the first time." She moved toward the door.

"Chrysabelle, wait. What I'm trying to say is... you need someone who doesn't care about consequences. Someone willing to break fae law. Or someone above it."

She stopped, Fi at her elbow. "And that's not you?"

He shook his head. "No. But—"

"Your brother. Augustine."

He snorted. "He won't help you. He could, but he won't. If it means risking his hide, he'll wish you well as he walks away. Especially if he thought I was behind your asking him."

"Then who?"

"There *is* a fae who's in your debt. Khell. The one you made Guardian. He has all the access you need."

"And you think he'll do it?"

"I have no idea. But it's worth asking."

She nodded and gave him a half smile, the bitterness in her mouth sweetening a little. "Thank you."

He scratched one horn. "You may not thank me after you go through with this. Just…be careful, okay? The Claustrum is no place for a non-fae." He laughed sadly. "It's no place for those who are."

Chapter Fourteen

Tatiana gazed across the office at Daciana. They sat looking at one another, neither of them saying anything since Lilith and the Castus had vanished. The smell of brimstone still lingered, clouding her mind as much as what she'd seen. Her child. But not. Somehow she had to make the best of this.

"Unbelievable," Daci finally mumbled.

Tatiana nodded, staring blankly into the room but still seeing the vision of Lilith in her head. "They've given her the power that should have been mine. Turned her into..."

"A monster," Daci finished.

Tatiana's gaze snapped onto Daciana. "Not a monster." No matter what her child had become, she was not a monster. "A new kind of vampire. A race above the nobility. I always said she was a vampire princess. Now she's become the vampire queen."

Daci recoiled. "Aren't you afraid of her?"

Yes. But so were the Castus, and unlike them, she wasn't about to show her fear. "She's still the child I held in my arms, isn't she? The baby I rocked to sleep? I'm the only mother that child has known. Why should I fear her?" Tatiana stood and walked to the helioglazed windows. The sun would be up in less than an hour.

"I don't know. She seemed very different. Even the ancient one seemed afraid of her." Daci shuddered.

Tatiana wrapped her hand in the raw silk drapes and leaned against the window frame. "He did, didn't he?" There was little point in denying what Daci had seen for herself. Then a thought occurred to her. "Do you know why that is? Because the ancients know Lilith's loyalties lie elsewhere. She called me mother. Recognized me instantly even though they tried to take her away from me."

Daci twisted, throwing her arm over the back of the leather settee to see Tatiana better. Some of the trepidation left her eyes. "She did. You think the ancients fear they'll lose Lilith to you?" She stood, visibly excited. "All that power. Yours to command." She rolled her lips in and a stifled squeal barely escaped. "We must call her back. You must talk to her, suss her out."

Tatiana glanced out the window again. A hint of purple colored the horizon. "I agree. Daysleep will be upon us soon. I would like to know where I stand before another day passes. For all we know, Lilith could be waiting for me to rescue her from the ancients. "

"For you to bring her home again." Daci's hand went to her mouth. "We must help her!"

Tatiana pushed away from the window and directed Daci toward the door. "Lock it. I don't want to be interrupted."

She looked crestfallen. "Are you dismissing me?"

"No. You were here the first time and Lilith didn't

object. You helped care for her as a baby; she must know that."

"Good." With a smile, Daci ran to the door and locked it, then leaned her back against it. "Ready."

Tatiana took her place in the middle of the room and opened herself to the possibility of a new future. A new, more powerful future. "Lilith, my child, if you hear me, come to me. Grace me with your presence."

A snap of electricity charged the air, lifting the small hairs on Tatiana's nape, and the shadows pulled together in the center of the room. Lilith stepped out of them. Or they became her. The change happened so quickly it was hard to tell.

"You called, Mother?"

Tatiana smiled and began carefully. If the ancients were listening, she didn't want them thinking she was trying to take Lilith back just yet. "Yes, I did. Thank you for coming. I thought we might sit and talk. Get acquainted now that you are grown. I've missed so much." The sadness in her heart over that was genuine. She'd lost years because of the Castus, a gap that felt unforgivable.

Lilith cocked her head to one side. "And that makes you unhappy? Why?"

Tatiana walked to the settee and sat. "Because you went from being a baby in my arms to a beautiful young woman and I wasn't a part of that. Watching you grow up was taken away from me."

"And you wanted to be a part of that?" Lilith seemed confused by the idea. "Why?"

"Because I love you, Lilith." Truthfully, Tatiana loved the child Lilith had been. This adult woman seemed like a very different creature, but that was to be expected. "I had hoped we would rule the vampire nation together, as mother and daughter. That we would be an unstoppable force."

"Love?" Lilith sat close enough for Tatiana to see the map of delicate blue veins beneath her translucent skin. "I don't understand love."

Daci snorted and came closer. "Love is not something the ancients know much of."

Lilith watched her. "You also knew me as a child?"

"Yes." Daci nodded and sat across from them on the matching couch. "You don't remember me?"

Lilith stared at her. "Perhaps."

Tatiana tried to help her remember. "Daci used to take care of you sometimes."

Lilith frowned. "There was another, a male..."

"Yes, Octavian," Daci said. "He's gone now."

"He was a traitor," Tatiana spat.

Lilith turned sharply. "A traitor?"

"He tried to give you to our enemies." Tatiana's fingers dug into the leather. "He was the reason you were taken from me."

Lilith seemed instantly curious. "What happened to him?"

Daci shook her head. "He killed himself so he wouldn't have to face your mother's wrath."

Lilith's eyes brightened. "Explain."

Daci laughed softly. "Most vampires are smart enough to fear your mother. She is a great and powerful vampire. That's why the ancients gave you to her to raise. If Octavian hadn't killed himself, your mother would have done it for him. Without hesitation."

"Yes," Tatiana said quietly. "No matter how much it would have hurt me."

"Hurt you? Because . . . you loved him also?"

Tatiana nodded. "Yes, but not as much as you. Not nearly as much. There is no greater bond than that of a mother and her child. I would do anything for you." She reached out and took Lilith's hand. Her skin had lost none of its baby softness.

Lilith looked down. "You love Daciana."

"Yes, but not as much as you." Tatiana stroked her thumb over Lilith's knuckles. "Do you wish to live with me again?"

Lilith lifted her gaze. Her eyes had gone almost completely black, the way nobles' eyes went silver. Then she was gone from Tatiana's side and seated next to Daciana. She'd moved quicker than Tatiana could track.

Daci reared back with a nervous laugh, her hand at her throat. "You frightened me. My, you move faster than any vampire I've ever seen."

Lilith's hand closed over Daci's arm. "My mother must love only me."

"What?" Daci pulled away but Lilith held tight. "I love you too, Lilith. I helped raise you, remember? I—"

"I remember you laughing with Octavian." Lilith tipped her head and bared her fangs. "Are you a traitor too?"

What little color Daci had drained from her face. "No, of course not." She struggled to get out of Lilith's grip.

Tatiana jumped up. "Lilith, she's not a traitor. Please let her go."

"Please?" Lilith sneered. "That does not seem like the word of a feared vampire."

"Let her go now," Tatiana commanded.

Lilith laughed. "That's better." She dropped Daci's arm. Daci slumped against the sofa, trembling. Tatiana relaxed, feeling like she'd just stepped back from the edge of a precipice.

Lilith's eyes narrowed as she spoke to Tatiana. "You care for her too much. I do not like it." With that, she drove her hand forward, plunged it into Daci's chest, and yanked out her heart.

Daci's eyes rounded a second before she went to ash, the heart in Lilith's hand dissolving at the same time.

Tatiana's jaw dropped as a pit opened up in her belly. She teetered toward numbness, unable to believe what had just happened. "What-what have you done?"

Lilith stood, wriggling her fingers to shed the last bit of ash. "She was unnecessary for your plan."

"My plan?" Pain wracked Tatiana's body and darkness edged her vision. Daci was *gone*. Her last remaining friend. A sob choked her throat and she fisted her hands to keep from striking Lilith, because she knew without question Lilith would kill her too. The creature before her was exactly what Daci had said she was. A monster. A monster Tatiana should destroy. Anger mixed with grief. *Would* destroy. But how? There was no one left to help her. No one vicious enough to face this hell-spawned beast. The word triggered a memory. There might be one person who could kill Lilith.

"Your plan for us to rule together." Lilith smiled. "Isn't that what you wanted, Mother?"

Tatiana forced herself to return the smile, but wasn't sure if the movement of her lips was a smile or a grimace. She hurt too much to care. "Yes," she whispered. The effort of speaking under the weight of such pain was almost impossible. "That's what I wanted." She looked for a way out and found her savior in the lightening horizon.

"The sun is almost up and I need to sleep." She stumbled toward the door. "You return to the ancients now and I'll call you when I need you again."

The happiness in Lilith's voice faded. "Why can't I stay with you?"

Nerves frayed, Tatiana snapped. Enough was bloody enough. "Because I said so and I'm your mother. Now go."

"Fine." With a huff, Lilith crossed her arms and disappeared in a small whirl of shadow.

Alone, Tatiana reached for the door handle, but missed, her vision blurry. Frustration and grief engulfed her. "Daci," she moaned. The sound of her friend's name sheared away the last of her composure. Unable to bear more, she crumpled to the floor and wept.

Chapter Fifteen

Creek was prepared for Chrysabelle to have blocked his entrance to Mephisto Island, but the guard at the gatehouse let him through. He didn't know what to make of the fact that she hadn't pulled him from the approved visitors list, but decided not to overthink it. He parked his V-Rod and jogged to the front door, glad for the chance to speak to her. The way they'd left things hadn't been good. He owed her an apology and an explanation.

Velimai answered his knock, giving him the same surly look she'd once reserved for Mal. Maybe the wysper still blamed him for Mal's death. Or Chrysabelle's unhappiness. Or the lack of world peace. "Chrysabelle here? I came to apologize, not cause her more trouble. Those days are over."

Velimai raised a brow.

Creek held his hands up. "I promise."

With a sigh, she moved out of the way. He followed her inside. A silver hard-shell roller bag sat by the door. She pointed to the living room, so he went and sat. She gave him a look that said *stay*, then she headed upstairs. He assumed to get Chrysabelle.

A few minutes later, Damian came down. Creek stood, wondering how the man would respond to him based on his sister's feelings toward Creek at the moment. "Good to see you back." He nodded toward the roller bag. "You finally moving in?"

"Good to see you too. That's Chrysabelle's bag." Damian stopped at the entrance to the living room. "She's upstairs and she told me to tell you she's not coming down if this is Kubai Mata business." He lifted one shoulder like he was sorry to be the bearer of bad news.

So much for convincing Velimai of his intentions. "It's not. I'm just here as me. I owe her some explanations and an apology."

If that surprised Damian, he hid it well. "Okay." He jogged back up the steps, returning a few minutes later with Chrysabelle in tow.

She eyed Creek warily, tugging at her tunic and smoothing a few loose hairs back into her braid. She was flushed and shiny with sweat.

"Didn't mean to interrupt your workout."

She shrugged and wiped her face with the towel around her neck before sitting across from him. "Damian said you're not here on KM business. That's the only reason I'm talking to you."

Creek sat. "I know. Thanks."

Damian walked toward the door. "I'll see you for dinner, Chrys."

She sat forward. "Don't go yet. Join us."

He glanced at Creek before answering her. "You got it." He took one of the club chairs at the end of the two big sofas, settling in like he was preparing to referee.

She turned her attention to Creek. "So what's going on?"

"A lot." He blew out a breath. "Not sure where to start, so I'll just dive in. I'm sorry for my part in Mal's death. I found out too late that I was possessed by a dark spirit, one who's since been...exorcised. She was also behind my persuading the mayor to set the curfew in place and the reason I sided against you and Mal in the mayor's office. For all of that, I'm sorry."

Chrysabelle's hard expression softened. "A spirit?"

"Yahla, the soulless woman. Damian and I set her free when we burned Aliza's house down. Apparently, Aliza had trapped her in the house and was using her as a source of power. Yahla attacked my grandmother too. Would have killed her if I hadn't gotten there in time." He dropped his head. He wasn't great at expressing emotion, but for Chrysabelle's sake he'd do his best. "I'm sorry I didn't figure this all out in time to save Mal. I know his death is my fault and I feel like hell about that."

A few seconds of silence passed before Chrysabelle spoke. "Mal's not dead."

Creek lifted his head, not sure he'd really heard what she'd said. "What? How?"

"When he drank from me, his full strength returned and he was able to scatter again. Except when he scatters, he turns to smoke. He escaped into one of the storm drains with a few burns."

Creek sat back, a little angry but mostly relieved. "Thanks for letting me think he was dead."

"What was I supposed to do? You weren't exactly on our side."

He nodded. "You're right. I probably wouldn't have told me either."

"Is your grandmother all right?"

"Yes. Thank you." He rubbed a hand over his Mohawk. "Speaking of not being dead, Octavian's in town. He's come to work for the KM here since he can't be of use in Corvinestri anymore."

Damian tensed. "What the hell? That bastard works for you guys? Does the KM know he used to beat me whenever Tatiana told him to?"

Chrysabelle shot her brother a pained look. "You never told me that."

"What was the point? I thought he was dead. But now . . ." Damian turned back to Creek, jabbing a finger in the air. "You tell him to stay out of my path. I'm not under Tatiana's thumb anymore, and KM or not, he's going to pay for what he did to me."

Creek nodded. "I hear you. Right now, he's working with the mayor, helping us keep tabs on her, so he's got no reason to contact you." He shifted uncomfortably. "I'll be perfectly honest; I have my doubts about him but I'm still KM and those doubts are strictly off the record." Damian's info only added to those reservations. "On the record, I'm sure he only did what he had to in order to keep Tatiana from being suspicious."

"I saw the pictures," Chrysabelle said. "What he did to Damian was above and beyond necessary."

Damian snorted, but otherwise kept quiet.

"I'm keeping as close a watch on him as I can," Creek said.

Chrysabelle inched toward the edge of the sofa. "Anything else?"

Before answering her, Creek glanced at Damian. He seemed lost in thought. "Just that…I'd like us to be friends again. If that's possible. I don't plan on being KM longer than I have to, but right now, quitting's not an option. I promise that if there's anything I can do to help you, I will. I feel like I owe you that much."

She nodded. "I appreciate that. That probably wasn't easy for you to say."

He shrugged. "Doing the right thing isn't always easy, but it's still the right thing."

She stared at him then, a strange, almost sad expression on her face. She smiled, but it too seemed sad. He felt like he should understand more about the way she was looking at him than he did. "Thank you." Her quiet answer did nothing to ease the sense he was missing something important.

"Something you want to tell me about?"

A quick shake of her head and whatever had been bothering her was gone. "No. Everything's fine."

She was a bad liar, but he understood whatever was on her mind wasn't something she was ready to talk about. "Okay, well, you know how to reach me if you need me." He got up to leave.

"Creek?"

He stopped and waited.

She looked away for a moment, her brow furrowing in thought. "There is something you could do for me." When she glanced up, her eyes held the same sense of loss he'd seen in his mother's when the judge had announced his sentence.

He sat back down. "What is it? I'll do whatever I can to help." She deserved that much.

Her fingers twisted together. "It's about Mal. I can't go into detail but he's not himself. He's... sick right now and the sickness is letting his darkness get the best of him. I've got the situation under control for the moment so there's no reason anything bad should happen, but if you see him out on the streets..." She swallowed. "He's not the Mal you know. He's dangerous." Her eyes met his again. "Please, keep him from doing something stupid. And don't hurt him any more than you have to. I need a little more time to get him better."

Creek nodded. Maybe it was better he didn't know the details. "I'll do what I can."

She smiled halfheartedly. "I know it's your job to protect the citizens of Paradise City. Try to think of Mal as one of those citizens who needs protecting from himself."

He stood. "You've got my word. I'll let you know if I see him, okay?"

She bent her head. Was she crying? "Thanks," she whispered. "And if I can't get him better..." Her voice broke.

"You want me to—"

"No." Her head came up, eyes sharp and liquid. "If it comes to that, I'll take care of him myself." She looked away again. "I owe him that much."

The plane's landing barely registered. Tatiana knew she'd arrived but the numbness of the last few days had erased the small sensations from her notice. She moved through the fog with as much purpose as she could manage, but the task before her was daunting. Bigger than anything she'd tackled alone before.

Which was why she had come to Paradise City to make

a deal with the man who'd saved her from the gallows when she was human. The man who'd turned her into the creature she was today and who she'd cut a swath of destruction through Europe with centuries ago. The man who'd been her husband and had since become her immortal enemy.

Malkolm Bourreau.

"We've landed, my lady." The fringe pilot stood beside her seat.

She nodded.

He stayed there, tipping his head slightly, trying to make eye contact. "What would you like us to do?"

She got up, but couldn't find the energy to focus on him. "Stay in the hangar with the plane."

"Yes, my lady." He went back to the cockpit.

Pulling herself up a little taller, she took a tiny scrap of fabric from her pocket. One of the guards had found it at Syler's estate. It matched the coat Mal had been wearing the night he and his whore had tried to steal Lilith from her. The fabric was little more than a few threads, but it was all she had to go on. She walked to the back of the plane and opened the bedroom door.

The Nothos she'd secured there raised its stinking head.

She held the fabric out. "Find this vampire."

The creature inhaled, nearly dragging the shredded bits into its nostrils. "Yes, my lady." And with that it took off, its loping gait carrying it through the plane and down the steps in a few strides. Tatiana scattered into a swarm of black wasps and followed it out of the hangar and into the night.

They went for miles, the Nothos running without tiring, stopping only to affirm the trail, then taking off again. An hour passed. Maybe two. If the creature didn't find Mal soon, she might have to seek shelter from the sunrise.

Then it stopped. Tatiana came back together beside it. "Here?"

It lifted one unnaturally jointed arm and pointed. "There, my lady."

She gestured behind her. "Take cover in that warehouse. Stay there until I need you."

"Yes, my lady." It loped away.

She inhaled. The stink of petrol and oil and rotting sea life almost hid the dark spice of vampire, but it was there. Hands on her hips, she stared at the abandoned freighter and a little of the numbness faded from her body. This encounter could very well end up with her death. She pulled the locket around her neck free from her clothing so that it could be seen. Mal would know what it was and that reminder might buy her a few minutes. Then she started up the gangplank.

Thoughts of her fine home filled her head as she boarded the ship. She'd come to offer him the life of his comarré in exchange for his help, but perhaps money would do more good. Judging by his living situation, he could certainly use it. Didn't the comarré have any money? Why wasn't she taking care of him? Or perhaps things were not that way between them. She ran her hand over one of the railings. Flakes of paint and rust rained into the water below. Maybe this wouldn't be such a hard bargain to strike after all.

Making her way cautiously inside, she kept her senses open for any sounds of movement. If Mal found her and killed her before she had a chance to explain…

Dim solars offered a little light here and there. Enough for her to pick her way, but the ship's interior was a maze of stairs and turns, four-way crosses, and dead ends. She inhaled again, finding his scent a little stronger and, this time, mixed with blood. She went after that. Blood was easy to follow, even though she'd fed from Aaron before she'd left.

Down a long hall she spotted an open door. Soundlessly, she made her way toward it and peeked inside. Mal lay on the bedroom floor, looking very much like he'd been dumped there. She nudged his leg with the toe of her boot.

Nothing.

She nudged harder. Still no response. She grabbed his arm, picked it up, and let it drop. It hit the floor with a dull thud. She'd never known him to be such a sound sleeper. She kicked his thigh. "Wake up! How can you daysleep when it's night?"

He still didn't move. Frustrated, she bent down and sniffed his open mouth. Sweet but a tiny bit bitter at the same time. "Bloody hell." Laudanum. Who had drugged him? Well, there was only one way to bring him out of it besides waiting for it to wear off on its own.

She tossed her jacket aside, pulled her sleeve up, and bit into her wrist, then held it over his mouth, letting the blood trickle in. When the wound closed, she did it again and was about to do it a third time when he came to. She jerked back into the shadows of the room.

He sat up and reached for his head, growling softly. He rolled his shoulders as if testing his body. "Damn it, not again."

"Exactly how often does this happen to you?"

A microsecond later, he was on his feet, his hand around her throat. Her feet dangled off the ground. "What the hell are you doing here? Did you do this to me?"

"I woke you up. I didn't knock you out." Her instinct was to shift her metal hand into a stake and turn him to ash, but she needed him. Instead, she held her hands up where he could see them and forced herself to remain calm. "Some thanks for saving you from your drug-induced coma."

He snarled, eyes reflecting silver. "Sounds like something you would do."

"It does, but I didn't." She tried to make a sincere face. "I'm here to offer you a deal."

"A deal? With you? You're the one who cursed me. Why should I have anything to do with you?" He scowled. "I should run you through right now and be done with it."

Sincere changed to pleading. "At least let me tell you why I've come first."

"And give you a chance to kill me first? I don't think so." He squeezed her throat tighter.

"Please," she croaked out. "I know we've had our difficulties in the past—"

"Difficulties?" He snorted.

"I swear on Sophia's grave, I come in peace."

He bared his fangs at her. "How dare you invoke my daughter's name?"

"*Our* daughter's name." She swallowed and lifted her chin as best she could. "I would never use her name for false purposes. I swear it. I'm offering a truce."

He stared at her for a few seconds, then relaxed his grip slightly and lowered her enough so that her toes touched the floor. His hand stayed on her throat. "Go on."

"In exchange for your help with one small matter, I promise to leave your precious comarré alone."

He laughed, his body language calming a little. "Why should I care what happens to her?"

Tatiana raised her brows. This was new and different. "So you don't then?"

"No. I'm done with her." He leaned in until his body pinned hers to the wall and all she could focus on was his face. And the hard length of his body against hers. Old, human memories surfaced. She swatted them down and tried to focus on what he was saying. "But she's my prize to take, understand?"

"Completely." Not at all actually, but she nodded anyway, her chin bumping his hand. So he was done with the comarré but she was still off-limits? Curious, but an opening was an opening. Tatiana slipped her hand up to cup his face. Hades help her, but she still found him attractive. Maybe more so now that she knew he wasn't smitten with the comarré. "Malkolm, we used to be so good together. We could be that way again. Help me and I'll restore your noble status. You can return to Corvinestri with me. Rule as my Elder. You'll never want for anything again. Power, money, blood, as much as you want whenever you want it."

A long moment passed. He dropped her to the ground and stepped back, his eyes narrowing as he assessed her. "What exactly do you want from me?"

She reached up to rub her throat but stopped before she showed weakness, resting her hands on her locket instead. "It's about the child whom you and the comarré came to take from me."

A flicker of silver crossed his gaze then disappeared. "What about it?"

"She. As you know the ancients took her from me."

"And you want me to get her back."

"Not exactly." She dropped her hands from the locket, settling one on the dagger at her waist. "I want you to kill her."

Chapter Sixteen

The *thump-thump-thump* of wings beating the air grew louder, but Creek was expecting Annika, so after his initial glance to confirm it was she, he stayed crouched on the rooftop where he'd set up his surveillance point.

Behind him, the sounds of her touching down barely registered. She squatted next to him, her wings now tucked away. "We have a problem."

Creek nodded. "You have no idea." He tipped his head toward the crime scene below. "Two murders in two days. And both pointing hard at a vampire killer."

"That's not what I'm talking about."

He looked at her. "What's up?"

The strobing blue police lights reflected off her protective shades. "Tatiana's headed here. Might already be here. Our intelligence gathering has become a little more difficult with Octavian out of the picture."

"Damn." Chrysabelle would need to know that. He wondered what Annika would do with Chrysabelle's news about Mal. Not that he was going to share that. He liked Annika, probably more than he should, and he'd even come to trust her as much as anyone could trust a KM sector chief, but therein lay the issue. She was still Kubai Mata and he was still trying not to be.

"Exactly. This could get ugly. We don't know her intent, but it's not hard to guess she's here to exact some kind of revenge on the comarré. I'm sure Tatiana blames her for what went down at the Dominus ball."

"Which we sent her to. Look, about Chrysabelle…" He hesitated, almost afraid to stir the pot further. "What's the KM's stance on her since she didn't bring the baby back?" They'd threatened to strip the gold from the ring of sorrows out of her skin if she failed on that mission, which she had.

"With Tatiana in town, we're going to let things ride." His shock must have registered on his face more than he realized since Annika continued. "Trust me, the KM aren't going soft, but the grand masters believe the ring's power might give the comarré the edge she needs to take Tatiana out once and for all."

"And if it doesn't?"

Annika stared into the street below. "You're assuming she'll live through a fight with Tatiana."

"She's done it before."

"She's had the vampire with her." Annika faced him again. "But we both know that situation's changed, don't we?"

He played dumb, something he hated to do, especially with his sector chief. "What do you mean?"

"We know he's still alive and we know something's changed between them. That's all I can say." Then she dipped her head toward the County Coroner's truck that had just arrived on the street. "Who do you think is responsible for these murders?"

"Not Mal."

She raised one brow over the rim of her sunglasses. "It wouldn't take much to return him to his previous state. Especially if he and the comarré have parted ways."

"They haven't. I just spoke to her and that's not the case." Was it? After everything Chrysabelle had said and the way she'd been acting, he wasn't so sure.

She shrugged. "Keep an eye out. That's the only directive I'm giving you for now." She stepped back from the lookout point. Her wings unfurled through the pleats in her jacket. "Just don't be surprised if our killer turns out to be someone we already know."

"Shall I hold dinner, Maddoc?" Isaiah asked.

Fi frowned. This dinner was specifically for Remo to get to know them better, but he wasn't here yet. Not a great start.

Doc looked at his watch. "No. Everyone else made it on time."

Barasa cleared his throat. "Maybe we could wait another minute?"

"Absolutely," Fi answered, shooting Doc a look. He hadn't been a fan of this idea, but she was determined to give it a go.

Frowning, Doc rolled his eyes. "Fine. Two more minutes and that's it."

"More than generous," Omur added.

"Very good, Maddoc." Isaiah nodded. "I'll keep things warm." He headed back to the kitchen, passing Channa, a female varcolai who'd been brought in to help serve.

She brought two wine decanters to the bar. "Can I pour anyone a glass?"

"A small glass of white," Fi answered. A little wine might help take the edge off, plus with Doc here, she wasn't as worried about drinking with Remo around.

A chime sounded, indicating the elevator was on its way up.

Isaiah reappeared on his way to the foyer. "At last, our missing guest."

"About time," Doc said. Omur and Barasa snorted in agreement.

"Be nice," Fi said softly. "We're trying to make friends."

Doc patted her hand. "I know. You're right. Sorry—"

"Out of my way." Remo stormed into the room, eyes gold with anger. "You." He pointed at Fi. "You murdered my sister and I have proof."

Fi's mouth gaped open. "What?"

Doc and his council members jumped up as Isaiah came running in after Remo. Doc stepped in front of Fi, flaring his arms out and clenching his fists. "You better step back before I—"

"Before you what? Murder me too? Look at my hand," Remo shouted. "Look at it." Fi stood as he shoved his palm at Doc. Tiny inflamed cuts covered it. The rest of the skin looked sunburned.

Doc's lip curled. "What does that prove?"

"Silver poisoning." Remo glared at Fi. "She gave me the vial of sand from the arena. I accidently crushed it in my hand." His pupils thinned to vertical slits. "That's when I felt the silver burning into the cuts. The sand was tainted. The fight was never fair."

Omur and Barasa exchanged a look. Doc shook his head. "This is as much news to us as it is to you."

"Your lies won't save her." Remo growled low and threatening. "Pride law says a life for a life." He pointed to Fi. "And I call for hers." Then he lunged toward her like he intended to make that happen.

Barasa and Omur leaped forward, grabbing his arms and taking him to the ground. Doc hoisted Fi over his shoulder and hurtled the couch. "Isaiah, now."

The butler followed them. Doc ran into the bedroom. Isaiah shut the door after them. "What can I do?"

Doc put Fi on her feet. "Tell her driver to meet her downstairs right now." He turned to her as Isaiah slipped out to call for the car. "Go to Chrysabelle's. It's the safest place I can think of. I'll make this go away."

"Is what he said true?" She stared into Doc's eyes, trying to find answers. "Was the fight unfair?"

Something broke, then someone cursed. Doc glanced at the door. "We don't have time for this—"

"Yes, we do." She grabbed his arm. "Answer me." His hesitation told her all she needed to know. "Who do you think did this?"

"No idea, but we'll figure it out."

"If the fight was unfair, then I didn't really win, did I?" She sat on the bed, her head reeling with the news. "Which means I'm not really qualified to be your mate."

"Cripes, Fi, of course you are. A hundred percent." He pulled her back to her feet. More sounds of scuffling and shouting carried through the closed door. "We'll get to the bottom of this, I promise, but right now I need you safe, okay? The car should be downstairs waiting for you." He hugged her hard. "I love you, baby. Don't worry."

"I love you, too." Her gut ached like she'd been sucker punched, but she went ghost and slipped into the night unable to shake the feeling she might never see Doc again.

"I'll only be gone for as long as I have to." Chrysabelle pulled on a tan leather jacket over the pale green sweater and jeans that were part of her new look.

Damian nodded. "Take whatever time you need. We'll be fine."

"Please, move into the house." She looked past him and out into the courtyard where Jerem was putting her roller bag into the trunk of the car. She glanced at the guesthouse before putting her hands on her hips and turning back to her brother. "Amylia can have the whole guesthouse to herself and you can get settled in here without me in your way."

"You've never been in my way." He smiled, but then his eyes narrowed and he moved to see past her. "You expecting company?"

"No." A car pulled through the estate's open gates. "That's Fi's car."

Sure enough, the car stopped and Fi jumped out. The moment she saw Chrysabelle she broke into a run. "Are you leaving? Wait, don't go yet."

The panic in Fi's eyes alarmed Chrysabelle. "I am, but I can wait. What's up?"

Fi came to a stop beside her. "I just found out someone put silver dust in the arena sand where I fought Heaven." She looked on the verge of tears. "That means I didn't win fair and square and now Heaven's brother is calling for my death to make things right."

"Pride law," Chrysabelle whispered. "How awful. What can I do to help?"

"Let me stay here?" Fi shook her head. "It's not safe for me at pride headquarters right now."

"Chrys, take her with you to New Orleans." Damian nodded toward the car. "Not like you don't have room and getting her out of town might be the best thing."

Fi's eyes brightened. "If you're going there to do what I think you're going there to do, you should totally let me come."

Chrysabelle bit her lip. "I don't know. I don't want to be responsible for what might happen."

"I can take care of myself, you know," Fi said.

Chrysabelle raised a brow. "I don't think one sparring session qualifies you as being able to take care of yourself."

"Please." Fi sniffed. "Nothing can touch me when I go ghost. Which I promise to do if anything bad happens."

"C'mon, Chrys," Damian said. "Let her go."

Chrysabelle said, "Fine," but a loud rumbling drowned her out.

"Hey," Jerem yelled. "Creek's here."

The KM parked his motorcycle beside Chrysabelle's sedan, notching his kickstand into place. He slipped his helmet off as he walked toward them. "Chrysabelle, can I have a word with you alone?"

"Sure." Creek's expression held no joy. Something was wrong. Chrysabelle shivered. "Fi, why don't you go inside with Damian and see if Velimai can pack you some snacks for the trip."

"So I can go?"

"Yes." Chrysabelle was already walking to meet

Creek. She spoke to him as soon as Fi shut the front door. "What's going on?"

"Bad news. There have been two humans murdered, both by vampires, and the KM think Mal's to blame."

Her spine went cold. "Why would they think that?"

"Because they know something's changed between you two. You didn't give me the full story the other day, did you?"

"No." She sighed. "It's not something I want to get into, especially if I can make it go away."

"That's not all." He shot a look at her car. "Are you going somewhere?"

"I have some out-of-town business to take care of." Out-of-town business that would hopefully bring Mal back to her.

"Good, that's good."

"Why?"

He glanced at the gate behind him before answering her. "Because as of last night, Tatiana is back in Paradise City."

Chapter Seventeen

Mal stared hard at the woman who'd once been his wife. And his captor. "You want me to kill a baby? You should know better than to ask me that."

Tatiana shook her head, her fingers again clutching the locket around her neck. "She's not a child any longer. The ancient ones fed her their blood and now she's an adult. More than that, she's a monster vampire. Unlike anything I've ever seen. Even the ancients are afraid of her."

He walked back toward the bed. This game of Tatiana's was starting to bore him. He had a comarré to deal with. "You're not as smart as you look, are you? Telling me the ancients are afraid of her isn't a great way to motivate me to the cause."

Desperation began to creep in around her eyes. He knew that look. He'd seen it many times before. If her next plea didn't work, she'd try to seduce him to her will. "The beast within you is stronger than she is. Would it be an easy kill? Perhaps not, but when's the last time the beast had a worthy opponent?" She smiled and took a few steps toward him, sashaying her hips. "You might even enjoy it."

He sat on the bed, giving her words some actual thought. "And if I do this, I get my noble status back. No other strings."

"No strings, but more than that." She trailed her fingers on the covers as she moved toward him. "I'll give you everything you've been missing. Think of it, the two of us, ruling the noble houses." She stopped when her knees touched his thigh. "Like the old days, but with more power and no fear of reprisal."

"You were the only thing I had to fear back then."

She looked stricken. "Lord Ivan forced me into betraying you. I never would have done anything to hurt you. I did it to protect you. To keep them from killing you." She tipped her head coyly. "I loved you, Malkolm."

"Fat lot of good that did me." He was almost enjoying this. Almost. "Why should I trust you now?"

"Because having a baby to look after, even for the short time I had Lilith, made me realize that..." She looked down and swallowed, letting a little half-sob escape her lips. "I missed what we had when we were a family."

Son of a priest, she was a good actress. She could have made a fortune on the stage. He leaned back and studied her. "I don't know." Actually, he did. He'd do it because it was a chance to regain everything he'd lost. "I need some kind of proof."

She reached up and opened the locket around her neck, then lifted the portrait so he could better see it.

Sophia. A tiny part of him felt ill.

Tatiana raised the portrait higher. "On Sophia's good name, I promise I will do nothing to harm you."

He refused to look at the picture. Couldn't, really. Instead, he stood and pushed past her to walk to the other side of the room. "I'll do it, but on my terms."

"Like what?" She actually sounded relieved.

He stopped beside his reading chair. At least twelve swords and sixteen daggers were mounted within arm's reach. He turned slowly, contemplating his options. Maybe he'd test her. "I want some good-faith money. Whatever you have on you."

Her mouth opened slightly. "I don't usually travel with money."

He crossed his arms. "You came here to persuade me to work for you and didn't bring any money. Did you think I was going to help you out of the goodness of my heart?"

"No, I—"

He held out his hand. "Give me the locket."

Her eyes rounded. "What?" She snapped the locket closed, pressing it against her heart. "No."

"No locket, no agreement." He told himself he wanted it because it was the thing she held most dear, not because it contained a picture of his only child.

Reluctantly, she unfastened the clasp and let it fall loose into her hand. She took a few slow steps toward him and held it out. "You had better kill Lilith."

"And you had better not lie to me." He closed the locket in his hand. "Again."

Octavian was working out beautifully, even better than Lola had anticipated. He seemed to know what she needed before she knew herself.

He looked up from typing the last of her notes into his tablet. "Anything else, Madam Mayor?"

"No, that's it. What else is on my agenda?"

"There's a report from the police chief about a couple of murders, but I took the liberty of skimming it and there's no new information, so I filed it. I hope that was all right." He looked at her, waiting for her approval.

She nodded. "That's fine." She checked her watch. "Seems we're done early."

He smiled. "I strive to be efficient. Would you like to see if any new e-mails have come in?"

"Not in the slightest." What she wanted was to loosen him up with a few drinks, and then see what she could find out about the ancient ones that might help her recover her granddaughter. So far, he'd been vague about what he knew of them. Almost scared to talk about them. "There are a few hours left before the sun comes up. How about we take the rest of the night off and have some fun?"

"Like what?"

She winked and said, "Follow me."

Half an hour later, the two of them and Luke Havoc stood in front of Seven. She leaned toward Octavian. "I've been here once before, but I was human then and didn't get to enjoy it. I have a feeling it'll be a very different experience now."

He seemed curious about the surrounding crowd. "This place is pretty popular, I take it."

"The taxes alone pay city hall's electric bill."

A bouncer opened the rope for them and welcomed them in. "Good evening, Madam Mayor. Have a good time."

Inside, they entered through a gorgeous pair of red double doors painted with crouching gold dragons. Through those doors and they were in the thick of the club.

A server came up to them almost immediately. She did a kind of half-curtsy that Lola found amusing. "What's your pleasure this evening? Which of our sins would you like to enjoy?"

Lola glanced at the doorways stationed along the perimeter of the club. Through the crowd of dancers, servers, and comarré, she could make out the words Vanity, Envy, Sloth, Wrath, Lust, Gluttony, and Greed above each door. She looked to Octavian. "Which one should we try?"

He pointed toward Greed. "What goes on in there?"

The server glanced back to see where he was pointing, then smiled. "Games of chance, sir."

He laughed and spoke to the mayor. "What do you say to a little gambling?"

She hooked her arm through his. Whatever he wanted to do was fine with her. She wanted him happy. "Let's break the house."

As she soon discovered, Octavian's talents extended past his office skills. In just a few hands of Baccarat, he'd won a tidy sum. His celebratory mood helped him down nearly a bottle and a half of the club's best champagne. Lola had done her best to sip hers and keep her head, but even with her vampire tolerance she was starting to feel a buzz. It was almost like the alcohol served at Seven was stronger.

She pointed at the growing pile of chips at Octavian's side. "You know what you should do with those?"

"What?" He leaned into her as he turned, booze sweet on his breath.

"You should buy yourself one of those." She gestured to a passing comarré. "I got Hector here, you know."

"That," he said heavily, "is a great idea." He stood a little straighter. "Where do we buy one? Whom do we talk to?"

Their server came up to them. "Do you need something, sir?"

"Yes. I want to buy a comarré."

"Very good, sir. The croupier will hold your chips until you're ready to play again or cash them out for you."

"Cash them out. I want to spend the money on a comarré."

"Excellent. If you'll just follow me." She led them through the gilded chain-mail curtain of Envy, then through another set of doors that were entirely gold-leafed.

The room inside was done in white with touches of gold and red. The heavy thump of the club's music filtered through, but it was so muted it seemed very distant. Luke stood just inside the door. He looked enormously bored with the whole evening. The server rang a small crystal bell, then turned to them. "Would you like another bottle of champagne while you wait?"

"Absolutely," Octavian answered.

Good, Lola thought. More champagne and a quiet place to talk. Just the setup she'd hoped for. "Luke, would you give us a few minutes alone?"

He nodded. "I'll be outside." He held the door for the server, then left after her.

Octavian settled onto a white silk sofa. He leaned into it, spreading his arms over the back. "This is quite the place."

She sat beside him. "Yes, it is. Did you have anything like this where you came from?"

"Not really. Most nobles like to entertain in their

homes." He drained his glass. "Fantastic parties." He sighed wistfully. "You can't imagine."

"Did the ancients ever come to those parties?"

The longing left his face quickly. "What?"

Soft, shushing footsteps interrupted them and a beautiful Japanese woman entered the room. Her face bore the hard angles of a noble vampire. She bowed before she spoke. "I am Katsumi Tanaka. I run the comarré operations here at Seven." She nodded at Lola. "Madam Mayor, welcome. I don't believe I've met your friend."

"This is my assistant, Octavian Petrescu."

Katsumi's smile faltered for a moment and her gaze widened on Octavian like she knew him, and then she blinked it away and smiled. "Another noble. How wonderful. Welcome, Octavian. Are you new to the city?"

"Yes." He crossed his arms. "Is that a problem?"

"Not at all." Katsumi dipped her head. "We are always happy to welcome new customers. I understand you're interested in purchasing a comarré."

His mood seemed to grow worse by the moment. "Yes, where are they? Bring them out."

Katsumi stiffened a little As though Octavian had insulted her. "We need to be sure our clients have the means necessary to purchase a comarré first." She held a palm-sized tablet out to him. "Would you please access your credit statement so I may verify you?"

"I have the money in cash." Octavian scowled and turned to Lola. "See what's taking that server so long with my money, will you?"

She gave him an ugly look. If she didn't need so much from him, she'd cut him down on the spot, but keeping him happy and helpful was her main goal until she got the information she needed. She forced a smile. "I'll be right back."

Luke was on the other side of the door. "Everything okay?"

"No. That fool thinks I'm his errand girl. And he's yet to give me any information about the ones holding Mariela." With every night that passed, the chances of getting her granddaughter back seemed to fade.

Luke shrugged. "Then teach him a lesson. Leave him here."

"Luke, I don't think..." She paused. Maybe leaving him would be a good reminder of her power for Octavian. Maybe then he'd be willing to answer her questions. She needed him, that much was true, but she also needed to keep the upper hand. "Let's get the car."

Chapter Eighteen

Katsumi knew the vampire with the mayor was familiar, but until she'd said his name, Katsumi couldn't place him. Then it all came back to her—the Dominus Ball. Octavian belonged to Tatiana. What was he doing here? Did the mayor know his past? His being in Paradise City was certainly information Dominic needed to know. And might even reward her for. She held her composure until the mayor left.

Unfortunately, the server returned with the champagne. Katsumi waited while the girl opened the bottle, poured Octavian another glass, then left them alone again.

Octavian sipped his bubbly. "The mayor will be right back with my money, so why don't you bring the comarré out for me to see?"

"I would be happy to, but we actually have a viewing room." They didn't, but she wanted an uninterrupted moment with him. "If you would just follow me, I'd be happy to show you those currently available."

With a sigh, he got up and went with her.

"Just through here." She opened the door to her office

for him, then shut it behind her. She leaned against it while he got his bearings.

"I don't see any comarré in here. This looks like an office." He turned, scowling.

"I know who you are," Katsumi said. "And if you don't tell me what you're doing here, I'll tell the mayor and every other noble vampire in this city exactly who you are and whom you work for."

His expression changed, his eyes silvering. "You don't know anything, especially about whom I work for."

"No?" She blinked at him. "Does Tatiana know you're here? Or did she send you? Are you working for her?"

Anger narrowed his eyes. "You talk too much."

"And you don't talk enough. You have ten seconds to answer me or"—her hand moved to the light panel—"I press this button and call security to have you removed. The head of our security is a shadeux fae. Nasty what one of them can do to a vampire, isn't it?"

Octavian lunged and Katsumi realized too late he wasn't nearly as drunk as he'd led her to believe. He grabbed her head in his hands and smashed it against the door, kneeing her in the belly at the same time. She doubled over in pain, lights swimming before her eyes. The soft shooshing sound of a blade being pulled from its sheath reached her ears. She went for the *kanzashi* stuck in her elaborately knotted hair, but a fiery pain pierced her body before she reached it.

She looked down, amazed to see the end of a slim wooden spike protruding from her chest. "You—"

But ashes had no voice.

* * *

Chrysabelle settled back as the plane began to descend. Darkness still cloaked the Ville Éternelle Nuit, the City of Eternal Night, as it was known to the nobility, called that because any vampire who set foot within the city limits of New Orleans would find they were impervious to the sun. The ability came from a witch who'd cursed the city in revenge of a broken heart. The fae, for whom New Orleans was a haven city, had been able to temper the curse so that upon leaving, all vampires immediately forgot most of what they'd experienced. The threads that remained had turned the city into a legend in vampire lore for being something remarkable. They knew it was special, just not exactly why or where it was.

The only thing special Chrysabelle wanted from the city was access to the Claustrum. By the time they landed and the sun rose, she'd hopefully have convinced someone to give it to her. Jerem, who'd accompanied them, sat near the front of the plane and rocked his head slightly to music on his MP3 player. She shook Fi gently. "Hey, we're here."

Fi's lids fluttered open and she stretched. "Cool. Can we get some beignets? I'm starving and I hear those things are like crack."

"You can do whatever you like after we check in, although I'll probably try to get a little sleep." Something she hadn't been able to do on the plane with everything going through her head. And regardless of what Fi thought, she had no intention of taking her into the Claustrum. That job and that risk were Chrysabelle's and Chrysabelle's alone.

Fi frowned. "Aren't you hungry?"

"I ate one of the sandwiches Velimai packed. I'm fine.

I just want to do what I came here to do and go home."
With Tatiana in town, she'd sent a message to Mortalis
asking him to stop by and check on things. She knew her
brother and Velimai could take care of themselves, but a
little extra protection was never a bad idea.

Fi patted Chrysabelle's arm. "I know it's not a vaca-
tion. I didn't mean to imply anything different." She
smiled apologetically. "So what's the first stop after the
hotel? Khell's?"

"Starting with the current guardian seems like the best
plan." She shrugged. "I did help him get that position,
after all."

"Then he owes you." Fi nodded. "I can't wait to meet
him. I bet he's an interesting guy."

"He looks a little like a math professor, but you won't
get to meet him. I need you to stay at the hotel. Or go
sightseeing or whatever else you'd like to do that doesn't
involve coming with me."

"What?" Fi made a face. "Don't even try that because
it's not going to happen. I've come this far; I'm not sitting
in some hotel room waiting for you to come back, wondering if you're okay, worrying that I'm never going to see
you again. No. Way."

"Fi, it's just that—"

"I'll stay ghost the whole time if that makes you feel
better. Plus, who else is going to watch your back?" With
a huff, she crossed her arms and put her feet on the seat in
front of her. "I am so going," she mumbled.

"It's just not a good idea—"

"Neither is your going alone. Stop arguing. We're
doing this together."

Chrysabelle let out a long, frustrated breath. "Fine, but

you're in ghost mode the entire time." She shook her head. "You really don't let up, do you?"

"To know me is to love me." Fi grinned. "By the way, you look nice in your new clothes. A lot more normal. Except for all the gold bits on your hands and face, but I'm guessing no one will look twice at you in New Orleans. They'll probably just think you're a street performer on the way to your job."

Within an hour of them deplaning, Jerem had them settled into the rental car he'd arranged, then drove them to the hotel, stopping only for the checkpoint, which they sailed through.

The last time she'd done this, Mal had met her in the city. And she hadn't been pregnant. How fast things could change in so little time.

At the hotel, Jerem turned the keys over to the valet but wouldn't let the bellboy touch the bags. It wouldn't take a genius to figure out that the long duffel held two swords and a leather roll of smaller blades. At least flying private made transporting weapons a lot easier.

Once in the penthouse, they separated into their bedrooms, each setting their alarms for the same time. The only place she knew to look for Khell was La Belle et la Bête, the oldest othernatural bar in the French Quarter. It's where she'd found him last time and she'd gotten the sense that he was a regular there, thanks to info Augustine had given her.

She didn't know if Khell would be there now, but chances were good she'd be able to persuade someone there into divulging his address. How much persuading that would take she didn't know, but she wanted to be rested for it.

Besides, there was little point in arriving at Khell's too

early and waking him or whatever his girlfriend's name was up. Chrysabelle needed him to be as amenable as possible, not cranky because she'd pulled him from his beauty sleep.

But when the alarm went off a few hours later, the sleep she'd managed had been fitful at best, disturbed by anxiety over what the outcome of this trip could mean if things didn't go well. Trying to push the worries out of her head only gave place to new ones.

Reluctantly, she tapped the alarm off, got up, and showered. She dressed in something that gave her a little more edge: black jeans, a long-sleeved gray T-shirt, and a darker gray leather jacket.

Then she unpacked her arsenal and strapped the daggers to her waist, where they'd be mostly hidden by her jacket. The sacres might upset a few patrons at the bar, so they'd stay here until she returned and knew she had passage to the Claustrum. They were definitely going with her then.

Fi walked into the bedroom sipping a large cup of coffee and wearing one of the hotel robes. Her hair was still a little damp. "Where to first?"

Chrysabelle sat at the dressing table and began to braid her hair out of the way. "La Belle et la Bête. Means beauty and the beast. It's an old othernaturals-only joint in the French Quarter."

"Sounds awesomely not awesome." Fi rolled her eyes. "Only fae would name a bar after a fairy tale. What is it, one giant tea party?"

Chrysabelle laughed, catching Fi's gaze in the mirror. "Not exactly. Last time I was there, the bartender was varcolai." She raised her brows for effect. "*Gator* shifter."

"For real?" Fi sat cross-legged on the bed. "So is this one of those deals where I have to stay in ghost form?"

She tied off the end of the braid and flipped it over her shoulder. "You might not even be able to see the building in your human form. It's got all kinds of fae magic protecting it."

"Hmm," Fi said. "This place might not be so bad after all."

Mal tucked the portrait of Sophia into his pocket. "You can't stay here."

Tatiana seemed perplexed by that news. "Why not? The sun will be up soon. Where else am I going to go?"

"Back to Corvinestri. I have something to take care of before I help you." Some*one*, actually. A gilded, blond someone he wanted out of his life for good. "When that's done, I'll come to you."

She laughed. "How exactly are you going to get to Corvinestri? You keep a private jet somewhere I don't know about?"

"I can borrow one." Dominic owed him. Or he'd steal it.

"You won't be able to get through the wards."

"So fix that. You already said you were going to return me to my noble status. Make that the first step. Otherwise, I'll have a hard time believing you."

"Fine." She lifted her chin. "Not that I'm not happy to get out of this hellhole you call home." She grimaced. "How do you live here?"

He picked one of his favorite daggers off the wall,

hefting it in his hand. "You didn't leave me with many options."

Her eyes went to the blade. "Yes, well, let's try to put that behind us, shall we? I've promised to rectify the situation. Let it go."

Let it go? She'd chained him in the ruins of an old fortress and left him to rot. He should just kill her now and be done with it, but the lure of access to all that wealth was great. And having power meant getting away with murder. Literally. He reluctantly tucked the dagger into his belt. "I'm ready for you to leave."

She sniffed. "What if someone tries to drug you again?"

"They won't. I'll only drink straight from the vein until I see you again." Which meant killing a few humans, but it wasn't like he'd never done that before.

"That's still not a guarantee."

"You're wasting dark. The sun will be up soon and you're *not* daysleeping here."

"What are you going to do? Throw me overboard?"

He raised one brow.

"Bloody hell." She grabbed the jacket she'd discarded and headed for the door. "You're supposed to be helping me."

She kept muttering to herself as she left the ship, her voice fading as he selected another blade for his last and final trip to see Chrysabelle. If he didn't take care of her now, she'd only end up following him to Corvinestri and with his new life as a noble before him, he couldn't take the chance that his unfortunate past would come back to haunt him.

Again the word "ghost" flitted through his brain. He shook it away. Too much to do to think about consequences.

First he'd need to find a meal. Going after the comarré hungry meant there was too much chance he'd lose control. He needed to be focused. To strike cleanly and swiftly.

But most of all, he needed the comarré dead.

Chapter Nineteen

Creek lay flat on the roof of the warehouse, a few of the ashes of the Nothos he'd killed still clinging to his clothes and souring the air. He kept his eyes trained on Mal's freighter. If Tatiana spent the day there, he'd sneak in and—no, she was leaving. How about that. Had she killed Mal?

He kept watching, waiting to see what she'd do. She seemed to be talking to herself. He caught a few choice curses and almost laughed. She was complaining about Mal, so maybe she hadn't killed him. A sharp whistle cracked the night air and he realized she was calling for the Nothos.

That wasn't going to go well.

When the creature didn't come, Tatiana cursed again, then scattered into a swarm of wasps and flew off. Apparently, she wasn't in a mood to wait.

Not long after, a second dark figure emerged on the ship's deck.

Mal.

Creek quietly crawled back from the edge and rappelled down the back of the building, where he crouched behind a stack of pallets. Mal was just stepping off the gangplank. He took off in a jog. Creek followed far enough behind that Mal didn't seem to notice.

They headed into Little Havana. Once there, Mal slowed to a walk. There were a few people out at this hour, some just coming home, some on their way to early-morning shifts, and some who never left the streets. Mal picked a woman in a hotel maid's uniform and started trailing her.

Creek kept up, his hood pulled low to hide his face. Once Mal looked back, but Creek ducked into a doorway and out of sight, and with the wind in his face, the tang of his KM-tainted blood stayed undetected.

Mal caught up with the woman when she cut through an alley. Creek caught up with both of them a second later, crossbow brandished. He wondered if Chrysabelle's words would make any more sense after this.

"Let her go, Mal."

The woman's eyes were wide in terror, her struggles pointless with Mal's hand over her mouth and his arm wrapped around her body. His eyes were dead black shot with silver. The beast was trying to get out.

He snarled, fangs gleaming. "I should have killed you when I had the chance."

"Let. Her. Go."

The woman whimpered. Mal opened his mouth wider and tugged her closer. Creek pulled the trigger and sank a bolt into Mal's thigh. Cursing, he dropped the woman. She scurried away, praying in Spanish.

Mal yanked the bolt out. Tendrils of black danced above the collar of his T-shirt. He laughed and shook his head. "Is that the best you can do?" Then he lurched sideways, hitting the concrete block wall of the alley. He tried to right himself and failed. The white came back into his eyes as he slipped to the ground. "What..."

Creek leaned down and took the bolt from Mal's hand. "What happened?" He wiped the blood off the titanium and onto Mal's jeans, then tucked the bolt back into his bandolier. "See, I've started coating a few of my bolts with a paste made of laudanum and hemlock. Works on both vampires and varcolai that way." And helped him keep his word to Chrysabelle. He smiled. "You should thank Chrysabelle the next time you see her, because she's the reason I'm going to be a nice guy and not leave you here to toast in the sun."

Mal grunted, and then his eyes rolled back and his head lolled to one side. Out cold.

With a sigh, Creek bent, hoisted Mal up by his armpits, then hefted him over his shoulder into a fireman's carry. He bounced once to adjust the weight. "Damn, you're heavy for someone who doesn't eat. She couldn't have fallen in love with someone a little lighter?"

He broke into a trot. The sun would be up soon, so he had no choice but to hustle if he was going to get Mal back on his ship and safe before morning.

Sweat trickled down his spine as he picked up speed. This definitely counted as his workout for the day.

The outside of La Belle et la Bête looked nothing like the fairy tale it had been named after. More like the building had been abandoned. Faded bits of gray-brown paint not yet worn off by time and weather still clung to the exterior. The three sets of louvered double doors on the first and second floors all had a few missing louvers and more peeling white paint. The simple balcony on the second floor didn't look sturdy enough to hold a houseplant, forget about a person.

Not a sound emanated from the closed doors, and not a single tourist strolling by even glanced at the place.

Fi, in transparent ghost mode, leaned in toward Chrysabelle and Jerem. "I hate to tell you this, but I think this joint is out of business."

"It's not, I promise," Chrysabelle said.

Jerem nodded. "I was here once. A long time ago. But I remember it looking pretty much just like it does now."

A tourist couple walked by. The man went right through Fi.

"Hey!" She shook her fist at him. "Ghost hovering here."

The man looked around like he'd heard something, but the couple kept moving.

"It's like they didn't even see me." Fi put her hands on her hips. "And you know, they didn't even look at you. I know the covenant's broken and humans are getting used to othernaturals, but how many people don't at least take a second look at a dude the size of Jerem, a woman covered in gold tattoos, and her friendly neighborhood ghostly sidekick?"

"I don't think they see us," Chrysabelle answered. "Mortalis said the place was covered with a diffusion spell. It keeps the mortals from thinking it's another French Quarter hot spot and protects the patrons from being stared at."

"Sounds right," Jerem said. "Why don't you let me lead?"

Fi bobbed at his side. "Cool with me."

"Yes, that's fine." Chrysabelle pointed to the right-hand set of doors. "That way, I think." Hopefully this wouldn't take long. Khell was the city's Guardian. That alone should make him fairly accessible.

Jerem pushed through the right-hand set of doors, Fi and Chrysabelle behind him. She stepped over the threshold. The doors swung shut and the wave of sound hit her. Patrons talking, ice clinking against glass, rollicking music, laughter, and a few random shouts here and there.

"Okay," Fi said looking around. "Definitely not out of business. That diffusion spell is pretty wicked. I'd never have known all this was going on in here."

"That's the idea," Jerem said. He kept his gaze on the crowd while he talked to Chrysabelle. "You want to do a walk-through? See if this guy's here?"

"I doubt he will be, but sure." The bar's insides only just exceeded its exterior. Apparently, people came here for the music, not the atmosphere. A jazz quartet with a gravely voiced singer played on a dais near the front. They looked like the same group that had been here the last time. House band, maybe.

And if they were here, maybe Khell would be too. She reached into her pocket for the plastic bills she'd stashed, palming them for easy transfer to whoever might give her the info she needed. She strolled among the tables, avoiding direct eye contact but skimming the crowd for the fae she'd helped make Guardian.

A body moved in front of her, blocking her path. "Well, now," the shifter drawled. "Long time no see, Goldilocks. What brings you back to our corner of the Vieux Carré?"

"I almost didn't recognize you on this side of the bar." Actually, she'd recognized him instantly. The scales flanking the bartender's neck and the bullet shape of his canines made him very hard to forget.

"Gotta keep my tables clean." He tossed a towel over his shoulder. "Who y'all looking for this time?"

"Same person. Just wanted to see how things are going for him." If the bartender remembered her, he must also remember what she'd done when she was here. How many othernaturals lived in this city and didn't know who the Guardian was?

The flash of red-green fire in his slit-pupil eyes didn't scare her the way it had the first time she'd seen it. He clutched at his heart, smiling. "I'm wounded. Here I thought you'd come back for me." Laughing, he tipped his head toward the back corner. "Khell's here. Why don't you ask him yourself."

"Thank you." She reached out and tucked the bills in her hand into his shirt pocket. "I appreciate it."

He glanced down at the money. "Much obliged." Then looked toward Jerem and Fi where they were still standing by the front doors. "I'll send a coupla sweet teas to your friends. Something to occupy themselves with while you do *business*."

She just nodded and slipped past him toward the spiral stairs in the corner. That's where she'd found Khell the last time. The fae were such creatures of habit. She traced a path through the crowd, which was thinner than she remembered, but maybe that had to do with the early hour.

And there he was. Same table, same black-rimmed glasses and brainy-professor look. Different girl, but still a redhead and still plenty curvy. Chrysabelle smiled and approached cautiously. If things weren't going well for him, he may not be thrilled to see her.

"Khell?" She kept her thumbs hooked into the pockets of her pants, close to the hilts of her daggers.

He stopped moving his head to the music and looked up, his gray eyes carrying a little more edge than she remembered. He studied her for a moment. "Chrysabelle. I didn't expect to see you again."

"Nor I you." Still no idea how he felt about her.

Then he smiled. "Nice to see you. Join us." He shoved the extra chair out with his foot. "What brings you to town? If you're here to find a new Guardian, I should warn you I'll have to kill you." He laughed, but his eyes were serious.

She smiled in a way that said she understood. "It's nice to know you're still ambitious." She took the chair.

"This is my lovely fiancée, Beatrice." He clinked his beer bottle against hers, then pointed it at Chrysabelle. "And this is the woman I've told you about. She's one of those comarré."

Chrysabelle smiled at the woman. "Are you ignus fae?"

Beatrice grinned. "You mean like his last girlfriend? Yes. But unlike her I'm here to stay." She winked at Khell as she stood. "I'm going to freshen up while y'all chat." She tipped her head at Chrysabelle. "Thank you for what you did for him."

"Sure." Chrysabelle waited until Beatrice left. "She's a little different than your last girlfriend."

"Why do you think I'm marrying her?" Khell sipped his beer.

"I'm a little surprised you're here. I thought being Guardian would keep you busy."

He shrugged. "It does, but I have lieutenants who run patrols, that sort of thing. This place has become my unofficial office." He tapped his thumb against the side of his bottle. "But I'm sure that's not what you came to talk about."

A multitude of scars and water rings marked the old wood tabletop. She traced one with her finger. "I need a favor. A big one."

He leaned in. "Name it. Anything I can do to help, I will."

She took a breath. "I need entrance to the Claustrum."

He sat back. A bead of condensation rolled down his beer. "Anything but that."

Barasa and Omur flanked a barely controlled Remo across from Doc's desk. He knew this whole scene could turn bloody in a flash if he didn't play it right. Just getting Remo from the holding cell in the basement to his office this morning had taken half of the on-staff security force. "I want you to know that I intend to put the full weight of the pride's capabilities into this issue."

Remo's chest rose and fell with emotion. "This *issue* is a murder. I want the police involved."

Barasa looked at him. "In a pride matter? That's not how we handle things."

Remo never took his eyes off Doc. "Perhaps I should call my father and tell him what's been going on. Tell him that his daughter was actually murdered and that upon discovering this shocking news, his son was treated to a night in the pride's jail."

Doc growled softly. "You attacked my mate. You're lucky a night in the basement is all you got."

Remo stayed quiet a minute after that. When he spoke

again, the edge of anger was gone from his voice, leaving only the gruff sternness and fresh pain of finding out the truth about his sister. "I want the police involved because I want an impartial third party heading up this investigation."

"So you don't trust us?" Omur asked.

"Would you if the situation were reversed?"

"He's got a point," Doc said. "If I consent to that much and allow the police to investigate, will you give me your word to let them do their job and abide by their findings while not endangering anyone else in this pride? That means no fighting, no accusations, nothing that is outside the lines of acceptable behavior for a council member."

Remo snorted softly. "Now you sound like my father."

"Then I must be doing something right. Your father didn't get where he is by making wrong decisions or bad deals." Doc sighed. Why on earth had Fi kept that vial of sand? But then, she had no idea what it held. What damage it could do. "So, your word?"

Slowly, Remo shook his head. "On one condition."

"Which is?"

"I will be a part of every discussion with the police or this council. I want to know everything that's going on firsthand. I find out something's gone on behind my back and I bring my father in."

"Agreed." Doc nodded at Omur. "Get Chief Vernadetto in here as soon as you can."

Chrysabelle stood on the wide wraparound porch of Augustine's home, the curved insets of leaded glass in the massive double doors sparkling in the late-morning sun.

Khell's reaction to her request had sucked all the hope out of her and now, looking at this big beautiful place, she knew in her heart that Augustine wasn't about to risk any of this for her, either. He hadn't helped her the first time she'd been here, so why would this time be any different?

Fi nudged her side. "This place is huge. Like, crazy big. This fae must be loaded, huh?"

A new voice answered. "It's not his house, darling."

They both turned to see an older woman coming through the front yard, a basket of freshly cut flowers dangling off one arm. The other hand gripped a crystal-topped cane. More crystals decorated her velvet and fringe caftan.

"Holy crap," Fi breathed. "You're Olivia freaking Goodwin. The vampire queen."

The woman laughed, her amber eyes sparkling in the light. "Only in the movies, *cher*. And those days are long past." She climbed the steps to stand beside them, her gaze coming to rest on Chrysabelle. She leaned her cane against her side, then reached out and clasped Chrysabelle's hand. "I remember you. You came here a while back with that handsome vampire. I like him." She looked behind Chrysabelle. "Is he with you?"

"No, Ms. Goodwin, he's—"

"Call me Livie. I told you that last time." She brushed past and opened the door, leaving it open as she traipsed into the hall. She set her basket of flowers on a bench in the foyer before heading deeper into the house. "Augie, get your lazy bones up! We have visitors, so put clothes on before you come down."

Fi's eyes rounded and she looked at Chrysabelle like she might explode.

"Keep it together," Chrysabelle whispered.

Fi nodded.

Livie turned around. "Are you two coming in or what? I'm not trying to share my business with the neighborhood."

"Yes, ma'am." Fi grabbed Chrysabelle's hand and stepped inside, dragging her along.

Livie didn't stop moving, so they followed. She swung a set of French doors open and went into the dining room. "I was just about to sit down to brunch. Have y'all eaten?"

"No, but—"

A hearty male laugh interrupted her. "Don't you know better than to turn down Southern hospitality?" Augustine sauntered into the room with the same devilish charm and air of nonchalance as he'd had during their last visit. His open shirt trailed behind him as he finished buttoning his jeans. He helped Livie into a chair, then kissed her on the cheek. "Morning, my love."

"It's nearly lunch, you lazy thing." Smiling, she reached up to pat the side of his head and ended up tousling his hair. That's when Chrysabelle noticed the stump of a horn.

Augustine caught her staring. "I grind them down."

"I wasn't..." Heat burned her cheeks.

He smirked. "Not all of us feel the need to be so blatantly fae all the time."

She nodded and paid closer attention to the way the silverware had been laid out. His horns, or what was left of them, seemed smaller than Mortalis's, but besides that and Augustine's skin being a paler shade of gray, the two fae were almost twins.

A maid, dressed in a black-and-white uniform, came

through a swinging side door. She set a vase of flowers on the center of the table. "Brunch will be right up. Beautiful flowers you got from the garden today, Ms. Livie."

"Thank you, Lally." Livie pointed the head of her cane at Chrysabelle and Fi. "As you can see, we've added a few to our party."

"We're really not here to eat," Chrysabelle said.

"Speak for yourself," Fi said. "When the one and only Olivia Goodwin invites me for brunch, I plan on eating." She beamed at Olivia.

Olivia laughed. "I like this one. What's your name, *cher*?"

"Fiona. But all my friends call me Fi. You can call me that too if you want."

Olivia reached one spotted hand across the table. "Give me your hand, Fi. If you don't mind. I like to read my guests."

Augustine laughed from his chair beside her. "Watch out, she's about to tell your life story."

Fi hesitated, sucking in her bottom lip. "Then I should probably tell you I'm a ghost."

Olivia drew her hand back slightly, her expression a little incredulous. "A ghost? Darling, you're as solid as the day is long."

Fi picked up her fork and held it flat on her open palm. A second later, the fork fell through Fi's de-corporealized hand and clattered to the table. Sunlight from the transom windows filtered through Fi's transparent figure. "I go both ways."

Augustine whispered something in faeish.

"Well, now, that is the singular best parlor trick I've ever seen." Olivia smiled and lifted her glass in toast.

"Here's to the most interesting brunch I've had in a long time."

Lally returned, setting several steaming dishes of food on the table, then went around filling coffee cups and juice glasses. While Augustine helped serve Olivia, she looked to Chrysabelle. "As wonderful as it is to see you, I'm sure you haven't just come for a visit." Her amber gaze took on an odd clarity and she dipped her head toward Chrysabelle. "Does your trip here have anything to do with that baby in your belly?"

Chapter Twenty

Creek hauled Mal through the corridors of the
freighter, finally dumping him in a section of one
that was completely free of sunlight. It would have to do.
If he tried to find Mal's actual room, chances were he'd
get lost in the ship and end up stuck here until Mal came
to and that had bad news written all over it. As it was, Mal
was going to be highly irate at being shot and drugged.
Common sense said the best thing to do was get scarce.

He worked his way out of the ship, but a few yards
from the door he'd come in, he heard the sounds of someone else on deck. He inhaled, looking for a scent, but
found nothing. He crept forward, wishing he knew the
freighter better so he could find another way out.

The door was open a crack, so Creek peered through
it. A vampire he didn't recognize was leaving a container
right outside the door. If not for the man's noble facial
structure, Creek wouldn't have known he was looking at
a vampire. It was like the man wasn't there at all, like he
created a dead spot in Creek's senses.

Paole. There was no other explanation. Which meant
this could be the vampire who'd turned the mayor. Creek

wished his crossbow wasn't collapsed. Snapping it open would make too much noise. Instead, he reached for his halm and jumped through the door, pushing it open at the same time that he whipped his halm out to full length.

He stopped just as the tip of the halm hit the vampire's chest. "Move and I'll run you through the heart."

The vampire froze. "Who are you?"

"I could ask you that same question." Creek nudged the container with his foot. "What's this?"

The vampire straightened as best he could. "A name, first."

"Creek. You?"

"Luciano."

Great, another Italian. Maybe Dominic knew him. "What's in the container?"

"Blood."

"Why are you bringing Mal blood?"

"I don't have to tell you anything."

"You don't have to live, either." Creek shoved the halm harder into Luciano's chest. "Who are you working for? Dominic?" The faintest hint of recognition flared in Luciano's eyes. "So you are. Why the blood then?"

Luciano looked like he'd rather sunbathe than answer, but he did anyway. "The blood is drugged. To keep Mal from killing anyone. The comarré requested it."

"Chrysabelle?"

"*Si.*"

"We're not enemies then. Not yet." Creek moved the halm, but kept it at full length in case the situation changed. "Why would Chrysabelle want to keep Mal drugged? And why would Mal kill anyone? He gets all the blood he needs from Chrysabelle."

Luciano sighed and glanced at the sky. "The sun comes soon. Perhaps we can talk elsewhere?"

"I like the sun. Explain."

With another very exasperated sigh, Luciano answered. "Mal's love for her was stolen by a fae. Now he is like he was before. A beast. A creature controlled only by his desire to feed." Luciano shrugged. "This comarré still loves him and does not want him to die. Not yet. Not if she can bring his love back. So until then...we feed him. Keep him sedated so he harms no one. Are you satisfied? Can I go? Otherwise I may be forced to kill you so that I do not perish as well." He smiled like that was funny.

Creek aimed the halm at him again. "One more question. Did you sire the mayor?"

Luciano's smiled faded. "*Cazzo!* Will no one let me live this down? Yes, what of it?"

Creek had orders to kill the vampire who'd sired the mayor, but Luciano was keeping Mal from killing anyone else with these blood deliveries. He'd have to explain to Annika what was going on so the situation could be reassessed. He jabbed his halm into Luciano's chest. "Sire anyone else and I'll kill you myself, understand?"

Luciano sneered. "Under what authority, human?"

Creek twisted the halm so that Luciano's shirt wound around the end in a tight knot, and then he pulled the vampire in close. "Under the authority of the Kubai Mata, bloodsucker."

He laughed. "The KM don't exist."

"You don't believe me, ask Chrysabelle. She's seen the brands on my back. Or maybe you should just take a nice deep inhale and get a whiff of the holy magic in my blood. I've heard it smells sour to your kind."

Luciano's nostrils flared, and then his eyes went a very fearful shade of silver. He nodded. "I won't sire any others. I swear on my mother's grave."

Creek yanked the halm back, tearing it loose from Luciano's shirt. A second later, he stood alone on the deck, the only reminder anyone else had been there the container of blood on Mal's doorstep and the breeze left behind in Luciano's wake.

Chief Vernadetto arrived just after lunch. Within half an hour, Doc had set him up with a conference room to use to take statements. Barasa and Omur waited with Doc in his office. They'd have their turns too, but he was up next. "This is a mess, you know. I've lied to Fi. I've lied to Remo. Now what, I'm supposed to lie to the cops?"

Barasa cleared his throat. "You have no choice. None of us do. We have to tell the same story or this house of cards will fall."

Omur nodded. "I'm sorry, Maddoc. I know this goes against your grain."

Doc snorted. "I used to run drugs for Dominic Scarnato. You think lying to the Five-Oh goes against my grain? It was the only grain I had for a lotta years." He sighed. "I just don't like doing it where Fi's concerned."

A knock on the door turned their attention.

"Come in," Doc answered.

Remo entered, looking less than pleased. "Vernadetto's ready for you."

Doc stood and went without a word. Vernadetto sat at the far end of the conference table with an e-tablet in front of him, the screen black, and a cup of coffee. Doc shut the door, then sat near him. "Chief."

"Maddoc." Vernadetto tapped the screen to bring it to life. "Where were you the night of the alleged murder?"

No small talk then. "In the stands of the arena."

"What was your relationship with the deceased, Heaven Silva?"

"Her husband by pride law."

Vernadetto nodded. "I remember that. Because you killed Sinjin, correct?"

"He challenged me. And I killed him in self-defense," Doc added.

"Yes, self-defense." Vernadetto scrawled something with his stylus. "Were you aware that the sand in the arena had been laced with silver dust?"

And so it began. "No."

"Do you have any idea who might have wanted to hurt Heaven?"

"To be honest, I didn't know her well enough to be able to answer that. She may have had enemies, but I couldn't tell you who. I can give you her tablet and password though. You can look through her contacts yourself."

"Thank you. That will help." More scribbling. "Who has access to the arena before a fight of this nature?"

Doc shrugged. "Pretty much anyone with access to the building. When the arena's being prepped, it's hardly ever locked."

"That doesn't make my job any easier." Vernadetto sipped his coffee. "I'll need you to provide me with a list of names of anyone who worked on the preparations and those on security."

Doc nodded. "I'll get that for you as soon as I get back to my office." He leaned in. "What's your take on all this?"

"I can't comment on an ongoing investigation." He tapped his tablet, darkening the screen. "But off the record, the evidence is gone, the site's been cleaned, and the suspect list includes everyone in the pride. Right now it's Remo's word against everyone else's." He looked at the door for a moment. "I like Fiona. She doesn't seem like the type to hurt anyone."

"She's not." Thank Bast for that cocktail party. Whatever impression Fi had made on Vernadetto that night, it had been a good one.

"I'm going to handle this case personally and while it will be a by-the-book investigation, I'll do what I can to wrap it up quickly and without a lot of noise."

"I appreciate that more than I can tell you."

Vernadetto nodded slowly. "I'll need to talk to Fiona, though, so wherever you're hiding her, get her unhidden fast."

Chrysabelle's mouth went dry. "H-how do you know I'm pregnant?"

Olivia swallowed a bite of Eggs Benedict. "When I touched you outside. Felt that new life in you like a kick to my gut."

"No one's supposed to know," Fi whispered, looking horrified.

"Too late," Augustine chimed. "You spend much time with Livie, you figure out real fast secrets don't stay secrets long. She's got enough haerbinger blood in her to make her dangerously interesting." He winked at her. "My kind of woman." Then he arrowed his gaze at Chrysabelle and leaned back in his chair. "So, who's the daddy?"

"The vampire," Olivia answered.

Augustine's chair thumped to the carpet. "How the hell is that possible?"

"He bit her while they were doing it," Fi said around a mouthful of sausage.

"Fi." Chrysabelle glared at her, instantly regretting letting her come. Why did Fi always have to say everything that came into her head?

"Sorry." She shrugged. "But it's true."

Augustine whistled long and low. "I bet that does have something to do with why you're here."

Chrysabelle set her fork down, not that she'd touched much of her food. Even the smell of things cooking made her queasy these days. "Let me explain." And so she did, for nearly twenty minutes, telling them about her visit to Khell and answering their questions as best she could without using Mortalis's or Amery's names.

Augustine threw his napkin onto his plate. "Let me get this straight. You want me to get you into the Claustrum?"

"Please. With Khell out of the picture, I have no one else to turn to and it's my only hope of making things right."

"You know what the consequences are for me if anyone finds out?"

"I do. And I'm sorry. I wouldn't ask if this wasn't so important." She exhaled, staring at her lap. "I really have no one else to turn to."

He stared at his plate for a while. "There is one person who could grant permission."

"I told you, Khell said if I asked again, he'd have me thrown out of the city."

"Not him."

She looked up. "Who?"

"The elektos Prime. If he okays it, and he might, considering the circumstances, I won't have to get involved."

Which she knew he preferred. Mortalis had made it clear his brother wasn't big on putting himself out there. "Who is the Prime?"

"We have a new one since you were here last. The shift in Guardian really shook things up." He pursed his mouth for a moment, making her dread his answer. "The Prime is Hugo Loudreux."

Every shred of hope she had dissolved. "He won't help me."

"Why not?"

"The last time I saw him, I threatened to kill him."

Chapter Twenty-one

Creek waited until Annika slid the door to the machine shop closed. "There's no way Mal's the killer."

"How do you know? Is this related to your recon on Tatiana last night?" She made herself at home in one of the easy chairs, kicking her feet up onto the cable spool table.

"Yes." He took the other chair, setting his bottle of water on the spool. His stomach growled in protest that he wasn't filling it with more. After his early-morning jog with Mal, he'd slept in and missed breakfast. "She brought at least one Nothos with her, but I took care of it as soon as I got there, then set up on the roof of the warehouse across from the freighter. Not sure how long she was inside, but she left a few hours before dawn. I thought she'd gone in to kill him, and was about to go in and check when he came out."

Annika's brows rose. "Unexpected."

"Absolutely. I trailed him, we had a run-in, and I ended up shooting him in the leg." No reason to tip off the KM about Mal not being himself until Chrysabelle had her shot at fixing him. "I've been tipping my bolts with a sedative, so he passed out right after. I carried him back to the freighter and as I was leaving, ran into a new vampire."

He sat back in his chair and stared into Annika's dark shades. "He's Paole. And he told me he was the one who sired the mayor, but that he did it in exchange for her lifting the curfew."

"So you eliminated him per orders."

"No."

Annika put her feet on the floor. "Creek, he's a threat. And you had orders." She tapped her fingers on the chair's arm. "Perhaps I have allowed our relationship to become...too familiar."

He bowed his head in deference. "I made a judgment call, and if I was wrong, I apologize, but after my conversation with him I don't believe him to be any more of a threat than you or I."

She shook her head. "How does this prove Mal's innocence?"

"I'm getting there." Creek sipped his water. "This Paole works for Dominic and Dominic has been sending Mal regular shipments of blood."

"Sated doesn't mean innocent. Some vampires can't resist the hunt and with Mal's past and whatever's going on between him and the comarré..." She shrugged. "It could still be him."

He rubbed the back of his neck and leaned forward. "No, it couldn't. The blood he's been getting is drugged. He's been knocked out cold every night there's been a murder."

Annika frowned. "Why would Dominic be sending him tainted blood?"

This was exactly what he hadn't wanted to do. Share Chrysabelle's business with the KM. It was that kind of garbage that got her so upset. He got up and walked to the kitchen, grabbing a protein bar out of his lean pantry. "Because of what's going on between Mal and the comarré. He's lost the ability to love her temporarily and it's made him...angry. To keep him from striking out, she's gotten Dominic to keep Mal sedated until she can heal him."

Annika stared at him long enough to make him uncomfortable. She now knew he'd kept information back from her. What she'd do with his subordination remained to be seen. "This is why you didn't kill the Paole."

He nodded.

"And this situation with Mal, when will that be resolved?"

He knew Chrysabelle was working on it, but what did that mean in real time? "I don't know, but soon."

"Creek, Malkolm is the most dangerous vampire in this city. You know his past. He was a terror. He's responsible for more human deaths than any other vampire we have record of. If he's gone back to that?" She stood and tugged her leathers into place, an air of reluctance around her unlike anything he'd seen before. "The comarré has forty-eight hours to return things to the status quo. If Mal still needs to be sedated by then...there is nothing I can do." Her mouth thinned to a hard line. "You will be ordered to eliminate him. No judgment calls allowed."

Loudreux's refusal to see her came as no surprise to Chrysabelle. She slammed the car door as she got back in. "I told you."

Augustine lounged in the passenger's seat beside her. "Still worth a shot."

Jerem started the car. Fi twisted around from the front seat to face Augustine. "That means you'll help us, right?"

His chin jutted forward and he turned to look out the window. "You've got to understand, I'm not exactly high on the Best Liked Fae in the City list already. A move like this would really put me in a tough spot."

Jerem grunted softly from behind the wheel. Chrysabelle understood. She was frustrated too. And despite what Mortalis had said, she was about to try something she probably shouldn't. Nothing left to lose, anyway. "That's pretty much how your brother said you'd react. He said you were lazy. What was that he called you?" She tipped her head like she was trying to remember. "*Bala'stro?*"

Augustine sat up straight, anger creasing his brow. "You tell Mortalis that he can shove one of his horns right up his—"

Fi snorted. "You don't like your brother very much, do you? What's up with that?"

Augustine's green-gray eyes darkened like a storm cloud. "He's been the source of a lot of misery in my life."

"Like what?" Fi asked.

Jerem laughed. Fi sure didn't give up easy.

Augustine took a deep breath and sat back like he was trying to calm himself. Then he arched like a cat in the sun and a languid smile spread across his face as he answered her. "Anyone ever tell you you remind them of a young Olivia Goodwin? She was a real looker back in the day." He shook his head and made a "mmm-mmm" sound. "They say there wasn't a mortal man alive who could refuse her charms."

Fi's mouth opened a little. "No, I, uh, no one's ever, I mean, no."

He continued. "'Course Livie had an unfair advantage with those couple percentage points of fae blood running in her veins." He lifted his chin at Fi, his lids suddenly too heavy to keep wide open. "You got any fae in you, pretty thing?"

She shook her head slowly, her gaze never leaving him.

His smile crooked up a little higher on one side. "You want some?"

"That's a married woman you're talking to," Chrysabelle told him. "And her husband's the leader of the Paradise City pride, so unless you want two hundred and some pounds of leopard hunting you through the streets of New Orleans, you should probably save your flirting for a woman who's actually available."

Fi swallowed. "Yeah." She twisted around to face the windshield, but the color in her cheeks was undeniable.

Augustine shrugged, clearly unrepentant. "No harm in talking."

"That's all you do, isn't it? Talk?" She huffed out a breath. "Jerem, how soon can we drop Augustine off?"

"We'll be there in a few more minutes."

She stared out the window at the beautiful, charmed homes lining the streets and spoke softly to herself. "I should have known Mortalis would be right. He always is. He said there'd be no help here, and sure enough—"

"All right," Augustine said. "I get it. You're trying to spin me up, make me prove my brother was wrong. Well you know what? He wasn't. I'm everything he said I was and more."

She looked at him, using whatever comarré charm she could muster. If that would even work on him. "You could change that. Just help me. Do this one thing and he can't say he knows what you're like anymore." She rested one hand on her belly. "Please. I don't want my child to grow up without a father."

"I had one. Occasionally. It's not all it's cracked up to be."

Chrysabelle stared at him. "I guess that explains it."

He stared back. "Explains what?"

Chrysabelle raised her brows. "Why you don't know how to be a man when the situation calls for it."

"Oh, burn," Fi whispered.

Augustine's scowl melted into something close to pain. He closed his eyes, tipped his head against the back of the seat, and bounced it off the headrest. "I know how to be a man. My father didn't. But I do."

Chrysabelle's insides went soft with hope. "Does that mean you're going to help me?"

"Damn it. Yes." He kept his eyes closed. "Make sure you tell Mortalis how wrong he was."

"I will." She wanted to grab him and hug him. Instead she smiled calmly. "Thank you."

He opened his eyes and slanted them at her. "Don't thank me until it's over."

She nodded, but inside she was ecstatic. And nervous enough to faint. "What do we need to do? Do you have time to stop by the hotel? I need my sacres. Those are comarré swords." Now she was just babbling. She shut her mouth.

"I know what sacres are. And yes, the hotel's fine. We can do it there. I don't want any of this traceable back to Livie." He sighed like he couldn't believe what he'd agreed to.

"I wouldn't want that either." She leaned forward and put her hand on Jerem's shoulder. "To the hotel."

He flipped on the signal to turn around. "Got it."

Chrysabelle sat back. "How soon can we do this?"

"Best time to pull a human through to the fae plane is twilight. Things get...thinner then." He studied her, all traces of his blithe attitude gone. The serious lines of his face spoke of pain and experiences beyond anything she could imagine. What had happened in his life? With his father? Between him and Mortalis? "I will take you to the entrance, but you're on your own from there."

"I'm going with her," Fi announced.

"Suit yourself." He cracked his head to one side. "You'll have an hour to do what you need to do. More than that and things get sticky. Getting you out gets harder the longer you're there. And trust me, you do *not* want to spend more time in the Claustrum than you have to."

"What's it like?" Fi asked.

He stayed quiet for a breath. "It's where the fae keep those of our own kind too horrible to be free." He smiled, but there was no charm in it. "It's where we keep the things that scare *us*."

Chapter Twenty-two

Son of a priest." Mal rubbed his throbbing head, wondering how much of it was from Creek's drugs and how much was because the sun was still an hour from setting. How many times was he going to wake up from daysleep feeling like he'd been on a bender? Enough was enough. What had the KM said? That he should thank Chrysabelle the next time he saw her.

Mal snorted. He planned on seeing her very soon, but thanking her wasn't on his agenda. Stupid git. If she knew what was good for her, she would have told Creek to bury that bolt in his heart.

He grabbed one of the protruding metal seams on the corridor wall and hauled himself to his feet. His right thigh ached where the KM's bolt had landed and his jeans were torn and crusted in blood. If he went out like that, he'd have every fringe in the neighborhood sniffing after him. He headed for the shower to clean up. He changed clothes when he was done, returning to his room long enough to tuck a short blade into one of his boots. The locket he'd taken off Tatiana sat on the small table by his reading chair. He didn't need to carry that reminder. He knew whose picture it held. More bad memories. That's all it was.

He strode down the hall toward the deck. The closer he got, the thicker the smell of blood grew. The voices went crazy as he stopped and splayed his hand on the door. Hot as blazes. Damnation, the smell of blood was strong. More than strong, it was making clear thought impossible. He had to have blood. No. He shook his head. *Blood blood blood.* He had no intention of drinking whatever was out there waiting for him, no matter how hard the voices pushed. Thanks to Tatiana, he was wise to Chrysabelle's ways. Who else would send him tainted blood? What else but the knowledge that he was incapacitated would embolden her to visit him? *Kill her drain her.*

Tonight he would be done with her once and for all, and then he'd take Dominic's plane and head to Corvinestri for retribution. Everything that had been taken from him would be restored. And if Tatiana broke her word, he'd kill her too.

The tingle of anticipation that signaled the sun had set washed over him. He pulled the door open. A container sat there, waiting. Fresh blood scent rolled over him, stirring the voices into a pitched frenzy. Maybe just a little sip…

No. With great effort to ignore the desire to feed, he hoisted the whole lot over the side of the freighter and was rewarded with a very satisfying splash. Nothing would keep him from his mission tonight.

Halfway down the gangplank he started to run. He was hungry and there was only one kind of blood that would quench his thirst.

Comarré.

* * *

"What do you mean she's not here?" Doc stood at Chrysabelle's front door. "I sent Fi here to keep her safe."

Damian nodded. "She's safe, I promise. She's with Chrysabelle in New Orleans. Come in if you want."

Doc walked in and looked at Mortalis, who sat on the sofa playing cards with Velimai and a comarré he didn't recognize. "You know about this?"

"A little. Fi will be all right, I'm sure. What Chrysabelle went there to do...she won't let Fi get hurt."

Doc rubbed a hand over his shaved scalp. "That doesn't make me feel any better. What did she go there to do?"

Mortalis set his cards down and took a breath. "She went to find someone to give her access to the fae that stole Mal's emotion."

Doc sat in the chair closest to Mortalis. "And do what? Reason with it?"

The shadeux shook his head. "Kill it."

Warmth built along Doc's bones. He dropped his head and pressed his forehead into his palm. He counted backward, one of the methods Barasa had taught him to help keep the fire at bay. "That sounds safe." After a deep breath, he looked at Mortalis again. "I'm not leaving this house until Fi gets back. And if anything happens to her, I'm holding you personally responsible. Why didn't you go with Chrysabelle? This doesn't sound like something she should do alone."

"I couldn't go. What she asked of me...I couldn't do."

"For real? Why?"

"Because if I took her where she needs to go and it came to light that I was involved, the elektos would sentence me to death." He glared back. "I have Nyssa to think of, you know."

"A death sentence? And Fi's with her." Doc's jaw went slack and the warmth returned as building heat. "Where the hell did she need to go?"

"The Claustrum."

Nothing Mortalis was saying was making Doc feel any better. "Which is?"

Velimai signed something.

Doc nodded at her. "What did she say?"

Mortalis lifted one shoulder. "She said it's not a great place."

Sparks snapped across Doc's fingers. "What. Did. She. Say."

Lifting his chin, Mortalis answered, "She said it's hell. On a bad day."

Only Fi and Jerem had eaten dinner. Chrysabelle's appetite was nonexistent, so she'd sat in the suite's living room, polishing her sacres and praying. She glanced outside. The sun would set in less than ten minutes. The time for prayer was over. Setting her swords aside, she walked onto the balcony where Augustine was.

He leaned against the railing, staring into the city. His lanky musculature reminded her so much of Mortalis. Pale red smoke trailed off a crude black cigarette tucked between his fingers, scenting the air with the aroma of burned fruit.

"Ready?" she asked.

He took a puff of the cigarette, then blew out the smoke before turning to face her. "Let's light this candle." He motioned in front of him. "Stand here."

She moved into place. He crouched down and sucked

on the cigarette again, this time blowing the smoke at her feet.

"What are you doing?"

He finished his exhale. "Covering your scent. The last thing you want to do is walk into the Claustrum stinking like a human. I'll need to do Fi, too. I know she's going in ghost form, but I don't want to take a chance."

"Humans stink?"

Smiling, he shook his head. "No. In fact, I happen to love the way humans smell. The women anyway." He closed his eyes. "All earthy softness and flowers and sex." Looking a little lost in some old memory, he opened his eyes. "But you walking into a place that's never known the slightest hint of human would be like dropping a spot of ink onto a white sheet. You won't go unnoticed. I'm trying to give you a little advantage."

"Thank you." She stood while he bathed her in smoke, the burned fruit smell getting stronger. "What is that? Not tobacco, obviously."

Before he could answer, Fi walked onto the balcony. "What's going on out here?"

Chrysabelle turned her head. "He's covering my human scent. You're next."

Fi settled into one of the deck chairs and stuck her feet up on the railing. "Mortalis was smoking that stuff. What's it called? Nekram?"

"*Nequam*," he said between breaths. "Mention my brother one more time and I'll find a reason not to do this." Chrysabelle stared down at him. Through his shaggy hair, the stubs of his horns darkened. "Turn," he said to Chrysabelle.

Fi grimaced. "Sorry." She watched him for a moment.

"Are your horns changing color? Hard to tell with them all short like that. Why do they do that?"

The red smoke curled around the front of Chrysabelle as he worked behind her.

Augustine's tone was cool and clipped. "I'm part smokesinger fae."

"Never heard of that kind," Fi said. "What else can smokesingers do?"

"Done," he said to Chrysabelle. She turned as he pointed to Fi. "You're up."

Fi took Chrysabelle's place. "You didn't answer my question."

"Fi," Chrysabelle admonished. "Augustine's a little busy." And clearly didn't want to answer anyway.

She sighed. "Aren't you at least a little bit curious? I've never met a smokesinger before. Especially not one as interesting as Augie."

Augustine smiled as he blew smoke over Fi. When he finished, he said, "Let me take care of this, and then I'll show you something."

"Cool." Fi looked at Chrysabelle. "See? Never hurts to ask."

With a shake of her head, Chrysabelle went back into the suite to strap on her sacres. As she left the bedroom, Jerem called out from the kitchen where he was washing up from dinner.

"Hey. You sure you don't want me to go with you? I will. Gladly. Just say the word."

"Thanks, I appreciate that, but your coming to help with transportation was enough. Besides, according to Augustine someone needs to stay here to guard the mirror in case the elektos figure out what's going on and try to do something." She leaned against the counter. "Not to mention I don't want to endanger anyone else if I can avoid it."

He racked a wet plate to dry. "Understood. No one will touch that mirror, I promise." He lifted his chin toward the balcony. "I don't think Augustine's as much of a slacker as he makes himself out to be. Covering you with that smoke? He knows what he's doing."

She looked out where Augustine and Fi were finishing up. Jerem's assessment made her feel a little better. "Too bad I don't."

"Just remember why you're doing this." Jerem drained the sink. "When I was in the military, focusing on my reasons for being there was what always got me through. You're strong and capable and you've faced tougher obstacles." A flicker of his inner bear danced golden in his eyes. "If anyone can do this, it's you."

She smiled. "You give a good pep talk."

The balcony door slid open and Fi and Augustine came back inside. Fi was almost bouncing with excitement. "Okay, let's see your trick."

"It's not a trick," he said. Still, he waited until Chrysabelle and Jerem came over. "I'm doing this only once."

Fi nodded, almost gleeful. "Do we need to stand back?"

"No. Just watch." He put his hands together, fingertip to fingertip, then slowly drew them apart. Tiny gray threads spun out between them. Then Chrysabelle realized it wasn't thread, but wisps of smoke.

"Holy crap, that's cool." Fi leaned in.

The lines of smoke began to twist and curl between Augustine's fingers until the shape became recognizable.

"A rose," Fi breathed in awe.

The form solidified further, and then Augustine flicked his wrist, breaking the connection. With that free hand, he grasped the stem. The moment he touched it, the stem went green and deep lavender filled its petals. He handed it to Fi. "Now you know something a smokesinger can do."

While she sniffed it, he looked at Chrysabelle. "Are you ready?"

"Yes."

"Good." He pulled a mirror off the wall and set it on the floor in front of them. "All right." He held a hand out to her and Fi. "Take my hands."

They did. Chrysabelle was surprised at how rough his skin was for someone who supposedly did nothing.

"Here we go." He stepped onto the mirror and pulled them through.

Chapter Twenty-three

Tatiana paced. Back and forth, back and forth, across the Persian carpet of her sitting room until she saw nothing but the problem in front of her. Mal should have been here by now, shouldn't he? Maybe. Maybe not. Maybe he wasn't coming at all. That meant she'd have to find a way to kill Lilith on her own. Was that even possible? The only ones who might know were the Castus, but would they tell her?

There was only one way to find out.

"Samael, my liege," she whispered. "If you can hear me, come to me *alone*. *Please*." Just saying the word grated her nerves, but fear overruled all else. She sank to the floor, her hands clasped in her lap, and spoke the words again. "Please, Samael, I need you and only you."

The room darkened with encroaching shadows and filled with the stench of brimstone. Never before had something so vile filled her with such relief.

He appeared before her, smaller than she'd ever seen him. More like the height of a man than the lord of darkness. His horrible visage, once a mask of terror, seemed... aged somehow. Tired. "What?" he snapped.

"Thank you for coming, my lord. Are you alone?" She looked behind him. There was no sign of Lilith, but that might not mean anything.

"Yes. Briefly. What do you want?" The skirt of shadows that draped him from the waist down bore none of the usual faces or reaching hands.

"It's about—"

"Don't say her name." He reached a hand out and placed it on Tatiana's head, weighing her down like a lead weight. *I know of whom you speak.*

His words echoed in her head. She stared at him. *I can hear you. In my head.*

And I you. What would you ask me of Lilith? I know that's why you've called me.

Tatiana nodded as best she could with his taloned fingers pressing into her scalp. *She...scares me, my liege. She killed one of my best soldiers without provocation. Do you mean for her to take my place? If so, I ask that you spare my life. I will leave without argument, just let me live.*

We do not mean for her to take your place. Something that sounded very much like a groan followed his words. *Neither did we mean for her to have so much power. She has become...more than we desired.*

That was all the opening she needed. *Is there a way to remove some of that power? I have always been your willing servant.*

There is only one way to deal with her. She must eat of the fruit of the Tree of Life in the Garden of Eden, a place we cannot go.

But I can?

Yes. Not only can you enter, but the Garden will

always be night for you. Whatever you need it to be, it will be.

Then I will go. Just show me the way. I will do whatever you wish me to.

He nodded and held out his other hand. A worn scroll appeared in it. *This map bears the runes that will open a portal to the Garden. Draw a circle with your blood, then write the runes inside it with your blood as well. A portal will open. When you go through, this map will show you how to find the tree you seek. She must go with you and eat the fruit there, as it cannot be removed from the Garden.*

She took the scroll, the paper crackling in her hand. *When I am ready, I will call for her.*

He took his hand from her head and stared into her eyes. "Do this and you will be greatly rewarded."

"I want your assurance you will approve my choice of Elder." She nodded.

"Granted." He leaned in, his red eyes piercing into hers with what could only be distress. "Do this *quickly.*"

"Yes, my liege," she whispered, but he was already gone.

Dominic sat back in his chair. Life was good, for the most part. His relationship with Katsumi was stronger than ever, in many ways due to her help on the recent mission to Čachtice. And since he'd given her *navitas* so she could be noble instead of fringe, she'd done nothing out of line. She had become very much the companion he'd always hoped her to be.

Luciano, despite having done the unthinkable in siring the mayor, was working out well. Revenues were back up since the curfew had been lifted. Just then, a soft roar rose from the Pits, muted by the French doors behind him that opened onto the balcony overlooking the fighting arena. He nodded at the sound. In fact, revenues had never been better.

He knew part of that was because Maddoc had lifted the long-standing ban on pride members patronizing Seven. That Maddoc would do such a thing with the bad blood between them spoke to his strength as a leader.

Dominic tapped his gold pen on the desktop. Perhaps it was time to make peace. He tapped the screen of his tablet and scrolled through his suppliers list. A gift maybe. To show he was open to reconciliation.

Someone knocked on his door. He wasn't expecting anyone. He reached for the blade he kept hidden under his desk. "Come."

Jacqueline, the slender brunette who acted as the house mother for his stable of comarré, poked her head in. "Mr. Scarnato?"

Even her tone was worried. He took his hand from beneath the desk and gestured toward a chair. "Come in, Jacqueline. What can I do for you?"

She shut the door behind her and walked toward him, wringing her hands. "I think something bad has happened."

Inwardly he groaned. *Mamma mia*, some nights, the comarré were more trouble than they were worth. "If there is fighting again, there will be punishment. You know I cannot abide the constant—"

"No, that's not the problem." She dragged in a breath. "I haven't seen Ms. Tanaka since last night. I was supposed to go over the quarterly numbers with her, so I tried her office. The door is locked, but she's not answering."

"That doesn't mean anything bad has happened." He pulled open a drawer. "I have a spare key."

"None of the comarré or floor staff have seen her since last night either and none of the doormen remember her leaving."

Dominic set the key on his desk and shut the drawer. "Come to think of it, she hasn't checked in with me either." Katsumi never went home without saying good-bye. He picked up the key, a sense of unease settling in his belly. "Come, we'll go open her office together. I'm sure she's just hard at work." But he wasn't sure at all.

He went as fast as he could without alarming Jacqueline. By the time they got to the office, a thousand scenarios, both good and bad, had worked through his head. He tried the knob, but it was definitely locked. He rapped his knuckles on the door. "Katsumi, are you in there? Answer me if you are."

But he was greeted with silence.

He notched the key into the lock and opened the door. It hit something metal as he pushed it open. A bitter, familiar odor rose up to greet him. He didn't need the lights, but he flicked them on anyway, not wanting to believe his eyes. Her *kanzashi*, the one he'd given her for protection right before they'd gone to Čachtice, lay on the floor.

Covered in ashes.

Chrysabelle gasped, prepared for whatever might happen. Then she realized they were already through. "That was fast."

Augustine dropped her hand. "That's why we travel that way."

Fi looked a little dizzy. "I'm going ghost."

"You should," Augustine said. "And you should stay that way until you're back out."

She nodded, instantly ghost and now hovering so she was eye level with him.

Chrysabelle glanced around but there wasn't much to see. The fae plane resembled an endless gray field capped with an endless gray sky. Here and there drifts of fog obscured the horizon with more gray. Wind moaned in the distance, a lonely, eerie sound that made her shiver. "Not what I thought it would look like."

"This is the landing for the Claustrum. There's a lot more to the fae plane than this."

"How do we get into the Claustrum?"

"Turn around."

She did. "Holy mother." A great black rock formation towered over them. An entrance was carved into it, the edges of it guarded with slivers of jagged stone pointing toward the center. "Those look like...teeth."

Fi whimpered.

Augustine nodded. "They are."

She didn't ask from what. She didn't want to know what creature had grown teeth that large.

"It's meant to intimidate any fae brought here."

Fi hovered closer to Chrysabelle. "Mission accomplished."

He started forward. They followed. The closer they got, the more she could pick out a path between the teeth. And the more the stink of unwashed flesh and refuse reached them.

Fi wrinkled her nose. "This place smells really, really bad. Like fish left in the sun. Then covered with sewage. And vomit."

Chrysabelle nodded. If she didn't keep it together, she'd be adding to that vomit. "Breathe through your mouth, that's what I'm doing." She slanted her eyes at Fi. "Why are you even breathing? You're in ghost form."

Fi's face was all twisted up. "I'm not breathing, but I can still smell it. I feel like I'm soaking in it."

Augustine kept moving, winding through the jagged teeth until they came to an enormous silver gate. He pointed to the ground beyond it. "See that path?"

Chrysabelle stared, shaking her head. "No."

"Close your eyes for a bit so they adjust to the darkness."

She did, annoyed at how much her senses were depleted. When she opened them again, she saw what he was pointing at. A faint phosphorescent strip about two feet wide disappeared into the tunnel. "Okay, I see it."

"Stay on it. Do *not* deviate until you find the raptor." He looked at her. "Repeat what I just said."

"Stay on it. Do not deviate until we find the raptor."

He nodded. "You step off that path and you may not return."

"Why?" Fi asked. Chrysabelle had never been happier about her curiosity.

"Because," he answered, "that is a safe line. It runs the exact right distance away from the creatures who are most likely to try to grab you and haul you into their cells. It's the path the wardens walk when they come here. Which isn't often, I promise you."

She pulled the cell number Mortalis had given her

from her pocket and held out the slip of paper. "How do I find this cell?"

"Numbers get smaller the closer to the bottom of the Claustrum you get." His finger stopped on a fae letter she didn't know. "This means the twelfth floor from the top. Can you read faeish?"

"No."

"Then you'll have to count as you descend. Floor and cell numbers are written in the same phosphorescence as the path. There's very little light beyond that, but you should be okay after a minute or two."

He took a pocket watch from his leathers. "You have fifty-two minutes left. I suggest you move." He grabbed the gate latch. "Just like the cells, this gate can be opened only from the outside. I'll be here to let you out when you return." Flipping the latch, he pulled the gate open. "If you go into the raptor's cell, be sure Fi stays on the outside so she can let you out. Fi, if you have to take solid form to do that, do it fast and be careful."

After a quick glance at Fi, who'd gone uncharacteristically quiet, Chrysabelle nodded. "Anything else I need to know?"

"No." He hesitated. "Good luck."

"Thanks." She walked through, nodded to him, and then, with Fi at her side, began the descent through the cavernous maw. Every edge of the rock jutting toward them seemed razor sharp. In a few spots, water dripped from the ceiling and patches of phosphorescent moss clung to the sides adding tiny spots of ambient light.

The deeper into the tunnel they went, the more sounds scudded up to meet them. Sounds that bordered on human, but weren't. Shouts, cries, calls for help, growls, and groans, weeping, clicking, snapping, and a low, ever-present hum. Just like the smell, there was no shutting the noise out.

Chrysabelle forced herself to focus on the reason she was here. That's what Jerem said had worked for him. Suddenly, the passageway turned and sloped down as it curved out and around. Time to descend. "Help me count, Fi. This is one."

The ghost nodded, but stayed quiet. From the look on Fi's face, she was struggling to keep it together.

"It's okay to be scared," Chrysabelle said. "I am."

"I hate the dark." Fi's voice wavered like a shifting wind. "Hate it."

"The dark's not so bad. Lots of good things happen in the dark."

"Like what?"

Two. "Haven't you and Doc ever done anything fun in the dark?"

Fi laughed. "I never expected *that* to come out of *you.* Thanks." She sniffed once. "That was the second floor."

"Great. Keep counting, okay?"

Except for Fi announcing the floors, they walked in silence the rest of the way. Maybe that was better, because if they could hear the occupants of the Claustrum, the occupants must be able to hear them, too. Not a pleasant thought.

And the farther down they went, the thicker and hotter the air became, until it clung to Chrysabelle's skin like wet wool. Breathing took thought and made her lungs work. She worried for the child she carried, praying this trip would have no lasting consequences.

"We're here. This is twelve," Fi said. Just as it had

at every floor, the glowing path forked off through the floor's entrance before continuing down the curving ramp toward the lower floors.

Chrysabelle checked the slip of paper again and nodded. The symbol above the entrance matched the one Mortalis had written. She held it up for Fi to see. "Here's the cell number."

"I hope it's not too far in."

"Remember, stay on the path."

"Right behind you."

Chrysabelle entered. Cells ran along either side of the path. In most, the shadows were too deep to see the occupants, but in some, the prisoners stood at the bars.

"That's a little girl," Fi whispered.

Chrysabelle stopped. "Where?"

Fi pointed to one of the cells. A child no more than five or six stood at the bars, weeping softly. "That can't be right, can it? A child?"

The little girl wiped her nose, tipped her head at Fi, then opened her mouth so wide half of her head disappeared behind teeth like ivory pins.

"Yikes." Fi jumped back, sliding through Chrysabelle's shoulder.

Holy mother. "Let's just keep our eyes on the numbers."

"Good idea."

But saying that and doing it were two different things. One cell held an abnormally tall, slender gray man built like a cypher fae but with a large head and eyes the size of billiard balls. One held a creature that had no discernible head at all but at least eight clawed limbs. Over and over it rammed into the bars, scuttling back like a spider to do it again. In another cell, some sort of fae sat on the floor draped in what looked like poorly sewn together human skins.

Occasionally, a small stream of liquid crossed the phosphorescent path and a new smell joined the existing ones. Blood. Waste. Other bodily fluids.

Chrysabelle shuddered just as Fi pointed again. "There. Look."

Quiet weeping reached her ears. "No more little girls."

"No." Fi shook her head. "It's the raptor's cell."

Chapter Twenty-four

Dominic stood alone in the middle of his office, but for all his awareness of the space he could have been anywhere. He shuffled blindly through the room with no real direction.

Katsumi was gone.

The loss tightened his throat and shoved knives into his chest, but not in the way that Marissa's death had. When Marissa died, so had his will to go on, at least for a few days. Now, he just felt...numb.

Hurt and numb. And if he really gave into what he felt, anger rose up in him like bile.

How dare someone come into his club and do such a thing? He was Dominic Scarnato. A man to be feared. A vampire to be reckoned with.

Something creaked. He looked down to find his hands squeezing the handles of the French doors that led out to the balcony overlooking the Pits. He nodded. A fight seemed like just the thing.

He opened the doors and walked out onto the balcony, stopping at the edge to rest his hands on the glass railing. The Pits were in full swing, as they almost always were.

Katsumi had loved them. She'd had a small team of fighters that she'd sponsored, taking great pride in their wins and the money they made her.

Shouts rose up from the crowd as they noticed him. The fighters battling seemed to suddenly fight a little harder. He backed away from the railing, in no mood to be the gracious host.

He would have to tell her fighters that their benefactor had been taken from them. Maybe he would give them each a small sum as a condolence. The thought almost made him smile. Katsumi would think him soft for doing such a thing. Not that she'd ever say such a thing to his face.

A fresh wave of grief swelled. She'd come so far since he'd given her the *navitas* she'd so desperately wanted. It was as if becoming noble had changed more than just her status. Her ambition hadn't faltered, but it had shifted, become less about her and more about… them.

And if he was truthful with himself, he *had* begun to love her. Not the kind of love he'd felt for Marissa. He'd never feel that way about anyone ever again. He'd never let himself. He couldn't. Her passing had destroyed the ability to give himself to another so completely. But life with Katsumi had become comfortable. Pleasant. Almost… effortless.

Companionship for his kind was never easy. Most nobles were too ambitious and too paranoid to ever allow another that close to them. But in the small world of Paradise City, without the influences of the nobility's politics, he and Katsumi could have lived many years with each other for company.

And now, some *faccia di stronzo* had taken that away from both of them.

He spun and pushed through the doors back into his office. Watching others fight was not enough. He needed to find whoever had killed Katsumi and put an end to him.

Only then might he find some solace.

Mal settled atop the security wall and inhaled. Comarré blood perfumed the air so heavily it almost intoxicated him. *Drink drink drink.* He would. Soon. He inserted the iron-mesh earplugs Tatiana had given him. Now the wysper could scream her head off and it wouldn't stop him from draining every last drop of blood out of Chrysabelle.

He walked the wall, looking for the best view into the house, but all the curtains had been drawn. Plenty of lights were on, though, and he could sense a number of heartbeats. She had company. He smiled. He'd feed well tonight. Good. This meal had to last him until he reached Corvinestri and was finally able to buy a comarré of his own. An obedient one, who did as she was told and nothing more. No meddling, no arguing, nothing but a warm vein when the need arose.

The guesthouse was dark. He followed the wall in that direction, jumping over the property's metal entrance gate to the adjoining wall and continuing until he could leap from the wall to the guesthouse roof. He landed with a thud and immediately flattened himself against the tiles. A few seconds later, the security lights clicked on and the front door opened.

He got lower, out of the sight line, and listened.

"See anything?" A male voice he didn't recognize.

"No." That low growl was unmistakable. Doc. "But I smell something."

Damn it. He hadn't counted on Doc being here. Maybe Doc could live. After all he'd done to keep Fi off Mal's back, he deserved that much.

Finally the door shut. The lights, however, stayed on. He crept to the peak of the guesthouse and looked over. No one had stayed outside to guard the house so he started moving again, this time toward the opposite edge of the roof. From there, he'd drop to the ground, being careful to stay on the path so he wouldn't trip the sensors hidden under the sod. Then he'd climb the building to the second-story balcony, wrench open the French doors into Chrysabelle's bedroom, and drink until there was nothing left to swallow.

Chrysabelle looked at the fae numbers written over the bars and nodded to Fi. "The numbers match what's on the paper. That's the raptor's cell."

"Where is it?" Fi whispered, peering into the cell's dark interior.

"It must be back in the shadows." The cell seemed empty, except... was that crying? Coming from inside?

"Raptor," she called quietly. "Come out where I can see you. It's Chrysabelle. The comarré whose gold you read."

The crying stopped, replaced by shuffling. The raptor hobbled into view, his enormous form outlined in the soft glowing light of the numbers over his cage. Smooth, murky green skin covered a shape that reminded her of the Nothos. Except for the lack of eyes. All the raptor had was a slanted forehead. He flared his wide, slit nostrils. "Comarré," it whispered, "is that really you or do I dream again?"

Fi gave Chrysabelle a look and circled her finger beside her head.

"It's me, raptor." Despite the creature's missing eyes she remembered very well that it didn't prevent him from understanding what was happening around him. With that in mind, she slowly pulled one sacre from its sheath.

The raptor reached through the bars, his long, narrow fingers uncurling toward her. "You've come to me. My love."

This time Chrysabelle returned Fi's look. *My love*, she mouthed. What was going on?

Fi shook her head.

Chrysabelle kept her voice to a whisper. "Stay on the path until I need you to let me out." Then she took a step toward the raptor. The smell of bleach wafted off the creature.

"Yes," he murmured, flexing his fingers. "Come closer, my dream."

She did, but only one more step. She was close enough now to see fully into the cell. There wasn't much room in there to swing her sacre. This was going to have to be a decisive strike. If the raptor had a chance to fight back, she'd have no defensible position. No place to hide.

He opened his mouth, flicked out a three-pronged black tongue from between multiple rows of teeth. An image of the Claustrum's entrance flashed in her head. He tasted the air in her direction. "Why have you waited so long to come to me?" he whined.

"I didn't know you wanted me to."

"Psst," Fi hissed. "Psst!"

Chrysabelle answered Fi without turning around. "What?"

"It loves you," Fi whispered loudly.

"Of course I love her," the raptor raged. He grabbed the bars and shook them, making them creak. "Why do you torment me this way?"

Farther down the corridor, other inmates howled in response.

"Shh, I'm here now. I'm here." She hadn't expected to have to mollify the creature she was about to kill. Holy mother, how was she supposed to kill a creature that loved her? Maybe she could persuade him to let Mal's emotion go? Trade some of her emotions for those of Mal's? She'd have to get the raptor to agree ahead of time as to what he'd take. "I'm going to come into your cell now. Is that all right?"

With a whimper the raptor sank onto his haunches and nodded his head. "Yes, yes, yes."

She shot Fi a look, then headed in, keeping a firm grip on her sacre. The cell door clanged softly behind her, a sound she never hoped to hear again. "Raptor, I am here to ask you a favor."

"Anything, anything." He was trembling now.

"Do you remember the vampire that was with me?"

He nodded, fingers waving in her direction but not coming any closer. "Darkness that one. All darkness."

"No, he's not. Or at least he wasn't. Not until you stole his emotions."

The raptor snorted, nostrils flaring again. "My payment." He pounded his fist against his chest. "My due."

"Yes, payment was owed to you, but you could have taken something else." That seemed to calm him, but she wasn't sure. Without eyes, he was hard to read.

"What else?" he asked.

"If I let you take emotions from me, would you let the vampire's go?"

The raptor slumped lower and covered his head with his long fingers. Minutes ticked by. Minutes they didn't have.

"Raptor? Will you do it?"

Lifting his head, he nodded. "Will do. For my love."

"You may only take my anger."

He sighed. "Not a fair trade."

"Please."

He went very still. "You say please to me?"

"Yes."

He inhaled, but it sounded like a sob. Then he reached out his hand. "Must touch."

"You agree to the trade? Anger for love."

"Yes." His fingers stretched closer. "My love's anger for the dark one's love."

She stuck her hand out.

His fingers wrapped her wrist. Suddenly, he let go of her, jerking back like he'd been shocked. "No," he howled. "You are ruined by his blood. His child." The raptor lurched to his feet, baring his teeth and hissing like a cat. "Ruined."

She backed up. "We had a deal."

"Chrysabelle!" Panic rang in Fi's voice.

"No deal, vampire whore." The raptor swiped at her.

She ducked, but he caught the side of her head. Blood trickled into her eye. She was vaguely aware of the surrounding noise level rising. He came at her again. This time she was ready. She dodged his punch and kicked his side, spinning him against the bars. He crashed into the stone wall and ricocheted off, falling forward. She jumped onto his back, both hands clenching the hilt of her sacre. Thrusting down with all her strength, she buried the blade in his back.

His long head jerked back, his mouth open to scream, but nothing came out but a gasp. Blood spurted up around her sword, and then he went limp. The raptor seemed to deflate, shrinking in size as she jumped to the ground.

The rest of the Claustrum began to wail. That had better mean the emotions he'd stolen were free again. They had to get back to Augustine now. She put her foot on the raptor's back and yanked her sacre out. "No one calls me a whore."

A quick tug and the knob of the French door came off in Mal's hand. He pushed the door open, hoping he'd get lucky and find Chrysabelle in bed. He didn't. But the scent of comarré blood was strong downstairs. *Blood blood blood.*

He went in that direction, the bloodlust in his system pushing him harder, making him as reckless as the voices urged him to be. He slipped down the stairs and stood in the foyer.

Doc saw him first. "Mal."

The shadeux fae jumped off the couch. "Velimai, a warning burst."

The wysper next to him opened her mouth and

screamed. Mal tapped one earplug. "Nice try, but I came prepared, although I realize now I should have killed you when I had the chance."

A blade snapped through the air and bit into Mal's shoulder, blazing pain through his body like he was on fire. He cursed and yanked it out, burning his hand in the process. He looked up. There was only one place that Golgotha steel could have come from. A comar stood in the kitchen doorway. Mal scowled at Damian. "Just like your sister. Where is the princess? Turn her over and I might let the rest of you live."

Doc shifted to his half-form, eyes green-gold and fingers tipped with razor-pointed claws. "I never thought it would come to this, but brother, I *will* take you down."

Mal opened his mouth as pain ripped through his body again, but it wasn't from his shoulder. It came from deep inside him, from where his heart had once beaten. He recognized it instantly. It was the throbbing ache of missing Chrysabelle, the agony of being separated from her, the gaping emptiness she'd once sealed away. The taste of her danced across his tongue, the silk of her skin slipped through his fingers, and her honey-sweet perfume filled his senses as though she'd never left his memory.

Longing followed, hard waves of it that stomped the howling voices down and shoved the beast into place. He went rigid as the balance returned and he realized what had happened. How he'd spoken to her, shunned her, hunted her. He closed his eyes, trying to quell the tide of sensation ripping through him.

Love came last and in such abundance that tears burned his eyes and he gasped for breath he didn't require. His need for her swallowed him in a flash of brilliance.

The room and its occupants disappeared until all he saw was her.

Every emotion he'd ever felt for Chrysabelle returned. The weight of it drowned him, beating him into the ground like a hammer. He couldn't speak. Couldn't move. Unable to bear the onslaught any longer, he dropped to his knees and collapsed.

Chapter Twenty-five

Lola rose as Luciano entered her office and moved out from behind her desk. "What a pleasant surprise. So nice to see you."

"And you." He kissed her cheek in greeting. "How are you? How are you adjusting to your new life?"

"I'm getting there. Growing more comfortable every day."

"And Hector? How is he working out?"

"Very well. His blood is exceptional." She nodded at Octavian, who was hovering at the door. "Thank you. That will be all." She sat back down at her desk but Luciano remained standing. "Is it possible that his blood can change over time?"

He stiffened. "What do you mean?"

"The taste of it seems to be changing."

Luciano stuck a finger into the collar of his shirt, loosening it. "Yes, of course, this is natural. You wouldn't know this as you are such a vampling, but it is typical. Think nothing of it." He waved his hand as if her concerns should be dismissed the same way.

She let it drop. "And how are you doing?"

"*Così-così.*" He tipped his hand back and forth

like a balance and sighed. "I wish I was here on better circumstances."

Octavian suddenly came in. "Did you call me?"

She scowled at his intrusion. "No. You must be hearing things." Hopefully after he closed the door he would go back to his desk and stay there. Since their night at Seven, she'd kept him at arm's length in punishment for his disrespect. He may be a more experienced vampire but he was still her assistant and she was still the mayor, and while she desperately wanted whatever information he could give her on the ancients, she would have to go about getting it from him another way. She turned her attention back to Luciano. "Why better circumstances? What's wrong?"

He pointed to the sitting area across the room. "Perhaps we can sit where it is more comfortable?"

"Of course, yes." She walked over to the loveseat while he took the club chair. "Can I get you a drink?"

"No, I'm fine, *grazie*." He planted his elbows on his knees and leaned in. "There has been a murder."

She nodded. "I know. Two of them now. The police are working on it, but unfortunately everything is pointing to a vampire killer."

He frowned. "No, not a human murder. A vampire murder."

"What? Where?"

"At Seven." He sat back a bit. "I know you and Dominic aren't on…the best of terms, but this is something that affects us all."

She waved her hand. "I agree. I'm sure we can move past what's happened in light of this news. Who was it?"

"A close friend of Dominic's who also worked at the club. Katsumi Tanaka. Did you ever meet her?"

Lola went still, her head going in a hundred directions as she searched for an answer. They'd just been there. Just met with her. What had happened after she and Luke had left? Could Octavian have done something? But no, he didn't seem the type. "Yes, but I can't say that I knew her. What happened?"

He shrugged. "When one of our kind dies there is so little evidence left. All we know is that her ashes were found in her office this evening."

"How awful." Truth would serve her best. It would take only a little questioning for him to find out she and Octavian had met with Katsumi, but Octavian was her link to the ancients. She had to protect him, at least a little while longer. "I just saw her last night. I was at Seven with my assistant. He even talked to her about the possibility of purchasing his own comarré, but he wasn't feeling well and we left before anything happened."

Luciano stared at her, dragging time out until the urge to speak again became nearly unbearable. It was a technique she knew well and often used at meetings. That knowledge saved her. She smiled back, despite his calculating gaze, and folded her hands comfortably in her lap.

Finally he stood. "Very well. I will inform my uncle that I've made you aware of the situation."

She walked with him to the door. "If there is anything I can do to help, please let me know."

He stopped before opening the door. "We will. It's good to know the mayor is on our side. With a killer on the loose, one can never be too careful or have too many resources." He let himself out.

She shut the door behind him, her nerves on edge. He didn't believe her. She felt it in her bones. What if

Octavian had done it? Would he kill her too? What did she really know about him, other than he had information she desperately wanted.

She couldn't take things slowly anymore, trying to piecemeal the information out of him. Steeling herself, she opened the door. "Octavian, will you come in here please? We need to talk."

The Claustrum erupted in a deafening roar. Fi ripped the cell door open, then went back to ghost form as soon as Chrysabelle got out of the raptor's cell.

"Out. Now," Chrysabelle mouthed, motioning for her to follow. Fi nodded and Chrysabelle took off running. She kept her feet to the path and her eyes straight ahead, only looking back to make sure Fi was still there.

As soon as they hit the ramp, she slowed to yell behind her, "Stay with me."

"I am," Fi yelled back. "Twelve floors. Let's go."

Chrysabelle nodded and took off again. Her heart pounded in her chest and by the seventh floor, her lungs burned with the effort of breathing the thick, hot air. Still she ran, counting the floors as they ascended. Finally, at twelve, she stopped and bent over, trying to catch her breath. This time, it wasn't just the wretched air. Something else about this place was wearing her out. Fi said something but she held her hand to her ear to show she hadn't heard over the wailing and crying and shouting.

"I said, what are you doing?" Fi pointed to the floor marker. "That's eleven."

"No." Chrysabelle shook her head, trying to enunciate. "This is twelve. I counted."

"So did I and this is eleven."

Chrysabelle checked the time. They'd been on the fae plane for fifty-three minutes. "Are you sure?" The margin for mistakes was zero.

Fi nodded, already floating farther up the path. "Yes, come on."

Chrysabelle went after her. When they hit the next floor, she knew Fi was right. The exit tunnel lay before them. Chrysabelle tried to keep up her speed, but it was like her feet were mired in quicksand. At least the noise had faded a little.

"How do you feel?" she asked Fi.

"Happy we're leaving. You?"

"Like I'm running out of juice."

"I noticed." Fi went ahead of her. "Do you want me to go get Augustine to help you? I could stay outside and open the gate when you get there."

"No . . . I'll . . . make it." But her breath came in gulps now.

Worry creased Fi's face. "I don't like this."

"We're . . . almost . . . there." Gray light filtered through the tunnel's darkness.

"Come on, Chrysabelle, you can do it. Think of Mal. He'll be waiting for you. And he doesn't even know about the baby yet. Think about how excited he'll be." Fi kept talking, encouraging her.

The gate lay ahead. On the other side, Augustine watched them. "Sixty-two minutes," he announced, shaking his head. "*Hurry* up."

"I'm trying," Chrysabelle answered. She stumbled and fell to her hands and knees. Every command she sent to her brain to get up was ignored. It wasn't happening, but that didn't mean she wasn't going to keep moving.

Motivated by the thought of her unborn child and reuniting with Mal, she crawled toward the gate.

"Sixty-eight," Augustine counted off.

"That's…not…helping." Lifting her head took too much effort, so she let it hang. She had to be close. The gate creaked open. That was a good sign, wasn't it? Maybe she should lie down for a second…

Strong hands closed around her arms and pulled her through. Augustine cradled her like a baby and carried her back to the field. "I told you no more than an hour."

She nodded, wondering how he could carry her when she knew she must weigh a thousand pounds. He set her on her feet, but she collapsed backward. The sky was so gray here. Like a storm was always on the horizon. Fi moaned.

"It's okay," he assured her. He reached into his jacket and pulled out a small round mirror, then tossed it on the ground.

"We're never going to fit through that," she whispered as he picked her up again.

"Fi, get corporeal and hold onto me."

Fi must have, because Chrysabelle blinked and they were back in the hotel suite.

"What happened?" Jerem asked. "Why are you carrying her? Is she hurt?"

"She's fine." Augustine deposited her onto the sofa. "We were there too long."

Jerem kneeled beside her. "She doesn't look fine."

"It'll wear off." He headed for the door. "There's no way the elektos doesn't know what happened so I need to get scarce. None of you hang here any longer than you need to, either." He glanced at Chrysabelle. "Nice to see you again. Next time you need access to the Claustrum? It's on Mortalis."

With that, he was gone.

* * *

Mal opened his eyes. And realized he was lying on the foyer floor in Chrysabelle's house. He sat up. A mostly familiar group surrounded him, except that there were an unusual number of weapons pointed at him.

He held his hands up. "I surrender."

Mortalis narrowed his eyes. "How do you feel?"

His hands went to his head. "Like hell."

"How do you feel about Chrysabelle?" the fae asked.

The sound of her name deepened the ache in Mal's chest. The voices droned in his brain, sad and confused and unhappy. "Like I can't wait to see her again."

Damian brought his sacre a little closer to Mal's face. "So you can kill her?"

"No." Mal scowled. "I love her." Then he remembered. "Son of a priest, I've been a total ass."

"Wasn't your fault," Mortalis said. "Not exactly."

Doc shifted back to human from his half-form. "What the hell just happened?"

"Mal just got his emotions back." Mortalis looked at him. "That's all that matters."

Doc raised a brow but said nothing else.

Mal got to his feet, wobbling slightly. Apparently getting all your emotions sucked out and then pumped back in made you feel like you'd been on a monthlong bender. "How did that happen? And where's Chrysabelle?"

"She had something to take care of," Mortalis answered. "But she should be home soon." He studied Mal. "Are you sure you're back?"

Mal nodded. The voices scratched around in his head, searching for remnants of old Mal. "I feel like I am. Except I really need to sit down."

They moved into the living room, but Mortalis stayed close. "If you're really back, take out those earplugs."

Mal reached up and popped them out. "I'd forgotten about those. Damn it. And about Tatiana."

"What about her?" Damian took the chair next to him. "We know she's in town."

"Not anymore. She's already gone back to Corvinestri. Where she thinks I'll be joining her."

Damian frowned. "Why?"

Mal explained everything that had happened, from Tatiana coming to see him to his encounter with Creek to the tainted blood Dominic had been sending.

Mortalis nodded. "Chrysabelle asked him to do that."

"It was a good idea. I can't imagine how many people she kept me from killing."

Doc frowned. "How many did you kill?"

"None." He tried to think, but ingesting so many drugs in so few days had left a few hazy spots in his memory. "At least, I don't think I did."

"Think harder," Damian said. "There have been a couple humans murdered in the last few days and everything I've heard says it was a vampire."

"Bloody hell." Mal racked his brain, trying to remember. He looked around. "I don't seem to have any new ghosts following me, so I'm going to take that as a good sign." He stood and stretched. "But if you want to stand guard over me while I sleep, be my guest. The sun will be up soon and I'm exhausted. Wake me when Chrysabelle gets home. I'll be in the hurricane shelter until then." Without waiting for a response, he headed down the hall.

He locked the door behind him and leaned against it. He'd remember if he killed someone, wouldn't he? But he couldn't answer that definitively. There was one way to tell. He stripped his clothes off and checked his skin for new names. Nothing but the usual that he could see.

He'd need a mirror to check the rest of his skin, but that would have to wait until the sun went down again. Until then, he needed to get unconscious and hope no new ghosts showed up to haunt him.

Chapter Twenty-six

"I wish Velimai had made enough sandwiches for the flight home. I'm starving."

Chrysabelle shook her head at Fi as she slid into the car beside her. "You're always hungry, but this time so am I. A little." She wasn't totally over the lethargy of being on the fae plane, but as it diminished, her appetite increased. It probably helped that they were back on the ground in New Florida. She was finally starting to feel safe again.

Jerem stuck his head in before closing the car door. "You want me to swing through a drive-thru on the way home?"

"Yes," Fi said just as Chrysabelle said, "No."

Chrysabelle smiled. "Fi, you know Velimai will have a better meal than anything you can get at a fast-food joint."

"Yeah, that's true." She waved at Jerem. "Thanks, but I'll be okay. Just drive fast."

He laughed and shut the door. A minute later, they were leaving the hangar behind and off toward the freeway.

Fi unclipped her seatbelt to scoot to the seat across from Chrysabelle. "How are you feeling? Better?"

"Yes. I think the residual effects of the fae plane have finally worn off."

"That was the scariest place I've ever been in." Fi tucked one leg underneath her. "We probably shouldn't tell Doc too much about it. He'll freak. I know him. And in your condition, you probably shouldn't be getting all stressed by being yelled at."

"I can handle Doc." Chrysabelle's hand slipped to her belly. "Whoa." She looked down. "Is it just me or does my stomach seem bigger?"

Fi nodded. "You're definitely showing a little. Maybe you should go back to your loose tunics. T-shirts and snug jeans don't hide much."

"You're the one who bought me these clothes."

Fi smirked. "Check the label. Those are maternity jeans. Why do you think you're still fitting into them?" She laughed. "You think all jeans are that stretchy?"

"They don't look like maternity jeans. Not that I've ever owned a pair before. Of any kind."

Fi yawned. "I'd say it was weird how fast this is happening, but considering this kid's parents, I guess it's not that weird at all. I wonder what your due date is. You should really go see a doctor."

Chrysabelle shot Fi a look. "And tell him what? I'm carrying a half-vampire baby? I realize with the covenant broken, othernaturals aren't a secret to humans anymore, but I doubt there's a doctor out there who's studied anything close to what's happening with me."

"Actually . . ." Fi's eyes took on a curious glow. "Barasa, he's one of Doc's council members and the pride's chief physician, he studied at a hospital that specialized in oth-ernaturals. If anyone could give you some insight into this pregnancy, I bet he could."

Chrysabelle thought for a moment. "Couldn't hurt to see him, I guess." She shrugged. "Might be a little strange, but normal hasn't been a big part of my life so far. Why start now?" She glanced down at her belly again. Soon everyone would know her secret.

"Something wrong?"

"Just thinking." She looked out the window.

"About?"

"If things didn't go the way they were supposed to with Mal...I'm not going to be able to hide this preg-nancy from him for much longer."

"You did everything you were supposed to. You killed the raptor, and the emotions were released. It's all going to be fine."

"What if he got his emotions back but isn't happy about this child?"

Fi rolled her eyes. "How could he not be happy about a baby?"

"He refused to turn his daughter into a vampire to save her life. He thought being a vampire was worse than death for a child." She stared at her stomach. "Now he's responsi-ble for bringing a vampire child into the world? Look at the trouble the last one caused. And now it's in the hands of the ancients. You think Mal's going to be thrilled about this?"

Fi reached over and squeezed her hand. "This is just the pregnancy hormones talking. I'll get you in to see Barasa tomorrow, I swear. I'll bet you feel a ton better after talking to him."

Chrysabelle nodded. "Maybe you're right. I'm going

to sleep a little bit." She closed her eyes, intending to work out the worst-case scenarios in case things weren't fine, but when she opened her eyes again, they were pulling into her driveway.

With the brilliant blue sky above them, the emerald green palms waving in the soft, salted air and the sun's warmth beating down on them, it should have felt like paradise. But without Mal…she shook her head and forced herself to smile. It was that or cry.

Tatiana read the Paradise City Press online, looking for anything that might give her an idea of Mal's whereabouts. She'd expected him here by now and nothing in the paper provided any reason why he might be late. Except for the mention of a few vampire-related killings. Could he have been brought in for questioning? Considering that the mayor had tried to put him to death once already, he was probably high on the suspect list. Yes, perhaps that was what was keeping him.

The tang of brimstone reached her nose. She spun around, realizing too late how dark her office had become. "My liege?"

"No, Mother. It's me." The voice came from behind her.

She twisted again. Lilith sat in one of her office chairs, one leg kicked up over the arm. Her jacket was made of dark red-brown leather and oddly cut, its edges left ragged and the seams joined with rough, looping stitches of ribbon in the same color. "Lilith, how nice to see you again."

She pouted. "Why haven't you called me? I thought you loved me."

"I do, my darling, so much, but I've been busy finding a father for you."

Her eyes lit up. "You have?"

"Yes. He's one of the most fearsome vampires to ever walk the earth and he's going to arrive very soon, and then do you know what's going to happen?"

She shook her head, looking very much the eager child.

Then he's going to help me kill you. "Then we're all going on a trip to the most beautiful place on earth."

"Where? I want to know *now.*"

Tatiana sat back and waggled her finger. "No. I can't tell you any more than that or you'll ruin the surprise."

Lilith crossed her arms and hurled herself back in the chair. "I *hate* surprises."

"No, you don't. You love them. Now be a good girl and let Mother get back to her planning."

But Lilith didn't budge. "I'm tired of the Castus. I want to live here with you."

Fear burrowed into Tatiana's gut like an icy worm. "And you will, but the house isn't ready for you yet. Your room is still a nursery. Do you want to spend your daysleep in a crib?" She made herself smile. "I want everything to be just right for you. Because I love you so much."

"It's taking too long. Kill one of the workers. That will speed the rest up."

"Yes, I suppose it would, but it might make the rest of them quit, too." Time to change the subject. "Is that a new jacket? I don't remember it the last time we visited."

"Yes." She smiled. "I made it myself."

That explained the crude construction.

Lilith spread her arms to give Tatiana a better look. "I skinned one of the Castus. He was always nagging me about taking too much blood from him." She rolled her eyes and shook her head. "So. Boring."

"You... *skinned* one of the ancients." Tatiana worked hard to keep the fear out of her eyes. "Did he hurt you when you were doing this? I don't see a mark on you." Surely the Castus fought back.

Lilith laughed. "Hurt me? How could he hurt me when he was dead?" She laughed some more, like she'd never heard anything so funny.

Tatiana realized her mouth was hanging open. She shut it and carefully sat back. Lilith had killed one of the Castus. In the more than five hundred years since she'd been sired, she'd never heard such a thing could be done.

No wonder the Castus were scared of this little monster they'd created. Lilith was unlike any creature that had ever existed. A nightmare made flesh. With the mind of a child.

Tatiana swallowed. The Castus expected her to provide them with the solution to their problem. She almost laughed. To think she was relying on Mal to help her. All she'd really done was sentence him to death.

Maybe both of them.

The sound of beating wings preceded Annika's arrival. She dropped into step beside Creek as he walked patrol through the neighborhood around City Hall. "We've got another death."

"Another human?" Creek shook his head. "This is getting serious."

"No, this time it's a vampire." She tucked her wings into her jacket. "An employee at Seven. Pretty high up. A woman named Katsumi Tanaka."

"Who'd she kill?"

"She was the victim."

His brows lifted. "Really? Someone must have had a serious issue to take her out. She's Dominic's right hand from what I know about her. Noble, too. He resired her a short time ago. *Navitas* or whatever they call it."

"Yes, *navitas*. She was the wife of a Yakuza boss when she was human and since coming to work for Dominic, she's made a name for herself running fighters through the Pits and now heading his comarré operations. There are a lot of people who might want her dead."

"But not that many who could take on a noble vampire."

Annika nodded. "So let's narrow it down."

"The mayor's a possibility." And he knew the KM were looking for a reason to remove her from office. "She's noble now, so she has the strength and ability and being Paole means she has the advantage of stealth. Katsumi being involved in the comarré operation could mean the mayor might want to take her out as revenge for the death of her daughter, Julia."

"Good. Who else?"

"This new vampire, Luciano. He's Dominic's nephew. He might see Katsumi as a threat to his succession at Seven. Plus, he's a loose cannon. We don't know much about him."

Annika scanned the streets as they walked. "Any others?"

He thought for a moment, wondering how much leeway she'd give him. He had his suspicions, but the KM was a tight group. They tended to protect their own pretty strongly. He shrugged. "I'm sure there are."

"You're thinking of a name. Who is it?"

"One I shouldn't say."

"Why?"

"Because you won't like it."

She paused, making him stop too. "Who?"

Nothing about her expression said she was going to let this go. "Octavian."

She didn't react. "Why would he kill Katsumi? It hasn't been ordered."

"Katsumi was part of the crew that went into Corvinestri to bring the vampire baby back. If he was at Seven, she could have recognized him, could have threatened to blow his cover."

"But why? What would she have to gain?"

He lifted one shoulder. "She's known for her ambition. If she could make it work for her, she would."

Annika started walking again. "He wouldn't kill her without an order to do so, and she's done nothing out of line to cause that to happen."

"Then it wouldn't hurt to ask him a few questions. I'm sure he's got nothing to hide." Actually, Creek thought Octavian had a lot to hide. Getting Annika's okay to dig might help him prove that.

"It's not your place to question a superior." She let out a gruff sigh. "Keep it casual, understood?"

If casual meant no excessive force, he could do that. In theory. He nodded. "Understood."

Chapter Twenty-seven

"Hi, Pete. Sorry, Chief Vernadetto. I know you're here on official business." Fi gave him a big smile, despite her nerves. Doc had briefed her on the ride home, so she'd been anticipating the chief's questions since she'd arrived.

"Good afternoon, Fiona. It's okay if you call me Pete. We're friends, right?" His smile didn't quite erase the sadness in his eyes.

"Absolutely we're friends." It was nice to know he still thought of her that way. She sat across from him, glad she'd been able to shower and change. There was something about an expensive dress and killer heels that gave her a real boost of confidence. *Killer* heels. She almost laughed. "How are you?"

"Fine, fine."

"Are you?" She looked at him closely. "Have you thought any more about what we talked about? You know, I have a lot of othernatural friends. If you want, I could ask around, see if any of them might know what you—"

"No, no, I'm good. I'm okay with not knowing too much, really." He lined his stylus up parallel to his tablet, even though it was already parallel. "How are you with everything that's going on?"

She didn't buy him being okay with not knowing his bloodlines, but for the moment she'd let it drop. "I'm dealing. I got a little freaked out when Remo attacked me, but other than that, I'm dealing." She leaned in. "I know you're here to talk to me about the fight with Heaven, but can we have a few moments off the record, just you and I?"

He nodded, seemingly grateful for the chance to take his police hat off. "Sure, what's on your mind?"

"You know how I asked you to do a little digging on Remo? I was just curious if you found out anything about him."

Pete frowned. "Unfortunately, due to this case, I can't say much about that." He sighed and tapped the stylus on the table. "I can tell you that Remo's record isn't spotless." He looked toward the door before going further. "He's got a pretty long rap sheet of minor run-ins, most of which his father has made go away. All small stuff, though. Fights. A DUI. A possession charge. Disorderly conduct. The typical bad boy who likes to party."

"What about pride issues? Those wouldn't be recorded in police records, would they?"

"No. Pride law is a separate thing unless it involves a legal issue. And each pride keeps its own records. What are you thinking?"

She held a hand up. "I'm not in any way trying to do your job—"

"I know that."

"What about possession of powdered silver?"

Pete went quiet, but kept tapping his stylus on the

table. Then the tapping stopped. "Is that against pride rules?"

"They treat it like a drug or a poison. Possessing more than an eighth of an ounce without a legitimate reason—which I don't think there are any—is grounds for a small fine and seizure of the powder. Second and third offenses have much more serious consequences."

Pete seemed to be mulling something over. "You think he might have tainted that sand himself then?"

She shrugged. "Not really, but he might have been involved in it."

"Why would he do that? Heaven was his sister."

"Whom he admitted he never got along with. Maybe he knew if Heaven was out of the way, it would open up a chance for him to come to the States."

"But why? That would be like a prince leaving his kingdom. Remo's father is one of the most powerful men in all of Brazil. Why would Remo want to put so much distance between them?"

Fi traced a circle on the table top. "Remo's the third born. I know that much about him. There was no chance he'd ever inherit that throne." She stopped drawing. "And Doc's a nobody to him. Maybe he thought he could come in here and take over this pride. Especially if he could throw suspicion about his sister's death on Doc or me."

Pete nodded. "That's interesting. And it gives me a lot to look into." He pushed his tablet forward a little. "I still have to ask you questions."

"I know. And I'm ready to answer." She'd said her piece, given him everything she and Doc had come up with in the car. Remo could definitely be behind this. And even if he wasn't, it would buy Doc and his council a little more time to do their own investigation.

Pete cleared his throat. "Where were you the night of Heaven's death?"

"Right there in the arena with her, getting the daylights beaten out of me. By her." Fi took a breath. "Next?"

"The sun will be down in an hour, maybe less." Chrysabelle pushed her dessert plate away. "I want to wake him up."

Not alone, Velimai signed as she began to clear dishes.

"I agree." Mortalis set his coffee cup down. "Let Damian and me go with you. Just to be safe."

Amylia smiled politely. "I feel like I'm intruding on personal business here. Thank you for dinner, it was lovely, but I'm going to go back to the guesthouse and let you have your privacy." She pushed her chair back.

Chrysabelle nodded, knowing how awkward this must be for the girl. "Thank you. You're welcome for dinner any time."

Amylia gave a little wave and left.

As the front door swung shut, Chrysabelle raised her eyebrows. "That was intuitive of her. Of course, she can't be that comfortable knowing there's a vampire in the house. I get it, but it is my house." She looked at Damian. "Sorry. *Our* house. I guess you're probably not crazy about him being here either."

"Amylia's...fine. As fine as she can be in this situation. And she understands about Mal." He flattened the crust of his key lime pie with his fork, turning it into sand. "She knows, like I do, that Mal helped you get me out of

Corvinestri. He kept you safe. And I know you have feelings for him. I'm not about to tell you whom you can and can't love." He looked at her. "I just hope for your sake, he wakes up like his old self again."

"Thank you." Having her brother on her side meant a lot. She pushed her chair back and stood. "Shall we?" She led them down the hall.

Mortalis stopped them at the door to the hurricane shelter. "Let me." He opened the door slowly, then tapped the light panel. Soft overheads filled the space with gentle illumination.

Mal sprawled on the couch, one arm hanging off, but otherwise stone still in the deathly repose of a vampire in daysleep. Mortalis pulled a small black dagger from his belt.

Damian unsheathed the sacre he'd grabbed along the way. "Just in case," he whispered.

She didn't like it, but she understood. "Mal," she called. "Can you wake up?"

No response. She went close enough to give his leg a shake. He wasn't usually a sound sleeper. "Mal. Wake up."

His eyes came open and he blinked a few times. The moment his gaze focused on her, he grinned. "You're home." He leaped off the couch.

Damian's blade came flashing down between them. "Not so fast."

Mal snarled, but his hands went up in surrender. "You have a death wish?"

Damian kept the blade in place. "Do you?"

"Enough." Chrysabelle itched to touch Mal, but first things first. "Mal, how do you feel?"

"Like if I don't get some alone time with you, I'm going to kill somebody."

Mortalis spun the blade through his fingers. "Not the answer we were looking for."

Mal frowned. "You know what I mean." He turned his gaze to Chrysabelle. "Damn, it's good to see you. I just want to hold you and make sure you're real."

He stared at her, his expression fraught with all the emotions that had been ripped from him, his eyes so silver they gleamed, and she knew in that moment that he was back. This was her Mal standing before her. "That might be a little uncomfortable." She pulled up the sleeve of her tunic top. "I'm wearing my body armor." It was the best protection she and the baby had against him if things went poorly.

His hands reached out for her, but he made no move to come closer. "I am so sorry. I shouldn't have let the raptor touch me. I should have fought." Anger and humiliation razed shadows across his face. He turned so she couldn't see his eyes. "That damned thing got the best of me."

Mortalis tucked his blade away. "There was nothing you could have done. And I'm the one who should be apologizing to you. I knew what that fae was capable of; I just never guessed what he'd go after."

"Put your sacre away, Damian." Emotion made it hard for her to say more. "I'm just glad you're back, Mal. So...glad."

He looked at her again, squinted, and pointed to her forehead. "Please tell me I didn't do that."

Her fingers went to the scratch near her hairline. "The raptor did."

Mal's jaw clenched and he slanted his eyes at Mortalis. "You brought that thing back? After what it did to me?"

"No." She held her hand out. "I went after it. I...killed it. I had no other choice."

Mortalis nodded softly. "That's why she wasn't here

when you arrived. And why your emotions returned to you." He looked proudly at Chrysabelle. "She did the impossible. To save you."

Dominic's patience had stretched to a new definition of thin. Katsumi's murder, much like Maris's, stirred a fire in him that could only be quenched by another death. He stared at his nephew as he entered the office. "What have you found out?"

Luciano settled into the chair across from him. "The mayor knows more than she is saying, but not much I think."

"She lied to you? You are her sire."

"And she is also *Americano*." He said the word with disdain. "She knows nothing of the old ways. Nothing of respect." He crossed one leg over the other, his pant leg pulling back to reveal a sheath of slim throwing daggers. "Do you know this new vampire that works for her? I spoke with the staff and he was definitely here with her that night."

Dominic waved his hand, one of his rings throwing flashes of red. "I don't know many of the fringe."

"He's not fringe. Not with that face and those eyes." Luciano nodded. "Definitely noble, and I could sense him before I stepped off the elevator, so not Paole either."

"What's his name?"

"She called him Octavian and I confirmed with both the server and the croupier who took care of them that night. Octavian Petrescu."

Dominic stared at Luciano but saw only memories. "Brown hair and eyes, medium build. No age on him. Sired less than a year, probably."

"*Si*, that could be him."

Dominic swore. "He works for Tatiana. *Porca troia*." He rested both elbows on the desk and steepled his fingers. "I want him brought in alive, and then I want word sent to her that her errand boy has been discovered. If she wants him back, she can come and get him herself. Otherwise, I will kill him."

Luciano's mouth bunched to one side. "Do you think she'll come? After all, she's not known for her compassion toward her fellow brethren."

"I saw them together at the Dominus ball. She loves him. She'll come. And when she does, I will kill both of them to make up for the deaths they have dealt me." He nodded slowly. "I must prepare my workroom. These deaths…" He smiled. It was good to have something new to focus on. "They will not be fast or merciful."

Luciano didn't get up. "*Zio*, there is another thing…"

Dominic settled back in his chair. When Luciano called him uncle, chances were good the next thing that followed would not be. "*Si?*"

"The other night, when I was leaving blood for Malkolm, I ran into someone." A rare sliver of fear ran through Luciano's eyes.

"And?"

"He claims to be Kubai Mata." Luciano laughed, but it seemed forced. "Of course, I know they do not exist, but still, who would make such a—"

"They do exist. His name is Creek. He hasn't been an issue for me, and from what Mortalis tells me, he's fairly levelheaded. I doubt you'll see him much. He tends to watch the fringe more. Now, go, I have work—"

"It's just that…" Luciano paused as if still absorbing

the knowledge that the KM were real. "He knows I'm responsible for siring the mayor. He said he had orders to kill me, but because of what I was doing for Chrysabelle in helping to keep Malkolm sedated, he would let me go. I was thinking, perhaps I should strike first—"

"No." Dominic shook his head. "You cannot kill him. His grandmother is not a woman I wish to upset, nor will I make an enemy of the Kubai Mata." He shooed Luciano away. "Out, find this Octavian and bring him to me. My need to avenge these deaths will not go unmet."

Chapter Twenty-eight

"Y ou killed the raptor? By yourself?" Mal stared in amazement at the beautiful woman across from him. The voices had retreated into a sullen, pouting mass, making them easy to ignore, especially with Chrysabelle standing in front of him. Her glow was more brilliant than he'd ever seen it and it wasn't just because he'd been away from her so long. She gleamed like she was lit from within.

She put her hands on her hips. "Is this the part where you scold me? I got a little scratch; that was it. A small price to pay for the return of your emotions."

He shook his head. "I'm not going to yell at you. I'm impressed. That thing was huge. And dangerous."

"And killing it was the only way to bring you back to me."

He ached to hold her. "I owe you my life. In more ways than one." He smiled. "How many times are you going to save me?"

She took a step toward him. "As many times as I have to." She held his gaze. "Damian, Mortalis, could you leave us alone? We can all agree Mal's not a threat to me anymore."

They left and Mal grinned. "I might be a threat to those clothes. How much of a burn do you think that body armor will give me while I'm tearing it off you?"

She laughed, but it faded fast. "You might want to sit. I have something to tell you."

"Later. I'm too wound up to sit."

She pointed at the couch. "Now."

Reluctantly, he sat. "Fine. But you've got two minutes. Then body armor or not, you're mine."

She didn't even smile as she took the other end of the couch, far enough that the silver mesh covering her body didn't cause his skin to itch. Much. "You should probably hear what I have to say first."

"I don't like the tone of your voice. Sounds serious."

"It is, but it's not bad news. I don't think."

"Just tell me." He swallowed. What had he done now? "I can take it."

She reached out, slipping her fingers through his. He closed his eyes at her touch, the warmth of her skin like a kiss. "I...I'm pregnant."

He froze.

"Did you hear me? I'm pregnant. That...*episode* in the plane's bedroom on the way home from Corvinestri? Well, it...worked." She looked slightly miffed. "As Fi would say, you knocked me up."

He stared at her. He knew he wasn't moving, knew he wasn't saying anything, but he couldn't get his body to respond and couldn't find words that made sense.

She tugged on his hand. "Aren't you going to say anything? Are you upset? Happy? I need to know how you feel about this."

Slowly, he began to nod. "Happy doesn't cover it. I

didn't even know it was possible. A child. *Our* child. I…" The cold realization of what that meant hit him. "This child is half vampire, half comarré."

"Yes. Part of each of us."

"Son of a priest." Fear crept in over his bones. "Look at what happened with Preacher's child. Julia wasn't even a real comarré. Can you imagine how many people will be after this baby? The lengths they'll go to lay hands on it?"

Chrysabelle's hands went to her stomach. "We'll protect it. No matter what."

"That goes without saying, but—"

"I already know Tatiana's in town."

"Not anymore. She was, but I sent her home."

Chrysabelle frowned. "*You* sent her home?"

"She came here to recruit me. Offered to restore my noble status and set me up as her Elder, in exchange for helping her."

"Helping her with what? It's got to be a trick."

"I don't think so. She told me the ancient ones fed Lilith, the baby, with their blood after they took her. They've turned her into some kind of monster. Grown-up Lilith has already killed Tatiana's Elder and she says even the ancients are afraid of what they've created. Now she wants my help getting rid of Lilith."

Chrysabelle crossed her arms. "I don't like this. She's setting you up to die."

"Maybe, but I told her I would do it."

"What? No." She grabbed his arm. "That was the old you. You can't."

He squeezed her hand. "I have to. Don't you see? If this Lilith is as powerful as Tatiana says, can you imagine the threat she'll be to our child? She must be dealt with. And in doing so, I'll be able to get close to Tatiana and take care of her, too. I *have* to go to Corvinestri. She's waiting for me. If I don't, I have no doubt she'll come back here."

She pulled her hand out from under his and slid a little farther away from him. "If you go, I'm going with you."

"Chrysabelle, right now Tatiana thinks you and I are done and that I care about nothing but my own advancement. She's got to *keep* thinking that for this to work." He snagged her hand and kissed her knuckles. "And you have the baby to think about." He smiled. "Our baby."

She glared at him, clearly unmoved by his affections. Damn, he'd missed her. "She won't know I'm there, and we'll be stronger working together. Besides, if Lilith is so powerful that the ancients are afraid of her, then the comarré need to know about this new threat. They need to prepare. We have been taught all our lives that the future holds a day when we will be called upon to rise up and destroy our hosts."

Her eyes took on a faraway look. "I believe that day has come."

"I need your help, Octavian." Lola hoped he could see the sincerity in her eyes, and the pain of losing her daughter and her granddaughter etched across her face. She also hoped inviting him to her home had not been a mistake. She folded her hands on her lap and sighed. "I am a woman in pain. A woman in mourning."

"Why?" he asked, leaning forward from his seat on

the big leather chair opposite her. She took that to mean concern. A good sign. "What's happened?"

"Since my daughter Julia's death, I have been searching for my granddaughter. She is a unique child, half vampire, half comarré. And I have been told that she is now in the possession of those known as the ancients."

Silver flickered in his eyes. "Yes, I've heard about this child. She was introduced to the nobility at a ball, recently. But I also believe what you said is true—she is now in the hands of the ancients."

Lola nodded. He knew of Mariela. "You must help me, then. I have no one else to turn to. No one else I trust."

"What help do you need?"

"I want to get her back." She looked into his eyes and tried to convey every ounce of pain she'd felt these last months. There truly was no length she wouldn't go to in order to get her grandchild back. He must understand that. "Tell me how to access these ancients."

His gaze went completely silver and he pushed back in his chair, shaking his head. "No. You cannot. They are ... unlike anything you know."

"But I do know," she said. "I know they are the creators of our kind, I know they are angels fallen from their first estate. And I also know that I am the one best suited to raise this child. I *must* get her back."

Again he shook his head. "What you ask is madness. They will kill you."

"How do you know?"

"Can you think of a reason they wouldn't?" He stood and began to pace. "A barely sired vampire wants to take their greatest possession from them?" He laughed. "Do you really expect them to hand her over to you?"

"I am her family. Her blood."

"None of that matters to the Cast—" He frowned. "The ancients. None of it. You would do yourself a favor to forget this child."

She jumped up. "Forget my grandchild? You are insane. Don't you have any family? Isn't there anyone you would fight for?"

He stopped pacing to glare at her. "I spent my life in the service of the nobles, only to give that life to them in exchange for this new one. The only family I've ever known has done nothing but take from me. Take and take and take some more."

Slightly surprised, she softened her tone. "I am sorry about that. No one should have to live that kind of life."

With a sigh, he collapsed into his chair again. "I apologize for raising my voice. I shouldn't burden you with my troubles, but I cannot see any outcome with the nobles that gives you the result you want. They are *hard* creatures. Frightening. Capricious. They are the father of our race and yet they treat us more like disposable playthings than children." His eyes met hers. "I worry for you. I have come to care for you in my own way, and I suppose that makes me foolish because we've known each other such a short time, but that is who I am. I wouldn't want anything to happen to you."

"That's very kind of you, Octavian." It warmed her heart to know she'd affected him so deeply in so few days. If she actually had. "But I cannot pretend my grand-daughter never exists. I cannot turn my back on her."

He nodded. "I understand."

"Then help me find a way to get her back."

"I will think on it. That is as much as I can promise right now."

"Think quickly." She sat back, her patience nearly at its end. "Luciano believes you murdered one of the employees at Seven. I told him you and I left early, that there was no way you could have been involved." She tipped her head and gave him her coldest stare. "Please, don't make me out to be a liar."

"I know it's late," Chief Vernadetto said. "I'm sorry to disturb you, but I have news I thought you'd both want to hear."

Doc nodded. "We appreciate your keeping us in the loop." The chief was a good man and whether or not he was doing this because of Fi, Doc didn't know, but it felt nice to catch a break once in a while.

"Totally, Pete," Fi added.

Isaiah set coffee cups in front of him and Vernadetto, then served Fi a cup of tea. He added sugar and a creamer to the table. "Anything else?"

"No, that's all. Thanks." Doc waited until Isaiah left before responding to the chief. He gave Fi's leg a little squeeze under the table.

Fi blew on her tea. "What did you find out?"

Vernadetto stirred sugar into his coffee. "As Fi knows, I dug a little deeper on Remo, but found nothing that led me to believe he was involved in his sister's death. However, we have now identified the source of the silver. A dealer down on Agramonte."

Doc turned his cup. Fi had told him about Vernadetto's info on Remo. "So? Whom did the dealer sell to?"

"That's the tricky part. This dealer is a remnant, part fae, and didn't want anything to do with this death. Claims not to remember much about the sale other than that the silver was picked up and paid for in cash by a messenger service. From that messenger, who also mysteriously can't remember any details, we were able to get one piece of information. He says one of your council members bought the silver."

Beside him, Fi stiffened. She shook her head and Doc noticed her hand was trembling. "No. I can't believe either of them would have anything to do with this."

Vernadetto dropped his head a little. "I'm sorry, Fiona. It's always hard when the news hits so close to home." He sighed. "I'm sorry, but I have to take Barasa and Omur down to the station for questioning. I just wanted to let you know first out of courtesy."

"I can't believe this." Doc stared at his coffee without really seeing it. "They've been so loyal." He shook his head. This wasn't the news he'd wanted to hear. "That probably doesn't help, does it?"

Vernadetto shifted uncomfortably. "You shouldn't say anything more. You'll be called to testify and I don't want to know more than I need to."

Doc nodded, swamped with heat. The two he'd trusted most. Losing either of them would hurt, but what if they'd been in it together? He couldn't believe it. What would Remo's father do when he found out his daughter had been murdered? The weight of it all pressed down on his shoulders, nearly bending him forward. Somehow, he held on and kept the witch fire at bay. "So that's it then."

Pushing his full cup gently away, Vernadetto stood. "Yes. I'm sorry."

"So am I." Without another word, Doc got up and walked away, leaving Fi and Vernadetto to say their goodbyes. He didn't stop until he got to the master bath, and then he shut the door behind himself and stepped into the massive marble shower.

Even with all Barasa had taught him about controlling the fire within him, there was only so much Doc could do, only so long he could keep a lid on what burned inside him. Not with the stress that seemed to grow at every turn.

At last alone, he erupted into flames.

Chapter Twenty-nine

C reek leaned against the door of Octavian's sports car as the vampire approached. His eyes silvered almost immediately, a pretty good indicator he wasn't happy to see Creek. "Something happening?"

Creek pushed off the car. "Just checking in to see how things are going with the mayor."

"I report to Annika. She knows how things are going."

He reached for the car door, but Creek blocked his path. "Can't a fellow KM be interested in how another operative is doing?"

"I'm doing fine. Your concern is noted, but unnecessary."

Creek stayed put. "I heard you and Lola hit Seven the other night. How was that? You two have a good time? Bond over a couple of cold ones?" He laughed. "I guess for vampires that would be a couple of warm ones."

Octavian stared at him. "What do you want?"

"Just a little conversation. One operative getting to know another." Creek dropped his grin. "What did you do there? Dance? Gamble? Taste some of that comarré blood? Maybe knock some heads together? Put a stake in someone's heart?"

"I've had enough of this." Octavian reached for the door handle again. This time when Creek stepped into his path, Octavian shoved him out of the way.

Creek grabbed Octavian's arms and threw him to the ground, then shoved his elbow down onto Octavian's throat, crushing bones. Octavian growled, but he stayed down. Creek calculated the time it would take to reach his weapons. "Did you kill Katsumi?"

"Get off me," Octavian wheezed.

Creek leaned in with more pressure. "Yes-or-no question."

"Screw you." Octavian stared daggers at Creek. "This is what the KM gets for hiring convicts. I outrank you, tribe. I can have Una's scholarship pulled. Think about that."

"So you read my file." With his free hand, Creek whipped his crossbow out from underneath the car, where he'd stashed it loaded and ready earlier. He pressed the tip to Octavian's chest. "Did you also read about how lies make my finger twitch?"

A little of the bravado drained from Octavian's face. "You wouldn't kill me. Annika would have your head."

"Annika sent me." He took his elbow off Octavian's throat and stood, tapping his fingernail against the crossbow's titanium frame, making a pinging sound. "Plus, I really enjoy killing vampires. The way they go poof into a cloud of ash? I can't get enough of that."

Octavian swallowed. "Yes, I killed her. It was necessary to the mission. She threatened to expose my cover."

Creek let the crossbow drop an inch. "See? That wasn't so hard, was it?"

Octavian jumped up and brushed the dirt off his suit, his anger returning fast. "If you think Annika isn't going to hear about this, you're dead wrong, you son of—"

Creek lifted his crossbow, pulled the trigger, and sank the bolt into Octavian's shoulder.

Octavian staggered back. "What the hell?" His knees buckled as the laudanum took effect.

"Lies *and* threats make my finger twitch. I always forget to mention that." Creek retracted the bow and tucked it away. "And don't worry, Annika's definitely going to hear about this." He pulled his phone out of his jacket pocket and hit STOP on the recording app, then held the phone up for Octavian to see. "Got it all right here. Now you just go to sleep and I'll be sure to keep you in a nice safe place until she decides what to do with you."

Octavian slumped against the side of the car, mumbling something.

Creek started the recorder again. "What was that?"

"I'm going to kill you..."

"Great, got it, thanks." Creek stuck the phone back in his pocket. "I'll make sure to tell her that, too."

"I'm going with you." Radiating brotherly protection, Damian leaned against the door frame of Chrysabelle's room.

"I appreciate that you want to, but you can't. Rennata will strip your signum off just like she did mine. I'm not letting that happen." She packed a small bag with a change of clothes. "This is really something Mal and I need to take care of once and for all. Besides, who will take care of the house and Amylia? I need you here."

"You need me with you. I can handle Rennata. Velimai can take care of the house and Amylia can take care of herself." He shook his head. "I'm serious, Chrys. I need to be there with you."

Chrysabelle wanted to argue, but she smiled instead. If this was how the big brother thing worked, she was okay with that. It was sweet, really. She left her packing to take hold of his crossed arms. "It's nice that somebody else wants to watch over me."

"That's what family does. Except you won't let me do it."

"Just in this instance. You can watch over me all you want when I get back. But you have to stay here. Trust me on this, I know best."

His frown deepened. "I don't like your going alone."

"I'm not going alone. I'm going with Mal."

He grunted. "You're going to the Primorus Domus alone."

"Yes, but I know what to expect now." She returned to her bag, zipping it shut. "I won't be spending a lot of time there. Just a few words with Rennata, and then I'm going to hide in the lower levels of Tatiana's estate until Mal is ready to strike. We've got it all worked out, I promise."

Jerem stuck his head in. "Plane's ready." He nodded at her bag. "Want me to load that?"

"Sure, thanks. Is Mal coming back from the freighter or are we picking him up on the way?"

Jerem grabbed the bag. "Picking him up."

"Let's go then." She kissed Damian's cheek as she passed. "We'll be fine." She gave his arm a squeeze. "But feel free to pray."

Within an hour, she and Mal were on board the plane and the pilot and copilot she'd hired were completing their preflight check. Mal took her hand as they sat side by side. "Nervous about going back to the Primorus Domus?"

"Yes. Obviously, my history with Rennata isn't good, but as I'm no longer under her control, there's not much she can do. Except not let me in."

His eyes narrowed. "I like the new look."

She plucked at the gray leather jacket and black jeans she'd chosen. "Fi's influence mostly." The top was one of her comarré tunics, picked especially for its ability to hide her belly. She rested her arm on top of his, twining her fingers between his. "I know you're going to fight me on this, but you need to feed. You need your strength for this trip."

His jaw tensed and she could feel a protest coming on. She spoke before he could argue. "Listen to me. I know you're worried that you're going to be taking blood from the baby, but I'm not tired and my body is producing plenty. I'd know if it weren't." She smiled sweetly. "Besides, we both know there's no point in arguing, because I will nag you until you break."

He snorted. "That's a given." He twisted to splay his hand across her rounding stomach. "Protecting you and this child are my main priority, so even if you think I'm going to protest, I'm not. I've already lost the ability to go to smoke since I haven't fed from you. Going against Tatiana and Lilith means I have to be at a hundred percent. If you think I can feed without harming the baby, then I trust you."

She raised her brows. "Are you feeling okay? That really doesn't sound like you."

He mocked an injured look. "Hey, I can change."

"Yes, but change with you isn't usually this good." A sly smile crept over her face and she bit her bottom lip. "Remember the last time you drank from me?"

His eyes shimmered silver. "Yes. You ended up pregnant."

"No chance of that happening again." She stood, grabbed his hand, and pulled him to his feet.

"Where are we going?"

"The bedroom. We've got time to kill anyway." She laughed, walking backward down the aisle.

"Is that what I am to you? Just a way to pass time?" His voice was low and teasing and sent a shiver down her spine. He pulled her up against him, cupping her body close. Leaning down, he nipped her ear. "I missed you."

"I missed you too." She cradled his face in her hands. "Don't leave me again. Swear it."

"I won't. I promise." He kissed her. "This time when we come home, we're not leaving. This is our last trip to Corvinestri. We're a family now and no one is going to interfere with this chance at happiness."

He looked her square in the eyes. "No one."

Fi found Doc sitting on the floor of the shower, flames dancing over his body, his head in his hands and his back against the wall. "Baby? You okay?" She'd thought the fire thing was under control. Apparently not.

"I can't believe this is happening. I don't *want* to believe Barasa or Omur is to blame for this. They've supported me throughout this whole mess, supported you and supported us being together, but I guess that support went too far."

He raised his head, then held his hand out and stared

at the blue fire shimmering over his skin. "And now you know the witch's curse never left me." He stood and punched his fist into the shower wall, cracking the marble. "Damn it. What kind of man am I to drag you into all this?"

"Stop it," she yelled. "You didn't drag me anywhere. I came willingly. Because I love you. I've always come willingly when you're concerned. Where we're concerned. This isn't about you; it's about us. Don't you dare fall apart on me." She blew out a hard breath. "And don't you dare punch that shower again. I love that shower."

He snorted, shaking his head. "You're crazy."

"I'd have to be to be with you, wouldn't I?"

He nodded. "I guess so." He leaned his head against the wall. The flames seemed like they were getting smaller. "What am I going to do about Barasa and Omur? Just the fact that they're being taken in for questioning will make them guilty in a lot of people's eyes."

She raised her brows. "Do you think they're guilty?"

With a long sigh, he shook his head. "I don't know. I don't want them to be, but what if they are? They had access. They had motive."

She came closer, but stopped before the shower's threshold. "Hire that retired JAG lawyer who was at the cocktail party and get him down there ASAP. As soon as he can get Barasa and Omur bailed out, we need to sit down together and figure this out."

He squeezed his eyes shut, his face a mask of concentration. A second later, the flames went out. He got up, walked out of the shower, and kissed her forehead. "I don't know what I'd do without you."

She punched him lightly. "Yeah, you're a lucky guy."

He laughed. "That's for damn sure."

She went up on her tiptoes and kissed him back. "Too bad Remo wasn't one of your council members sooner or they'd be hauling him downtown too."

Doc's mouth came open and he stared at her like she'd just said something crazy smart. Then he snagged her hand and started leading her out of the bathroom. "You're a genius."

"I am?"

"My council members. Fritz. Don't you get it? Fritz was a council member, but he quit because he was loyal to Sinjin. If anyone knows who might have wanted to kill Heaven, it's him. As soon as I call that lawyer, I'm going to talk to him."

"But I thought he moved out after he quit?"

"He did, but no one ever really leaves the pride." He winked at Fi. "Or I guess I should say, the pride never really leaves them."

Chapter Thirty

Creek would have been lying if he'd said he didn't enjoy trussing Octavian up like a pig for a roast. He cranked the winch one more time, lifting the vampire into the air in the center of the machine shop. He knew living in this place would come in handy someday. Being able to hang Octavian off the old pulley system was a great way to keep track of him.

Swinging gently in the air, Octavian mumbled something. Apparently, the laudanum was starting to wear off.

"Sorry, can't hear you through the gag. I'd take it off, but you threatened to kill me so getting close to your fangs seems like a bad idea." He locked the chain in place, then stood in front of Octavian, staring up at him. "Annika will be here soon, so just hang in there. No pun intended." He laughed. "Okay, maybe a little bit."

The metal door behind him squealed. He turned to see Annika coming in. Her gaze was aimed at Octavian. "What the hell is this? Get him down right now."

"Sector Chief, good to see you." He imagined the eyes hidden behind her permanent shades were probably glaring at him now.

"I said get him down." She didn't bother shutting the door behind her, just stood there, hands on her hips, waiting.

"Listen to this first." He pulled out his phone and played the recording he'd made.

She took it all in, her expression changing very little. When it was over, she pointed to Octavian. "Get the gag out of his mouth. I need to talk to him."

Creek unhitched the chain and lowered Octavian to the floor, then carefully removed the gag. He tossed it aside and stepped back. "He's all yours."

Octavian rolled his shoulders. "You're going to pay for this, you stupid—"

"Octavian, enough," Annika snapped. "Killing a vampire without orders is a breach of conduct. Such a death can only create issues for all involved. You know how these things can affect—"

"She was going to blow my cover," Octavian argued.

"You shouldn't have gone to Seven in the first place." Annika scowled. "And you had no order to kill her. You broke a rule."

Octavian shook his head slowly and began to laugh. "I am so tired of your rules and regulations. I've given my life to the KM and what did I get back? Heartache. I was forced to betray the woman I loved and now I'm stuck in this dump of a city? I don't think so."

For a moment, his body seemed to ripple, and then he burst apart into a swarm of clicking metal scarabs. The tiny gunmetal wings whirred through the air as his restraints fell to the ground. The cloud of beetles streamed out through the open door and into the night.

"Stop him," Creek yelled. "Turn him to stone." But it was too late. Octavian was gone.

Annika shook her head. "Wouldn't have worked. I couldn't make eye contact." She ground her teeth in frustration. "Bring him in alive. Do nothing else until that's accomplished." She started to leave, then stopped. "Let the mayor know Octavian is now considered a threat. Tell her whatever you like, but don't disclose that he's KM."

Creek nodded. "Will do."

"One more thing."

"Yes?"

"Watch yourself. If he stays in the city, I'm sure you'll be a target."

"Where else do you think he'd go?"

She frowned as her wings unfurled. "Back to Tatiana. That's why we need him contained."

Lola dropped her head back and licked her lips. "Thank you," she sighed.

Hector nodded and smiled, holding his wrist up with a handkerchief pressed to the bite mark she'd left behind. "It is my pleasure." He stayed at her side.

She lifted her head enough to look at him. "Something else?"

"Are you pleased with me? With my blood, I mean?"

She nodded. "Of course." The taste had changed, but Luciano claimed that was nothing to be concerned with so she'd let it drop. In fact, Hector's blood seemed to invigorate her more than usual these days. "Is there a reason I shouldn't be?"

"No, my lady. I just always want to make sure you're happy with me. That's all." With a little dip of his head, he went to the end of the sofa and took up his usual spot.

A strange buzzing, clicking sound distracted her from any further thought on the subject. "What is that?"

Hector shook his head. "Sounds like bees, my lady. Do you want me to shut the windows?"

"No, it's such a nice night, I love having them—" A swarm of something spilled into the room and a dark form appeared before her. "What in the hell!" She jumped off the sofa. Octavian stood in the middle of her home office. "How did you do that?"

"It's called scattering. Some vampires can do it, some can't." He pointed at Hector. "Leave us."

Hector looked at her for direction. She stood her ground. "He goes nowhere until you tell me what this is about."

Octavian looked peeved, but so what. She was driving this bus. He made an unhappy noise. "I've done some *thinking*, like you asked me to."

That hadn't taken nearly as long as she'd thought it would. "In that case...Hector, give us a few minutes." She sat back down while he left. "So. How do I contact these ancients?"

"Forget them. They've given your child to another vampire to raise."

"What?"

"I can take you to her."

Lola stood. "When can we leave?"

"Do you have access to a private plane? We can't go commercial, obviously."

"I can find one."

He nodded. "As soon as you can arrange it, we can leave."

She clutched the back of the nearest chair. "I could be meeting my grandchild by this time tomorrow."

"That's right. Imagine being able to hold her for the first time. Being able to bring her home."

Her hands were trembling. "At last. This is what I've been working for."

"What you've sacrificed for," he added.

"Thank you, Octavian." She'd misjudged him. "I owe you."

He smiled. "Just seeing you with her will be payment enough." The smile vanished. "I'll be at the private airport waiting. Get that plane as fast as you can and meet me there. The longer it takes, the less chance we have of making this happen."

She was about to ask why when he scattered again and flew out the window.

Tatiana's home was enormous, but Mal also knew it was the Dominus estate. Its size and grandeur came because of its status, not from the vampire who currently lived in it. Still, to think that the woman who'd once been his human wife, a woman who'd eked out her living by stealing and conning, a woman who'd ended up on the gallows to pay for her crimes, now resided in a mansion that could house hundreds... He shook his head. There was no justice in the world. He was certainly proof of that. *Loser loser loser.*

He snorted softly. The voices were really having a hard time adjusting to his old self being gone. He almost felt sorry for them. Almost.

Having to pretend to be on her side was going to be undiluted torture, but if it meant a safe future for his family, he would play his part with every ounce of imagination he had. He reached for the heavy door knocker, then paused. Old Mal wouldn't knock.

Hefting his bag in one hand, he shoved the door open and walked inside. "Tatiana," he bellowed as he walked through the main hall. "Where are you?"

A moment later, a female servant ran into the room. "May I help you?"

"Who are you? Where's Tatiana?"

"I'm Kosmina, my lord. My lady is in her study. If you'll just wait a moment—"

He walked past her. "Which way?"

She hurried to catch up with him. "I'd be happy to get her for you. Who did you say you were?"

Farther down the hall, a door opened and Tatiana stepped out. She raised her brows, but her surprise quickly turned into a smirk. "I was beginning to think you weren't coming."

"Well, you were wrong. As usual."

Kosmina went to Tatiana's side. "I'm sorry, my lady. He just barged in and—"

Tatiana held her hand up. "It's fine. I'd expect nothing less from him." She strode toward him, sashaying her hips in that way of hers, a not-so-subtle smile playing on her lips. "So happy you decided to join me. I'd hate to put you on my naughty list again."

He grabbed her hand as she reached for him. "Let's get one thing straight. I'm not here for you. I'm here for the payoff. Understood?"

"Just like the old days." She laughed, wrapping her fingers around his. "If that's what gets you through, it's all right with me."

Kosmina cleared her throat. "Is there anything I can do for you, my lady?"

"Yes," Tatiana purred, never taking her eyes off Mal. "Take Lord Bourreau to the guest suite. The one in the north wing." She slipped her hand from his, only to trail her fingers down his arm. "I own a comarré. I'll send her in to feed you."

That was news to Mal. "Why do you own a comarré?"

The mirth left her face and her eyes silvered. "She belonged to my late consort. And since he won't be needing her anymore…" She smiled again but it was noticeably forced. "Consider her my gift to you."

"You know I can't drink from the vein." Unless it was Chrysabelle's. He had no intention of trying that feat on anyone else. Just the idea of drinking another's comarré's blood felt like cheating, especially after being with her on the plane. All for the cause, he reminded himself.

She shrugged. "Bleed her, then." She waved her hand as she walked back to her study. "Be back here in one hour. We have much to discuss." She snapped her fingers. "Kosmina, our guest."

"Yes, my lady." But Kosmina answered to a closed door. She curtsied toward Mal. "If you would just follow me, Lord Bourreau. Shall I take your bag, sir?"

He wanted to say no, that it was ridiculous for a woman to carry his bag, but that wasn't the proper response. He tossed his bag in her direction, inwardly cringing at his actions.

She caught it, but just barely. "Very good, sir."

He followed her to his quarters, noting they were only two halls away from Tatiana's. He would have liked more space between them.

Kosmina opened the door and went in, dropping his bag on the bed. "Shall I unpack you, sir?"

"No." The room was everything he'd expected it to be. Completely overdone and stuffed with priceless antiques and art. Tatiana must have wept with joy when she'd been able to move in here.

The servant didn't leave. "H-Have you known Lady Tatiana long?"

Interesting. And brave. He studied the fresco on the ceiling. Blue sky, white clouds, darting swallows. Vampires loved to remind themselves of what they'd lost, didn't they? "Since she was human."

Kosmina's eyes went wide. "Are you *Malkolm* Bourreau? But that means you're..."

He turned to face her. "That's right. I'm Tatiana's husband."

Chapter Thirty-one

Chrysabelle hoped Mal was having better luck than she was. Rennata may have allowed the comarré here to let her in, but she had yet to show. So far, she'd kept Chrysabelle waiting for almost half an hour. Maybe she wasn't coming out at all. Maybe this was some strange new punishment. Chrysabelle got off the couch and walked toward the passageways that led back into the heart of the Primorus Domus. Could she still access those halls or did becoming disavowed change that?

"Thinking about visiting your old cell?"

She turned at the voice. "There you are, Rennata. I was beginning to think you weren't coming."

"I shouldn't have." Rennata stared at her with more hauteur than Chrysabelle thought possible in one woman. "I had to see for my own eyes that you dared come back here. Your sense of what's appropriate astounds me."

"Get off your high horse, Rennata. A bigger problem exists than me being in your precious house. An *actual* threat. A vampire greater than any other that has ever been created has arisen out of the ranks of the ancients. The kind of vampire that makes other nobles fear for their existence." She paused to let the information sink in. "The time has come for the comarré to rise up and join forces against this new vampire."

Rennata was quiet for several seconds, and then her face cracked into laughter. "Oh, give me a moment to catch my breath." She wiped at her eyes. "You do live such a drama-filled life, Chrysabelle. How do you manage to always be in the center of so much excitement?"

Chrysabelle strode forward and grabbed her by the shoulders. "This isn't a joke, you foolish old woman. You know Tatiana's vampire baby, Lilith? I'm sure you've heard of her. The ancients decided to feed her their blood and in doing so, turned her into a full-grown monster."

Rennata batted her away. "Take your hands off me. If that was true, why wouldn't I know about it? We know about Lilith of course, but she's a baby."

"If the ancients don't want it known, why would you?" Chrysabelle's insides felt like fire. All her life she'd been trained for the moment of uprising, knowing it would come, just not knowing when. Now Rennata was acting like the threat of Lilith was no threat at all. "What must be done to alert the rest of the comarré?"

Rennata narrowed her eyes. "Nothing. Because we're not going to alert the rest of the comarré. You're going to leave and be thankful you're getting out of here without a scratch on you." She lifted her chin. "Remember that, because it won't happen again."

"No, it won't, because I'd kill you first this time." Chrysabelle leaned in. "Try me. I killed a fae a few days ago just for being in love with me."

Rennata jerked back. "You've lost your mind."

Chrysabelle turned and started toward the right-hand corridor. A cluster of comarrés stood there watching, but scattered like mice at her approach. "Maybe. I'll let the Aurelian decide."

Dead silence for a heartbeat. "You are insane. How dare you visit her when you're disavowed."

Chrysabelle kept going. "She's already tried to kill me." She patted the hilt of one sacre standing over her shoulder. "But I've learned to anticipate."

Rennata raced to join her. "You can't do this. I won't allow it."

"Put your hands on me and you'll regret it." She stopped outside the carved double doors that guarded the house's portal to the Aurelian. Every comarré house had one, but few comarré ever used it. They were taught to fear the Aurelian, to respect her for her age and wisdom and her part in the creation of the comarré, whatever that might be.

Chrysabelle put her hand on the door, then gave Rennata one last chance. "You coming? Why not let the Aurelian decide this?"

"I don't take my orders from her." Rennata's angry words sliced through the hall's quiet.

Chrysabelle shrugged. "If you're not curious..." She pushed through the door.

Rennata followed. "I'm only coming to keep an eye on you."

"Suit yourself." As soon as the door swung shut, a flash of light flooded the space. Chrysabelle blinked. And met the Aurelian's eyes.

"You." Nadira rose from her chair. "I thought I killed you."

Rennata glanced at Chrysabelle, then immediately dropped to her knees. "She barged past me. I couldn't—"

"Quiet," Nadira snapped. She walked out from behind her worktable, laden with scrolls, maps, books, and an assortment of objects, but kept her hand on the hilt of the massive sword resting atop the whole mess. "I said I thought I killed you."

"You did," Chrysabelle answered. She hooked her thumbs in her pockets, pushing back the sides of her leather jacket so the twin daggers at her waist could be seen. "But death doesn't seem to stick to me ever since I melted down the ring of sorrows and used that gold to replace the signum Rennata stripped out of my back."

Nadira's mouth came open. She closed it slowly, swallowing. "You foolish child. No wonder you didn't die." Her fingers tightened around the sword's hilt. "What do you want of me?"

Chrysabelle smiled. It was nice to hear a little bit of fear in the Aurelian's voice. "I'm so happy you asked."

Doc parked his car a few streets away, praying to Bast that the alarm system kept it from being jacked. In this part of town, there were no guarantees. He checked the address on his phone again, hoping the file on Fritz was up to date.

He climbed the four flights to apartment E. There were voices coming from inside—sounded like an argument— but the building wasn't exactly built for privacy, meaning too many other conversations overlapped. Picking out more than a few words was impossible. He knocked twice, then waited.

A few moments later, Fritz came to the door. Behind

wire-rimmed glasses, his eyes widened. "Maddoc Mays." He almost shouted Doc's name. "What are you doing here?" Still too loud for normal conversation.

Weird, but then Fritz was an odd dude. "I'm not here to hurt you, if that's what you think. No need to freak out. I just want to talk."

Fritz didn't budge. The door was only open about eight inches. He glanced to the side of the room Doc couldn't see, his body language twitchy and nervous. "We can talk right here."

The dude needed to calm down. "I'd like to come inside. I've already told you I'm not going to hurt you."

"I don't want to—" The sound of breaking glass came from inside.

"Are you in trouble?" Doc didn't wait for an answer. He shoved Fritz out of the way and ran inside. Every room was visible from the apartment's tiny living room. The kitchen window had been broken.

Doc ran over and looked through the window. He caught the top of a head as someone made their way down the fire escape. The person wore a ball cap and was dressed in all black. The lack of streetlights made it impossible to make out more detail. He dashed back to the front door and past Fritz. "Call the cops. I'll catch the intruder."

He shifted into leopard form halfway down the first flight of steps. By the time he got out of the building and turned down toward the alley where the fire escapes ended, the intruder was disappearing out the other end.

Doc poured on the speed, pushing himself through the dark streets as fast as he could go. What few solars existed in this part of town were mostly broken. The runner smelled like varcolai, but that was all Doc could make out. Finally, he got close enough to swipe one big paw across the intruder's back, tearing through his jacket and shirt. Blood welled from the four thin slices.

The man glanced back. A bandana covered his nose and mouth. There was no way Doc could ID him from the sliver visible between the ball cap and fabric. When the man saw Doc, he leaped into the air, shifted into a jaguar, and blasted forward. Police cars barreled down the street ahead of them, screeching to a stop as they blocked the road. The jaguar sailed past the cops as they jumped out of their cars.

One stepped into Doc's path, tranq gun pointed right between his eyes. "One move and I drop you."

Doc shifted back to his human form, pointing after the intruder. "Damn it. That's the one you want, not me."

The cop took one hand off the tranq gun to click a receiver button on his collar. "Suspect has been apprehended."

"Cripes. I had the cops called. I'm not the one you're after," Doc explained.

Both hands back on the gun, the cop ignored him. "Sir, you have the right to remain silent. Anything you say can and will be used against you in a court of law..."

"When are we going to meet her?" Lola paced the hangar. Being in Romania felt no different than being in New Florida. Not yet anyway.

Octavian scowled. "I told you, as soon as the sun sets and the car service can take us into the city. Your impatience won't make that happen any faster."

"I can't take this waiting. I want to go get her now. She

could be in trouble, she could be hurt, she could be—" Lola stopped. "Do you think she senses I'm here?"

"Shut up," Octavian snarled. "Your incessant talking is driving me mad."

"How dare you speak to me that way? I'm still your employer, you—"

Eyes silver, he backhanded her, cracking her lip and knocking her back a few steps. "I told you to be quiet and if you haven't figured out that you're not the one in charge by now, then you're dumber than you look."

She put a hand to her face, but the pain there was nothing compared to the anger building in her heart. The coppery flavor of her own blood coated her tongue. "I should—"

"You should do nothing if you want your grandchild back."

She nodded, fuming inside and planning his demise. Once she had Mariela.

His eyes gleamed with a determination she hadn't seen before. "You will be quiet and do as you're told. Understand?"

She nodded again. She understood that when she had Mariela safe in her arms and they were back in Paradise City, she would turn him over to Luciano. If she didn't kill him herself. Octavian had to be the one who'd killed Katsumi. Clearly, he was capable of it. And now, here she was, trapped with him in this strange place. Only the thought of rescuing Mariela kept her from attacking him.

When the car arrived after sunset, she got in when Octavian told her to, sat where he said to, and kept her mouth shut. She hadn't become mayor by being stupid but if that's what he wanted to think, let him. Throughout her political career, many men had underestimated her: opponents who had fallen short as the tallied votes came out in her favor, as her initiatives were passed and her ordinances put into action.

She watched Octavian, waiting for the first sign of weakness. Maybe she wouldn't wait until they were back in Paradise City. Maybe all she'd turn over to Luciano was ashes.

Chapter Thirty-two

A report on Creek's scanner app had led him to this section of town, but the soft *whuffs* of an animal in pain stopped him. He crept down the alley, almost to the end before he saw the creature. Behind a stack of trash cans and recycling bins lay an enormous spotted cat. It sprawled on its side, panting hard. Creek turned on his flashlight and scanned the animal's body. Four narrow parallel gashes marked its back. The report about a burglary in progress lost its appeal.

The creature growled at him. Creek lifted the hand not holding the flashlight and backed up a step. "Easy there, not an enemy. You need help?"

The growling stopped, replaced with another *whuff*.

"I have no idea what that means. You want me to call an ambulance? Or a vet? I don't know what you varcolai do in cases like this." He flicked the light over the gashes again. They looked smaller.

He nodded. "I get it. You're healing. You just want to be left alone, right?" He started to back out of the alley. "No worries. I was looking for someone else anyway."

He cut out of there, but found a spot across the street to

park himself. The blood scent was bound to draw fringe; the least he could do was keep them off the shifter. Over the next few hours, a few drifted into the alley, but they retreated to the sounds of menacing snarls. The shifter obviously didn't need his help. Creek was about to head out when a man limped out of the alley. Creek didn't recognize him, but snapped a few pics on his phone anyway. In this town, sometimes things were exactly what they seemed, and sometimes they weren't. He hung a while longer, hoping the lingering blood scent might even lure Octavian, but no such luck.

He resumed his patrol route. Might be time to pay Dominic a visit, let him know what had happened with Octavian. Creek had no desire to step foot into Seven, but Dominic wasn't the kind of man to take a death like Katsumi's easily. He probably already had his own people working on it. Damn it. That might mean Luciano.

Creek turned back toward his apartment and broke into a run. He needed his bike. He had to get to Seven fast. Better Dominic found out about Octavian from him than discover it on his own and take matters into his own hands.

A vampire set on revenge was a very dangerous thing.

"I'm here for a very good reason, Nadira." Chrysabelle addressed the Aurelian like an old friend, something she definitely wasn't, but Chrysabelle had learned from Mal that throwing people off guard was a great way to keep them guessing. Plus, it helped mask her fear. The Aurelian might not be able to kill her again, but that wouldn't stop Nadira from trying. "The Castus have raised a monster that sets even the nobles on edge. I want the comarré alerted so this new threat can be dealt with swiftly. The moment for them to rise up has come."

Nadira relaxed, but only slightly. "What monster is this? I've heard nothing."

"The vampire baby. They fed her their blood and grew her into some kind of super vampire."

Nadira nodded, dropping her head for a moment. "I did not know they had brought her back into this world."

"You knew about this?" Chrysabelle threw her hands up. "What's being done?"

"Nothing," Nadira answered. "We knew, but there was no sign they would bring her out of the Castus plane and back to the mortal one. You know this for sure, that she's been seen?"

"She killed one of Tatiana's soldiers."

Nadira peered at her, uncertainty in her eyes. "How do you know this?"

"It came from Tatiana's mouth. She told it to someone who wouldn't lie to me."

"Who is that person?"

This was going to go over big. "Malkolm."

Nadira's lip curled. "The vampire who twice dared breach my sanctuary."

Chrysabelle jabbed a shaking finger at Nadira. "The second time it was to save my life. I should kill you myself for what you did." She took a breath, forced herself to calm down. Yelling at the Aurelian wouldn't accomplish the task at hand but it might start a fight. "And in case you're wondering, I found Damian, no thanks to you."

"It was not my place to help you. Those records are sealed for a reason."

Stupid, worthless…she took another calming breath

since the first one hadn't worked. "Are you going to raise the comarré forces?"

Nadira turned and pulled a large book off the shelf behind her, then sat and paged through it. At last, she looked up. "No. This is not the time."

A muscle in Chrysabelle's jaw spasmed in anger and she realized that the fear the Aurelian had once instilled in her was completely gone. With a quiet but determined voice, she spoke. "What good are you, Nadira? You offer me no help. You never have." She slid one of her sacres from its sheath. Rennata inhaled loudly. "I would be well within my rights to consider you my enemy, wouldn't you say? You are an obstacle in my path." She leveled the sword at Nadira. "Do you know what I do to obstacles?"

The rise and fall of Nadira's chest increased. "Rennata, curb your comarré."

"She's mine no longer." Rennata's voice quavered. "She's been disavowed. As you know. As you commanded."

The anger rising through Chrysabelle's body found a level spot and an eerie calm settled over her. A sense of imperviousness came with it. Perhaps that was from the ring of sorrows sewn into her back. "You already know she can't dictate what I do. No one can. That should make you very afraid, because there is nothing keeping me from killing you." She lifted her sacre a little higher. "Unless you'd like to give me a reason not to."

With a gulp, Nadira lifted her hands in surrender. "I-I can help."

"Can you?" Chrysabelle asked. "Because I have yet to see proof of that."

"I will not call upon the comarré to rise, but I can aid you in the fight against your enemies."

"You give me aid? Why should I believe you?"

"I cannot speak lies. You know that."

"No, but too often you speak too little and use twisted words." Chrysabelle tipped her sacre to flash light in Nadira's eyes and stepped forward. Metal met flesh. "What help can you give me? Will it be enough to save your life?"

Squinting, Nadira pulled back against her chair as far as she could to avoid the blade under her chin. "Sheath your weapon."

"No. What help?"

Struggling to look down, Nadira began scrolling through the book still open on her desk. At last she settled on a page. The words were written in a language Chrysabelle couldn't read, but at the center was a beautiful drawing of a tree unlike anything she'd ever seen. "You must lure your enemy to the Garden of Eden, then make her eat of the fruit of the Tree of Life."

"And I'm supposed to find the Garden of Eden how?"

"Move your weapon. Please."

Chrysabelle pulled the blade back a few inches.

Nadira stood, then opened a small drawer in the edge of the table. From it, she retrieved a short dagger.

Chrysabelle whipped her sacre up against Nadira's neck again. Rennata whimpered. Chrysabelle ignored her. "Put the blade down."

Nadira trembled, but held tight to the dagger. "I need it to cut this page from the book."

Chrysabelle eased her sword back. If Nadira was willing to damage one of her precious books this information might actually be worth something.

She cut the page out, tossed the blade away, and

handed the yellowed paper to Chrysabelle. "The signum along the edges will open a portal to the Garden's gates the same way you've used the signum on your back to open a portal to me. The map will guide you to the tree once you're there."

Chrysabelle nodded at the paper. "Roll it up and secure it." Nadira did, then handed it back. The sudden realization of the task before her sank in. "I have to get Tatiana through a blood portal? How is that help?"

Nadira pursed her lips. "You'll figure it out. Steal something from her. She will follow."

Chrysabelle tucked the scroll into her jacket. "I thought humans were banned from entering the Garden. Are you sure I'll be able to enter?"

Nadira started to say something, then shook her head. "You will be able to enter. I give you my solemn vow."

Chrysabelle raised her sacre between them. "And if that vow proves worthless, I will pay you one final visit. Do I make myself clear?" Nadira nodded. Chrysabelle pointed the weapon at Rennata. "You do anything to tip Tatiana or Lilith to this plan and so help me, holy mother, I'll strip the gold from your body the way you did mine. Every. Single. Signum."

Then she sheathed her weapon, spun on her heels, and left them to stare after her as she walked away.

Tatiana sighed. Hades, Mal could be difficult. "What is wrong with you? Was the taste of the comarré that unpleasant?"

Mal cleared his throat and leaned back in his chair. "It was fine."

Not very convincing, but perhaps he didn't like drinking from a secondhand comarré. "Then stop swallowing."

Mal swallowed again, probably just to annoy her. "Can we get back to the subject at hand? I don't believe she killed one of the ancients. It's not possible."

Tatiana twisted her hands in her lap, the metal one reflecting light like a mirror. "I saw the skin around her shoulders with my own eyes. I swear to you, it was real. I've seen them often enough to know what their flesh looks like." She forced herself to sit still. "I told you she was dangerous, but even I had no idea just how much. However..." She leaned forward and dropped her voice. "*They* told me what to do."

"*They*." Mal raised a brow. "As in the ancients."

She nodded. "Proof of how worried they are about her, don't you think?"

For an instant, he looked skeptical. "Absolutely. What did they tell you?"

"We must take her to the Garden of Eden and get her to eat from the Tree of Life."

He stared dumbstruck, then laughed. "And how do we get there? By unicorn? The Garden of Eden is a myth. They're lying to you. Probably trying to see how much you'll fall for."

"It's not a myth." She reached down between her body and the side of the chair and pulled out the scroll Samael had given her. Carefully, she spread it open, revealing the hand-drawn map with the ornately illustrated tree at its center. "They gave me this."

He studied it, nodding once or twice, then leaned in.

"Let's say this really is a map to the Garden and we go there. How do we get in? Isn't it guarded?"

Her nerves settled with the realization that despite his skepticism, he was with her in this. "The ancient one assured me we would be able to enter."

He sat back again, stretching one arm along the back of the sofa. "Then that's the plan. Their word is good enough for me."

She rolled the scroll up and stuck it back down in the cushions. "Are you ready to meet *her*?"

His body language stayed loose and relaxed. "Yes."

He'd better be. There was no turning back after this. She stood and lifted her hands. "Lilith, my darling girl, come to me."

Darkness clouded the room as if someone had dimmed the lights, and then that darkness converged into a human form. From that, a woman-child emerged, shedding the darkness like a butterfly leaving its cocoon. Or a parasite leaving its host. She tipped her head and looked at Tatiana. "Hello, Mother."

"My darling." Tatiana fought to keep her smile in place against a new onslaught of nerves. This had to go well. "I'd like you to meet Malkolm Bourreau, the vampire I was telling you about."

Her attention shifted to Mal. He stood, but kept his distance. He nodded at her. "So you're Lilith?"

She walked toward him. "And you are one of the most fearsome vampires to walk the earth."

The whites of his eyes began to turn black. Tatiana recognized that as a sign of him loosening his hold on the beast inside him. He was showing Lilith who he was. Good. "I've heard that said about me."

Unfortunately, his show of power didn't seem to affect her. Maybe she just didn't realize what it meant. "That's what Mother says." Lilith looked over her shoulder. "Don't you, Mother?"

"Yes," Tatiana answered. "He is the perfect vampire to join our family."

Lilith stuck out her bottom lip. "Why? What makes him better than any other vampire?"

"I didn't say he was better. I said he was perfect for our family." Tatiana wanted to slap her, but refrained out of respect for her own life. "He was my human husband and the father of my mortal child. He knows how to be a father—"

Mal put his hand up. "I'll handle this." He rolled his shirt sleeve back and held his black-inked forearm out. "See those names, Lilith? I am covered with them." He pulled up his shirt, revealing a taut stomach covered with more black script.

Lilith sighed like a bored teenager. "So."

Mal picked his shirt up a little higher, showing off more ink. "Each name represents one of my kills."

Tatiana watched as Lilith's eyes widened and a tiny smile lifted the corner of her mouth. This child she'd once held in her arms was a bloodthirsty savage, something she might have approved of if that savagery wasn't so capricious.

Lilith reached for his skin. "So many . . ."

He tucked his shirt back in before she could touch him. "That's not all. I have the ability to transform myself into a beast owned by darkness. A beast that has taken on and destroyed hordes of Nothos."

Lilith clapped her hands. "Show me."

"No."

Her face fell. "Yes. Now. I want to see."

Mal leaned forward, eyes going dark with the beast. "I said no." The harshness in Mal's voice surprised Tatiana, but then she realized he spoke with the beast's voice too. Her satisfaction level rose. She hadn't expected him to understand so quickly just how firm a hand Lilith needed.

Lilith flopped onto the couch to pout some more.

Just then, someone called Tatiana's name from another part of the house. The sound of it gave her chills. She turned toward it, suddenly trembling. "That voice," she whispered. Her hand went to her throat. "Octavian."

Chapter Thirty-three

Getting into Dominic's office had taken some doing until Creek had run into Mortalis. A little explanation and the fae had escorted him through the crowd without stopping. He even seemed mildly amused when Luciano jumped out of his chair as Creek walked through the door.

Creek held his hands up. "I'm not here to kill you. I just need to speak to Dominic."

Luciano sat back down and Dominic gestured toward the other chair in front of his desk. "Sit."

Mortalis stayed by the door. Creek took the seat. "Thank you for seeing me."

Dominic nodded. "You and I have never had problems." He glanced at his nephew.

Creek smiled. "No, and I'd like to keep it that way. Which is why I'm here." He shifted a little, choosing his words. "I understand you had a death here recently."

"To be clear, a murder. Katsumi Tanaka. She was a good friend and a trusted employee." Dominic's mouth tightened. "What about this brings you here?"

"You have my sympathies." Creek wasn't an idiot. She

was more than a good friend to Dominic. She'd been his lover. He'd cared for her enough to give her *navitas* and raise her from fringe to noble. "I know who killed her."

Dominic's face shifted from human to vampire. "I already know," he growled. "Octavian. He used to be—"

"Tatiana's consort," Creek finished. "How do you know this already?"

"You think I am *stupido*? That I can't find out who comes into my establishment? What they do here? Where they go? I know everything that happens here. Everything."

"I'd expect nothing less," Creek said. Damn it. This was going downhill fast.

Dominic's eyes narrowed. "The question is, how do you know it was Octavian?"

"Because I got him to confess."

"You have him? Where is he?"

Luciano jumped to his feet. "I'll bring him back. Just tell me where he is."

Creek popped his jaw to one side. "That's the problem. I had him tied up, but the sedation wore off and he scattered and escaped so now I'm looking for him too. If we work together, we have a better chance of finding him."

"Agreed." Dominic's face went back to human. "I never thought I'd see the day that a noble vampire and a Kubai Mata would join forces, but I never thought I'd end up anathema, either." He smiled, but the expression held sadness. "I understand you spared my nephew's life as well. For that, I am grateful."

"There's one more thing," Creek said.

"*Si?*"

"I'm under orders to bring him in alive."

Dominic rolled his tongue over his fangs, taking his time before he spoke. "Then I would suggest you find him first."

Mal raced after Tatiana, but Lilith flew past them in a blur, laughing like a child playing games. When he skidded to a stop alongside Tatiana, Lilith already stood in the foyer, assessing the visitors. Son of a priest. What was the mayor doing here? And with Octavian? There was no way this was going to end well. The voices cheered.

"You're dead," Tatiana said. Her face was a frightening blank.

"No, I'm not, my darling." He took a step toward her, but she retreated. "I can explain."

She lifted her metal hand to point at him. "You betrayed me."

Lilith studied the group, gaze flicking from face to face. "Who is this, Mother?"

The question brought a look of contempt to Tatiana's face. "This is Octavian. The one who knew you as a baby. The one who betrayed... *us*."

"As a baby?" Octavian turned toward Lilith, staring at her face. "It can't be. Is this our child?"

Tatiana bent forward, screaming, "She's not your child!"

The mayor shrank back into the corner, her anxious gaze pinned to Lilith. "It can't be," she muttered.

Lilith's eyes went completely bloodred, swallowing up the white. "You." She stalked toward Octavian. "Mother said you were a traitor. That you tried to give me to her enemies. That you're the reason I was taken away from her." Lilith hissed at him, spittle flying from her mouth. "You're a bad vampire. I don't like you."

She grabbed him by his shirt and tossed him against one of the stone columns flanking the doors.

"No," he yelled, but the impact silenced him, crumpling him to the ground in an unnatural heap.

Lilith picked him up again and shook him. "You hurt my mother."

Blood trickled from Octavian's mouth as he tried to lift his head, tried to protest.

Before he managed a word, Lilith opened her mouth and bit down on his limp neck. She yanked back, tearing a section of his throat out and spitting it onto the polished marble flooring.

She dropped his body as it went to ash, and then she turned to Tatiana, gore covering her mouth and chin. Her lower lip trembled. The white had returned to her eyes. "Was that wrong? Are you mad at me again?"

Tatiana looked like she'd gone into shock. She stood there, staring at the space Octavian had just occupied. Her eyes weren't even silver, just hollow and round. "I..." She moved her mouth but no words came out.

Lilith howled, covering her face with her hands. "You *are* mad!" The light shifted with her wails, as if retreating from her. Shadows broke free from the corners of the room and surrounded Lilith in darkness. When they cleared, she was gone.

Tatiana swayed toward Mal, her body collapsing. Mal grabbed her before she hit the ground. Her head lolled back. She was out cold.

"Was that... *creature* my granddaughter?" the mayor whispered.

"Yes," Mal answered. "What are you doing here? Never mind; you need to get out of here. Do you have a car outside?"

She nodded, arms wrapped around herself. "So you're not dead and my granddaughter is a psychotic vampire. You have some explaining to do."

"Later. Have the driver take you back to whatever hangar your plane is parked in and then get on it and go the hell home. Tell no one you came here, what you saw, or anything about me being here. Understand?"

Again, she nodded. Tatiana moaned softly.

"Now," he told the mayor. "Go while you still can."

"This isn't over," she hissed, but she slipped out the door and disappeared into the night. As soon as he heard the car drive away, he yelled for help. "Kosmina!"

Before long, the head of staff came running. "What's wrong?" She gasped when she saw Tatiana in his arms. "What's happened to my lady?"

"Octavian was here." He gestured toward the ash. "But as you can see, Lilith took care of that." And if Lilith was that quick to act, Tatiana was right. She had to be dealt with. He could only imagine what she'd do if she found out there was another vampire child on the way.

Chrysabelle found a spot in the recesses of the wine cellar and settled in. The stacks of crates and barrels hid her completely from anyone approaching. Now all she had to do was wait. She lay down, tucking one arm beneath her head as a pillow. Cold seeped up through the stone floor, making her wish Mal would hurry.

A low whistle opened her eyes. She sighed in frustration. She hadn't meant to fall asleep.

Again, the whistle broke the deep silence of the wine cellar. She pushed to her feet, her body aching a little from lying on the cold ground. Mal had fed from her on the plane, strengthening her with the exchange, but the truth was, being pregnant was using up her reserves faster than normal. She whistled back, soft and low.

"Chrysabelle?" Mal's voice came from farther away.

She slipped out from behind the barrels as he came around the stack of bottles in front of them. She smiled and held her arms out. "I'm so glad you're here. I need you to kiss me."

Without a word, he pulled her into his arms, bent his head, and covered her mouth with his.

Long seconds passed before she broke away. "Thank you. That's already helping."

He gave her a strange look. "Glad to know I can be of service."

She poked him. "I was a little low on energy. Much better now." And she was. One kiss and she felt revitalized. "What's going on up there?"

"A lot. I've met Lilith. Tatiana wasn't lying. She's a nightmare from hell. The mayor and Octavian showed up—"

"Holy mother."

"Indeed. Lilith figured out who he was. Apparently Tatiana told her that Octavian had betrayed them and was the reason she was taken away from Tatiana, so Lilith bit his head off. Literally." Mal grimaced. "Damn, it was nasty. I do *not* want to go like that."

This was so not good. "How did Tatiana take all this?"

"She passed out. Shock, I guess."

"Did Lola pass out too? I don't like that she knows you're alive now. Hopefully she won't try to kill you again."

"I saved her life, so she owes me. After Tatiana passed out, I told the mayor to go back home as fast as she could. She didn't argue, although she expects an explanation. I think seeing what her grandchild has become may have changed her mind about wanting custody of her."

Chrysabelle almost laughed, but then she imagined how devastating that realization must have been for Lola. Family seemed to mean a lot to her. Something Chrysabelle understood. "Where's Tatiana now? Does she suspect anything's changed?"

"She's resting and I promise, she has no idea I'm not on her side." He took Chrysabelle by the arms, staring into her eyes. "How are you holding up?"

"I'm fine." Tired, but still fine. "Anything else?"

"Yes. The ancients met with Tatiana and told her how to deal with Lilith. She's got to eat from the Tree of Life—"

"In the Garden of Eden." Chrysabelle pulled the page from her inside pocket and held it up. "Except I was told Tatiana had to eat from it. I don't know how we're going to get her to go through the portal, though."

He took the map and studied it. "Looks the same as Tatiana's. You won't have to worry about getting her through your portal. She was given instructions for opening her own. She and I will go through that way with Lilith." He stared at her page a little harder. "Who gave you the info about the tree?"

"Same person who gave me the map. The Aurelian.

She wasn't happy about it either. Well, maybe a little. Mostly because I didn't put my sacre through her."

"And now she knows you're alive." Mal frowned. "You trust her? She has no reason to help you."

"Sure, she does. I threatened to kill her." Chrysabelle waved the paper. "She cut this page from one of her books. Seems to me like a good sign she's sincere. Do you trust the ancients?"

"Good point." He squinted at her. "You look tired." He lifted her and set her on one of the upturned barrels. "Rest while you can. No arguing."

"No arguing." A lot of smiling, though. Mal was definitely back to being his usual, protective self. "I guess we have no choice but to get them there and make them both eat from it. How we're going to get Tatiana to eat something she thinks is meant to kill Lilith is beyond me."

Mal leaned against another barrel, but reached over to take her hand. "Leave that to me. I'll make it happen."

"What's our next move, then?"

"You take the plane home, then open your portal there and follow this map. I'll stall Tatiana and Lilith for a day so you can get there ahead of us, and then I'll get them through the portal from here and I'll see you inside the Garden of Eden." He shook his head as he handed the map back. "There's a phrase I never thought I'd use."

"Tell me about it." She tucked the map into her jacket again. "Assuming I can get into the Garden without a problem, I'll find a place near the tree to wait."

"Be safe."

"I will. I promise." She slid off the barrel and tucked her hands into her pockets. "And then, when it's all over, you'll come back with me through my portal."

He stood, threading his arms through hers and kissing her forehead. "I can't wait until we're home again and all this is behind us."

"Me too."

A bottle fell somewhere in the stacks, shattering with a pop. Mal's eyes silvered and he leaped into action, disappearing in a flash of movement. He returned, a woman struggling in his grasp. "We have a spy."

Chrysabelle whipped a blade out and shoved it under the woman's chin. "Who are you?"

"Don't kill me," she begged. "I'm just a servant. I heard nothing."

Mal held her tight. "She's Kosmina, Tatiana's head of staff." He shook his head. "We'll have to kill her."

"No, please. I can help you," Kosmina pleaded.

"Help?" Chrysabelle asked. "How?"

All traces of fear left Kosmina's eyes. "I am..." She lowered her voice. "Kubai Mata."

Chapter Thirty-four

"And that's when they arrested me," Doc finished. He'd given Fi the whole rundown on his evening at Fritz's, which had turned into a day at the police station answering questions, making a statement, then filling Vernadetto in on what had happened.

Fi shook her head. "Unbelievable. I knew something was up when you didn't come home and I couldn't get a hold of you. It was nice of Pete to call me and let me know you were okay."

"Yeah, Vernadetto's not a bad guy."

Fi got a strange look in her eyes. "No, he's not. He's a really decent man, actually." She sighed. "So, any idea who the guy at Fritz's was?"

"I couldn't see him. He was average build and average height. Nothing much to go on, except he was varcolai. Jaguar."

"How many jaguars in the pride?"

He shook his head. "Probably several hundred."

"Crap," she muttered.

"Exactly. And when the cops showed up with their flashing lights, I just didn't get a good enough look." Whoever it had been, they had *not* wanted to be identified.

"But you cut him."

"Yeah, but by now he'd be healed. They weren't that deep, and it's been too long." Doc shrugged. "Vernadetto promised he'd send some guys down to talk to Fritz, see what they can find out. Hopefully we'll hear something soon."

She snuggled against his side and turned the holovision on. "I'm glad you're okay."

He kissed her head. "Thanks, baby."

"Did you see Barasa and Omur when you were there?"

A local news station flickered to life. "No. According to Vernadetto, they've already taken them to the detention center. The lawyer says they're charging them with homicide." He let out a long, unhappy breath. Damn it. Things couldn't get worse.

"It'll be okay. We'll figure something out." She grabbed the remote and started running through the channels.

He gave her a squeeze but said nothing. They both knew her words were empty. An hour into whatever movie she'd picked that he couldn't concentrate on anyway, the phone rang. A minute after it stopped ringing, Isaiah came in.

"Excuse me, Maddoc, but that was Police Chief Vernadetto. He's on his way up."

Fi turned the holovision off and twisted to face him. "I hope he found out something good from Fritz. Not that Fritz has any reason to help us, but he wouldn't lie to the police after you tried to help him, would he?"

"No idea. Never got to know the man. He quit a few days after I became pride leader."

She frowned. "I wish there was something I could do to make this all better."

"Me, too."

The private elevator chimed and Isaiah soon brought Vernadetto in. He nodded in greeting. "Fiona, Maddoc. May I sit?"

"Please." Fi patted the seat beside her, then scooted over closer to Doc.

Vernadetto sat where she'd indicated, adjusting his gun belt as he did. "I sent my best investigators over to speak with Fritz about the incident and see what he could tell them about this situation with Heaven." He inhaled. "Fritz was gone. A few things were missing, enough to indicate he's in the wind."

Doc leaned forward. "We'll find him. The pride has ways of tracking its members."

"Be that as it may, right now Fritz is a dead end." He held up a finger. "However, the officers searched the apartment. They found a wooden box with silver dust in it. Not enough to be measurable, but that's definitely what the container held."

"Are you saying you think Fritz is involved in Heaven's death?" Doc shook his head. "I don't buy it. Fritz was Sinjin's man. He wouldn't have hurt Heaven."

Vernadetto shrugged. "People do a lot of things you wouldn't suspect. Maybe he was just the supplier. We're pulling his financials, digging through his computer, looking for anything to indicate a connection."

"To Barasa and Omur?" Fi asked.

"To anyone," Vernadetto answered.

So much for that, Doc thought. "What about the intruder?"

"No prints on the broken glass other than Fritz's. Unless you think you can work with a sketch artist, we don't have much to go on there." Vernadetto stood. "I wish I had better news, but until something new comes along, that's all I've got."

"Thanks, anyway." Doc stood to walk him out. "How much would it help if you could talk to Fritz?"

"Hard to say. Depends on how much he'd give up. But it's kind of a moot point with him being gone. Until we find him..." Vernadetto shrugged.

"Understood."

After the elevator doors closed, Doc leaned his head against them. He had to find Fritz. But the regular trackers the pride used would take time. Time they didn't have. And if Fritz had left the city, Doc would need someone with a broader scope of influence. There was one person who could access that kind of information. The more Doc thought about it, the more he knew it was the way to go. Sure, he might have to work an angle or two to get the help, but there was a time in his life when he'd been all about angles.

The sounds of the holovision drifted out from the living room. He lifted his head. "Babe?"

"Yes?" Fi called from the other room.

"I have to go out." He grabbed his jacket and tugged it on. "Back as soon as I can."

Lola wrapped herself in a blanket and stayed there as the plane took off, but nothing seemed to stop her body from trembling. Over and over she saw Octavian being killed before her by a woman Malkolm claimed was her granddaughter.

How was Malkolm alive? She'd seen him die on the holovision. Obviously, that had been some kind of trick. What was he doing in Corvinestri now? And why was it such a secret that he was there? Was he in league with her granddaughter?

No, not her granddaughter. A monster. The two didn't mesh in her brain. The images of the infant she'd expected to find and the grown woman she'd seen were so diametrically opposed that there was no way she could reconcile the two.

That couldn't be her Mariela. That…horrific creature was not the sweet, innocent baby Julia had given birth to. "Please," she whispered. "Don't let it be her."

She shuddered again, remembering the red eyes and vicious fangs. There was no way she wanted anything to do with that hell-born thing, even if it was her blood kin. Which it couldn't be. No, this whole thing had to be some sort of…game. Octavian must have set her up. Or Malkolm had, to get his revenge on her. She huddled farther into the darkest corner of the plane. Despite the shades being drawn, she could feel the sun on the verge of rising.

Maybe Preacher would know what to do. Maybe she should confess her sins to him and tell him everything that had happened. Or maybe…she should keep this whole business a secret. One she'd take to her grave.

Covering up with the blanket, she let herself drift into daysleep. It was the only way she knew to forget.

"Bloody hell," Mal growled. "No way you're KM. That's a lie to save your skin." *Kill kill kill*. He shut the voices out enough to hear Kosmina's response.

"No, it's not. I swear." She shook her head. "I can prove it." She looked at Chrysabelle. "Your patron, Algernon, he was a KM agent. Did you know that?"

"Yes. That's how he came to have the ring of sorrows." Chrysabelle caught Mal's gaze. "If she knows that…"

Mal shook his head. "If Algernon was KM, why didn't they come after you? Wouldn't they have thought you had something to do with his death?"

Kosmina shifted uncomfortably. "After a while, the KM knew Chrysabelle wasn't responsible for that."

"After a while?" Chrysabelle asked. "So you were watching me?"

Kosmina shrugged. "The KM has eyes everywhere. And as you know, Octavian belonged to them too. We worked together. He brought me in to replace him as head of staff when Tatiana turned him. I'm the reason Tatiana thought he was dead. I covered for him. Otherwise she would have flayed him alive."

"How did you cover for him?" Chrysabelle asked.

"At the ball, after you two ran out of the suite—that was you two in disguise, wasn't it?"

"Yes," Mal said. Figuring that out didn't take help from the KM. "Go on."

"When Tatiana went after you, Octavian left through the servants' quarters. I scattered ashes on the floor where he'd been and, when Tatiana returned, told her that he'd taken his own life out of fear of her." She drew in a ragged breath. "She would have killed him. It was the only way to get him out safely."

"What about the other female servant?" Chrysabelle asked.

"Oana? She was Lilith's wet nurse. With Lilith out of the picture, Oana was no longer necessary. I paid her to go away." Kosmina glanced at Malkolm. "And she knows I'd kill her myself if she ever spoke a word of what happened."

Mal eased his grip on the double agent. She was telling them more than she had to. Enough that her story sounded genuine. "Why would Octavian come back here? He'd have to know Tatiana would kill him for what he'd done."

Kosmina pulled out of his grasp entirely and tugged her uniform back into place. "Not long after he brought me in to replace him as head of staff, I started to see signs that his loyalties were drifting. He truly loved Tatiana. And the life she provided." She shook her head. "It's not the first time an agent has shifted sides."

"More than once?" Chrysabelle asked. "How long have you been KM?"

Kosmina cast her eyes toward the door to the cellar. "All my life. My whole family is."

"Son of a priest." Mal's brows shot up. How deep was the KM in Corvinestri? "And do they all work for nobles?"

She nodded and lifted her gaze toward Chrysabelle. "We do the job the comarré were meant for, but have fallen away from."

"Don't look at me," Chrysabelle said. "I tried to raise a force to help us and got shot down. Also, I'm not comarré anymore."

"I know," Kosmina said. "We're aware you were disavowed." She started toward the exit. "I have to go. I have things to do before . . . I have things to do."

Mal stepped into her path. He wasn't done asking questions. "Why did you follow me down here?"

Kosmina's expression shifted into one that was pure soldier. "To determine why you were suddenly on Tatiana's side, and if necessary, kill you. Which reminds me…" She pulled a snuffbox out of her pocket and handed it to him. "Put a pinch of that under your tongue."

"You? Kill me?" Mal laughed softly as he took the box and opened it. Fine white powder filled the small metal square. A citrusy aroma wafted up from it. "What is this?"

"The antidote to the *solis basium* currently coursing through your system."

The voices stilled completely. They were trying to figure out if what she said was true. "What the hell is *solis basium*?"

Chrysabelle licked her bottom lip. "Means something like 'sun kiss' in Latin, doesn't it?"

Kosmina nodded. "And without that antidote, you'd find yourself inexplicably drawn to walk outside and greet the dawn tomorrow morning."

Mal snorted skeptically. "There's nothing in my blood. I'd know if you drugged me." *Sick sick sick*, the voices whined. *They* believed her.

"Would you?" Kosmina asked. "Because you drank the comarré's blood without question."

Chrysabelle looked at him. "What comarré?"

"The one Tatiana provided for Octavian," Kosmina answered. "Tatiana offered her to Malkolm so he wouldn't go hungry."

"I didn't drink *from* her," Mal said. "You know I can't do that. But I did let her fill a goblet for me." He could tell this was bothering Chrysabelle. "I had no choice. I didn't want Tatiana to get suspicious."

She nodded, but said nothing.

He looked back at Kosmina. "You're telling me her blood held the drug?"

"Like I said, put a pinch under your tongue and you'll be fine." Kosmina gave him a final glance before heading toward the door.

"Wait," Chrysabelle called. "What about . . . what you heard?"

Kosmina stopped and met her gaze. "The plan to get Tatiana and the other one to the Garden of Eden? I'll help in whatever way I can without blowing my cover, but my time here is short. You don't have to worry about me getting in your way."

"That's not what I meant," Chrysabelle said.

Kosmina shrugged. "That's all I heard. Now I really must go." She left, closing the door behind her.

Chrysabelle's hands shook. "She knows about the baby. She's going to report to whomever she reports to and the KM are going to come knocking again, expecting something from me." Her hands went to her belly. "If they think they can use this child for their purposes, they are sorely mistaken."

Mal nodded. "That's for damn sure." He tipped his head to touch hers. "No one is going to lay a hand on you or this child, understand? I won't let it happen."

She blew out a breath. "I know." She smiled up at him. "I'm okay. Hormones, you know?" She laughed softly. "You should be used to my crazy by now."

"Speaking of crazy, can you believe she drugged me?" He slipped his hand into Chrysabelle's, glad the mood had lightened, but feeling like he owed her a little more explanation. "I know you're not happy that I drank blood from another comarré, but I didn't have much of a choice."

"You'd better take that antidote." Her mouth thinned, but she squeezed his arm. "And you're right. I'm not happy about the other comarré, but I also understand. You did what you had to do." She offered him a wisp of a smile. "It's all for the end game, right?"

"Right." The end game that would finally free them to live a peaceful life raising their child.

Her gaze shifted back to the exit. "When we get back to Paradise City, we need to have a long talk with Creek and come to some kind of understanding."

Mal stuck a pinch of the white powder under his tongue. It tasted like sugar, not much like an antidote to anything. "The only understanding that matters is that they leave us alone. If someone has to die to make that happen, so be it."

Chapter Thirty-five

The knocking on Creek's door fired up his internal alarm system. He wasn't expecting anyone, Annika included. And with Octavian in the wind, there was no such thing as being too cautious. He snapped his crossbow into place, locked a bolt into it, and slid the door back half an inch. "Who is it?"

"Doc. Chrysabelle's friend. The varcolai."

Creek opened the door farther as he dropped the crossbow. "How do you know where I live?"

Doc gave him an odd look as he came in. "You know I'm the leader of the Paradise City pride now, right?"

"Yeah, I'd heard that." Creek slid the door shut, then led Doc to the kitchen. "I take it you're telling me you have access to the kind of people who can find people like me?"

"Actually, all I had to do was ask Chief Vernadetto." Doc looked around the machine shop. "Interesting place to live."

Creek removed the bolt from his crossbow, stored it, then collapsed the bow again so that it resembled a length of titanium pipe. Notching it back onto his holster, he leaned against the counter. "What can I do for you?"

Doc stopped checking out the makeshift apartment to look at Creek. "I need help finding someone and I thought you might have the resources. Mine don't extend much beyond the city. I can call on other prides, but they tend to be territorial and keeping tabs on another pride's business is frowned upon, you dig? Plus, I don't really want to tip my hand that I'm looking for this cat."

Creek nodded. "Sure. Who is this person?"

"Name's Fritz Haber. He was one of Sinjin's council members, but quit when I took over."

"Didn't like the new regime, huh?"

"Didn't even give it a chance. Anyway, he may be connected to the death of Heaven, Sinjin's wife."

None of that made sense. Creek shook his head. "I thought Heaven was your wife. And didn't Fi kill her? In that challenge battle?"

Doc pointed to one of the battered club chairs. "You mind?"

"No, go ahead. You want something to drink?" Creek was about to go out looking for Octavian again, but this was getting interesting.

"No, I'm cool, thanks." Doc sat. "Fi won that fight, but as it turns out, Heaven died because someone laced silver dust into the arena's sand. It got into Heaven's system and..." He exhaled. "She couldn't take it. Heart shut down. Silver does some pretty nasty stuff to varcolai."

"I guess that's thrown a wrench into the works." Creek kicked his feet up onto the cable spool coffee table. "If it was silver, I guess you know it wasn't a vampire or another shifter."

"I wish that was true. Two of my council members, Barasa and Omur, are currently being held by police because the messenger who delivered the silver dust will only say he delivered it to a council member, but says he can't remember which one. He's human and says we all look alike to him."

"Idiot." Creek rolled his eyes. "Where's this Fritz fit in?"

"Cops found a box with traces of silver dust in his apartment."

Creek nodded. "Then he's the council member who ordered the stuff."

Doc leaned back. "I don't know. Fritz was Sinjin's right-hand man. If he was going to do anything to fix that fight, he would have worked out a way to make Heaven the victor."

Creek tapped his fingers on the chair's arm. "You think that box was planted?"

Doc stared at his hands, nodding slowly. "Could be." Suddenly he sat forward. "You know, I went to see Fritz, thought maybe I could talk to him shifter to shifter, ask him if he knew anyone who might have wanted to hurt Heaven. When I got to his place, he acted all freaked out, like he didn't want to let me in for reasons beyond just who I was—and pride law dictates that if the pride leader requests your presence, you had best present yourself, so not speaking to me would have been a dumb move."

"Dumber than quitting the council?"

"Quitting the council only removed him from his standing in the pride. Not speaking to me would have been considered a personal offense. I could have him removed from the pride altogether for that."

Creek nodded. "Got it."

Doc spread his hands. "I'm standing at his door, right, trying to get him to let me in and I hear glass breaking.

Fritz is already twitchy, so now I'm thinking someone's in there, threatening him or who knows what. I bust through the door in time to catch somebody going down the fire escape. I chase the guy, but don't catch him because on my way out, I tell Fritz to call the cops." Doc rolled his eyes. "They show up and guess who gets tapped?"

"Damn," Creek said. "Not your night."

Doc sat back. "Dude vanishes. Me? I'm wearing bracelets and get to spend the night downtown. You know they can hold you for twenty-four hours without charging you?"

Creek shot him a look. "Yeah, I'm intimately acquainted with the penal system."

"I guess you are." Doc shook his head. "I almost had that guy too. Got a swipe in, but couldn't hang on to him."

"A swipe?"

Doc held his hand up and shifted to his half-form, popping inch-and-a-half claws out of his fingertips.

"Double damn." Suddenly it was Creek's turn to sit up. "Are you saying you sliced the guy?"

"Yes. Across the back."

"The field of suspects just got narrower."

Doc sighed. "Not really. Varcolai heal too fast for there to still be a mark on him so any chance of identifying him that way is long gone by now."

Creek shook his head as he reached for his phone. "I saw this guy. I was out on patrol, heard the report over the police scanner, and headed toward the action. I ran across a wounded varcolai lying in an alley. Leopard, I think. Whatever is big and spotted." He raised one shoulder. "Sorry, I don't know the breeds well enough to say. Anyway, this cat had four slices across its back. I left it alone, but hung out across the street because I thought the blood scent might draw some fringe, which it did, but the few vamps that sniffed around didn't stay long."

He pulled out his phone and tapped the screen. "A couple hours later, a guy walks out of the alley. I took a few pictures because you just never know." He pulled up one and held it out for Doc to see.

Doc's mouth opened and his eyes glimmered green-gold. He cursed softly under his breath.

Creek set the phone on the table. "I take it you know this guy?"

"Hell yes." Doc picked up the phone, still staring at the photo. "That lying piece of Brazilian trash. That's Heaven's brother, Remo."

After saying good-bye to Chrysabelle, Mal had one mission left. Delay Tatiana's plans until Chrysabelle had enough time to get to the Garden of Eden ahead of them. Fortunately, Tatiana was so focused on what had happened with Octavian, the plan to get Lilith to the Garden had been put aside for the moment.

"How could he," she snarled, stomping across the sitting room like the madwoman she was. "He was dead. I saw the ashes. Kosmina told me he killed himself because he knew he'd end up dying at my hands for his betrayal. Then he comes back here? Not dead and thinking I'd somehow forgive him for—" She stopped and stared at Mal, but her gaze was wild and unfixed. "Kosmina," she whispered. "How did she see him kill himself when he wasn't really dead?"

Kosmina's words about her time here being short

suddenly made sense. She'd probably slipped away, knowing her story about Octavian would be revealed as a lie now that he'd shown up. "Must have been some kind of black magic."

If Tatiana even heard him, she didn't show it. She yanked open the doors to the sitting room and charged out into the hall. "Kosmina," she bellowed. "Now!" Then she stomped back in and returned to muttering.

Shockingly, Kosmina appeared a few moments later. "Yes, my lady?" She didn't look at Mal once.

"Octavian was here." Tatiana's eyes were white-hot silver.

She nodded, head down, hands clasped. Ever the dutiful servant in appearance. "Yes, my lady. I saw him."

"Just like you saw him kill himself?"

Kosmina blinked once, but didn't falter. "Yes, my lady. Surely he tricked me with magic. I am very sorry."

"Sorry?" Tatiana trembled with visible rage.

Mal sighed like the whole thing bored him, but the voices were on the verge of chaos. It was like they could smell the potential for bloodshed. "Can we get back to business?" They still hadn't discussed how they were going to persuade Lilith to go with them to the Garden. "Yes, it's shocking that Octavian showed up, but who cares about what this kine saw or didn't see?"

She looked at him. "Don't you get it? This *kine* was in league with him." She pointed at Kosmina with her metal hand, the fingers melding until they stretched forward into a short blade. "She must have known he was working against me." New pain flared in her eyes. "Which means he was really working for you."

With new determination, she stalked toward Mal.

"Was he? Was Octavian working with you and the comarré whore to steal Lilith? Tell me. There can be no secrets between us if our plans are going to work."

The word "whore" caused Mal's anger to tick upward. The voices cheered. The urge to take Tatiana by the throat and shake her until her neck snapped itched along his nerves. How did Kosmina stand it? "No, he wasn't working for me. And I doubt very much this servant could have helped him in any way. You're wasting time. We have a *task*."

"That task can wait." She whipped around and jabbed her sword hand under Kosmina's chin. "Tell me what you know or so help me, I will slice you from ear to ear."

Kosmina lifted her head slightly as her eyes went strangely blank. "I know nothing."

Tatiana's blade pressed into Kosmina's skin until a drop of blood rolled down the shining metal surface. "You lie."

Kosmina went up on her toes, struggling to rise above the cutting edge. "No, my lady, I know nothing."

Mal stood. "You're wasting my time on these foolish games, Tatiana. An old lover returns and your focus is gone. I've had enough." He took a few steps toward the door, hoping to pull her focus off Kosmina. Even if the KM agent had been prepared to kill him, he didn't want her blood on his hands. "You said you wanted my help, but I'm here and you've done nothing to make use of me. Instead, you're distracted. I'm tired of waiting on you. If you want to do this on your own, so be it."

Tatiana paused, her sword hand lowering an inch or two. "Mal, wait. Don't you see? Her disloyalty must be punished."

"Being tricked by Octavian does not make her disloyal. It merely makes her gullible. She's kine. If you expect more, you're a fool."

Some of the rage left Tatiana's eyes. She dropped the sword from Kosmina's throat and it became a hand again. "I suppose I do expect too much." She took a step toward him. "And we have so much work ahead of us."

He nodded. "We should focus on that."

"We should," Tatiana agreed. "This isn't something I need to deal with. I'll give her over to some of my household guards, have them see what they can get out of her while we're gone."

Behind her, Kosmina's face took on the same soldier-like expression he'd seen in the wine cellar. Her hand went from the pocket of her uniform to her mouth, and then her jaw popped as she bit down. "Go to hell, vampire."

Tatiana spun around as Kosmina began to convulse. Foam bubbled from her lips and she fell to the ground. After a few seconds of twitching, she lay still.

Tatiana kneeled and felt her throat. "She's dead. Bloody kine traitor."

Son of a priest. "Look at it this way," Mal said. "She saved you the effort."

"Hmph." Tatiana stood, her silver gaze directed at him. "And you were trying to protect her."

"No." He came to her side, intent on damage control, and took her by the shoulders. "I was trying to protect you."

"Me?" She frowned. "From what?"

"From Lilith's wrath. You haven't spoken to her since the incident with Octavian and when she disappeared, she was convinced you were angry at her. How much more time will you let go by before you console her? Do you really want her to stew longer than necessary? The more upset she is, the harder it may be to convince her to step through that portal with us."

Tatiana's hand went to her mouth. "Bloody hell. With this thing with Octavian, I'd completely forgotten."

He released her. "You've got to call her to you, soothe her, and persuade her to come with us to the Garden. Make it seem like something special." He narrowed his eyes. "She's growing stronger, isn't she? More volatile?"

Tatiana nodded and shifted her face back to human. "Thank you."

Those were the last words he'd expected out of her mouth, but with Tatiana, nothing was a given. "For what?"

"For keeping your head when I'm losing mine." She hugged him, causing him to stiffen. He forced himself to relax, but her touch was so repulsive it took effort. "I never should have let you go, Mal. We're so good together, you and I."

It was pointless to remind her that she hadn't let him go; she'd left him to rot. "Yes, well, I'm here now."

And the sooner he could rid the world of her and her hell-spawned child, the sooner he'd be gone.

Chapter Thirty-six

Chrysabelle slept as much as she could on the way home. The child in her belly had definitely begun to sap her strength, something she would need when she entered the Garden. She yawned and stretched as Jerem pulled the car around to the front of the house. The sun was just coming up.

Velimai opened the door, her gaze shifting from Chrysabelle's face to her stomach and back up again. Her hands started moving. *How are you feeling?*

"Tired, but I'll make it." Behind her, Jerem brought her bag in. "Thank you. Take a few days off, okay? You've earned them."

He nodded, smiling. "Thanks, boss."

After he left, Chrysabelle glanced up the steps. "Damian moved in?"

Yes. He's in the suite at the very end of the south side.

"How's Amylia taking it?"

"She's doing fine." Damian came down the stairs. "How was your trip? Tatiana dead yet?"

"No, not yet. Mal and I have some work to do before that's accomplished, but we're close." She gave him a hug when he approached. "I'm glad you moved into the main house. I like having you here."

"I'm not sure I'm staying, though. The trust lawyer dropped off some paperwork while you were gone and I was reading through the list of the Lapointe Company holdings. Our mother was a very savvy businesswoman. Among the properties she purchased is a penthouse on Venetian Island." He grinned. "I was thinking I might move in there. If you wouldn't mind my taking that place."

"Mind? I didn't even know about it." She smiled, but her heart sank. She'd wanted him to stay here. To share the house. But maybe that was selfish. And not something he was interested in. "And it's not up to me anyway. It belongs to both of us. If you want to live there, then that's what you should do." Her smile faltered. "Venetian Island rings a bell with me for some reason, but I can't recall it now. Either way, if that's what you want, I'm happy for you."

He pointed to the back of the house. "You know you can see Venetian from here. It's just the next island up. We can go back and forth by boat."

"Have you visited the place yet?"

"No, I wanted to talk to you about it first."

She tipped her head. "And are you taking Amylia with you?"

He laughed. "Don't think I don't hear the sly tone in your voice. I might. It's not like that between us, but she has become a friend and we certainly know what the other one is going through. Besides, you know I feel responsible for her."

Velimai came out from the kitchen. *Breakfast is almost ready if you're hungry.*

Chrysabelle's stomach growled. "Famished." She

hooked her arm through Damian's. "I'm so glad you're here." The only upside of him moving out was that she could keep the secret of the baby a little while longer if she wanted to, but that seemed a small victory. He was her family. Fi was right. He deserved to know, but telling him scared her. Things were so good between them; she hated to do anything to ruin it. Would he understand? "There's something I want to talk to you about after breakfast, okay?"

"You got it." He patted her hand as they walked into the kitchen. "You need any help with the rest of your plan for Tatiana?"

"I might." She sat as Velimai brought platters to the table. "Do you know about the comarré ability to open portals?"

"You mean like the secret doors and passageways beneath the noble estates?" He filled both their glasses with orange juice from a pitcher.

"Something like that, except it involves blood." She took a sip. "I'm going to open one tonight and use it to travel to the Garden of Eden."

His eyes widened. "Really?"

She nodded. "You're welcome to watch if you'd like. It's probably not a bad skill for you to learn. I'm going to prepare a few things, catch a few hours of sleep, and then I'll be ready." She took a plate of bacon from Velimai, who then sat across from Damian.

"I wouldn't miss it." He helped himself to a slice of raisin toast. "Is that what you wanted to talk to me about?"

"Yes." *Coward.* "No." She put her fork down and made herself look him in the eyes. *Just say it.* "I'm pregnant."

He stopped buttering his toast and stared at her.

She looked down at her plate. "I know, it's a lot to take

in, but you're my brother and you should know. You'd figure it out in a few more weeks anyway, the way I'm starting to show."

"It's Mal's?" He put the bread down. "Of course it's Mal's. Stupid question. Are you okay?" He glanced at Velimai. "You already knew about this?"

"She knew," Chrysabelle answered. "She figured it out before I did. And yes, I'm okay. Mal's feelings for me have returned and things are wonderful between us. I just want to know how you feel about it."

A slow, unsteady smile built on his face. "I'm...I'm going to be an uncle."

Setting everything up and getting Vernadetto to arrive had taken a few hours, but he and a few of his officers had finally joined Doc in his office. Doc stood to shake his hand as he came in. "Thanks for coming, Chief. I promise you, this will be worth your while." He nodded to Creek, already there. "I understand you know Creek already. He's the one who helped me figure this out."

Creek stood and shook the chief's extended hand. "Chief."

Vernadetto looked at him. "You staying out of trouble's way?"

"If by trouble, you mean the mayor, then yes."

Vernadetto snorted. "She has gone in an interesting direction."

Doc held a hand up, trying to shift the conversation before Creek revealed too much. Until Doc knew the outcome of this meeting, the file Creek had given him might be his only leverage. "Let's focus on what's about to happen. After you and your men set up in the conference room, I'll call Remo up here. Creek and I will lay the evidence out and see what happens. You'll be able to follow along on the tablet in there thanks to the camera we set up."

Vernadetto nodded. "And if he doesn't give us something we can use?"

Doc glanced at the officers. "If it comes down to it, we may use some...extra persuasion."

Creek crossed his arms. "You have a problem with that?"

Vernadetto shrugged. "If you can do it without leaving marks, that would be better. Harder to prove if there's nothing to show."

"Got it." Doc opened the door to the conference room. "I hope to Bast this works."

The officers filed in, Vernadetto behind them. "For Fiona's sake, I hope so too."

Doc shut the door, then went to his desk, hit the speaker button on his phone, and punched in a number. It rang twice before Remo picked up.

"What?"

No respect whatsoever. Fire built along Doc's muscles. "Council meeting."

Remo laughed. "With one council member?"

"I'm making do."

"All right. I'll be up."

"Soon," Doc said.

More laughter. "What are you going to do? Start without me?"

Doc hit the button to disconnect and looked at Creek. "You may have to stop me from killing him."

Creek blew out a breath. "You know that's not really my area of expertise."

Doc nodded and sat at his desk to wait. "Just make sure there's enough of him left to stand trial."

Damian nodded appreciatively at the penthouse's foyer as he got off the elevator. The place was posh and seemed to be decorated in the style of the Primorus Domus with its gilding and ceiling mural. He studied the painted ceiling and snorted softly as he recognized the source. A copy of *The Feast of the Gods* by Bellini. How appropriate for a comarré. He brushed his fingers over the lion's-head door knocker hanging off the bronze double doors. Oddly masculine, but he'd never known his mother, so he was in no position to judge her taste.

He held up the key the attorney had given him, waving it in front of the scanner. The bolt slid back and he tucked the key away. If the rest of the apartment looked anything like the foyer, he'd have to gut it and start over. He'd never be able to live in a replica of the place that had sold him into slavery. Of course, gutting the apartment would take money he didn't have. Money he'd have to take from his mother's estate.

He scowled at the thought. It felt so foreign to him to even think about a mother. Or a sister, for that matter. A sister who was pregnant with a vampire's child.

He'd let Chrysabelle think he was happy for her, but in his gut, happiness wasn't what he felt. He knew nothing about the vampire other than Mal had come with her to rescue him, but Damian hadn't seen him since she'd returned from Corvinestri.

He might not have known Chrysabelle long, but his instincts to protect his sister had already kicked in. Any man, vampire or otherwise, who would create that

kind of relationship with her only to disappear had a lot
of explaining to do. Damian had endured nearly a hundred and twenty-two years of training. Killing a vampire
who'd dishonored his sister wouldn't be hard.

He rubbed a hand across his mouth, trying to calm
himself. Chrysabelle was a grown woman. It wasn't his
place to interfere unless it was clear she was in danger and
that hadn't happened. Yet.

It was good this apartment was here. He should give
her some space, especially with the baby on the way. Yes,
they were family and they needed to get to know each
other, but it was obvious she was going through something right now that only time could help. Besides, she'd
risked her life to save his. He owed her that much.

He put a hand on the door and pushed.

The apartment inside was beautiful. Clean, modern
lines and tall windows that looked out over the sparkling
blue waters of the bay. The door swung softly shut behind
him as he walked toward them to look out.

He planted himself before the glass and whistled
softly. "Nice view."

"Thank you. Can I ask what brings you here unan-
nounced?"

Damian spun. "Dominic. What are you doing here?"

The vampire nodded. "Glad to know you remember
me." He tightened the tie of his silk robe. "And I believe
I'm the one who should be asking you that question."
Small sparks of silver lit his eyes. "How did you get in
here?"

Damian fished the key from his pocket and held it up.

The silver disappeared from Dominic's eyes. "From
Marissa's attorney, no doubt."

"So you know my mother owns this place?"

He smiled bitterly. "I should. I'm the one who gave it to her." He pointed at the sleek leather chairs in the sitting room. "Please." He turned toward the hall. "Isabelle. We have a guest."

A moment later, a slender, lavender-eyed female in a clingy black dress glided toward them. Everything about her looked human, except for her lifeless, unnaturally colored gaze and weirdly plastic skin. "Hello, guest," she intoned. "Would you like a beverage?"

"No, thanks." He eyed the woman as he sat.

Dominic laughed. "To answer the question undoubtedly in your head, no, she's not human. She's a symbot." He turned to Isabelle. "Lower the shades, please." He glanced at Damian. "I hope you don't mind, but even with the helio-glazing, the sun is too bright for me this time of day."

"That's fine." What a surreal conversation. He watched Isabelle while Dominic took the chair across from him. His hair was rumpled and stubble darkened his jaw.

"I take it I woke you from daysleep. Sorry about that, but I'm surprised. I hardly made a sound." And most vampires went comatose during daysleep.

He shrugged. "Years of working at Seven. I sleep when I can and have trained myself to do it lightly. I have... enemies. I'm sure that does not shock you."

"No. But I'm not one of them. I didn't know you were living here."

"Few do. Which is what I was striving for." He nodded to Isabelle as she finished lowering the shades. "That is all."

With a soft whirr, she disappeared back down the hall.

Damian leaned back. "You said you bought this place for my mother?"

Dominic nodded. "It was our first real place outside of Seven and the safest place money could buy at the time. I had the deed put in her name because..." He smiled. "It was a good gift, no?"

"You had the deed put in her name because why?"

Dominic's smile waned. "Because I knew she would leave me. And I wanted her to have a place to call her own." He ran his finger along the seam of the chair's leather. "I tell you this because you deserve to know the truth. You are her child."

"But you live here now?"

"After she bought the estate on Mephisto Island, she sent me a key to this place. She knew I needed time away from Seven, knew how much I had enjoyed spending time with her here." A hint of a smile returned, but it carried the weight of the past. "It was her way of trying to mend things between us, I think."

Damian sat, not knowing what to say. What had Maris done to Dominic that had left him in such pain?

Dominic sighed like the burden of his years pressed down on him. "I will have my things moved out in the next few nights."

"Why?"

Dominic lifted his head, eyes confused. "You came here to see about taking this property for your own, didn't you?"

Damian shook his head. "Just checking out the places on the list." Dominic had been instrumental in rescuing him. He wasn't about to kick the man out of a place that held such memories.

Dominic's eyes narrowed, doing nothing to hide the sudden spark of life that filled them. "You are a good man,

Damian Lapointe. Your mother would be proud of you." He stood and extended his hand. "If you ever need anything, I am here for you, just as I have been for Chrysabelle."

"Good to know." Damian rose, dug out the key the attorney had given him, and held it out to Dominic.

Dominic took the key. "*Grazie.*"

Damian headed for the door. "I won't keep this a secret from Chrysabelle, however."

"No, no," Dominic added, walking with him. "There must be truth between the members of a family." He lifted one shoulder. "She has been here. This is not such a secret to her anyway."

Damian paused, his hand on the door lever. "There is one thing I'd like to know before I leave."

"*Si?*"

"The vampire Malkolm. Do you trust him? Should I be worried about him and Chrysabelle? He won't hurt her, will he?"

"Malkolm? There is nothing to worry about there. I trust few people, but Mal is one of them. And he loves your sister." Dominic's eyes took on the faraway look again. "If your mother and I had what he and Chrysabelle have, she never would have left me."

Mal's presence was a comfort, something Tatiana had never expected to feel. Maybe it was because everyone else in her life was gone. Maybe it was his familiarity. No matter what their past was, their history had started well. They had loved one another, hadn't they? It was hard to remember exactly what her feelings for him had been all those centuries ago. They had at least understood each other.

Now, they were once again traveling the same path. She glanced at him and smiled weakly, not quite ready to call the maelstrom that was Lilith back into her life. "It's funny, isn't it?"

"What?" He stood across from her, leaning on the bar in that loose, easy way of his, but she knew well that in the blink of an eye he could become a killing machine. How many times in their early days had she seen it happen? Reveled in his ruthlessness? Drank from his spoils?

She closed the distance between them down to half. "What tore us apart was Sophia's death. Now we've come back together to kill off a child."

His heavy-lidded gaze didn't falter. "Calling her a child is like calling a Nothos a puppy."

She laughed softly. "Yes, of course, but you see the irony."

"And you see that I'm not here for the mission so much as the end result. I want my status back and the wealth you promised me. An estate of my own. The position as Elder. Forget anything you promised me and you *will* be sorry."

She touched his chest lightly. Playfully. "Your place as Elder is already secured. The ancients promised me I'd be rewarded for this task and their approval on your ascension to that position is guaranteed."

"Do you trust them?"

She jerked back, his words bordering on blasphemy. "Of course. Don't you?"

"I find it odd that they would have the child eat of the tree and not you as well. It seems to me that the child has no need for that kind of power." He lifted one shoulder in a lazy roll. "I only wonder if she wasn't listening when he spoke to you. If perhaps he said that knowing you'd understand to do the opposite."

She went very still. "I don't know."

"Yes, you do," Mal said. "You know I could be right. You said yourself that the ancients were afraid of her. How do you know she's not orchestrating this whole thing in an effort to get rid of you? And if she eats the fruit before you, she'll pitch a fit if you try to have one of your own."

"Hades," she whispered as she turned away. Doubt flooded her thoughts. "What am I going to do?"

"You'll eat the fruit first. It's all you can do. Once you eat it, she'll insist on having one as well."

She looked at him sharply. "And what if it proves fatal?"

"It won't." He dug into his pocket and held out a small metal box. "Because I have this."

"What is it?"

He lifted the top off, revealing a fine white powder. "Protection against any kind of holy magic." He smirked. "The comarré gave it to me a while ago." He sniggered. "Now that's irony, don't you think? Me using her gift to me to save you?"

"That's absolutely delicious." She clapped her hands, then reached out and ran her fingers down his body. "The estate you'll inherit sits on the next property over. It comes with the job of Elder, as you know. I didn't live there long, but it's a beautiful property. You'll enjoy it. And I'll enjoy having you close again after all these years. Of course, I wouldn't be unhappy if you wanted to spend more time here. With me."

He grabbed her hand and stopped it from moving. "Why would I want to do that?"

She wriggled her fingers free and leaned into him, the solidness of his body a welcome memory. "You cannot deny that there is still something between us."

"Animosity. Bitterness. Deep-seated resentment. Take your pick."

"Oh, Malkolm. You can't still be harboring ill will toward me? Not after we've been working so well together."

He went quiet, watching her, only a flicker of silver in his eyes.

She poked him. "See? You know it's true."

"I suppose," he grunted. "Things have been going... well." He shifted, putting some space between them. "But you can't expect me to just forget everything you did to me."

She leaned back against the bar where he'd just been, planting her elbows on the marble top in a way that pushed her breasts forward. "You should at least give me the chance to make all that up to you."

"All I need is what I've been promised."

He'd fold. She knew what he liked, how to motivate him to do her will. And once they were rid of Lilith, she'd have nothing else to worry about. Then she could put all her efforts into wooing him back to her side for good. She shrugged like it didn't matter whether or not he gave her a second chance. "Shall we get on with it, then?"

He crossed his arms. "Please."

She tipped her head back. "Lilith, my angel, come to Mother. I've got a very special surprise for you..."

Damian waved to Chrysabelle on his way from the car to the guesthouse. "I'll be over in a few minutes. Don't open any portals without me."

"I won't. I promise." She nodded as the gates began to open. "Vel, we have a visitor."

Fi's sedan pulled through the gates. A minute later, Fi

hopped out, then waved to Velimai and Chrysabelle as she ran up to the front door, a shopping bag swinging from her hand. "Hey, I was just going to drop this off." She lifted the bag. "I can't stay long. There's a lot of craziness going on at headquarters. You didn't kill Tatiana yet, right?"

"Right. She's not dead yet. But soon. I'm meeting Mal in a few hours." If everything went as planned.

"Ooo, the final showdown." Fi's eyes brightened. "This is perfect timing then." She shook the bag. "I have just the thing for you to wear."

"I thought we were done shopping." Chrysabelle let Fi drag her upstairs.

"This wasn't shopping. This was custom made, which is why it wasn't ready until now."

"That sounds expensive."

"It was, but don't worry about it. The pride's loaded. Think of it as my and Doc's wedding gift to you and Mal."

"What? We're not getting married."

Fi laughed. "You will be. You'll see." She opened the door to Chrysabelle's quarters and handed her the bag. "Go try it on."

If Fi smiled any harder, her teeth might pop out. Chrysabelle peeked into the bag but all she could see were swathes of tissue paper. "What is it?"

"Scared?" Fi laughed again and sat on the bed. "Don't be. It's just exactly the right outfit for crushing Tatiana. She sees you in this and she'll be so freaked out, you'll probably catch her off guard."

"Okay, yes, now I'm scared." Chrysabelle started to take the bag into the bathroom with her, then stopped and looked back at Fi. "You know you're the first female friend I've ever really had outside my mother and Velimai. And I know we didn't exactly get along at first—"

"You were trying to kill the vampire who was keeping me alive."

Chrysabelle nodded, laughing softly. "True. But I'm really glad we got past that."

Fi grinned. "Me too."

Chrysabelle's smile thinned out. "I just want you to know that I'm thankful for our friendship. In case things don't go well with Tatiana."

Fi frowned. "I'm thankful too, but you shouldn't say crap like that. You're going to kick Tatiana's fangs right out of her mouth, you got it?"

"Got it."

"Good. Now get in there and change. I have to get back soon and I want to see this thing on you."

"Going!" She hustled into the bathroom, where she removed the tissue-wrapped outfit from the shopping bag. She laid it on the counter next to the map of the Garden and the gold pipette she'd be using to draw blood to form the portal. She pulled back the first layer of tissue.

Red leather, worked into beautiful patterns and burnished with black so that the leather took on an almost antique look. It reminded her of some of the outfits she'd seen Mortalis in. She ran her hand over the skins. Super soft but so very different from the kind of clothing she was used to. She shook her head. "Oh, Fi," she whispered. "You silly girl."

Reluctantly she undressed and put the pants on. They clung to her form, but were surprisingly flexible and fit over her swelling belly as if they'd been measured for her yesterday. She shrugged. Fi said they'd been custom made. The top looked more like an engineering project in the back, straps crisscrossing her shoulders and lower back in an intricate pattern. The front was a solid piece. Almost like a breastplate, and it too fit like it had been molded to her body.

She tugged the laces tight at the back of the top, tying them off before looking at herself in the mirror.

A warrior stared back at her. A gold-gilded, red-leather-clad warrior. "Holy mother."

"You like it?" Fi called.

"I . . . I don't know. It's different. And it shows a lot of signum." And it was too tight to hide the one thing she didn't want Tatiana to know about. She turned sideways to see exactly how pregnant she looked in the outfit.

Oddly, her stomach was perfectly flat. She ran her hands down over her belly. She could feel the curve of it. Why couldn't she see it?

She opened the bathroom door. "Fi, why—"

"Holy crap, that's freaking awesome." Fi bounced on her knees on the bed. "You look like you're going to kill someone. Like you've already killed someone. A lot of someones."

Chrysabelle held up her hands. "Take a breath. Why can't I see my stomach in this?" She turned sideways and studied her reflection in the bedroom mirror. "Look. Nothing shows, but I can feel it. So strange."

Pure delight gleamed in Fi's eyes. "Not really that strange when you consider who made it."

Chrysabelle glanced over at her. "Who?"

Looking extremely self-satisfied, Fi laid down on the bed, propped on one elbow on her side. "The same fae that makes all of Mortalis's leathers. Nyssa hooked me up with him." Her gaze went to Chrysabelle's stomach. "The reason you can't see your belly is fae magic, plain and simple. I figured it would come in handy in case you needed to hide the pregnancy for these next few months."

"Or just from Tatiana." Chrysabelle's hands coasted over her abdomen. "Amazing."

"So what do you think?" Fi asked. "Are you going to wear it to face down Tatiana for the last time? I know I'd be afraid of you if you came after me in that outfit."

"Why red? I know I've been trying to wear more color, but red?"

A satisfied gleam sparked in Fi's eyes. "Red means stop. It's a warning of danger. It's the color of blood. There were a lot of reasons I chose that color." She crossed her arms. "So are you going to wear it?"

Chrysabelle took another long, hard look at herself. "Believe it or not, yes."

The front door slammed. "Chrys, where are you?" Damian called out.

"In my bedroom," she answered.

He walked in. "Are you ready to—holy mother, what do you have on?"

Chrysabelle planted her hands on her hips. "My Tatiana-killing outfit." Fi snickered at that. "Am I ready to what? Open the portal? Yes."

He stared open-mouthed another second, then shook his head. "That looks like a Tatiana-killing outfit."

"Fi's choice. She did well, didn't she?" With a wink at Fi, Chrysabelle continued. "How was the penthouse? Are you going to move in there?"

"It's nice, but not my style. If it's okay with you, I'll stay here a little bit longer."

She frowned at him. "What's okay with me is if you don't leave at all. I really don't want you to go."

"You're sure? I just thought with things about to change the way they are, that…I don't know. You'd want your own space."

"Damian, the space I want has you in it."

He nodded and smiled. "Then I'll stay."

"Good. Thank you." She rubbed her forehead. "I'm glad that's settled. One less thing to worry about, especially since I really need to open that portal and get to the Garden."

Fi hopped off the bed. "That's my cue to leave. I told Doc I wouldn't be long." She gave Chrysabelle a hug. "Get it done and bring Mal home."

Chrysabelle hugged her back. "Will do."

Fi waved to Damian as she left. "See you later, D."

Chrysabelle shot her brother a look. "You ready?"

"Absolutely. Are you? Do you have everything you need? Are you sure you don't want me with you?"

"I'd love to have you with me, but I'd rather have you here protecting the portal." And out of harm's way.

"Understood. I know with our training you can handle yourself. I just can't help but worry about my sister." He smiled. "Give her hell, Chrys." He laughed. "Or at least send her there."

Chrysabelle returned his smile. "That's exactly what I intend to do."

Chapter Thirty-seven

Doc nodded to Creek after Remo was seated. "Show him the pictures."

Creek tapped the screen of his phone, and then held it out for Remo to see.

He studied the picture for a long second before his angry gaze rose to meet Doc's. "You are having me followed? On what grounds?"

Doc fixed his gaze on Remo and held it there. One way or another, Remo was going to tell the truth. "I'm not having you followed. Creek took those while on surveillance for another matter."

"So." Remo shrugged. "What is it supposed to prove, other than I often take walks through the streets?" He sat back. "Is this the council meeting? If so, I fail to see what a photo of me out walking has to do with anything."

"Those photos were taken after I chased you out of Fritz's apartment."

"I don't know what you're talking about." Remo laughed nervously. "Who is Fritz?"

"You know who he is. He's the council member you

replaced. The one you're trying to frame as Heaven's murderer."

Remo started to stand, but Creek put a hand on his chest and pushed him back into his chair. "Don't be rude. Your pride leader's talking to you."

"Get your hand off me. I'm done with this," Remo snarled.

Doc rapped his knuckles on the desktop. "You leave and you're done with this pride, you get me?"

Remo shut up.

Doc continued. "What this proves is that you're not the innocent you make yourself out to be."

Creek set the phone down on Doc's desk. "I saw you in that alley in your animal form. You had four scratches on your back."

"Do you have pictures of them also?" Remo asked.

"No," Creek answered.

"His word that he saw them is good enough," Doc said. "Because I know where those scratches came from. I put them there when I chased you out of Fritz's apartment."

Remo had the nerve to look bored. "I said I don't know what you're talking about."

Doc took a breath and tried to remain calm, tried to pull the frustration from his voice. "Look, all I really want to know is why you did it? Why you'd kill your sister? I can't make it work in my head."

Remo's face didn't change. "I loved my sister and I resent the implication that I would hurt her."

"Why'd you frame Fritz? What does that get you?"

Remo sighed and stood. "I believe the time has come for me to consult with my father on this." He moved toward the door.

Doc decided to call his bluff. He leaped over the desk and blocked Remo's path. "You're right. Maybe we should call your father. Maybe he's the one behind all this." Yellow flickered in Remo's eyes like a flame, then went out. Doc pushed harder. "That's more likely, isn't it? You wouldn't have the brains to think up something like this. Or the connections to make it happen. No, this definitely wasn't something you're capable of, because killing a family member? That would take stones bigger than what you're carrying around. Rodrigo Silva–sized stones."

Remo's lip curled. "My father wouldn't have the guts."

"You're the one who wouldn't have the guts." Doc leaned in until they were almost nose to nose. "You couldn't even get this position without him."

Remo's eyes went gold and he snapped his jaw, baring his teeth. "I should have killed you too."

He swung, but Doc grabbed his arm and threw him against the wall. Remo staggered back, swinging again. This time Doc caught Remo by the waist, took him to the ground, and held him there. "Why'd you kill her? Why?"

Beneath Doc's grasp, Remo snarled and fought. "To push you and your useless human wife out of power, you stupid *Mané*."

Doc jerked him to his feet. "I don't know what the hell you just called me, but I'm sure it wasn't good." He shoved Remo up against the wall. "How does getting me out of power help you?"

Remo snarled. "Fritz was going to call for fresh blood to be voted in."

"Fresh blood?" Doc stared at the murderer in his grasp. "As in you?"

"Yes. On the strength of my family name and with

the sympathy of my sister's death, every vote would have been mine. I would have taken over this pride and run it the right way. Restored the power it had under Sinjin and doubled it."

Doc's lip curled. "Under Sinjin, this pride was being punished for his whims."

"And now it's better that the pride is run by a street hood like you?"

Heat built in Doc's bones but he was in no danger of losing control. He'd won this. "Considering you laid the plans that killed your own flesh and blood, I don't think you're in any position to be insulting your pride leader."

"You're not my pride leader." Remo spat the words out. "You're a pretender and that's all you'll ever be."

"If Fi hadn't given you that vial of sand, how were you going to make all this happen?" Doc forced a smile. "Because honestly, you don't strike me as smart enough to have made this work otherwise."

Remo snapped, but Doc held him back. "I would have planted the tainted sand, then had my sister's body exhumed and reexamined, but your stupid wife saved me the trouble."

New warmth crackled along Doc's nerves. He leaned his full body weight onto his forearms, pressing into Remo so hard that the other shifter's breath went ragged with effort. Then he put his mouth next to Remo's ear. "Do you know what they do to pretty boys like you in prison?" Doc shook his head. "Bad, bad things."

"Damn straight," Creek said.

Shaking with the effort of controlling his fiery temper, Doc dropped Remo, stepped back, and called for the police chief. "Vernadetto, come get this piece of garbage."

Vernadetto and his officers charged out of the other room.

"Was that enough?" Doc asked.

Vernadetto nodded as two of the officers cuffed a struggling Remo. They went to the ground with him, but Vernadetto had been smart enough to bring varcolai officers. They could handle Remo. "With Creek's pictures and testimony, yes. Plus, I'm guessing if we search Remo's quarters, we'll find the evidence he intended to plant."

"You need a warrant for that?"

Vernadetto shook his head. "Not if you give us permission."

"Done."

Vernadetto smiled. "I'll have Barasa and Omur released within the hour."

"Thank you." Doc stared at the man who'd created so much chaos in his and Fi's life. "One more thing."

"What's that?" Vernadetto asked.

Doc walked over to where Remo now stood between two officers, hands cuffed behind him. Doc punched him in the gut, lifting him off the floor. Remo doubled over, gagging in pain.

"That was for trying to frame Fi." He nodded to the officers. "Get that disgusting animal out of here."

Chrysabelle kneeled on the bathroom floor, the pouch containing the gold pipette in one hand and the scroll in the other. She glanced up at Damian. "After I open this portal, it must remain untouched. If the circle is broken, the portal will close and Mal and I will be trapped there.

Also, some sound may filter through, but unless I call your name, stay on this side."

He'd gone to retrieve his sacre while she prepared and now wore it sheathed across his body. He nodded, resting his hand on the leather strap that crossed his chest. "No one will touch this circle."

"All right. I'm going to begin." As he came around to her side, she closed her eyes and bent her head. *Holy mother, give me strength to accomplish this task. Guide Malkolm as well, and help him do and say all the right things. And please, protect this child I'm carrying.*

She opened her eyes and removed the thin gold pipette from the pouch with a steady hand that belied her trembling nerves. No matter how many times she'd done this, it was never easy.

Hopefully, this time would be the last. After this, she and Mal would be able to live a peaceful life. With that thought and a deep breath, she lifted the pipette with the small, tapered end facing her. She inhaled and forced the thought of the pain out of her head, and then she wrapped her left hand over her right and plunged the pipette into her chest.

To his credit, Damian didn't flinch.

The stabbing pain sucked the breath from her body, but she steadied herself with purpose. This was a small price to pay for a life without Tatiana. Index finger over the pipette's open end, she slid it from her chest. Blood trickled from the wound and trailed down beneath her leathers.

Using the pipette like a fountain pen and her blood for ink, she traced the portal onto the marble. Circle finished, she copied the signum from the edges of the torn page.

When she was done, she sat back. Just as before when she'd drawn the portal for the Aurelian, the blood began to spread inward, filling the circle until a perfect, shimmering circle of blood sat before her.

The surface rippled like it had been touched by a breeze. A flash of golden light gleamed across the blood and the heady perfume of flowers rose up from it. Without question, she knew the scent came from the Garden. The portal was open.

She stood, tucked the map through the strap of one of the sacres crossing her chest, and stepped through.

"Lilith, please."

After Tatiana's third attempt to bring Lilith to them, Mal retired to the couch. From there, he watched her, his amusement growing in time with Tatiana's frustration, but he finally decided to put an end to it. "How many more times are you going to call her?"

Hands fisted at her sides, she glared at him. "You have a better idea?"

"Yes." He stood and freed a little of the beast so that it spilled into his voice. "Lilith." The sound came out of him like a thousand voices speaking at once. "*Now.*"

The darkness swelled, shadows leaking into the center of the room from the corners until they coalesced into a familiar shape. She stepped out of the gloom, arms crossed, anger contorting her face. "What?"

Mal approached her. "Your mother's been calling you."

She eyed him warily. "So?"

"When she calls, you come." Part of him couldn't

believe he was speaking to this monster this way and the other part of him couldn't believe it was working.

Lilith sniffed. "She's mad at me."

"No, she's not. In fact, she's got something very special planned for you."

A little of the pout disappeared from her bottom lip. "What?"

"Not until you apologize." He pointed back at Tatiana. "Now."

"Sorry," she mumbled.

He leaned in, the beast still in his voice. "Like you mean it or that special thing goes away."

She pulled away from him, shrinking toward Tatiana. "I'm sorry for killing Octavian without asking."

Surreal didn't begin to cover this. "That's better," Mal said.

Tatiana's smile was shaky, but otherwise convincing. "Thank you, Lilith."

Lilith grinned and pressed her hands together in front of her chest. "What's the special thing?"

Tatiana moved closer to Mal. Was she that afraid of Lilith or trying to present a more unified front? "My darling, Malkolm and I have decided to take you to the most beautiful place on earth. The Garden of Eden. Won't that be exciting?"

Lilith looked doubtful. "Why? What's exciting about it?"

Mal wanted to roll his eyes, but didn't. Tatiana wasn't selling this very well. He sighed. "Because your mother has missed so much time with you, she wants to make up for that by allowing you to choose a very special present from the Garden. All the animals there are tame, so you can pick anything you like as a pet."

Tatiana smiled like Mal had just come up with the best idea ever. Which, clearly, he had. "That's right. Any animal you like. You pick it and we'll bring it back here to live with us."

Lilith's eyes brightened. "You mean after that we're all going to live here together?"

"Yes," Tatiana answered. "You'll stay here with us from then on."

She squeezed her hands together. "And I can have any animal I like?"

"Any one at all, my darling. I used to have a cobra. I might get another one while we're there."

"No," Lilith shouted. "Only I get a present."

Tatiana stiffened and she held her hands up as she laughed unconvincingly. "All right, my sweet, only you get a present."

If he thought he'd have a chance, Mal would have killed them both right there. A more irritating pair he couldn't imagine. "Go rest now, Lilith. We'll call you in just a short time to join us, but we have some final preparations to make before we can leave." They'd already decided that Lilith shouldn't see the portal being drawn. If anything went wrong, that wasn't information she needed to possess.

"You promise not long? I hate waiting."

Tatiana nodded. "We promise. Not long at all."

"Fine." She narrowed her red eyes at them. "But you better not be lying."

"Go now, Lilith," Mal said. "Or we won't call you at all."

"Hmph." But she crossed her arms and disappeared.

Chapter Thirty-eight

Sand and rocks covered the earth in every direction except the one directly in front of Chrysabelle. Before her stood a set of gold filigree gates unlike any she'd ever seen. They soared over her, the tops of them disappearing into the clouds scuttling across the blue sky. The wall they were attached to was made of trees; trunks and branches and swathes of leaves all woven into an impenetrable barrier.

The sweet aroma that had wafted through to the other side of the portal was nothing compared to the air now. It was like she could taste the sweetness of the fruit and flowers perfuming the breeze. She closed her eyes and inhaled.

"Beautiful, isn't it?"

With a jerk, she opened them again. A being with four wings stood in front of her. A drape of the deepest blue covered him and a soft glow surrounded his body. He had a kind but strong face.

"Who are you?"

"I am Eae, the cherubim who guards this gate." He held his hand out to his side and a flaming sword appeared in it. The blade twisted of its own accord, spinning slowly.

"You're not going to let me pass, are you?"

He smiled with the ferocity of a lion. "Your blood decides that, not me." He stepped to the side and the gates began to open. "And yes, you may pass. Just know that you may not remove anything from the Garden and you bear the consequences of anything you eat."

She nodded, shocked that he wasn't trying to stop her. "I understand. Thank you." She hesitated. "There are others coming. Vampires. Two females and a male."

His face shifted into something fiercer, almost hawk-like. "Nobles?"

"Yes."

He scowled.

"Will they be able to pass?"

More scowling. "Yes."

She glanced at the sun shining in the sky. How was Mal going to know when it was night here? "This sun will affect them just like the sun anywhere else, right?"

"Yes," Eae said. "But they will never see it. The Garden is whatever its inhabitants need it to be. For them, it will be night."

"And for me?"

"As you may abide either, you will see it as night when they arrive."

She sighed with relief. She'd know exactly when Mal got here. "So you know, the male is on my side. But the females with him can't know I'm here. Please don't say anything to them about me, but if you can somehow let the male know I've arrived, that would be okay with me."

He nodded. "I will do what I can."

"One more thing?" She prayed she wasn't overstepping her bounds. "The portal I came through…" She glanced behind her. It shimmered on the ground, a brilliant red circle undeniably out of place. "Is there any way to hide it from those coming?"

"Sand."

"Sand?" She picked up a handful and sprinkled it on one side of the portal and the edge disappeared. "Okay, sand." She quickly covered the rest of it.

A quick thank-you and she hurried into the Garden, unsure how much longer the gates would stay open.

Once past them, the world around her was unbelievable. Not a single cloud obscured the sky on this side of the wall and the brilliant sunlight picked out every color of the flowers and trees and wildlife, making her feel like she was walking through a kaleidoscope. Mist drifted through an abundance of lush, tropical trees and plants in every imaginable shade of green. Beneath her feet, a mossy path wound into the distance. She reached down to touch the grass. The tiny springy blades were silky soft.

Here and there, enormous chunky-barked trees arched over the path, shading the way with dinner-plate-sized leaves in deep bluish-green. Where the mist cleared, sunlight filtered through in a dappled pattern and lit up an array of unusual fruits hanging from vines. Electric bright flowers bloomed everywhere and the scent wrapped around Chrysabelle like welcoming arms.

Birdsong, light and more musical than any she'd heard before, floated around her. The subtle buzz of busy insects hummed along in harmony. There was no sense of anything being afraid of her. She passed rabbits sitting near the path, but they just blinked up at her without running away.

A shadowy length of spotted skin rippled behind

some of the foliage. A leopard emerged from a clump of tall spiked red flowers and sat, looking at her with a vaguely curious expression. Chrysabelle froze. This was no varcolai.

But it *was* the Garden of Eden. Wasn't it supposed to be peaceful here? Everything in accord? "Nice leopard," she whispered, keeping her hands very still at her sides.

The beast made a snuffling sound, then got up and came toward her. She held her breath. It brushed along her hip, pushing its big head into her hand, then kept going, disappearing back into the thick. She exhaled, relief sweeping through her.

Glancing back the way she'd come, she saw the gates were closed. She took one more long look around, trying to take in the unfettered majesty of the place, and then she pulled out the map that would guide her to the Tree of Life.

Making note of a few landmarks, she started forward again. From where she was, there was no sign of the tree wall that she'd encountered at the entrance, which gave her the sense that the Garden was much bigger than she'd imagined. And every turn of the path brought more beautiful sights. A waterfall threw a rainbow into the air a few yards from the walkway. Some sort of tiny antelope drank from the pond below it. There were blooms the size of basketballs. Dragonflies that could have carried housecats. Trees that sported too many kinds of fruit to count.

She walked for a while, until she came to a crystal-clear pool of water surrounded by a few tall rock formations. Near one edge, water bubbled up, evidence of the spring at its source. The shape of the pool matched the one on the map, so she turned, walking around it. A trio of scarlet and emerald hummingbirds jetted past.

As she came around one of the rock outcroppings, the vegetation cleared in a circular area, almost like a natural arena. Long tendrils of ivy and flowering vines softened the edges of the surrounding rocks and a cloud of yellow butterflies fluttered through the space. At the center stood a grand tree, perfect in every way, from the thickness of its smooth, golden trunk to the deep, brilliant green of its heart-shaped leaves.

Small, apple-like fruit hung at even intervals, their skin so dark red they almost looked black and so shiny they seemed made of glass. She approached cautiously, unsure what to expect, but nothing impeded her progress. She reached out and touched one of the fruit. It was as cool and smooth as the glass it looked like.

The desire to eat one was overwhelming. Perhaps that was the nature of the tree? She took a few steps back. She didn't have time to question anything. Mal could be here with Tatiana and Lilith at any moment. She needed a place to hide and watch, a place from which she could strike quickly in case either of them didn't eat the fruit.

This beautiful, peaceful garden would be the final battleground and as much as she hated the thought of marring this perfect landscape, if it meant safety for her child, she would do it gladly.

She stared up at the tree. The leaves and fruit were so thick that beyond the first few branches, nothing else of the tree was visible. She smiled, nodding. The element of surprise often turned a battle early. With that thought propelling her, she grabbed the nearest branch and began to climb.

* * *

"You're sure?" Tatiana asked. She kneeled on the floor of the sitting room where they'd rolled up the carpet to reveal bare wood. The scroll sat next to her, unfurled.

"Yes," Mal said. "Turn part of your metal hand into a fountain pen, then use your blood to draw the portal. I've seen the comarré do it. I know it's the way."

Tatiana sniffed. "I hate that she was such a part of your life. You did kill her, didn't you?"

"I'm here, aren't I? Stop wasting time and get on with it." Every moment with Tatiana was like a year away from Chrysabelle. All he wanted was to be with her again and have this nightmare behind them. Then he wanted to press his hands to her belly and feel his child within her.

"Why are you smiling?"

Damn it. He was. "I was thinking about how nice it will be when this is over with."

Tatiana smiled back, tipping her head coyly. "Won't it?" She lifted her metal hand and a fountain pen formed between her fingers, and then she lifted her wrist to her mouth and bit down. With a soft curse, she dipped the nib into the blood spilling from her vein.

"Make a circle large enough to step through," Mal said.

"I know." Tension edged her voice.

He let her continue without speaking again. She drew the runes into the center of the circle, stopping twice to reopen the vein in her wrist as it healed.

Finally, she sat back. "I don't see how this is going to—bloody hell, look at that."

The blood began to spread, filling in the empty spaces as it expanded. Mal nodded. "You did it." Amazing, considering how little she liked following directions.

She got to her feet as the pen in her hand became fingers again. "Now what?"

"Wait..." Mal studied the portal. The blood touched the sides of the circle and a flash of gold gleamed across the surface. "There. It's open."

Her lids fluttered and her mouth opened. "Do you smell that? Like watermelon and fresh-cut grass and flowers."

"And sunlight," he added. The perfume flowing through the portal dug into his brain and picked out his few remaining memories of summer, a smell so rich and so rare it almost buckled his knees.

Beside him, Tatiana wept a single tear. She swiped at it. "I haven't smelled that since... I don't know when."

He turned away, ignoring the wrenching longing that had come alive in his chest. *Chrysabelle is already there, waiting for you*, he told himself. "Call Lilith. The sooner this is over, the better."

She opened her mouth.

"Wait." A thought struck him. "How do you know it's going to be night when we go through? It doesn't smell like night to me."

"It's okay," she answered. "The ancient one reassured me that the Garden becomes whatever you need it to be. I assume when we step through, it will change to night if it's not already."

"I hope you're right." Because if she was, the shift would alert Chrysabelle that they'd arrived and she'd be able to take cover until the right time. "Go ahead, call the little monster."

"Mal." Tatiana glared a warning at him, then put on a mask of happiness. "Lilith, my darling, come to me. We're ready for our trip."

Without hesitation, a sliver of shadow invaded the room and turned into Lilith. "I'm here." Her eyes were round with excitement and Mal wondered how the Castus hadn't realized that feeding their blood to a child would end up creating such a mad, twisted being. In a way, he felt sorry for Lilith. Her true family, her childhood, and her slim chance at some kind of normal life had been ripped away from her. He knew what that loss felt like from a father's point of view, but did she? Did she remember anything of her life before she'd become a pawn in this horrific game?

Perhaps death would be a welcome end for her. "Thank you for obeying so quickly," he told her. "Tatiana, why don't you go first, then Lilith, then I'll follow."

"No," Lilith barked. "I'm going first. It's my present."

Tatiana stepped back in surrender. "You go first, then."

Mal pointed at the portal. He couldn't have been more over this whole thing if he tried. At least Lilith going first was a great way to test if the sun was still up. "There. Go."

With a flounce, Lilith tossed her head and stepped into the circle. She disappeared. Tatiana looked at him. "Maybe we could just erase the portal and be done with her that way?"

Mal raised one brow. "She can travel in and out of the ancients' realm without effort. What would keep her from leaving the Garden that way?" Again, he pointed to the portal. "Hurry up, before she kills something on the other side."

Sighing, Tatiana followed after her. As soon as she disappeared, he stepped through.

And found them waiting for him in the middle of a desert. At night.

"There's nothing here," Lilith grumped. She stuck her hands on her hips as she turned to look at him. "What kind of—" Her mouth rounded into a circle. "Look!" She pointed and he and Tatiana turned.

A set of gates to rival any he'd ever seen rose up from the sand and vanished into the evening sky. Walls made of trees joined the sides and rounded out of sight. The air in front of the ornately filigreed gates shimmered like a heat mirage and a soldier appeared. Not a soldier exactly. He'd never seen a soldier with wings.

The creature came toward them. Lilith hissed. The creature opened his mouth and roared at her, blowing them all back a few steps. Then he pointed a wicked, flaming sword at her. It spun on its hilt, the flames flowing out like hungry tongues. "Demon spawn," he said. "Do not urge me to battle."

Mal yanked Lilith behind him. "Quiet, you." He bent his head slightly, trying to show respect. "We only wish entrance to the Garden. Will you let us in?"

The creature stared at Mal, losing some of the animosity he'd directed at Lilith. "Your blood decides that, not me." Behind him the gates began to open. He gestured to Tatiana and Lilith with the sword. "You may pass. You will not be permitted to remove anything from the Garden and you bear the consequences of anything you eat."

Tatiana grabbed Lilith's hand and dragged her forward. Mal hesitated. The creature hadn't indicated he could go through.

The soldier watched Tatiana and Lilith slip through the gates, then turned to Mal and lowered his sword. "You are not the first to enter these gates." His voice was soft. "Do you understand?"

Mal nodded, happiness replacing the frustration in his belly. "The comarré," he whispered.

The creature gave a single, short nod and held his hand out toward the gates.

Mal raced forward, catching up with Lilith and Tatiana, hopefully before they realized he'd lagged behind.

"Magnificent, isn't it?" Tatiana turned in a slow circle, a look of wonderment shining on her face.

"Glorious." But Mal's attention was on Lilith, who'd already strayed from the mossy path underfoot and was reaching for something in a tree. "Lilith," he called. She ignored him. "Lilith." She didn't even glance in his direction. He strode over to where she was.

And realized she was pulling a bright blue snake out of the tree. "Son of a priest, leave that alone."

She whipped around to face him, her hands still locked on the serpent, her eyes going full red. "You said I could have a pet."

"And you can, but we've only just entered. Don't you want to see what else there is?"

As his logic sank in, the whites returned to her eyes. She let go of the snake. "I guess."

He made himself smile at her. "That's a good girl. Come on, now, let's see the rest of this place."

He put his hand on her shoulder and herded her back to the path and Tatiana, who was still ogling the landscape. He pointed, showing Lilith a large purple lizard hugging a tree branch farther up the path. She raced off to look at it up close, giving him a moment to pull Tatiana back to reality. "Could you join me here? How far until we get to the tree?"

"What? Oh." She sighed and took the map out. "We

follow this path for a while, then leave it after we come to a large spring."

"Then let's go before *someone* gets distracted again and we have to drag her by her hair."

Tatiana nodded and with her help, they soon made it to the spring. He'd only had to forcibly herd Lilith three more times.

They turned off the path, Lilith straggling behind to pull the heads off flowers and throw them into the water. "Lilith, look." Tatiana pointed into the clearing ahead where a tree sat dead center.

Even without the map and the foreknowledge that it was the Tree of Life, Mal would have known it was something special. It was too perfect, too cleanly shaped to be something ordinary. The fruit hanging off it gleamed like black glass, looking more deadly than life-giving, but then, that was why they were here. Why he was here. To finally rid himself of the woman who'd wanted nothing but the worst for him for many, many years.

He surreptitiously scoped the area for Chrysabelle. It was impossible to pick out her scent with the garden's heavy perfume, but he knew she was here, just not where. Behind one of the monolithic rock formations or clusters of trees skirting the clearing? Ivy and flowering vines curled up the trunks, joining some and distorting others to the point where it was difficult to see the separation between the trees. She could be anywhere. His gaze landed on the tree again and as he stared at it, he realized there was a faint glow emanating from it.

Chrysabelle was in the branches. He hoped Tatiana just chalked it up to being part of the tree's supernatural specialness. Or maybe she'd be too distracted to even notice.

Fortunately, that distraction chose that moment to run past them. Lilith went straight to the tree's lower branches and the fruit hanging there. "What are these? I want one."

Mal leaned over to Tatiana. "Take yours now. Hurry." Then he approached Lilith to divert her for a moment. "They're some kind of fruit, but they don't look ripe."

Her bottom lip poked out right on cue. "But I want one."

At the sound of crunching, he and Lilith turned. Tatiana stood just a few feet away, one of the black apples cradled in her metal hand, the snowy white flesh revealed by the bite she'd taken.

"Delicious," she purred, eyes closed. Juice dripped down her chin.

"I want one," Lilith screeched, reaching toward the nearest fruit.

Tatiana's eyes opened, fear silvering them until they glowed. "Lilith, I don't think you should have one of these."

But Lilith shoved Mal out of the way so hard he hit the ground with an audible thud. She snatched one of the apples and shoved it into her mouth, chewing like a greedy little pig.

Tatiana made a show of trying to pry it away from her, but Lilith met her with a foot to the stomach and pushed her down, too. "My apple," she cried, bits of white flesh flying out of her mouth.

She opened her mouth to say something else, but only a choking sound came out. Then she fell to the ground.

Chapter Thirty-nine

Doc wrapped Fi in a hug like she hadn't had in a long time. She leaned in and held on, the tension of the last few days gone from his body. He was her big kitty cat again, relaxed and happy. A deep purr rumbled out of him. She squeezed him once more before tipping her head back. "I still can't believe Remo would kill his own sister just to tip the scales toward him becoming pride leader. What are you going to tell Rodrigo?"

Doc kissed her forehead before pulling her down onto the couch with him. He laid back, his long, hard body suddenly the most comfortable thing Fi had been in contact with lately. "The truth. I owe him that much."

She put her hands on his chest and pushed up. "You sure that's the best thing to do?"

He nodded. "Yes. Lies only complicate things. Rodrigo's a good man. He understood about Heaven. He won't be happy about what Remo's done. In fact, if he's mad about anything it will probably be that we can't hand Remo over to him now that the police have him in custody. Issues like this need to be taken care of internally."

"It *is* pride business."

"I know. But turning Remo over to the cops was the only way to get Barasa and Omur released. Remo knew what he was doing when he insisted on bringing the police in." Doc rolled his head from side to side. "He's a slick one. He knew taking it public would keep him out of his father's hands if things went south."

"Which they totally did." Fi lay back down, tucking her head under Doc's chin. She loved the way the heat of his body seeped into hers. "You're out a council member again."

Doc cursed softly. "Remo screwed us more ways than I can count. Replacing him isn't going to be easy. He might not have been well known, but he had the weight of the São Paulo alliance behind him. And despite Barasa and Omur being cleared, they'll never be clean enough for those in the pride who still resent me for taking out Sinjin." His hands fisted and his body suddenly became almost too hot to touch.

Fi jerked back. "You're not about to go nova on me, are you? Your skin is like fire."

He took a deep breath, closing his eyes for a few seconds. "No. I'm good." He blew out the breath slowly. "Flames just get harder to control when I get riled, you know?" He gave her a pitiful smile. "Sorry, baby."

She leaned against the couch but kept one hand planted on his forearm. "Does a council member have to be a pride member? Or even varcolai? Can it just be anyone the pride leader appoints?"

"Remo was proof they don't have to be an existing pride member. They become an honorary member through the appointment. I don't know about someone who's not varcolai." He squinted at her, his skin cooling beneath her fingers. "What's going on in that pretty head of yours?"

She smiled. "What's it worth to you?"

He laughed.

She tapped a finger against her temple. "This is pure gold, kitty cat. I'm going to need a lot of high-quality persuasion to spill it."

His eyes went green-gold, the pupils thinning down to slits. She shivered with anticipation as he pulled her down to him. "Good thing I'm all about high quality." He nipped at her chin, scraping his teeth down her neck and causing her to moan. "You should probably tell me your idea now, though."

"Why?" she breathed. She wasn't sure which one of them was on fire now.

His deep laugh reverberated against her throat. "Because when I'm done *persuading* you, you probably won't be able to talk."

"Oh. Oh! *Ohhh…*"

The juice coated Tatiana's tongue with the flavors of warm honey, cinnamon, and smoke. After she'd swallowed the first bite, a gentle hum had vibrated through her body. Almost like a tiny electric shock, but completely pleasant.

It felt very much like power to her, the kind of power Lilith didn't need. But maybe she'd been wrong. She pushed to her elbows on the ground beside Mal. "Is she dead?"

"I don't know." He flipped to his feet and stood over Lilith's body. "She looks dead, but she hasn't gone to ash."

Panic swept through Tatiana. She stared at the apple's small white core. "What if it kills me too?" She tossed the fruit and dug in her pocket for the little metal tin of white powder. Frantically she opened it and dumped it into her mouth. She coughed, spewing dust as she rolled to her side. It tasted like sugar. She clutched at her throat. "I think I'm dying." She clawed hysterically at the ground. "Water. I need water."

Mal shook his head. "You're not dying." He sighed, disappointment crystalline in his eyes. "Unfortunately."

Tatiana went still. She *wasn't* dying. "Now is not the time for snide remarks, Malkolm."

A gasp stole their attention. Mal turned, moving out of the way enough for Tatiana to see Lilith quivering on the ground.

"She's having a seizure." New fear chilled Tatiana. Death could still be coming for her.

Lilith's body shook so badly her features blurred. She bent and bowed up off the ground, limbs flailing.

Mal swore softly. "She's shrinking."

She was. Right before Tatiana's eyes, Lilith was growing smaller and smaller. Tatiana grabbed her own arms and legs and palpitated them, but they seemed to be the right size. She tried to listen to her body, to feel for anything that might be changing internally, but there was nothing. In fact, she'd never felt so good.

She glanced back at Lilith. She was no more than the size of a toddler now, and the tremors seemed to be subsiding. Tatiana got to her feet. "What's happened to her?"

"I have no idea," Mal answered. He looked at her. "How do you feel?"

"Good. Really good."

He squinted at her and was about to say something when a piercing wail erupted behind him. Again they turned. Lilith was sitting up, sobbing, swamped in clothes that were now vastly too large for her. Tears trailed down her pink cheeks. She blinked, her brown eyes big and wet, and reached toward Mal like she wanted him to pick her up.

"Holy hell," Tatiana muttered. "She's a child again."

"More than that," Mal said, his nostrils flaring. "She's . . . human."

Creek stood in front of the machine shop, unlocking the big sliding door, when the familiar sound of leathery wings beating the night air reached his ears. He pushed the door back and left it open after he went inside.

A moment later, Annika joined him. She closed the door as her wings disappeared into her jacket. She walked past him and sat. "Octavian's dead."

Hello to you too. Creek took the other chair. "How?"

"He and the mayor showed up at Tatiana's house in Corvinestri."

"The mayor?" Creek hadn't expected that. "No wonder I couldn't get in to see her. Or find Octavian."

"None of us could," she said. "As to how he died, Lilith figured out who he was and killed him before Tatiana could even react, apparently." She picked at one of the holes in the fabric on the chair's arm. "It's all for the better. We would have had to kill him anyway."

Creek nodded slowly. The meting out of KM justice wasn't something he always agreed with, but in this case, he would have been totally on board.

Sighing, she leaned forward, her arms on her knees. "There's more. Our contact overheard a conversation between Malkolm and Chrysabelle."

"Chrysabelle's in Corvinestri?"

"Was. We believe she's already returned home to complete the rest of her and Malkolm's mission."

Now he really felt lost. "They had a mission?"

"Self-imposed. They're luring Lilith and Tatiana to the Garden of Eden and putting an end to both of them there."

"The Garden of Eden? That's a real place?"

"Very. And almost impossible to get to unless you know how to open a portal. Even then, humans can't get in."

"But Chrysabelle's human."

"Mostly. And now that we believe she's carrying Malkolm's child, we—"

"What? Chrysabelle's pregnant?"

"Didn't you know?" She raised one brow. "We thought you were privy to everything that went on in the comarré's life."

He got up and went to the kitchen for a beer. It was better than letting Annika watch the anger on his face. "You know I'm not. Being the KM's messenger boy has destroyed my relationship with her."

"You sound upset."

Brilliant deduction. "I am." He left it at that. Any more and he'd only succeed in putting himself in a worse mood. But pregnant? How was that even possible? If the KM thought he was doing anything to help them put their hands on Chrysabelle's child, they were dead wrong. He changed the subject. "I hope they get rid of Tatiana once and for all."

She nodded. "Me too. But Lilith's the real issue. If they can't make this happen, the KM's main focus will shift to her. After what our contact shared, we now know that she's the greatest threat to mankind that's ever existed."

"Why can't your contact there do something to stop Lilith?"

Annika stood, wing tips emerging from her jacket. "Because our contact activated an emergency message alert. Our receiving it means she was unable to stop the system from sending it, which most likely means she's dead." She walked toward the door.

She? But he knew better than to ask. If Annika wanted him to know more, she would have already given him the info. "Before you go..."

She stopped at the door. "Yes?"

It was now or never. "Does anyone ever leave the Kubai Mata?"

"Besides dying?"

Obviously. "Yes."

"You can buy your way out or fight your way out." She stared at him. "Thinking about retirement?"

He nodded. "You might say that. We both know I don't have the funds. Whom would I have to fight?"

She snorted softly, then pushed the door open. "Me."

Not the answer he wanted to hear. "And *if* I win, what happens to my family and my record?"

The amusement left her face. "The money goes away, Creek. The mortgage on the house becomes your mother's and grandmother's responsibility. Una's scholarship won't be pulled, but it won't be renewed next semester, either. As for your record, it stands the way it is. You've been cleared of the charge. The KM won't put you back in prison unless you give them a reason to."

The next question stuck in his throat. "Would I have to...kill you to win?"

She went quiet a moment, like she couldn't believe

he was contemplating this. "No. You'd just have to best me." Her fingers strayed to the temple of her shades. "You should know that there's no cure for being turned to stone by a basilisk."

He nodded. "Good to know." Horrible to know. It pretty much meant the brawl would be over almost immediately unless he could fight her without looking at her, which didn't seem possible.

She tipped her head at him, then stepped through the door and flew into the night. He leaned back in the chair and rocked his head back to stare at the ceiling. The chains he'd strung Octavian up with still hung from the ceiling. At least that was one issue he'd no longer have to deal with. Dominic would want to know.

He sat up. Dominic. If anyone could make the impossible possible, it was an alchemist. Creek grabbed his jacket and his keys. Anything was worth a shot.

Chapter Forty

Chrysabelle watched from her perch in the branches as Tatiana lunged for Lilith. Fortunately, Mal got there first. He snatched the child up, brought her close to his face, and inhaled. "She's definitely human."

"She can't be." Tatiana reached for her, but Mal pulled Lilith away. "Give her to me," Tatiana commanded.

He turned slightly, his eyes silvering. "For what reason?" Lilith wrapped her little arms around his neck. The blouse she'd been wearing as an adult now dangled off her like a christening gown.

Tatiana held out her hands. "Because she's my daughter."

Chrysabelle had heard enough. Tatiana's time had come to an end. She dropped out of the tree, landing behind Tatiana. "No, she's not."

Tatiana whipped around, putting Mal and Lilith at her back. "Chrysabelle." She looked at Mal. "You said she was dead. That you killed her."

Mal shook his head. "I guess it didn't take."

Tatiana let out a shriek of anger, but spun back to face Chrysabelle. "What are you doing here?"

"I'm here to do what the Tree of Life didn't."

Chrysabelle reached back, grabbed the hilts of both sacres, and unsheathed them in one graceful sweep. Their beautiful blades gleamed like water in the moonlight, the hilts humming and ready for the battle ahead. "I'm going to kill you."

"Like hell you are." With a snarl and flash of fang, Tatiana thrust her metal hand out, transforming it into a long, wicked blade. Toothy serrations ran down one edge. "Bring it, blood whore. I've wanted to cut you apart for a long, long time."

Chrysabelle circled toward Mal, pushing Tatiana away from him and whatever Lilith had become. In his arms, she seemed like an innocent. Chrysabelle snuck a look at them. Heaven help her, but Mal looked so natural cradling Lilith, whispering soft words that had stopped her tears. Chrysabelle's pride in him soared. He would be a wonderful father, no matter what his reservations were. Renewed by the surge of emotion, she raised her weapons and beckoned to Tatiana. "Let's go, vampire. Your time is up."

Slowly, Tatiana worked farther away from Mal. She spun her sword hand in a figure eight, the metal leaving trails of light in the air. "How wrong you are, comarré."

Chrysabelle shook her head. "The only wrong thing here is that your ashes are going to dirty up this place." Satisfied that Mal and Lilith were out of danger, she lunged.

Tatiana blocked the thrust and metal met metal. The clang scared a flock of small birds near the perimeter, filling the night sky with the rustle of wings. Tatiana twisted, bringing her sword around.

Chrysabelle ducked and the blade whistled over her head. She kicked a leg out, knocking Tatiana off balance.

She fell, but caught herself with her physical hand and flipped back to her feet in a split second.

Plenty of time for Chrysabelle to reposition. She sliced both sacres through the air as Tatiana righted herself. The tips of the blades caught the front of her throat, opening a red line that closed almost as soon as it formed. "First blood," Chrysabelle taunted. "And I'll have the last blood, too."

Tatiana retaliated with a downward strike, but Chrysabelle danced out of the way. Pain burned along her upper arm. She glanced down to see blood spilling from a slice on her bicep.

"Too bad you don't heal as fast as I do," Tatiana gloated. Behind her, Mal growled. Tatiana laughed. "Don't worry, my love, I know you wanted to be the one to kill her, but looks like that fun is going to be all mine."

"My love?" Chrysabelle smirked. "Is that what you're calling my fiancé these days?"

Mal's mouth opened slightly and he stilled. Then a smile as bright as the sun he'd never see broke over his face. "Is that a yes?"

Chrysabelle winked at him. "We'll talk about it."

"Fiancé?" Tatiana whirled around. "What the hell is she talking about? Explain this, Malkolm, or I swear, I will kill you when I'm done with her."

It was all the opening Chrysabelle needed. She tossed one sacre into the air, caught it in a reverse grip and drove it forward like a lance. The blade pierced Tatiana's back and slid through her body like a needle stitching silk until the hilt met flesh. Chrysabelle leaned in to whisper in Tatiana's ear. "That's for Maris." Then she grabbed the hilt with both hands and yanked up, slicing through

Tatiana's rib cage before loosening her grip to shove Tatiana forward.

Tatiana fell flat on her face, but pushed to her knees, struggling to get a foot on the ground so she could get up. Chrysabelle danced around to face her. The first few inches of the sacre's blade stuck out of Tatiana's chest, dripping blood that turned to ashes as it fell. Chrysabelle shook her head. "Too bad you didn't turn your back on my mother. Then she could have taken you out a long time ago."

Anger gleamed in Tatiana's eyes and blood trickled from her mouth. She lifted her sword hand to strike, but Chrysabelle stepped back from the wobbling figure. Tatiana took one step forward. "You stupid whore. You've ruined everythin—"

The sacre fell to the ground as Tatiana's ashes floated down after it. They covered the weapon in a gray shroud.

It was *over*. A sob shook Chrysabelle in a hard rush of joy and the rising sense that she'd finally avenged her mother. "We're free," she whispered across the clearing to Mal. It seemed as if another person took over her body and began moving her feet, walking her toward him, and then something inside her clicked and she ran.

He set Lilith down and caught Chrysabelle up in his arms. "You did it." He kissed her. "I knew you could." He leaned back. "I didn't know you were going to do it dressed like a dominatrix, but the look is growing on me."

Laughing, she returned his kiss with tears streaming down her face. Tears of happiness and pain and redemption. Beside them, Lilith's little hand patted Chrysabelle's leg. She glanced down to see Lilith sucking her thumb. "What are we going to do with her? I'm not even sure what happened to her."

Mal followed Chrysabelle's gaze. "She's got family in Paradise City. We take her back with us."

Lilith lifted her arm to point at something behind Chrysabelle, her little face scrunching into a tearful mask. "No," she shouted. "No!"

Chrysabelle and Mal looked where she was pointing. "Holy mother," Chrysabelle whispered.

Mal uttered a curse, then shook his head. "You can say that again."

"I'm pleased about Octavian." Dominic lifted one hand and frowned. "Not as pleased as if I'd been able to kill him myself, but one can't be too picky when it comes to things like this."

"I get it," Creek said. "If I'd had anything to do with it, I would have brought him back for you to deal with." A lie, but one that would hopefully put the vampire in a giving mood. He shifted in his seat. Luciano hadn't moved from the chair next to Creek's other than to nod at whatever Dominic said. "There is something else I'd like to talk to you about."

Dominic raised a brow. "The Kubai Mata has need of me?" He smiled indulgently. "This I must hear."

"Not the KM, exactly." Creek knew this was a bad idea and yet he couldn't help but try. "I need your help. Me, personally." He watched Dominic's face but the vampire showed no reaction. Creek continued. "I have a chance to gain my freedom from the Kubai Mata, but it won't be much of a chance unless I have some help."

Dominic twirled a gold pen between his fingers. "What can I do? I am a vampire. Not exactly friends with the KM."

"I've never done anything to harm you. In fact, I spared your nephew's life." Beside him, Luciano sniffed. Creek looked at him. "You sired the mayor for your own personal gain. I'd be surprised if the KM were the only ones who considered you a threat after that."

Dominic held up his hand. "That transgression was Luciano's doing alone. For sparing his life, I thank you." He tapped the point of the pen on the desktop. "So you mean to collect on that debt?"

"That wasn't my intention. Just to ask for your help. I have to fight a battle against a creature I'm no match for. I was hoping you might have some kind of spell—"

Dominic's eyes flared silver. "I'm an alchemist, not a witch."

"Got it." Creek nodded. "And one of the most talented alchemists who ever came out of the House of St. Germain, from what I know."

The silver in his eyes faded. "What is this creature you're to fight?"

"A basilisk."

Dominic raised his eyes to look Creek in the face. "A basilisk." His tone reeked with disbelief. "Have you actually seen this beast?"

He leaned back and crossed his arms. "Seen her, talked to her, even had dinner with her at my grandmother's house. She's my KM sector chief."

Luciano mumbled something in Italian and Dominic nodded. "My nephew says not only should such a creature not exist, but they are the last ones who should be in charge of protecting mankind." He picked up the pen again. "And you know she is what she says? You've seen proof?"

Creek had prepared for this. He dug into his jacket,

pulled out the cockroach Annika had turned to stone and tossed it onto Dominic's desk. "She is what she says. Without question." He nodded at the insect. "I saw her make that."

Dominic dropped the pen and picked up the bug, rubbing his thumb over the body. "She did this?"

Creek nodded.

Luciano cursed and panic colored his words. "This creature lives in Paradise City? What defense do we have against her? I have no desire to spend my eternity locked in a stone prison."

"Full circle," Dominic muttered, staring at the insect.

Creek leaned in, hoping for some kind of advice or secret he could use against Annika. "What does that mean?"

Dominic shook his head. "Nothing." He dropped the cockroach. "Which is exactly the amount of help I can give you."

Disappointment tightened Creek's gut. "You realize if something happens to me, she'll take over until they find a replacement. And she's not as understanding as I am when it comes to the goings-on in this city."

Dominic narrowed his eyes. "It's not that I won't help you. It's that I *can't*. There is nothing I can do against a basilisk without some kind of original material." He tapped a finger on the stone bug. "This is not enough."

Creek shrugged. "What the hell is original material?"

"Bones, blood, skin—"

"Scales?" Creek interrupted.

Dominic pursed his lips and nodded. "Scales would work well. Very well."

Creek stood. "I'll be back."

"*Uno momento*." Dominic raised a finger. "If I help you and you succeed, what does this benefit me?"

Creek stopped himself from scowling. Of course Dominic would want something in return. "Besides my not executing Luciano?"

Luciano sighed.

Dominic smiled gently. "I am a businessman, no? Surely you understand that my skills do not come cheap."

"I don't have any money. If I did, I'd be buying my way out, not risking my life in a fight."

Dominic picked up the cockroach again, hefting it in his palm like he was weighing it. "Since losing Katsumi, I am short-handed here. If you are free from the KM, you will also be unemployed, yes? I assume you will need some source of income."

A cold shiver went through Creek. "I will." Desperately.

"I will help you and when you win your freedom, you will come to work for me. You will be fairly compensated, I assure you. Do you agree?"

"What do you get out of it?"

Dominic offered him a faint smile. "I am aware of your skills. I would much rather have you on my side than against me."

He was getting out of bed with one master to get in bed with another. What choice did he have? Taking care of his family had always been his goal, but at what cost to his own life? To his sense of justice? "Can I give you an answer when I return?"

"*Si*." Dominic tipped his head slightly, his fangs glinting white in the blackness of his mouth. "But we both know you'll say yes."

Chapter Forty-one

From the pile of Tatiana's ashes rose a ragged whirlwind. Even in the bright moonlight, the swirl of gray dust cast a sinister shadow on the grassy plain.

"What the hell—" Mal shoved Chrysabelle behind him. She'd done enough to protect him. Now it was his turn to get them home. *To die.*

"Doesn't make sense," Chrysabelle said. "There's no wind." She scooped Lilith up and the little girl clung to her.

"This isn't wind; it's something…else. Son of a priest." The whirlwind took shape. Tatiana's shape.

With a shiver, the ashes became flesh and blood again. Tatiana shook herself a second time, then stared at him, an unnaturally bright smile on her face. "Well, now, my dear faithless husband. You weren't expecting that, were you?" She laughed and brushed at her sleeves. "I wasn't either, but isn't it a fun surprise?" She gestured at the tree. "Everlasting life on a grander scale than I could have imagined. I'm so glad you convinced me to eat one of those little black apples."

The beast roared for release. Instead, Mal charged forward, caught Tatiana in his arms, and took her to the ground. Her laughter rang in his ears as he yanked a knife from his belt. She rolled out of his grasp and got back to her feet.

She shook her finger at him like she was scolding a child. "What are you going to do? Kill me? Weren't you watching? That doesn't work on me anymore."

He jumped to his feet and threw the blade. It sunk home just shy of her heart.

On the perimeter, Chrysabelle clutched Lilith a little tighter.

Shaking her head, Tatiana tugged it out and grimaced. "That hurt, Malkolm. Not as much as your betrayal, but then that's all you've ever been good for, isn't it? Causing me pain." She flung the dagger back.

He caught the knife by the hilt, inches before it pierced his chest. "I saved your life."

"Phft. That old song." She walked to the tree, picked another black apple, and stuck it in her pocket. "Screw what that guard said. I'm taking a few of these home with me."

"No," Chrysabelle answered. "You're not leaving here. This is where your reign of terror ends."

Tatiana shifted her attention to Chrysabelle. "You do know that I'm going to kill you, don't you? What chance do you have—"

Mal's dagger drilled into Tatiana's neck, cutting off her words. She dropped the apple and he attacked, taking her down and grabbing the dagger's hilt. He wrenched the blade down, severing her spine. She went limp beneath him, then turned to ash a second time.

He stood, wiping the bloody blade on his pants. "There. It's done."

But before he could walk back to Chrysabelle's side, the ashes lifted into the air, swirling just as they had before, taking on Tatiana's shape once again.

The knife fell from his hands. "The Aurelian never mentioned this, did she?"

"No," Chrysabelle said, her voice thick with hopelessness. "Nadira's big on leaving out details."

He nodded as Tatiana's form became flesh and blood. "If we ever get out of here, I'm killing the Aurelian next."

"Thanks for coming, Chief. I know it's late." Doc shook Vernadetto's hand as he walked into the office. The man had done a lot for them and if this meeting went well, he'd be doing a lot more. Fi gave the man a hug. Amazing her effect on people. If anyone was cut out to be the pride leader's wife, it was Fi.

She stepped back by his side. "Nice to see you on better circumstances, Pete."

"You too, Fiona." Vernadetto looked at Doc. "I can't imagine what other information you have to give me about Heaven's death. We found enough evidence in Remo's apartment that the case is officially closed. But Fi said it was important, so—"

"It's not about Heaven's death but I didn't want to say too much over the phone." Doc gestured to the sitting area. "Come on in and we'll talk."

He shut the door as Fi and Vernadetto got comfortable on the couch, and then he sat across from them in one of the chairs. He leaned forward. "Can I get you a drink?"

"No, thanks." Vernadetto grinned nervously. "Better keep my wits about me until I know what's going on."

Doc sat back. "But I'm guessing you have a pretty high tolerance for alcohol, don't you?"

Vernadetto nodded, smiling sheepishly. "Runs in my family."

"Most varcolai can outdrink a human three to one," Fi said quietly.

The color drained out of Vernadetto's face. "I don't know what you're talking about."

Before Doc could say anything, Fi grabbed the chief's hand. "Don't be mad at me, but I told Doc what we talked about at the cocktail party. What we've *been* talking about. I can't keep secrets from Doc anymore. Not anything, not after what we've been through." She glanced at Doc, then went on. "Did you know the mayor had Creek investigating you?"

Vernadetto's head snapped up. "What the hell? After everything I've done for her?"

Fi laughed reassuringly. "That's what we thought. Anyway, Creek and the mayor aren't exactly getting along these days. He gave us the file. All the info he'd collected on you."

Vernadetto started to breathe through his mouth. "I don't like this. He had no right. He should have given that to me."

"I agree, but he gave it to us because he knew we might need a bargaining chip." She smiled and shook her head. "Obviously, everything worked out with Remo and we didn't. We wouldn't have anyway. Your business is your business. And I promise you, neither of us has looked at what's in the file."

He calmed, but stayed wary. "You haven't?"

She pulled the large envelope out from under the sofa and placed it on his lap. "It's still sealed."

Vernadetto clutched it, but kept it on his lap. He stared at the single *V* written in pencil on the front. Seconds ticked by in silence.

Doc cleared his throat. "Based on what Fi told me, I'm sure you're a remnant. You know what that is, right?"

He nodded, still mute.

Doc tipped his chin at the envelope. "After you digest what's in there, Fi and I would like to talk to you again. Make you an offer."

Vernadetto said nothing.

Fi bit her lip. "Are you mad because I told Doc about you? Please don't be, Pete. With all this going on, I couldn't not tell him. And I swear, we just want to help you."

Vernadetto inhaled a deep shuddering sigh. "I'm not mad at you and I don't need to open this." He raised his head and looked Doc squarely in the face. "I already know what I am."

Creek turned the engine off before he hit the turn that would take him to his grandmother's house. He coasted, then hopped off and walked the bike in. She'd be asleep by now, his mother probably an hour or two from getting home after her shift at the hospital, but the sooner he did this, the sooner he could be free. Or as free as a man could be who'd just sold his soul to a new devil.

Unless leaving the KM wasn't the right thing to do after all.

A soft light shone from the back of the house and he smiled as he parked his bike. The earthy tang of cigarette smoke told him Mawmaw was up and waiting. Once again, she'd known he was coming. Tucking his helmet over the handlebars, he ran a hand over his Mohawk and said a prayer that she'd know what to do. She always did. She was his rock when everything else was quicksand.

She deserved a grandson who was around more, able to help her when she needed it, not one who was off doing the bidding of a shadowy organization hell bent on... whatever they were hell bent on. The KM and their damn money. At least they made it possible for him to provide for his family that way. How would he replace that money if he left? That was the thing that weighed heaviest. He could handle prison again if he really had to, but leaving his family broke was unacceptable, especially when their financial situation had been caused by his legal troubles to begin with.

He skirted the house and went around back. Mawmaw sat in her rocker, the faint light from the cherry of her cigarette brightening her face more than the gas lantern sitting on the railing. Pip curled at her feet. The dog lifted his head enough to sigh, then went back to sleep. Creek nodded at her. "How are you, Mawmaw?"

"Good." She exhaled, the smoke pale in the lantern's light. "You should sit. You have a lot on your mind."

He took the rocker next to hers, his body as comfortable on the worn wood as in a feather bed. "I have a decision to make. One that will color my future."

She took a long drag, then blew the smoke out in a thin stream. "Go on."

"The organization that freed me—"

"The ones who make you hunt the blood eaters."

"Yes, them. They also make me do other things. Things I'm not happy about. Things that have hurt people I call friends." An owl hooted. He stared out at the swamp.

"But?" she said, waiting.

"But they're also the ones who made Una's scholarship happen. The mortgage payment the bank gets for this house every month? That's not from me. It's from them. The raise mom got after I joined them…" He shook his head. "They own me."

She turned to look at him, anger in her eyes. "No one owns you, Thomas. You're a child of this land. Remember that."

He nodded. "I know, Mawmaw, but telling them I'm a child of this land isn't going to mean squat. They expect my service. It's the price I agreed to."

She looked away from him and crossed one arm over her body to prop up her other elbow. "What are you here for if you have all the answers?"

"Because I don't have all the answers. Especially now. What I do have is an opportunity to get free."

She raised her brows like she knew there was more to it. Because she did know. She *always* knew.

Damn it. "Free of *them*, anyway. It would mean aligning myself with another who could be just as bad."

She ground out her cigarette in an old coffee cup filled with sand. "You battle two wolves. One known, one unknown, but both are wolves."

"How do I know which one is the most dangerous?"

"If you refuse to attack, which one will attack you first?"

He sat silently for a moment. There was no way the KM would let him ignore their directives. Dominic on the other hand would probably rather keep some kind of working relationship between them. "The wolf I know."

She nodded slowly. "Then that is the one you must kill."

"What about the money?"

Her thin shoulders lifted in a shrug. "There is always a way. Now go, kill the wolf before it kills you."

"Okay." He reached over and squeezed her hand. "Thank you. For everything."

She slipped her hand out from under his, reached into the pocket of her house dress, and pulled something out. "Here," she said, holding her closed fist over his hand.

He turned his palm up.

She dropped three waxy, dime-sized disks into his hand. "You're going to need those."

He pinched one between his fingers. They were hard and rough. "I almost forgot to ask about them."

She pulled out another cigarette and lit it up, making him wait. After an inhale, she released a few smoke rings. "They're what you came here for. Basilisk scales."

He squeezed them tight in his hand. "I love you."

She smiled. "I know."

Chapter Forty-two

Chrysabelle held tight to Lilith's hand. Panic tingled down to the tips of her fingers. Tatiana was almost herself again. "What are we going to do? How many times do we have to kill her?"

Mal glanced back the way they'd come. "Maybe we should just run for it."

"And have her follow us?" She shook her hand. "No way. This ends here. It has to." She nodded toward the tree. "The angel guarding the gate said nothing can be removed from the Garden. She's got one in her pocket. Maybe if she tries to leave with it, he'll kill her."

Mal nodded. "It's worth a shot. As soon as she's herself again, we'll run and let her chase us. I'll take Lilith." He scooped her into his arms.

Chrysabelle nodded. "Good." Tatiana would probably use the child for blood if they left her. She shuddered at the thought.

Lilith patted Mal on the head, but it didn't faze him. "Anything's better than Tatiana having her, although I don't know if the mayor will still be interested in Lilith now that she's human again."

A ragged breath left Chrysabelle's lungs. Completely real again, Tatiana walked toward them. "Here she comes."

Mal turned, putting himself between Tatiana and Chrysabelle. "Stop right where you are."

"Why should I listen to a thing that comes out of your lying mouth?" Tatiana kept walking. She thrust her hand forward like she was going to make a sword out of it, but it was flesh now. Healed by the tree, maybe. She frowned and shook her fingers, but they stayed fingers.

"Because I have a deal for you." Mal held his ground. "And you're apparently out of weaponry."

A deal? Chrysabelle wished she knew what Mal had planned, but she trusted him.

"That's rich. You have a deal for me." Tatiana stopped and put her hands on her hips. "And for your information, I'm happy to have my real hand back."

Mal ignored her comments. "Let us take the child and Chrysabelle won't stop you from taking fruit from the tree back to Corvinestri with you."

Tatiana bent in laughter. "Oh, that *is* good. The comar-ré's going to stop me? She couldn't even kill me."

"No, but she *does* have weaponry and she could spend the rest of eternity lopping your head off. That's got to hurt, and who knows, that apple you ate might run out at some point." He hefted Lilith a little higher onto his hip. "What do you say?"

"I say you're a liar and not to be trusted."

"The life of a child is at stake, Shaya." At the use of her human name, the snarl left her face and a flicker of sadness filled her eyes. Mal nodded. "You know me well enough to understand that, in this, I speak the truth."

She swallowed. "I still want the comarré dead."

Chrysabelle exhaled hard. "The feeling is mutual, you—"

"Understood," Mal interrupted. "But that's for another time and place."

Fi shook her head. "But you said you didn't know what you were."

"I know," Pete said quietly. "I didn't want to lie to you. You really do remind me of my niece and you're such a sweet kid. Plus, you had enough to deal with. You didn't need to know the city was being protected by a freak."

"You're not a freak," Fi said. Not that she knew what he was, but honestly, what could be considered freaky these days? "Doc changes into a leopard, I'm a ghost, the city's lousy with vampires and fae and other varcolai. I can't imagine what you could be that makes you think you're stranger than any of that."

He sighed again and looked at Doc. "You're lucky to have this one, you know."

Doc nodded. "I know. That's why I married her." He smiled at Fi.

She winked back, not really wanting to change the subject. "Pete, this whole building is filled with full-blooded, feline varcolai. A remnant isn't going to scare anyone."

Pete laughed. "Like I said, sweet kid." He bounced the envelope on his knees as if weighing the contents. "I'm not a remnant. I'm full-blooded." He reached into his shirt and pulled out a gold chain. A well-worn, highly polished gold disc hung from the end. At the circle's edge was an inscription too small for Fi to read. "This keeps me from changing. I've worn it since I was fourteen." He swallowed. "Since the first and last time I changed."

Doc caught Fi's gaze. His eyes were full of questions. She gave him a small nod, then returned to Pete. "It's beautiful. It looks very old."

He dropped it, not bothering to hide it beneath his shirt again. "It is. Passed down to me from my grandfather, the last of us to manifest the change before me."

She leaned in. "Pete, what are you?"

He moved like he might get up. "You wouldn't believe me if I told you."

Doc snorted. "You realize whom you're talking to, right? This is your chance to get this off your chest, bro. You're among friends. I swear it on the life of this pride."

Pete seemed to consider Doc's words. He nodded. "Okay. It would be nice not to keep this secret any longer. Maybe you could even help me." He shrugged. "Not that there's much use for someone like me."

He leaned over and stuck his hand under the table lamp. "What do you see beneath my hand?"

Fi looked closely. "Nothing."

"Exactly," he said. "I cast no shadow." He inhaled and lifted his chin, his gaze flitting between them. "I'm a doppelganger."

Chapter Forty-three

Once Tatiana had agreed to Mal's proposed deal, he'd put Lilith down and told her to hold Chrysabelle's hand. Now the little girl walked with her as she led the way back to the gates of the Garden. Mal followed behind, acting as a buffer between them and Tatiana in case she changed her mind about their strange truce. If she was able to leave with the fruit, their only other hope was that she'd be killable, permanently, once they got her outside the Garden. She glanced back, meeting Mal's eyes, trying to let him know with a look that she understood his plan.

He gave her a quick nod in return.

Lilith tugged on Chrysabelle's hand. "Birdy!" She pointed as a scarlet macaw sailed overhead.

Chrysabelle smiled and nodded. "That's right." The little girl's small hand clutched hers tighter and her own child kicked in her belly. Soon, the hand she was holding would belong to her own flesh and blood. The child that she and Mal had created. She looked back again, this time at Tatiana. Chrysabelle could not allow that evil to harm her family. Tatiana could *not* return to Corvinestri and her power-hungry, blood-spilling ambitions.

At some point, she would find out about the baby Chrysabelle was carrying and that information would shift Tatiana's full attention onto her. Just as Tatiana had stolen Lilith, she would throw her weight into stealing Chrysabelle's child.

It would not happen. It could not. Lilith had been put through hell, stripped of her childhood to be used as a pawn and turned into a monster. Chrysabelle studied the child at her side. She seemed so innocent now, as if the fruit had somehow cleaned the evil from her soul, but looks could be deceiving. What if darkness still lingered in her heart? Would it manifest someday? Would this child become a threat to Chrysabelle's own?

She knew Mal wanted to take Lilith back to the mayor so she could be raised by family, but that might not be the right decision. Chrysabelle didn't want to turn her over only to have to kill her someday when her true nature resurfaced.

The gates loomed ahead and, as they approached, began to open. The moon still gleamed from the same place in the sky as when night had first fallen while she was hiding in the tree. Had it moved at all? Did it move? Who knew how this place worked?

A new glow beckoned from the open gate. Eae maybe? She squinted, trying to see through the halo of light, but then a second figure appeared, one that was easily recognizable as Eae.

She slowed and Mal came up beside her. He spoke softly. "Is that a second guard?"

"Maybe." She shook her head. "I don't know."

"Go cautiously."

She nodded and started forward again. With each step, the face of the second guard became more readable.

She inhaled as recognition hit her and the scene of her mother's death flashed before her eyes. "Michael." The name came out on a breath and as she averted her eyes, a sudden wave of inadequacy struck her. The glory that surrounded the archangel pressed on her, showing her in a flash of memories how she'd fallen short in her duties as a comarré since she'd last seen him at the breaking of the covenant.

She fell to her knees as he approached, overwhelmed by such deep emotion that standing seemed impossible.

"Get up, child," he said.

She shook her head. "I don't think I can." Not yet. Not while this inexplicable guilt pushed her to the verge of tears. Once again, her pregnancy emotions were besting her. *Her pregnancy.* Holy mother, what would he think of that? As if he didn't already know.

He crouched down before her. "Look at me, Chrysabelle."

Reluctantly, she raised her head. The suffusion of light faded enough for her to see him clearly. His face still glowed, but this time, with kindness.

He smiled. "Everything you're feeling belongs to you and you alone. I am proud of what you've accomplished. Nadira should have offered you help when you went to her."

"S-she did. In a way." Why Chrysabelle felt the need to protect the Aurelian, she had no idea.

Michael shook his head. "Not enough help. Not the right help. You were correct. The time for the comarré to rise up had come."

"Then why didn't Nadira do more?"

He stood. "She is a stubborn woman, too old to bend

with pressure, too full of her own importance. But she—and Rennata—are mine to deal with now. Nadira I can only chastise, but Rennata I can, and will, replace. Something I should have done years ago." He shook his head ominously. "But know that by your actions, you have averted the crisis." He held his hand out to her.

She took it and let him help her to her feet. His skin was like water, cool and soothing. "How can that be?" She glanced back at Tatiana. Both she and Mal hung a few feet away. "My enemy still seeks me."

Tatiana scowled, but Michael laughed. "Your enemy is contained."

Tatiana laughed right back. "You don't scare me."

His countenance radiated authority. "Don't I? Then you're ignorant. But I'm not here to scare you, demon."

She sniffed. "Then what are you here for?"

Michael glanced at Chrysabelle before answering Tatiana. "You have two choices, demon. Remain within these gates for your eternity or walk through them and die."

She laughed. "You think you can kill me? That doesn't work anymore, but nice try." She started forward, pushing past Chrysabelle and Lilith.

Michael turned as Tatiana approached the gates. "Walk through those gates and you'll kill yourself."

Tatiana stopped. "What does that mean?"

"You ate of the Tree of Life."

Her hand slid into the pocket of her gown, no doubt to clutch the forbidden fruit squirreled away there. "Which is why I come back to life now. I get it."

He smiled in the way of people who know far more than those they're speaking to. "Your new immortality only works *within* these gates. Your human side died cen-

turies ago when you were sired. Eating the fruit of the
Tree of Life killed your vampire side, except on these
grounds where there is no death." He nodded past her.
"Out there, beyond the Garden's boundaries, you will last
no longer than the time it takes for your foot to touch the
ground."

She lifted her chin defiantly. "I don't believe you."

He held out his hand and one of the Tree's apples
appeared in his palm. He pulled back and tossed it
through the gates. The moment it crossed the threshold, it
exploded into dust.

Tatiana's mouth opened and she glared at Mal, then
Chrysabelle. "You knew this. You *knew* this and you
tricked me." She flew toward Chrysabelle, but Michael
stepped into her path.

"Neither of them knew." Michael bent his head. "Will
you stay? Or will you leave?"

Tatiana backed away from the gates, circling outside
of Michael's reach. Her eyes shone silver and she growled,
baring her teeth. She pointed at Lilith. "If I have to stay,
so does Lilith. She ate the fruit also."

Chrysabelle grabbed the little girl and pulled her close.
"No, please, Michael, don't make her stay. She's only a
baby and Tatiana will—"

He held up his hand. "The child may leave."

Tatiana screamed in frustration. "No! She ate the
fruit, too."

Michael nodded. "The child was born human *and*
vampire. When she ate the fruit, her vampire side was
killed just as yours was, but her human side remains. All
that my fallen brothers did to her has been erased." He
walked toward the gate. "You are free to leave, demon."

Tatiana sputtered, but Chrysabelle didn't wait to hear what she had to say. With Lilith's hand firmly in hers, she grabbed Mal's hand with her other and pulled both of them after Michael.

Tatiana followed, cursing, but stopped the moment they stepped over the gate's golden threshold. Slowly, the doors began to close.

Chrysabelle turned, putting Lilith behind her, and stared into Tatiana's angry metallic eyes until the gap disappeared and the entrance was sealed. A scream went up that shook the gates, echoing into the stillness of the desert night.

Chrysabelle leaned into Mal, exhaling the breath she'd been holding. "It's over. She's never getting out of there."

Mal put his arm around her. "Not alive."

She twisted to face the archangel. "Is that right? Are there any loopholes? Any possible way she might escape the Garden?"

"No." He held a hand out toward Eae, who was now making Lilith laugh by hiding his face behind his wing. "Even if she did, she wouldn't make it past the guardian."

Relief unlike anything Chrysabelle had felt before overwhelmed her. She swallowed, trying to find her voice. "Thank you."

"You did it, my child." He smiled gently. "You've always been the light of your kind."

She wiped at her eyes. "But not anymore." She put a hand over her belly, feeling the swell that her leathers hid. "You must know what I've done."

"What we've done," Mal corrected her. He stuck out his chest as if defying Michael to call his unborn child a mistake.

Michael glanced at Mal, then back at her. "I do know. The child you carry will be the best of both of you and the greatest protector of the human race." His smiled faded. "But this child and your union with the vampire are also what separate me from you."

Chrysabelle shook her head. "I don't understand."

"The vampire's blood courses through your veins. His child grows in your belly. You have become one with him." Michael smiled wistfully. "You must understand my position does not allow me much truck with vampires."

"Or any, I'd guess."

He nodded and came close enough to cup her face in his hands. For a long moment, he just gazed at her. "My beautiful warrior child," he whispered. Sadness dimmed the light in his eyes. "I also came because I wanted to say good-bye to you. My daughter."

Creek tossed the basilisk scales onto Dominic's desk. "How soon before it's ready?"

Dominic picked up the scales and smiled. "Well done."

"How soon?" He wasn't that anxious to fight Annika, but putting it off was only going to make him feel worse.

"No more than a day." Dominic tucked the scales into his vest pocket and nodded toward a chair. "Sit, please."

"I didn't plan on staying that long."

Dominic shrugged and took a sip from an ornate goblet on his desk. A nauseating mix of blood and wine by the smell of it. "And your answer?"

Creek took a few breaths. And sat. "My grandmother is a healer. A very powerful woman in our tribe. She's fairly well known in Seminole circles."

Dominic nodded. "Rosa Mae Jumper's power and reputation extends beyond your tribe, I can assure you."

It shouldn't surprise Creek that Dominic knew about his grandmother and yet, it did. The woman was a constant revelation. "She's the one who gave me the scales. And the reason I'm willing to work for you."

"*Bene, bene.*" Dominic stood and extended his hand. "I am not such a monster as you think I am. You will see."

Creek hoped that was the truth. He shook the vampire's hand, inwardly cringing at the man's cold touch. At least Dominic knew Creek hadn't made the decision to work for him alone. And if Dominic really knew Mawmaw, he'd think twice about the kind of work he gave Creek to do. "When should I be back?"

"I'll bring it to you." Dominic arched a brow. "I'd like to keep an eye on my investment."

And so it began. "You know where I live? Little Havana. The old machine shop near—"

"Sixteenth Avenue. I know the place." He gave Creek a curious look. "I'll be quick." He checked his watch. "No more than three hours from now. Will you be ready?"

Creek nodded, but even that felt like a lie. "See you then."

As soon as he got outside, he sat on his bike and took out his phone to text Annika. *My place in three hours.*

He tucked the phone into his pocket and pulled on his helmet, revving the bike's engine as he glanced over his shoulder for traffic. His pocket vibrated before he could take off. He dragged the phone out again and checked the screen.

Annika had already texted him back: *Done.*

When he arrived home, he knew why her answer had

come so quickly. She was already there, perched on the steps leading up to the sleeping loft. "Have you made your decision then? I assume that's what you called me here for."

He nodded. "I have." He took a breath. "I choose to fight." The exhale came easier. "I have no desire to fight you. None. But I want my freedom more." He shook his head. "I can't do this job anymore. I can't."

She nodded. "I know. You're a good man, Creek. The Kubai Mata wouldn't have selected you if you weren't." For an instant, the corners of her mouth turned up in a miserable smile, and then the expression vanished. "When do you want to do this?"

He turned enough so that he didn't have to look at her. He felt like he was betraying a friend. "Tonight."

"You'll need a second."

"A second?"

"Someone to stand with you."

Dominic would be here, but he didn't want to be indebted to him any more than he already would be and there wasn't anyone else he wanted to witness what was about to happen. "I'm fine alone."

She shook her head slowly. "You have to have one."

"Why? Is it part of the rules?"

"No," she said, the tone of her voice almost painful. "It's so someone can take care of your body."

Chapter Forty-four

Chrysabelle knew her mouth hung open, but didn't care. "You're my father?"

"Yes," Michael answered.

"That's why I was able to enter the Garden, isn't it? Because I'm not completely human."

Michael nodded. "The angelic heritage is also what makes comarré blood so irresistible to vampires, and why, to vampires, comarré glow."

Behind her, Mal made a sound of disbelief.

"So you and my mother were...that is..." She shook her head, mostly to empty it of the images starting to form there.

"No." His gentle smile eased her discomfort. "Conception was never physical. That's not necessary for my kind."

"Did my mother know?"

"No. None of the comarré chosen to bear children knew about their angelic partners, or do to this day." He looked at Mal. "It's a necessary secret and must remain so. Can you imagine if the nobility knew the comarré living in their homes were direct descendants of their embittered enemies? The ancients would have every one of them murdered."

Mal put his hand on her back. "So why tell us?"

"Because if there is anything you both excel at, it's keeping secrets, and this is one that must be kept."

"What about Damian?" Chrysabelle asked. "Can I tell him?"

Michael thought for a moment. "I would prefer you didn't."

"Again," Mal said. "Why tell us at all?"

Michael sighed. "Because I will not be able to see Chrysabelle again after today. Her relationship with you...complicates things."

Mal growled. "Are you trying to say I tainted her?"

"Mal." She turned slightly and rested her hand on his chest, trying to stave off the sudden spark of fear that he might challenge Michael. And lose.

"You cannot pretend not to understand the ramifications of the two of you being together." The sudden fierceness in Michael's eyes erased all previous softness. "I am the leader of the heavenly armies. Even the appearance that I might be acquainted with a child of my fallen brethren is unthinkable." He held up his hand when Mal opened his mouth. "Your child, however, *will* know me. And you will never be without whatever protection I can manage."

He turned to look back at the Garden. "Although I don't imagine you'll need much of that now." His gaze landed on Mal again. "I know you love her. Take the utmost care of her and this child she will soon give you."

"Or what?" Mal asked, challenge ripe in his question. "You'll kill me?"

Michael spread his wings, blocking out the view of the garden behind him. "No." He smiled and nodded at Chrysabelle. "She'll do that herself."

Mal snorted and the tension between them dissipated. "Duly noted. It's not like she hasn't already tried."

Chrysabelle exhaled. She'd never felt quite so exhausted. "Thank you for telling me who you are. And for everything else." She glanced at Lilith, still being entertained by Eae, and a thought occurred to her. "If I'm never going to see you again, there is one thing I'd like to ask of you. A favor."

Michael thought for a moment, then nodded. "What do you desire?"

She tilted her head toward the Garden. "The fruit that turned Lilith into a child again... would it restore the humanity to any vampire in a similar situation?"

He shook his head. "It will not work for Malkolm."

"I'm not asking for him."

Michael thought for a moment, glancing back at Lilith and Eae. Then he nodded. "It would."

"Would you allow me just this once to take one with me? I give you my solemn vow it will be used for the purpose intended and nothing else."

"If it isn't, that person's life will be forfeit."

"Understood."

He held out his hand to her. In his palm appeared one of the gleaming black apples. "This will be one more secret between us."

She smiled and took the apple. "Thank you, Father."

Michael stepped back and lifted his eyes skyward for a moment before nodding at her. "Peace be with you." He glanced at Eae, shifting their attention to the guardian. "Peace to you."

"Peace to you," the other angel responded, enfolding Lilith in his wings at the same time as a burst of lightning and booming thunderclap shattered the silence. Chrysabelle cringed at the sudden noise. When she looked up, Michael was gone.

Eae opened his wings and Lilith giggled. Apparently, he'd shielded her from Michael's raucous departure.

Mal's cool fingers laced through hers. "You okay? That was a lot of heavy information."

"I'm fine." Mostly she was. Processing everything Michael had told her might take a few days. Her father was an angel. Not just an angel, *the* archangel. She was about to make the leader of Heaven's army a grandfather. With a half-vampire child. Heavy didn't begin to cover what she was feeling.

"You think Lilith will remember any of this?"

"I don't know. If she does, someone's going to have to explain it to her someday."

Mal squeezed her hand. "This was one strange trip for all of us. And considering the things we've seen, that's saying something."

"Mm-hmm." Her hand went to her belly as a spell of light-headedness made her wobble.

Mal caught her in his arms as she leaned into him. "What's wrong? You just went white. Are you sick? Is it the baby?"

"I'm just tired is all. Growing the first human-angel-vampire hybrid isn't easy."

He smiled, then quickly wiped it off his face when she scowled at him. "I can't imagine it is." He picked her up in his arms, something she'd normally protest, but normally, she didn't feel like she was on the verge of passing out. "Where's that portal?"

Eae stepped forward, holding Lilith's hand, and pointed. "Under the sand."

"Thanks." Mal leaned down and put his mouth to her ear. "Let's go home, mama. For good this time."

She smiled as her eyelids drooped. "Best idea you've had."

"Doppelgangers are extinct," Doc said. Maybe they *should* have looked at those files. Vernadetto might have something mental going on.

"Are you sure?" Fi asked. "What is a doppelganger? Like that evil twin thing?" She glanced at Vernadetto. "Are you evil? You don't seem evil."

"No, I'm not evil and doppelgangers are *not* extinct. Not that it matters." The man lowered his head. "I should go."

Doc wasn't about to let him drop this bomb and leave. "You can't just tell us doppelgangers exist, you are one, and then split. You owe us some kind of explanation."

With a long exhale, Vernadetto leaned back and put the envelope next to him. "I know doppelgangers are real because I come from a long line of them. My family has done everything in its power to kill the line. We don't marry other varcolai. We do our best not to reproduce. And we never, ever let the change take over."

"Why? What exactly is a doppelganger?" Fi's eyes were as big as streetlights. There was no way she was letting this drop. He knew his girl too well.

Vernadetto answered. "It's kind of like what you said, Fiona, a twin, but a doppelganger is actually a rare form of varcolai."

She glanced at Doc. He nodded. Rare was an understatement. She looked back at Vernadetto. "So you can shift?"

Vernadetto sighed. "Into any type of creature we want so long as we know what it looks like."

"Holy crap." Fi squealed, a noise Doc recognized as barely bottled excitement. "You mean you could turn into Doc in his leopard form? Or me when I'm a ghost?"

He nodded, doubt clouding his eyes. "Exactly like that."

"Double holy crap." Fi grinned. "That is wicked cool."

Doc laughed. "She's right. It beats my being a leopard all day long."

Vernadetto shook his head. "It's not cool at all. It's horrible. The being we mimic usually dies within a few days of contact with us. We're like...omens of death. It's why my family has kept the power hidden and tried to erase the line. We never shift. Never. That's what the amulet is for. It reflects our own image back to us so that the urge to change is virtually removed." His fingers went to the chain. "There's some deeper magic than that involved, but those are the basics."

Fi patted his hand. "Denying your nature is no way to live your life. Your power can't be all bad."

He stood and paced to the other side of the room. "I became a police officer to do some good with my life." He stopped at the windows and looked out onto the city. "I have no intention of doing anything to harm the life I've built as a human."

"What if we knew someone who might be able to help you?" Doc asked.

Vernadetto turned. "Like who?" Doc held out his hand and let the blue flames erupt from his fingers. Vernadetto drew back. "I thought that was...taken care of."

"Not taken care of so much as I learned to control it. Barasa's got a shaman's background and some higher education on dealing with othernatural issues. He helped me. He could probably help you."

Relief washed over Vernadetto's face, but it was fleeting. He turned back to the windows. "I'm a cop. I know what the pride charges for *services* like that. I can't afford that kind of help."

"You can if you're a member of the pride," Doc said. "Then it wouldn't cost you a thing."

Vernadetto laughed bitterly. "I don't know what you're getting at, but—"

"About that offer I mentioned." Doc leaned forward. "It would make you an honorary member of the Paradise City pride."

Vernadetto looked at him. "How is that even possible?"

Fi laughed, unable to contain herself. "You have to say yes."

His expression softened when he looked at Fi. "I don't know what it is yet."

"We need you," Fi said.

Doc nodded. "She's right. We do." He paused. Vernadetto had to agree. He was exactly what the pride needed to regain confidence in Doc's leadership. "I'd like you to become one of my council members."

Vernadetto stared at them. "I don't know what to say."

"Well, duh," Fi said. "Say yes."

He smiled. "Okay. I'll do it."

Chapter Forty-five

Dominic arrived exactly when he said he would, his sleek sedan pulling quietly to the curb outside the machine shop. Creek leaned against the building near the entrance. Mortalis got out first and opened the door for Dominic. With his dark suit and precise grooming, he stood out in this section of town like a Rottweiler at a cat show.

Mortalis tipped his head to Creek. He nodded back. Maybe he'd ask the fae to be his second, because he certainly wasn't asking his mother or grandmother. Neither of them needed to be responsible for carting his dead body out of here if it came to that. Which he prayed it wouldn't.

Dominic buttoned his jacket as he approached. "Surely we aren't doing this out here?"

"No. Just wanted to make sure you didn't attract any extra company." Creek rolled back the machine shop's heavy door. "Come in."

He shut it again after the vampire and the fae entered. "Everything turn out all right?"

"*Si.*" Dominic pulled out a small glass vial from his jacket and held it out to Creek. "This will protect you."

"Thanks." He took the vial, turning it so the cloudy liquid inside sloshed. He twisted the top off. "There's something else."

"*Si?*"

"I need a second for the fight. Someone to take care of things if the outcome doesn't go my way." Creek put the vial to his lips and drank. Tasted like chalk. "I wouldn't ask this of you, but I was hoping Mortalis might do it."

The fae nodded, but Dominic spoke. "It will be handled. Neither of us is leaving until this is over."

"I didn't think you were going to stay."

Dominic smiled. "And leave my new investment alone? Not yet I think."

Creek tossed the vial toward the kitchen sink. It shattered against the stainless steel. Dominic wanted to see if his investment was going to live or not. Understandable. "What if she makes eye contact with you?"

"Mortalis and I have taken the necessary precautions."

Creek pointed to the sleeping loft. "Regardless, you might want to watch from up there." He pulled his phone out and checked the time. "She'll be here soon."

A knock rang out from the door.

"Or now." As Dominic and Mortalis headed upstairs, Creek went to let Annika in. "Right on time."

"This isn't something to be late for." She came in, phone in hand. She tapped the screen as he secured the shop again. It lit up with a document. She held it out to him. "I need you to read this and press your thumb to the signature box when you're done."

He took the phone. "What is it?"

"Your termination agreement."

He scrolled through it. Page after page flew by. "Give me the bullet points."

"You agree to hold harmless the Kubai Mata in any past, present, and future events. You agree to deny all knowledge of them and their operations, as they will of you. Furthermore, you understand that any and all sub-sidies provided to you by the KM will cease to exist the moment you sign off."

"Una's scholarship?"

"As discussed, it terminates at the end of her current semester."

"But not before."

"Not before." She nodded at the phone. "It's all in there."

At least that would buy him a few months to scrounge up the plastic to pay that bill. "What about the brands on my back?"

She scowled. "We're not the comarré, Creek. I'm not going to cut them out of you if that's what you're asking."

Yeah, actually, it was. Good to know. He lifted the phone. "Anything else in here I need to know about?"

"The KM has the right to call on you in the future, but you also have the right to refuse. If you agree, you'll be paid on a case-per-case basis."

"I'm never going to say yes."

"I know." She smiled. "I also know you should never say never." She tipped her head back like she was looking up. "Either one is a good choice for a second."

He pressed his thumb to the screen. A second later, the phone buzzed, and then the one in his pocket did the same. He handed Annika's phone back to her as he pulled his out. A copy of the document was in his mail.

She pointed at the device. "You can keep your halm and crossbow as parting mementos, but I'm going to need that back."

He held up the phone. "Then how am I going to keep a copy of that agreement?"

"Send me a copy," Dominic called down. "I'll make sure he gets it."

Annika nodded and began typing in the e-mail address Dominic gave her. Creek set his phone on the cable spool. The rumble of an old, gas-burning engine died outside and a car door slammed. The sounds of the neighborhood. He glanced around the machine shop. Yes, it was a dump, but it had been home for a few months. Now he was without a place to live and stuck with a new job that had the potential to be just as bad as his old one. Maybe this hadn't been the right decision.

The shop door squealed on its track and a familiar face peeked through the gap.

Creek's gut knotted. "What are you doing here?"

Mawmaw's thick, black-rimmed glasses made her eyes seem bigger than they really were. "Is that any way to greet your grandmother?"

"Now's not really a good time."

She squeezed in through the narrow opening, tugging her overstuffed purse along behind her. "Don't say things that make you look ridiculous. Now's the perfect time." She shifted her gaze to Annika, then shot a quick look at Dominic and Mortalis. "I see all the players are here."

"Players?" Creek's level of confusion jumped up a notch. "What do you mean?"

"What I mean is that you're not going through this without family to support you." She plopped her purse on the coffee table and took a seat. "Now." Her eyes narrowed on Annika like she was trying to defeat the sector chief herself. "Let's get on with it, shall we? I ain't getting any younger."

Mal stepped through the portal to find Damian waiting. The smell of his blood roused the voices, but only slightly. After time in the Garden, they seemed subdued. Almost awed by the experience. Perhaps it had been the realization that he could have ended his existence—and theirs—with the Tree of Life's fruit.

The comar's hackles went up at the sight of Chrysabelle in Mal's arms. "What happened? What's wrong?" His gaze dropped to the little girl holding on to Mal's pant leg. "Who is that?"

"Quiet," Mal said. "She's sleeping." Chrysabelle sighed deeply. "She's exhausted." He tipped his head toward Lilith. "And this is Lilith."

His brows shot up, disbelief rounding his eyes. "Lilith? As in the big, bad vampire everyone was worried about?"

"Yes. Long story, but first I need to get your sister in bed so she can rest." Lilith crowded Mal's leg.

Damian backed away.

"She's not a vampire anymore, Damian. She's a child again. An innocent." Chrysabelle stirred, so he dropped his voice as much as he could without losing the urgency. "All the ancient evil that twisted her up is gone."

"You're sure?"

"Positive. Now move."

Hesitantly, Damian opened the bathroom door and

stepped to the side. "Get Chrysabelle in bed. I'll take care of the portal."

Without another word, Mal carried Chrysabelle into the next room, Lilith toddling along at his side. He led her to a chair. "You sit here."

She shook her head, reaching for him. "No. You stay."

"I'm not going anywhere, I promise. I'll be right back, okay?"

Halfway to a full-on pout, Lilith threw herself into the chair. Then she crossed her arms and stared at him angrily. He sighed. He remembered that look from Sophia.

Shaking his head, he eased Chrysabelle onto the bed, then started undoing the elaborate leather gear she wore. The outfit was the last thing he'd expected her to wear, but she looked like a warrior goddess in it. Maybe that was the point. And now they both knew she really was a warrior. At least the daughter of one.

Half angel. He shook his head again.

Velimai walked in as he unbuckled the last strap. She stopped dead in her tracks and pointed to Lilith, mouth open in wonder.

"Explanation to come, but first I need something for Chrysabelle to sleep in."

Velimai nodded, eyes still on Lilith. She went to the dresser and came back with a slip of white silk that seemed more like something he should be taking off Chrysabelle than putting on her. The fabric snagged on Velimai's rough skin as she handed it over. When he took it, her hands started moving.

He grimaced. "You know I don't understand signing."

Velimai crooked her fingers and held them up to her

mouth like fangs, then made an hourglass shape in the air and gave him a questioning look.

"Tatiana?" He loosened Chrysabelle's top.

She nodded.

"Contained. Permanently." He tugged the sheet over Chrysabelle before slipping the leather free. As soon as they were off, her belly swelled beneath the covers.

His mouth opened and he stared. "How ... she didn't look pregnant at all in the Garden."

Velimai signed something else.

Mal growled. "Damn it, fae, go get your tablet."

Rolling her eyes, Velimai left, her hands moving the whole time.

"Everything okay?" Damian came out of the bathroom, drying his hands on a towel.

"Other than that I can't read fae sign language, yes." He glanced at the bathroom. "Portal gone?"

"Completely." A quick look at Lilith and he tossed the towel over his shoulder. "What was it like?"

"Beautiful." And informative, but Damian would never be privy to the information Chrysabelle had received.

"I'm sure it was, but I meant killing—"

"She's not exactly dead but she is contained. I'll explain soon." Mal adjusted the covers over Chrysabelle as he canted his head toward Lilith. Her crossed arms hung limp near her waist and her chin bobbed toward her chest. "I guess I need a bed for that one too."

"There's a guest room a few doors down. I can put her in there and then meet you downstairs."

"Good." Mal turned off the bedside lamp. "Then we'll talk there."

Damian scooped Lilith up and took her to the other room. Mal met Velimai on his way down the steps and brought her to the kitchen with him. He grabbed a bottle of whiskey off the bar on the way in. Velimai found glasses as Damian joined them at the table.

Mal filled the glasses, but Velimai ignored hers to scrawl on her tablet. *The child is Lilith?*

"Yes, that's her. She ate fruit from the Tree of Life and it killed off her vampire side, leaving her mortal one intact. She survived it because she was born both vampire and human, never sired. She's a hundred percent human now. And the only family she has left is here in Paradise City. That's why we brought her back."

Velimai nodded. *Tatiana?*

"She also ate fruit from the Tree and it also killed off her vampire side, but because her human side was already dead, she had no choice but to remain in the Garden if she wanted to live. There's no death in the Garden. But if she leaves it, steps just one foot beyond its borders, she dies." Somewhere down deep, the beast shifted uncomfortably at the reminder.

Velimai's brows rose as she got up from the table, her lips pursing in a satisfied way. She leaned against the counter, taking slow sips of her whiskey.

"It's done then." Damian held his by the rim, turning it, but not drinking. He stared into the amber liquid as if he expected it to do something.

"Yes. Finally." Mal tossed his back. The burn felt good. Reminded him that he was back on solid ground. He tipped his glass toward Damian. "Only works if you drink it."

Damian kept his hand on the glass, shifting his eyes to

look at Mal. "Now that Tatiana's taken care of, what are your intentions with my sister?"

Mal almost smiled, but didn't. "You mean am I going to make an honorable woman out of her?" *Drain her.*

"Yes." Damian wasn't amused.

Mal refilled his glass. "Absolutely. And I think she agreed while we were in the Garden, but she passed out before I could confirm it. I can't force her to marry me."

Damian sat back. "So you've asked her?"

"Several times."

"And she's said?"

"No. Not now. I need to think about it." He downed the shot, mollified that the truth had sucked the anger out of Damian. "All her usual avoidance techniques."

"You want me to talk to her?"

"Depends." Mal stared at the comar.

"On what?"

"On what your advice to her would be." Mal let a hint of silver into his eyes. "I know you can't be thrilled about her relationship with me. What I am and what she is are two very different things and that's got to make you a little crazy. Especially after what my ex-wife put you through."

Damian stared back, a thousand painful memories filtering through his eyes. He stayed silent long enough to make Mal uncomfortable. "You love Chrysabelle."

"I do. And she loves me back."

The comar shrugged. "She's as free to do what she wants as I am. If she's happy, who am I to stand in her way?" He picked his glass up and sipped.

"Very forward thinking of you." Mal lifted his glass in toast. "I appreciate that."

Damian set his drink down. "So do you want me to talk to her or not?"

"Sure. But it won't do any good."

"It might. I *am* her brother." The comar smirked. "And about to be brother-in-law to a vampire and uncle to a half-vampire child. Holy mother, I never saw any of this coming."

Velimai snorted.

Mal looked at the fae. "Don't laugh, wysper. That means you and I are going to be like family, too."

She widened her eyes and made the sign of the cross, cringing in mock horror.

Mal shook his head. "My kid is going to be seriously screwed up living in this house with you people."

Damian laughed. "There's only one way to solve that."

"What's that?" Mal asked.

Damian raised a brow, his eyes slanting toward Velimai. "Move in."

Chapter Forty-six

"Mawmaw, I appreciate it, but you really can't be here." Creek scraped a hand over his head. "How did you even know anything was going on?"

His grandmother flicked her gaze onto Annika. "Your sector chief invited me."

Creek spun to face her. "You had no right."

She shrugged. "I wasn't sure you'd have a second."

He clenched his hands. Fighting a woman seemed a little more doable right now. "I was starting to feel unsure about my decision to leave the KM." She'd done this on purpose and he knew that, but it didn't make her actions any easier to take. "Not anymore. Let's do this."

"As you wish." She smiled, infuriating him further. Damn, she was good. He'd always been on her side, and hadn't ever really seen this aspect of her, but she hadn't gotten to be sector chief by winning the KM lottery. She unzipped her jacket and threw it on the floor, revealing a set of biceps that would make most teenage boys weep with jealousy.

He pulled his shirt off. Behind him, Mawmaw inhaled sharply, reminding him she'd never seen the brands the KM had burned into his back.

They began to circle each other, her smile never faltering. "You really mean to do this, don't you?"

"I wouldn't be here if I didn't."

Her hand lifted toward the button that raised the shades blocking her stone gaze. Before she reached it, he twisted into a roundhouse. His foot connected with her shoulder, knocking her sideways. She bent back, catching herself with one hand and pushing upright.

Instead of retaliating, she straightened, put her palms together in front of her chest, and bowed to him. Then she looked up toward the sleeping loft. "That's enough. I'm satisfied." She held her hand out to Creek. "It was a pleasure working with you. I hope you find what you're looking for."

Uncertainty settled over him. He stared at her. "What the hell are you talking about? What happened to fighting my way out? Was this some kind of test? What?"

She snagged her jacket off the floor and put it on. "A small test. To make sure you were serious about leaving. That you wouldn't back down." She looked past him at his grandmother before continuing. "I also wanted to make sure those scales got used up." She lifted her face to the loft. "I assume you used all of them in whatever potion you made to protect him?"

Dominic didn't answer.

Creek held his hands out. "So the whole fight was just a setup?"

"No, the fight was real." She turned to leave.

None of this was making any sense. "But you stopped it."

"Because your bond price has been paid." She yanked the door open. "You have twenty-four hours to vacate the premises. Enjoy your new life." Without a glance back, she slipped out and was gone.

Creek turned to face his grandmother. Dominic and Mortalis were coming down the steps. "One of you want to tell me what the hell just happened here?"

The three of them ignored him as if he wasn't even there.

Dominic nodded in deference to Creek's grandmother. "I trust this settles things between us."

"Settles what things?" Creek asked. Nothing but crickets.

She stood and held out her hand. "It does."

The vampire lifted Mawmaw's hand and kissed the back of it. "As always, a pleasure."

Frustration pushed Creek. He grabbed his crossbow off the kitchen counter and aimed it at Dominic. "Somebody start explaining or it's going to get dusty in here."

"Thomas Creek," Mawmaw snapped. "Put that down this instant."

"Not until I get an explanation."

She raised her eyes to Dominic. He nodded, then lifted a hand. "*Por favore*, there is no need for the weapon." He stiffened, as if bracing for Creek's next move. "I paid your bond price."

Creek held the crossbow where it was. "I didn't ask you to do that."

"No." Dominic lifted his chin. "Your grandmother did."

Creek let the crossbow drop. "Why would you do that, Mawmaw? I will never be able to work that off." She'd doomed him to the same life he'd just left. Always owing, never able to get free.

"There is nothing to work off," Dominic corrected. "The debt was owed to your grandmother. She simply asked me to do this with the funds instead."

Creek stared at his grandmother and slowly shook his head. "You'd better start from the beginning."

Still yawning, Chrysabelle padded through the hall toward the sound of sniffling that had woken her. She found Lilith sitting up in bed, sucking her thumb, cheeks wet with tears. Chrysabelle sat on the bed next to her and took hold of the little girl's free hand. "What's wrong, pumpkin?"

"Mama," she sobbed. "I want mama. Wanna go home."

Chrysabelle opened her mouth, but there was no answer for this problem. Not one that involved Tatiana. "We're going to take you home soon, baby. Don't cry, okay? I'll be right back."

She hurried out into the hall. "Mal? Where are you?" There were voices in the kitchen. His and Damian's. And laughter. Good to know they were getting along. She headed down the steps.

"I'm here," he answered, meeting her in the living room. "You didn't sleep very long."

"Lilith was crying. It woke me up." She sighed. "She wants her mother and to go home."

Mal nodded. "Poor kid. She's been through a lot. You get dressed, I'll tell Jerem we need the car."

"Thanks." She ran back upstairs and dug through the bags Fi had brought her, utterly grateful for them. At this point, she doubted her belly would fit into any of her old comarré trousers. She came back downstairs in new maternity jeans and an ivory tunic sweater, Lilith's little hand firmly in hers. "Is the car here?"

Velimai and Damian were sitting in the living room. *Just pulling up*, Velimai signed.

"You want us to go with you?" her brother asked.

"No, thanks. We won't be long. Sun will be up soon anyway."

Mal opened the front door. "Ready?"

She nodded, then looked down at the child beside her. "Let's go, honey. Let's get you home."

Thumb secured in her mouth, Lilith followed gamely along and finally let go of Chrysabelle's hand to hop into the car. Chrysabelle went in after her, then Mal. Lilith patted the seat beside her and commanded, "Sit."

"Me?" Chrysabelle asked.

"Uh-uh. Hims." Lilith pointed to Mal.

"Yes, ma'am." Mal did as he was told. He grinned at Chrysabelle. "Bossy, isn't she? Kind of reminds me of someone..."

"Hush," Chrysabelle whispered, laughing a little. Mal was a different man with Lilith. A man who was going to be the exact kind of father she'd dreamed he'd be. Sweet, gentle, protective, loving. Her smile grew. Actually, he was the same with Lilith as he was with her. "You're so good with her."

A flicker of sadness shot silver through his eyes. "Sophia was..." He swallowed. "She was everything good in my life. The thought of being a father again..." He glanced out the window. "I feel like I'm getting a second chance."

"I know." Sentiment made her voice husky. Her hand drifted to her stomach. There were more emotions in her soul than words in her brain. "I know."

She sat watching Mal and Lilith until Jerem finally pulled the car to a stop. He powered down the glass divider. "We're here. Mal, if you want, I'll go in with Chrysabelle."

He nodded. "I want." He looked at Chrysabelle. "You have your blades?"

She patted her sides. "One on each hip, but it's not going to come to that." She reached out to Lilith. "Time to go home."

Lilith tugged on Mal's hand. "Him come."

"I can't, Lilith. Only very special people can go into that building and I'm not one of them, but you are. You and Miss Chrysabelle, okay?"

She stuck her lip out. "No kay."

He took her small face in his hands. "You'll see us again. I promise. Now be a good girl and go with Miss Chrysabelle."

Lilith threw her arms around him. He hugged her back, then handed her over. "I hate that I can't go in there with you. Anything happens and you need me, I'm coming in. To hell with the consequences."

Jerem opened the door and held out his hand to Chrysabelle. She passed Lilith to him, then scooted closer to the door. "Nothing bad is going to happen. Promise." She kissed his cheek and got out. Jerem shut the door.

She glanced at him. "Stay behind me, okay?"

"Will do," Jerem said. "I know you want to handle this alone."

"That and I don't want any unnecessary casualties." When he nodded, she turned her attention to the building in front of her.

The hallowed structure loomed over them, a symbol of power and sanctuary at the same time. Chrysabelle hoped the sanctuary part was still true. She inhaled and took Lilith's hand. "All right, kiddo. Let's go find your father."

Chapter Forty-seven

M adam Mayor?"

Lola looked up from the news program she was watching. The holovision rarely had anything good on it these days. One of her security guards, Andrew, stood stiffly in the doorway of her den. He was one of the first fringe she'd hired, a good worker and second in command of the night shift. "Yes?"

"One of the patrols trailed the comarré from Mephisto Island to Little Havana." He put a hand to his ear, pressing the receiver closer. "They're there now. At Preacher's. The vampire Malkolm is with her." He listened again, then nodded. "They have a child with them."

She sat up, pushing Hector's head off her lap. "How can that be? A child? How old?"

He spoke into the mouthpiece on his lapel. "Approximate age of the child?" After a beat, he nodded again. "Young. Maybe two, ma'am. What would you like the patrol to do?"

"Nothing. Just watch."

"Very good, ma'am. Have a nice evening."

She waved him off and as Andrew left, she dropped

her head back to stare blindly at the ceiling. Why on earth would Chrysabelle take a toddler to Preacher's? Was she trying to pass the kid off as Mariela? And for what purpose? The Mariela she'd seen at Tatiana's was grown. And a monstrous, killing machine. She shuddered at the memory. Her grandchild. It was...horrific.

Still, that didn't explain what Chrysabelle was doing with a child of that age. Were she and Malkolm up to some kind of revenge? Against her? If so, why now? Why not do something to her at Tatiana's when they'd had the chance?

She sat up again. Unless that hadn't been Mariela at Tatiana's. Maybe he and Chrysabelle had had possession of her granddaughter all along and never intended to tell her. Anger drove her to her feet, almost knocking Hector off the couch.

"What's wrong? Are you leaving?" he asked.

"I have business to take care of. I won't be long. Follow me." She strode down the hall, Hector trotting behind like a puppy. "Andrew," she yelled. "Here. Now."

The guard came running back. "Yes, ma'am?"

"Tell the patrol no one leaves that church. Detain them by any means necessary, but the child is to remain unharmed at all costs." When he nodded, she continued. He fell into step beside her. "Bring the car up front immediately. As soon as I'm suited up, we're going out there."

"Anything else?" He broke off toward the front of the house, but waited for her word.

"No. I'll be five minutes."

"Very good." He bolted for the door, already sending orders out through his radio.

She diverged into her room and opened the newest

section of her closet. A Kevlar vest, tested to withstand direct blows to the heart, hung waiting. She shed her blouse, then lifted it, hefting it over one arm. Hector jumped in to help, getting her strapped in quickly.

"I hate when you wear this. It frightens me," he moaned.

"Nothing's going to happen to me; it's just a precaution."

"I still worry," he said. "You should feed before you go, for the protection. My blood is stronger than ever with the new vitamins I've been taking."

Vitamins? That might explain the change in taste. She didn't know anything about these vitamins, but if they could make her stronger she was all for them. "I fed this morning. That will have to do. I don't have the time now." She tugged on a sweater over the vest, then grabbed her gun and slid in a clip of silver bullets. Just having the gun tucked into her shoulder holster made her skin itch from the silver being so close, but that was a small price to pay to have some protection. She added a light jacket to cover the holster, then turned to Hector. "Don't let anyone into the house until I get back, got it?"

"Yes." He frowned. "I could come with you. Help you."

"No. Don't make me say it again." There was no time for his drama now. She left the room, knowing he'd follow.

The car was waiting when she walked through the front door. Hector hung back, moping. She forced herself to smile at him. "Just think, I may be coming home with my granddaughter."

He clapped his hands. "Why didn't you say so? Go get her!"

She got into the car and one of the guards shut the

door. Nerves skipped along her skin. "That's exactly what I intend to do," she said to herself. "And this time, I won't leave any loose ends."

Mortalis stood guarding the door when Creek returned from fetching the Cuban coffee Mawmaw had insisted on. A neighborhood like this must house a few of Dominic's enemies; no wonder he'd wanted Mortalis to keep a lookout. Creek gave the fae a nod as he walked back into the machine shop. Mawmaw had declared Creek's brand of coffee too weak to wake a fly. He imagined what she really wanted was a chance to speak to Dominic alone before everything came out.

"Here you go, Mawmaw. Cream and extra sugar, just like you asked." He handed her the coffee, then sat on the cable spool.

"Thank you, Thomas." She popped the top and blew on the steaming liquid. She tapped the arm of the chair where Dominic sat as if she were calling a meeting to order. "Go ahead, tell him what he wants to know."

Jacket unbuttoned but still looking uncomfortable, Dominic began. "When I came to New Florida with Marissa, Chrysabelle's mother, things were not good for us. We were forced to leave Corvinestri with little more than the clothing on our backs. Marissa was severely injured during the fight required to gain her freedom."

"Libertas," Creek said.

"*Si*." He crossed one leg over the other, picking at the crease of his pants. "She was paralyzed from the waist down." Not a spark of silver in his eyes. Instead, he seemed to stare blindly at a spot on the arm of the chair. "None of that mattered to the way I felt about her. I loved her regardless. I knew her feelings for me were not as strong as mine for her, but I understand now why that was. Everything she did, she did in the hopes of saving her daughter."

He smiled a little. "Marissa was such a fighter, so strong-willed and so beautiful." One hand drifted to his chest. He shook his head and his hand came back down. "Like I was saying, she was paralyzed. We went to every doctor we could, spent money we didn't have on therapies and untested cures, and all of it? *Per niente*. In vain."

He scowled. "Half of those doctors were worthless to begin with, but I was willing to try. For her, anything. But eventually the debt was too much. Marissa insisted we stop trying. That she'd come to terms with what had happened to her and she just wanted to move on."

"I could not accept that there was nothing I could do." Tipping his head back a little, he stared into the heights of the ceiling. "Then one night, about a year after she'd given up, I heard about a woman who might be able to help us. A healer."

"My grandmother?"

"Rosa Mae Jumper." Dominic looked at Mawmaw. "She was not happy to see me when I showed up on her doorstep."

Creek snorted. "You're lucky she didn't stake you."

Dominic canted his head as if remembering. "She almost did."

Mawmaw brushed her hand through the air. "It helped that he came bearing gifts."

Creek raised a brow.

"I brought her a vial of my blood," Dominic answered.

Mawmaw nodded. "I knew if he was willing to give me that, he wasn't there to hurt me."

"I told her everything. Including that I had no money to pay her with. In return she gave me a remedy and the promise that I only had to give her a favor if the medicine worked." He shrugged. "How could I pass that up? I went home and started slipping the potion into Marissa's evening tea as your grandmother instructed me."

He sighed. "It had no effect. Or so I thought. When I went with Mal and Chrysabelle to Corvinestri to rescue Marissa from Tatiana's clutches, I found out she could walk. She'd been hiding the ability for who knows how long. I knew right then your grandmother's remedy had worked."

"How did you know it was her remedy that did the trick?"

Dominic narrowed his eyes. "I am an alchemist. I have a feel for these things. I *knew*." A pained look crossed his face. "Also, it wasn't long after I started giving her the remedy that she began to pull away from me. I believe now that it was because she wanted the freedom to retrain without having to continue the pretense of her injury with me."

Creek just nodded, a little awed by Dominic's story. The man wasn't exactly the monster he'd believed him to be.

"After we returned to Paradise City, after Maris was buried and I'd made my peace with her death, I went to see your grandmother again. To tell her what had happened and to acknowledge that I owed her a favor. She told me when she needed it, she would let me know."

Creek leaned back, studying his grandmother. The short, gray-haired woman in the chair across from him suddenly looked very different. He shook his head as he spoke to her. "My bond price was the favor."

She held the thick paper coffee cup with both hands. "It would have been a not-guilty verdict, but Dominic couldn't make that happen. And not because he didn't try."

Dominic balled one fist. "Human courts..." He snorted in disgust.

Mawmaw poked her finger into her knee. "This, however—this was something he could do."

Dominic stood and buttoned his jacket. "And now that it's done, I should go."

Creek got up. "Does Chrysabelle know anything about this?"

"No. Not even Marissa knew the real reason she regained her legs. Some things don't need telling." Dominic raised a brow. "This is one of them."

Creek nodded. "Fine. But what about us? Our agreement."

"I assume you still want a job?"

"I do."

"Then I'll expect you at the club by sundown."

Creek looked up at the sleeping loft. "Considering I have to be out of here in twenty-four hours, I can be there a lot sooner than that."

Dominic bowed to Mawmaw. "A pleasure to see you." She nodded back at him, and then he walked toward the door. As he passed Creek, he tossed him something.

Creek caught it. A key. "What's this for?"

"Your apartment at Seven. Yours for as long as you work for me." He pushed the door back. "Mortalis, we have an appointment to keep."

Chapter Forty-eight

Chrysabelle lifted her hand to knock on the door of the old church, but it creaked open before she touched it. Preacher glared at her from the dim interior, his gaze skipping briefly over Lilith to shoot straight to where Mal waited in the car. After a long, hard look, his gaze returned to her. "Comarré. What brings you here?"

About the greeting she'd expected. "I have great news. Can we come in?"

"You can." His gaze stayed on Mal. "That's it."

"The child comes with me."

He glanced down at Lilith and crinkled his forehead but stepped aside to let them pass. He swung the door shut as soon as they were in. "What's this great news?"

"First, how about you lose the attitude?" How was she ever going to leave this child with Preacher if he didn't cool it? "I'm not the enemy."

Preacher sneered. "The vampire out in that car is."

"No, he's not. In fact, he saved this little girl's life. And she happens to like him very much."

Preacher crossed his arms, but the tone of his voice softened a little. "What's it to me?"

"You're starting to make me regret this decision." Chrysabelle leaned in until only a few inches separated them, then lowered her voice. "She's your daughter, you self-loathing hypocrite."

The scowl on his face melted into disbelief and his eyes focused on Lilith. He shook his head, the scowl coming back. "That's a dirty trick and it's not going to work on me. That child is human. My daughter is not."

"She is now." She put her hand on Lilith's shoulder where the little girl hung onto her leg. "This *is* your daughter, rescued from the clutches of the ancient ones."

Doubt clouded his eyes. "Mariela has a birthmark on her hip shaped like a crescent moon."

Chrysabelle nodded and crouched by the little girl. Lilith looked on the verge of tears. This all had to be so confusing for her. At least Velimai had been able to get her some decent clothes. Chrysabelle patted her hair. "It's okay, baby. Can I just look at your tummy and see if you have a spot there?"

"M'kay." She pulled up her dress, showing off a pair of pantaloons, then pointed at her side. "Here."

Chrysabelle tugged the pantaloons down half an inch, revealing the crescent-shaped mark. She looked up at Preacher. "Satisfied?" But his eyes were already filling.

He dropped to his knees in front of them, his dog tags clinking softly. "Mariela," he whispered. "My Mariela. At last. I don't know how she's grown so fast, but I don't care." He looked heavenward. "Thank you." Then he held out his hands to her. "My sweet girl. I'm your papa."

Mariela looked at Chrysabelle. She nodded. "He is."

Mariela shook her head, her bottom lip thrust out.

"Wait," Preacher said. "Give me a sec." He disappeared into a back room, returning with a speed only made possible by his vampire abilities. He held out a stuffed pink giraffe. "Remember Gigi?"

Mariela's frown disappeared. She put her hand on the giraffe's head. "Gigi."

"That's right. And I'm papa. Remember?"

Mariela smacked one of his hands with her own like she was playing a game, then loudly pronounced, "Vampire."

He laughed and nodded. "Yes, I am." Then he glanced at Chrysabelle. "And so was she. So how isn't she a vampire anymore?" He shook his head. "She's changed so much. She's so... big."

Chrysabelle let go of Mariela as the little girl tucked Gigi under one arm and took hold of both of Preacher's hands. "You can thank the ancients for her growth spurt. As for the vampire half of her, it's a bit of a story, but it's gone for good."

He looked up. "How is that possible?"

"It has to do with the Tree of Life and the—"

"The Tree of Life? *The* Tree of Life?" He scooped Mariela into his arms, kissed her face, and stood. "In the Garden of Eden?"

"That's the one. She ate fruit from the Tree and it killed off her vampire side, making her completely human again."

A single tear tracked down his face. He pressed his mouth to Mariela's cheek in a long kiss. "Thank you. Thank you for saving her." He hugged his daughter tightly, causing her to squeal. "Parenting a human child is not going to be easy for me, I know, but I will do the best I can."

"Do you wish that you could be human again too?"

He nodded, obviously too choked with emotion to speak.

Chrysabelle reached into her pocket and pulled out the gleaming black apple Michael had allowed her to leave with. "It just so happens, I can help you with that."

He stared at the fruit. "What is that?"

"Apple!" Mariela shouted. She reached for it.

Chrysabelle pulled her hand back. "No, no, little one. You've had yours." She nodded at Preacher. "She's right. It's an apple from the Tree of Life."

He shook his head. "How did you get that?"

"It was a gift from my . . . from the Archangel Michael. For this exact purpose."

He glanced at the fruit with new appreciation, holding out his free hand.

She drew the fruit back slightly. "First, I have to know something. When you turned yourself into a vampire through that accidental blood transfusion, did you die before you were transformed? The way it usually happens?"

"No. I was conscious the whole time."

"Then, from what I understand of how the Tree works, eating this should kill off your vampire side and restore you to your full humanity, just like it did with Lilith. I mean, Mariela. But eating this also means you'll age, lose your extra strength and speed. All your vampire abilities will be gone."

"But I'll be human?"

"Yes."

He stared at the apple. "You're sure about this? That it won't kill me?"

"Not a hundred percent, no." She shrugged. "I'm sorry,

I can't promise you better than that. I just thought you'd want the chance. If not..."

He grabbed the apple. "I do." A muscle in his jaw tightened. "If this doesn't go good, what happens to Mariela?"

"I can...take her to the mayor. Let her grandmother raise her."

"The woman who lied to me about Mariela being dead? No. You raise her. Promise me."

Chrysabelle hesitated. That had not been part of any scenario she'd run. She was about to have a child of her own. Raising two couldn't be that much harder, could it? "I promise. But it won't come to that."

He set Mariela down, but hung onto her hand, giving it a squeeze. "Give me a minute, sweetheart." He took the apple. One last look at Chrysabelle, as if seeking assurance, then he bit into the fruit.

Juice ran from the corner of his mouth and the scent of spice and honey mingled with the waxy essence given off by the bank of votives near the altar. He took another bite and a shudder racked his body. He dropped to the ground, groaning.

Shouts erupted beyond the doors—Mal's voice and a female one she couldn't quite place at first until she heard the word "granddaughter." A second later, a loud pop rang out followed by a guttural roar that sounded very much like Mal.

She had taken one step toward the exit, ready to fly to his side, when the church door flew off its rusted hinges. Wood splintered like confetti. Lola stood at the threshold, trembling, a gun in her hand. Chrysabelle imagined the shaking must be the pain of being so near sacred ground. Or nerves. Then she looked past Lola.

Jerem stood behind Mal, who was on the ground. An armed group of fringe guards surrounded them. Jerem's eyes glowed with varcolai rage and Mal's eyes were bright silver. Suddenly she realized blood dripped from Mal's thigh.

Rage narrowed Chrysabelle's vision. "You shot him? You stupid—"

"Next bullet goes through his heart." Lola pointed at Mariela. "Unless you bring the child to me."

Chrysabelle didn't need to see Mal shaking his head no in order to make her next move. She hoisted Mariela under one arm, hooked her hand through Preacher's belt, and dragged them deeper into the sanctuary. "This child belongs with her father. And I can pretty much guarantee you'll be dead before there'll be a next bullet."

Preacher wasn't moving and Mariela began to cry.

"That is my granddaughter. She belongs with me." Lola stepped a foot inside the church. The hand holding the gun shook so badly she almost dropped it, but she somehow put another foot forward. "And I intend to bring her home."

Memories flashed in Lola's brain at the sight of the child in Chrysabelle's arms, memories of another little girl. Julia. And seeing this child now, there was no question she was Mariela. She was Julia's twin at that age.

Her dead heart ached to possess her grandchild. To show everyone she was right, that she was the one best suited to raise her. So much so that the nerve-crunching pain razoring through her body couldn't keep her out of the church. She pushed forward. The moment she crossed the threshold, her body went up in white-hot waves of agony. She hesitated, knowing she should turn back, knowing death lay in her path, but unable to stop moving. Something inside her had clicked on, pushing her forward. Tiny teeth gnawed on the soles of her feet with every step, but still she went deeper in.

She clenched the gun in her hand harder, trying to stop the shaking. "Give her to me," she commanded. "I'm her grandmother."

"And Preacher is her father. That bond comes first," Chrysabelle said. "You want to see Mariela, you work it out with him."

She raised the gun at the comarré. "I sacrificed so much for her."

Chrysabelle shook her head, her expression full of disgust. "You told Preacher she was dead."

"Only because I know what's best for her." Unable to hold on any longer, the gun fell out of her hand. And Preacher, who Lola had assumed dead by the way he lay crumpled on the floor, started to stir. His movement spurred her on. Her tortured steps grew ragged and off balance. He would fight her. Blame her. Accuse her of lying. He didn't understand that she was the only one who could properly raise Mariela. She reached her hands out even as shots of lightning-fast pain danced through her muscles, making her twitch. The ability to care about her own life had vanished. "Give her to me. I have to have her. I did all this for her." Tears streamed down her face. "For her."

"You became a vampire for your own reasons." Chrysabelle shook her head, fear reflected in her eyes. "Get out of here. Save yourself."

But Lola knew that was impossible.

Preacher pulled himself up using one of the pews. He stared at her with a horrified look. "You foolish woman. You're killing yourself."

"Just like you killed my Julia?" Red edged her vision and the tang of smoke filled her nostrils. She stumbled to her hands and knees. Pain shot through the contact points and she clenched her jaw to keep from crying out, but a jagged sob left her anyway. A cry for her own life. For the life of her granddaughter. For everything she was about to lose and powerless to stop. If only she could get Mariela.

Preacher picked Mariela up and turned her face away. "You know I didn't kill Julia."

Julia. Where was Julia? Pain fogged her memory. She reached out again. The hand in front of her looked . . . odd. The cuticles were black, the rest of the hand shriveled and gray. She stared at it, trying to understand whom that hand belonged to. Her? That was her hand? The drive to keep moving forward burned in her brain.

The skin burst into flame. A second later the pain exploded through her body. She tried to get to her feet, but her nerves were a melted mess of stinging nettles. "Mariela," she whispered as her throat filled with smoke and her vision went dim.

Then an incredible lightness filled her. And she turned to ash.

Chapter Forty-nine

Son of a priest." Mal shuddered at what he'd just seen. He was a few yards from the front door and the church's proximity caused his body to ache more than the silver bullet Lola had put through his leg. He couldn't imagine the pain of dying the way she just had. One of the fringe guards retched and the rest stood staring, their job of guarding him and Jerem forgotten. He pushed to his feet and not a single one of them did a thing.

Chrysabelle looked up from the ashes that marked where the mayor had been incinerated, tears streaking her cheeks. She swallowed, her body racked as a sob overtook her. Then her eyes met his. She skirted the mayor's remains as she walked stiffly into Mal's arms.

He held her while she wept soundlessly, held her until the last sobs left her. Finally she lifted her head. "How could she..."

"Greed. A false sense of reality. Who knows?"

"She said she did it all for Mariela—that's Lilith's real name—but I don't know if I believe her. She seemed as power-driven as Tatiana at times. That poor little girl. At least she won't be used as a pawn anymore."

"Mariela's safe now." Mal wiped a tear off her cheek. "How's Preacher?"

"Human. The apple worked." Chrysabelle swallowed and smiled weakly. "How are you? She shot you?"

"It hurts like hell, but it went straight through. I'll have a scar, because the bullet was silver, but I'm already healing."

"Good." She turned a little and looked back at the church. "Preacher will have to move. He can't raise a child in an abandoned building."

Mal nodded. "The mayor never mentioned any other family, so I'm pretty sure Mariela is her only heir. With the inheritance due her, Preacher will have everything he needs to take care of her just fine."

"I hadn't thought about that." She took a deep breath and raised her face to his. "We should go home. We have guests coming."

He smiled. "I'm not sure I like this plan to domesticate me."

She planted her hands on her hips, pulling her sweater tight across her expanding belly. "Too bad, because as you may have noticed, there's no turning back."

He grabbed her hand and turned toward Jerem and the car. "Home. Before she starts making up a chore list." He helped her into the car.

"Hey," she said. "That's actually not a bad idea…"

Tatiana lost track of how many times she'd walked the perimeter of the Garden. In fact, she wasn't sure she *had* walked the whole thing. The landscape seemed almost to change before her eyes, blooms appearing where there'd been none before, plants increasing in size, streams narrowing or widening. The place was maddening in its beauty. Frustratingly dense and colorful. For someone who'd lived so many of her years in the subtle gray world of night, this unnatural brilliance without the benefit of sunlight wrought havoc in her brain.

And the idea that there was no way out? Impossible.

Her building frustration needed venting. She tipped her head back and screamed for Samael, even knowing while she did that there was no way he could come to her. Not here. Not to the place of the original sin. He was banned from this place, just as she was chained to it.

She grabbed a tree branch and ripped it free, tossing it as far as her rage could manage. Instantly, another grew in its spot. "I hate this place!" She shook her fists to the sky.

An eternity here would drive her insane. She fell to her knees. Hot, angry tears seared her skin. An eternity here would drive her to her death.

Maybe that was the point. Maybe this was how she would die. Killed by the inescapable splendor of the most beautiful place on earth.

A hawk sailed overhead. If only she was that free. Her tears stopped. She pushed to her feet and got her bearings. The gates were behind her. She ran to the right as fast as she could, finally encountering the wall of trees she sought.

Here, at the edge of the Garden, multiple rows of trunks merged into what seemed to be one giant hedge. She found a low branch and pulled herself up, picking her way through the dense lattice of branches. Higher and higher she climbed, squeezing through narrow slivers of space until she felt satisfied she'd gone high enough. She inched forward on one thick branch. So far, so good. A tiny spring of hope welled up. Could she escape this way?

Her hand coasted along the branch as she got ready to move farther along, when something sharp and searing bit into her fingers. She yanked her hand back. The ends of her fingers were gone, tiny bits of ash stuck to her skin.

A new wave of pain struck as the flesh began to grow back. She crumpled against the branches, hugging her hand to her body as a pit of desperation opened in her chest.

There was no way out.

Not unless she intended to die.

Within half an hour of Mal and Chrysabelle returning to Mephisto Island, Doc and Fi arrived. Chrysabelle sent them into the living room with Mal since Dominic and Mortalis were already in there. Hopefully, they were adult enough to keep the peace between themselves, although Dominic seemed to have softened toward Doc since he'd become pride leader and lifted the ban on pride members patronizing or working at Seven.

As soon as Damian came back from checking on Amylia in the guesthouse, she and Mal could make their announcement official.

A knock at the door called her out of the kitchen, where she was helping Velimai get drinks. Velimai looked up, questioning.

"I'll get it. I don't know why Damian didn't just come in." She wiped her hands on a towel and went to answer the door. But the security camera showed a different face than the one she'd been expecting.

She opened the door and slipped outside so whatever conversation was about to take place wouldn't disturb her guests. "What do you want?"

Creek held up his hands. "Nothing bad, I promise. I just wanted to tell you I'm not Kubai Mata anymore."

"You're not?" He did seem different. Perhaps a little worn around the edges, like he'd had a few hard days and nights. And yet, there was a lightness about him she couldn't recall seeing before. "How did that happen?"

He laughed a little, staring at the ground. "My grandmother. And Dominic." He shook his head. "Doesn't matter. What matters is I'm free of the KM and I thought you should know."

"I'm happy for you." She smiled. "Happy that we can be friends again. What are you going to do for work?"

He tipped his head back toward Dominic's sedan. "My new employer's already here." His smile faded. "Look, I didn't mean to interrupt. You obviously have something going on and I wasn't invited, so let me get out of your—"

"Creek. Hey, how are you?" Damian grinned as he walked toward them from the guesthouse. "I didn't know you were coming."

Creek shook his head. "I'm not. Just leaving."

"Stay," Chrysabelle said. "There's no reason for you not to now."

He glanced up. "You sure?"

"Yes. Come in." She led the way and when he and Damian were seated, Mal came to join her at the front of the room. She let him speak first.

Mal slipped his arm around her waist before he began. "As you know, the bond between Chrysabelle and myself has grown significantly over these last few months."

"We noticed," Fi said. "Mainly because you stopped trying to kill each other."

Mal laughed along with everyone else. "No promises there, especially since we're about to enter a new..." He looked at Chrysabelle. "Stage? Phase? I told you I'm no good at this."

She took his hand. "What Mal's trying to say is that we've decided to get married."

The reactions ranged from Fi whooping to Doc pumping a fist in the air to Creek's open-mouthed shock.

Dominic nodded, clapping enthusiastically. *"Molto bene.* When do you propose to make this official?"

"Soon," Mal said.

Chrysabelle nodded, her hand going to her belly. "Because I'm pregnant."

The room went instantly quiet. Until Fi leaned back and announced, "I already knew."

"So did I." Creek shook his head. "So does the KM, but I swear I had nothing to do with it. They told me."

Mal looked at Chrysabelle. "You were right about Kosmina."

She looked back at Creek. "Do you think the KM will leave us alone? Leave our child alone?"

He took a breath. "I don't know, but your child isn't going to be a threat to them. And"—he looked around the room—"you have a lot of powerful friends." Then he tipped his head slightly. "What about protecting this baby from Tatiana? If you have a plan to get rid of her and you need help, I'm in."

"Thank you, but Tatiana has been taken care of," Chrysabelle answered. "She's been imprisoned in the Garden of Eden by her own hand. Any attempt to leave, any breach of the Garden's boundaries and she'll die. She's no longer a threat to any of us."

Creek exhaled. "Good. I'm…happy for you." He looked at Mal. "For both of you. You deserve it after what you've been through."

"Thank you." Mal looked around the room. "To all of you. We wouldn't be here without you. We've shared losses together. Fought battles together. It's only fitting we should also share this joy." He laughed. "I'm still not used to that word applying to my life."

"Joy is a good word, bro," Doc said. "And it's about time you got some."

Chrysabelle smiled and hooked two fingers in the front pocket of Mal's jeans as she continued to talk. "You've all become our family." Her other hand cradled her belly. "We already know this won't be an ordinary child. We're going to need your help. We hope you'll still be there for us." At the sight of the solemn expressions staring back at her, she laughed. "What I'm really saying is getting baby-sitters for a half-vampire, half-comarré child isn't going to be easy."

Laughter answered her. She looked at Dominic, then Doc. "Mal and I really want you two to put the past behind you and come to some kind of peace. We can't have our child's godfathers fighting with each other."

Fi nudged Doc with her elbow. He nodded. "I've already lifted the restrictions Sinjin set in place. If Dominic shows some kind of good faith on his end, I'm ready to move past everything that's happened."

Dominic stroked his chin. "Allowing your pride members access to Seven was a big step for you and I appreciate it. What kind of good faith do you want me to show?"

Doc glanced around the room. "I'm about to announce a new council member. Police Chief Vernadetto."

"A human?" Mal asked. "That is progressive."

Doc shook his head. "Vernadetto's not human. He's a rare type of varcolai, but he'll make that announcement soon enough."

Dominic held his hands out. "I don't understand what this has to do with me?"

Doc continued. "When Vernadetto makes his announcement, he's also going to lay the groundwork for his mayoral campaign. He plans to run against the mayor in the next election. I want you to endorse him."

Dominic nodded. "Done." His expression went strange. "I have a feeling he'll win without much trouble."

As the two men shook hands, Chrysabelle nodded. "You're absolutely right. Mostly because the mayor's dead." Mal's arm went a little tighter around her waist. "She basically killed herself trying to get her granddaughter away from Preacher, who, by the way, is no longer a vampire."

"She was too long on hallowed ground," Mal added. "Went to ash right in the middle of that church he lives in."

Doc grimaced. "I understand trying to get her granddaughter, but at the cost of her own life? That's harsh."

Dominic cleared his throat. "I believe my nephew may have played a part in that. I found some things missing from my laboratory and when I asked him about it, he confessed he'd been feeding the mayor's comar vitamins that were laced with certain alchemical substances. He purposefully tainted her comar's blood to weaken her mental stability in hopes that she would cause her own end." He shook his head. "Apparently, he was successful. It was his way of making things right with me."

For a long moment, no one said a thing. Finally Chrysabelle spoke up. "I guess we've dropped enough bombs for one night, huh?"

A chorus of voices agreed with her.

Fi stood. "Well, after all that news, I could use a drink, even if Chrysabelle can't join us in the alcoholic stuff. Who's with me?"

The somber mood was broken with several affirmative answers. Mal kissed Chrysabelle's temple as laughter and talk filled the room. She looked up at him. "I think we're going to be all right."

"I know we are."

Doc came up and shook Mal's hand, slapping him on the back and drawing him away as Fi hugged Chrysabelle.

Mortalis approached, Nyssa at his side. "Congratulations."

We're thrilled for you, Nyssa signed.

Chrysabelle leaned forward as the shadeux kissed her on the cheek, and then Nyssa hugged her too. "Thank you, both."

Hours later, as everyone left, Chrysabelle stood at the door waving and watching the last car go through the gate. Mal came up behind her and put his hands on her shoulders. She put one of her hands over his. "We have good friends. A little strange, but good."

He laughed. "Agreed." His thumbs kneaded her back. "How are you feeling? Tired?"

"A little." With a contented sigh, she turned in his arms. "But there's one person left to tell and I can't rest until that happens."

He kissed her. "Then let's take care of that."

Chapter Fifty

Mal helped Chrysabelle out of the car. The wind had picked up, carrying the tang of the sea and the charge of a coming storm. It whipped her hair past her face, turning her into a warrior goddess once again. *His* warrior goddess, made even more beautiful by the child she carried. He smiled at her, again wondering what he'd done in his life to earn this second chance.

"I won't be long," she said. Jerem stood a few yards away, ready to escort her.

"Take all the time you need." He tucked one wind-blown lock behind her ear.

She stayed put. "The sun will be up soon."

"And the car windows are helioglazed." He leaned in, narrowing his eyes. "Don't rush on my account. I mean it."

"Okay," she said with an appreciative smile. She squeezed his hand, then nodded to Jerem and began to make her way through the rows of headstones.

Mal leaned against the car and watched her go. The prickle of the hallowed ground scratched at his bones and made the little hairs on his skin stand up, but it was a tiny price to pay to accompany his wife-to-be to see her mother.

What would Maris think if she knew her precious daughter was about to marry a vampire? And not just any vampire, but a vampire who'd gotten a child on her? His gut told him she wouldn't like it.

Jerem hung back a row as Chrysabelle kneeled at Maris's grave. The wind carried a few of her soft words to Mal's ears. "Love...marry...baby."

He tipped his head back and studied the clouded night sky. Here and there a star shone through, but otherwise the heavens were closed off to him. Centuries ago, he might have taken that as a bad omen. Hell, even now it seemed like some kind of sign.

Maris, if you're up there, you have to know I love her. And the child she's carrying. I know I'm not the man you would have chosen for Chrysabelle. I know this isn't the life you wanted her to have, but I'm not leaving her. Ever. I also know I don't deserve her any more than I deserve this second chance, but I'm not going to waste it.

If you could have gotten to know me...He shook his head. This was stupid, talking to a woman who wasn't there. Who probably would have done everything in her power to keep him away from her daughter. Including trying to stake him.

He lifted his eyes to the sky again. *I will protect them with everything I have until the end of my days. I promise you that.*

Thunder rumbled, long and hard enough to shake the car. Lightning shattered the Western horizon but the rain held off. The corners of his mouth turned up with a hint of a smile.

Chrysabelle came jogging back. "I think it's about to pour."

"Did you say everything you wanted to?"

She nodded, but her eyes were sad. "I wish she was still here."

"Me, too."

Surprise replaced the sorrow. "You do? Even though you know she probably wouldn't have liked you very much."

"I could have changed her mind." He reached for the car door.

Thunder rumbled over their heads. She glanced at the sky. "There's a storm coming."

He nodded, his gaze traveling to her belly. "There always will be. And just like always, we'll weather it." He opened the car door just as the first fat drops of rain pelted them.

She slid into the car, but he hesitated, flicking his gaze skyward once again. No matter what Maris thought, no matter who came after them, no matter what price he had to pay, he would keep Chrysabelle and his child safe.

It wasn't a question of if. Trouble *would* find them again. And until it did, he'd be waiting. Watching. Prepared to fight. Ready to protect.

From this day forward, last blood would always be his. Always.

The End

Glossary

Anathema: a noble vampire who has been cast out of noble society for some reason

Aurelian: the comarré historian

Castus Sanguis: the fallen angels from which the othernatural races descended

Comarré/comar: a human hybrid species especially bred to serve the blood needs of the noble vampire race

Dominus: the ruling head of a noble vampire family

Elder: the second in command to a Dominus

Fae: a race of othernatural beings descended from fallen angels and nature

Fringe vampires: a race of lesser vampires descended from the cursed Judas Iscariot

Kine: a vampire term for humans, archaic

Libertas: the ritual in which a comarré can fight for his or her independence. Ends in death of comarré or patron

Navitas: the ritual in which a vampire can be resired by another, to change family lines or turn fringe noble

Noble vampires: a powerful race of vampires descended from fallen angels

Nothos: hellhounds

Patronus/patron: a noble vampire who purchases a comarré's blood rights

Remnant: a hybrid of different species of fae and/or varcolai

Sacre: the ceremonial sword of the comarré

Signum: the inlaid gold tattoos or marks put into comarrés' skin to purify their blood

Vampling: a newly turned or young vampire

Varcolai: a race of shifters descended from fallen angels and animals

Acknowledgments

Writing never gets easier. There are good days and there are tough days; both are hard, but on either kind of day, my support system never fails me. All those who've helped me in some way deserve thanks. My apologies for those I've forgotten to mention, please forgive me.

To begin with, I want to thank my Creator for the blessings He's given me.

This series wouldn't have happened without my amazing, supportive agent, Elaine. She's the reason many of the great things in my writing life happen.

Big ups to my editor, Devi, for pushing me to delve deeper into the madness I put on the page and to her assistant, Susan, for always being there to answer my questions. You both rock, as does the entire publishing team at Orbit, including Alex, Ellen, Laura, and Lauren.

I have to also give a shout-out to Nekro, the amazing talent behind the art for these covers. I could not be more indebted for your work on them.

Massive thanks to the Writer's Camp chicks, Laura and Leigh, for their support, their friendship, and their ability to yell at me with kindness when I'm shopping online instead of writing. To Rocki and Louisa, whose friendship gets me through each day and every trial.

To all my readers, you guys are awesome and the reason I do this!

Lastly, tremendous thanks to my parents and my brother for their continuous support and to my husband for being my number one fan. I couldn't do this without you.

extras

orbit

meet the author

KRISTEN PAINTER'S writing résumé boasts multiple Golden Heart nominations and praise from a handful of best-selling authors, including Gena Showalter and Roxanne St. Claire. A former New Yorker now living in Florida, Kristen has a wealth of fascinating experiences from which to flavor her stories, including time spent working in fashion for Christian Dior and as a maitre'd for Wolfgang Puck. Her website is at kristenpainter.com and on twitter as @Kristen_Painter.

introducing

If you enjoyed
OUT FOR BLOOD,
look for

RED-HEADED STEPCHILD

Sabina Kane: Book One

by Jaye Wells

Sabina Kane is half-mage, half-vampire and all attitude. Despite her red-headed stepchild status in the vampire community, she remains loyal to the vampire leaders who raised her to be an assassin.

When a routine mission uncovers startling secrets that could destroy the uneasy truce between vampires and mages, Sabina must find a way to prevent an all-out war. Helping Sabina navigate this treacherous world are a

*high-maintenance hairless cat demon, a prognosticating
nymph who used to work in faery porn, and a mysterious
mage with an agenda...*

Digging graves is hell on a manicure, but I was taught
good vampires clean up after every meal. So I
ignored the chipped onyx polish. I ignored the dirt caked
under my nails. I ignored my palms, rubbed raw and blis-
tering. And when a snapping twig announced David's
arrival, I ignored him too.

He said nothing, just stood off behind a thicket of
trees waiting for me to acknowledge him. Despite his
silence, I could feel hot waves of disapproval flying in my
direction.

At last, the final scoop of earth fell onto the grave.
Stalling, I leaned on the shovel handle and restored order
to my hair. Next I brushed flecks of dirt from my cash-
mere sweater. Not the first choice of digging attire for
some, but I always believed manual labor was no excuse
for sloppiness. Besides, the sweater was black, so it went
well with the haphazard funerary rites.

The Harvest Moon, a glowing orange sphere, still
loomed in the sky. Plenty of time before sunrise. In the
distance, traffic hummed like white noise in the City of
Angels. I took a moment to appreciate the calm.

Memory of the phone call from my grandmother
intruded. When she told me the target of my latest assign-
ment, an icy chill spread through my veins. I'd almost
hung up, unable to believe what she was asking me to
do. But when she told me David was working with Clovis Trakiya, white-hot anger replaced the chill. I called

up that anger now to spur my resolve. I clenched my teeth and ignored the cold stone sitting in my stomach. My own feelings about David were irrelevant now. The minute he decided to work with one of the Dominae's enemies—a glorified cult leader who wanted to overthrow their power—he'd signed his death warrant.

Unable to put it off any longer, I turned to him. "What's up?"

David stalked out of his hiding place, a frown marring the perfect planes of his face. "Do you want to tell me why you're burying a body?"

"Who, me?" I asked, tossing the shovel to the ground. My palms were already healing. I wish I could say the same for my guilty conscience. If David thought I should apologize for feeding from a human, I didn't want to know what he was going to say in about five minutes.

"Cut the shit, Sabina. You've been hunting again." His eyes glowed with accusation. "What happened to the synthetic blood I gave you?"

"That stuff tastes like shit," I said. "It's like nonalcoholic beer. What's the point?"

"Regardless, it's wrong to feed from humans."

It's also wrong to betray your race, I thought. If there was one thing about David that always got my back up, it was his holier-than-thou attitude. Where were his morals when he made the decision to sell out?

Keep it together, Sabina. It will all be over in a few minutes.

"Oh, come on. It was just a stupid drug dealer," I said, forcing myself to keep up the banter. "If it makes you feel any better, he was selling to kids."

David crossed his arms and said nothing.

"Though I have to say nothing beats Type O mixed with a little cannabis."

A muscle worked in David's jaw. "You're stoned?"

"Not really," I said. "Though I do have a strange craving for pizza. Extra garlic."

He took a deep breath. "What am I going to do with you?" His lips quirked despite his harsh tone.

"First of all, no more lectures. We're vampires, David. Mortal codes of good and evil don't apply to us."

He arched a brow. "Don't they?"

"Whatever," I said. "Can we just skip the philosophical debates for once?"

He shook his head. "Okay then, why don't you tell me why we're meeting way out here?"

Heaving a deep sigh, I pulled my weapon. David's eyes widened as I aimed the custom-made pistol between them.

His eyes pivoted from the gun to me. I hoped he didn't notice the slight tremor in my hands.

"I should have known when you called me," he said. "You never do that."

"Aren't you going to ask me why?" His calm unsettled me.

"I know why." He crossed his arms and regarded me closely. "The question is, do you?"

My eye twitched. "I know enough. How could you betray the Dominae?"

He didn't flinch. "One of these days your blind obedience to the Dominae is going to be your downfall."

I rolled my eyes. "Don't waste your final words on another lecture."

He lunged before the last word left my lips. He plowed

into me, knocking the breath out of my chest and the gun from my hand. We landed in a tangle of limbs on the fresh grave. Dirt and fists flew as we each struggled to gain advantage. He grabbed my hair and whacked my head into the dirt. Soil tunneled up my nose and rage blurred my vision.

My hands curled into claws and dug into his eyes. Distracted by pain, he covered them with his palms. Gaining the advantage fueled my adrenaline as I flipped him onto his back. My knees straddled his hips, and I belted him in the nose with the base of my hand. Blood spurted from his nostrils, streaking his lips and chin.

"Bitch!" Like an animal, he sank his fangs into the fleshy part of my palm. I shrieked, backhanding him across the cheek with my uninjured hand. He growled and shoved me. I flew back several feet, landing on my ass with a thud.

Before I could catch my breath, his weight pinned me down again. Only this time, my gun stared back at me with its unblinking eye.

"How does it feel, Sabina?" His face was close to mine as he whispered. His breath stunk of blood and fury. "How does it feel to be on the other end of the gun?"

"It sucks, actually." Despite my tough talk, my heart hammered against my ribs. I glanced to the right and saw the shovel I'd used earlier lying about five feet away. "Listen—"

"Shut up." His eyes were wild. "You know what the worst part is? I came here tonight to come clean with you. Was going to warn you about the Dominae and Clovis—"

"Warn me?"

David jammed the cold steel into my skull—tattooing

me with his rage. "That's the irony isn't it? Do you even know what's at stake here?" He cocked the hammer. Obviously, the question had been rhetorical.

One second, two, ticked by before the sound of flapping wings and a loud hoot filled the clearing. David glanced away, distracted. I punched him in the throat. He fell back, gasping and sputtering. I hauled ass to the shovel.

Time slowed. Spinning, I slashed the shovel in a wide arc. A bullet ricocheted off the metal, causing a spark. David pulled himself up to shoot again, but I lunged forward, swinging like Babe Ruth. The metal hit David's skull with a sickening thud. He collapsed in a heap.

He wouldn't stay down long. I grabbed the gun from his limp hand and aimed it at his chest.

I was about to pull the trigger when his eyes crept open. "Sabina."

He lay on the ground, covered in blood and dirt. The goose egg on his forehead was already losing its mass. Knowledge of the inevitable filled his gaze. I paused, watching him.

At one time, I'd looked up to this male, counted him as a friend. And now he'd betrayed everything I held sacred by selling out to the enemy. I hated him for his treachery. I hated the Dominae for choosing me as executioner. But most of all, I hated myself for what I was about to do.

He raised a hand toward me—imploring me to listen. My insides felt coated in acid as I watched him struggle to sit up.

"Don't trust—"

His final words were lost in the gun's blast. David's body exploded into flames, caused by the metaphysical friction of his soul leaving his flesh.

My whole body spasmed. The heat from the fire couldn't stop the shaking in my limbs. Collapsing to the dirt, I wiped a quivering hand down my face.

The gun felt like a branding iron in my hand. I dropped it, but my hand still throbbed. A moment later, I changed my mind and picked it up again. Pulling out the clip, I removed one of the bullets. Holding one up for inspection, I wondered what David felt when the casing exploded and a dose of the toxic juice robbed him of his immortality.

I glanced over at the smoldering pile that was once my friend. Had he suffered? Or did death bring instant relief from the burdens of immortality? Or had I just damned his soul to a worse fate? I shook myself. His work here was done. Mine wasn't.

My shirt was caked with smears of soot, dirt, and drying blood—David's blood mixed with mine. I sucked in a lungful of air, hoping to ease the tightness in my chest.

The fire had died, leaving a charred, smoking mass of ash and bone. *Great,* I thought, *now I have to dig another grave.*

I used the shovel to pull myself up. A blur of white flew through the clearing. The owl called out again before flying over the trees. I stilled, wondering if I was hearing things. It called again and this time I was sure it screeched, "Sabina."

Maybe the smoke and fatigue were playing tricks on me. Maybe it had really said my name. I wasn't sure, but I didn't have time to worry about that. I had a body to bury.

As I dug in, my eyes started to sting. I tried to convince myself it was merely a reaction to the smoke, but a voice in my head whispered "guilt." With ruthless determination, I shoved my conscience down, compressing it into a tiny knot and shoving it into a dark corner of myself. Maybe later I'd pull it out and examine it. Or maybe not.

Good assassins dispose of problems without remorse. Even if the problem was a friend.